D0791540

JUSTIFICATION FOR MURDER

JUSTIFICATION FOR MURDER
ELIN BARNES

Paperless Reads ®

This is a work of fiction. All companies mentioned in this book are fictitious, and any resemblance to actual persons, living or dead, is purely coincidental.

©Elin Barnes 2013
Cover: Virginia Sardón and Mischa Lluch
Cover photo: Lucia Ybarra

www.elinbarnes.com

Published by Paperless Reads

ISBN: 978-0-9899880-1-8

This book is dedicated to my mom. Thank you, I couldn't have done this without you!

CHAPTER 1

Tuesday

Harper Johnson looked down at the woman bleeding on the floor. He drew a line through the first name on his list of three with a pen. The ink was red and the tip was broken, so it bled unevenly as he ran it through the letters. When he was done, he folded the piece of paper and stuffed it back in his pocket.

She hadn't put up too much of a fight. He surprised her in the bedroom, where he'd expected to finish the job, but she had hit him hard with the hair dryer and run downstairs to the kitchen, probably hoping to find something to defend herself with. But Harper had anticipated this and hidden the Wüsthof knives in the fridge before he went upstairs to confront her.

When he appeared in the kitchen, she was searching frantically, but she found nothing and froze. He closed the distance between them slowly and deliberately. She started to scream, but before the voice carried too far, he leaped toward her and smashed her head with the aluminum bat he'd been swinging. She dropped to the floor with a heavy thud.

Harper kneeled down on one knee. While leaning on the bat, he checked her pulse. It was faint, but she was still alive. He stood and placed one foot on each side of her waist and, holding the bat with both hands, he took a deep breath and drove it down with all his strength. Evelyn Shaw's skull cracked, spilling brain and blood onto the kitchen floor.

Harper looked at her and felt a pang of pity. Then, with a whisper he said, "Better you than me" and started raiding her place so the police would think it had been a robbery gone bad. He went back upstairs and looked for jewelry. He took everything he found regardless of its apparent value and stuffed it inside his large black duffle bag. He then searched the closet for furs, but this being California, he wasn't surprised to not find any.

Back downstairs, Harper took her laptop, cell phone and the small Bang & Olufsen sound system that held a prominent place in the living room. He opened the sliding doors to the backyard and walked outside to find the kitchen window. He took a rock from the flowerbed and broke the glass. He slid the window open, returned the rock to where it had been and walked back inside. Harper closed the blinds so nosy neighbors couldn't see the body lying there. He took a final look around and, finding nothing else that could fit in his bag, left through the back door.

Harper drove out of Scotts Valley and as soon as he entered Santa Cruz, he stopped by the first dumpster he found and threw in there everything he had stolen, then drove home to wash the blood off his bat.

CHAPTER 2

Saffron clenched her teeth and looked around. The fancy restaurant with the light classical music and the overly obliging staff was perfect for a couple in love. The place was empty, though, and Saffron wondered if Ranjan had chosen it in case she made a scene. Sipping her wine, she thought about what she wanted to say, or if there was even anything to say.

"Saffron?" Ranjan pressed, but when she looked at him, he didn't push further.

He drained his glass and not waiting for somebody to re-fill it, he poured the rest of the bottle. Before she could say anything, the waiter came out of nowhere and asked, "Can I entice you to any dessert tonight?"

"No. The check, please," she said, curter than she'd intended.

Ranjan reached out to touch her hand, but she moved it as if the contact would burn her. Saffron had decided to remain civil with him in the restaurant and have the fight when they were alone in the car.

They waited outside for the valet to bring the Audi A8. The light rain felt icy on her face and she shivered in the crisp night but moved away when Ranjan tried to wrap his arm around her.

"I'll drive," she said, snatching the keys from a guy who looked more like a club bouncer than a valet.

"I can drive," he assured her.

"You're drunk. I'm driving," she said, already getting behind the wheel.

They remained silent as they left Santa Cruz. Saffron concentrated on the car's movements as it took each curve, smooth and controlled like an old waltz. The Audi gripped the asphalt of Highway 17 on each twist, screeching slightly over the rain but not sliding an inch. The speedometer danced between fifteen and twenty miles per hour over the speed limit. The engine roared, only purring when she slowed down slightly to take the curves.

"I didn't know you were such a good driver," Ranjan said.

Saffron ignored the compliment and accelerated again. The rain splashed against the windshield, and the wipers moved back and forth rhythmically. She hoped the swaying would have a soporific effect on her boyfriend. She needed him to be quiet. She decided she didn't want to have the fight anymore, she just needed time to think.

"Saffron, you have to talk to me." He slurred a little, the effect of wine finally evident in his voice.

She maneuvered the car around a sharp bend and passed the only car they'd seen in miles. Nobody liked to take Highway 17 in the rain. Her jaw muscles tensed again as she gritted her teeth, her knuckles tight on the wheel.

"You need to understand that I have to do this for my family." Ranjan looked out the passenger window. The trees were moving too fast, and Saffron saw him pressing his hand against the pit of his stomach.

"Saffron—"

"Stop it," she said. Her hands started to ache. She rubbed her right hand against her thigh. She switched and did the same with the left. "You need to stop talking. You've said enough."

He shook his head. The only reason she hadn't walked out on him at the restaurant was because they'd taken his car. He'd pitched the evening as a romantic dinner in Santa Cruz, but it had turned out to be anything but that. She saw him fix his eyes on the road twisting in front of him.

"Can I turn the radio on?" she asked before he could start another plea. Without waiting for a response, she reached out for the knob. Diana Krall was finishing a sad song about a love that ended. "How appropriate," she said and saw Ranjan's face twitch.

Saffron shifted her eyes back to the road and was momentarily surprised by a pair of high beams in the rearview mirror. She hadn't seen any cars trailing them, especially not at the speed she was going. The car, at least a foot taller than Ranjan's Audi, was coming up fast behind them. She considered slowing down but decided to change lanes instead. The car followed. She lifted her foot from the pedal. The car got closer. She could see it was dark, maybe black or navy. Before the next curve, it turned on its floodlights and almost blinded her.

"What's going on?" Ranjan asked, turning to look behind him. Saffron saw him swallow hard, as if he was trying to hold down the threat of vomit.

"I don't know. I think this guy's crazy." She looked to the right, but there were no exits, no side roads. "Look for a place where we can pull off."

"It's almost midnight and there're no lights. How do you want me to do that?"

She didn't answer. The car was now only a few feet behind. Saffron saw a short straightaway and accelerated to almost thirty miles per hour over the speed limit. The car followed, as if they were connected by an invisible line. It got closer. She swerved and moved back into the slow lane, slamming on the brakes as soon as she was on the other side of the white lines.

The dark car stayed on the left, and before Saffron managed to get behind it, with a quick twist of the wheel, the driver had rammed them, pushing them off the road.

The Audi screeched, jumped over a shallow ditch, losing its grip on the asphalt, and slid in the fresh mud. She tried to maneuver it back into the road, but the wheels were slick over the grit, tree leaves and loose branches. Saffron tapped on the brakes, but before she was able to slow down enough to regain command of the vehicle, the other car slammed against them again.

The right tire got stuck in the ditch. She turned the wheel but the Audi wouldn't respond. Before she could try something else, they hit a fallen tree and the car jumped and rolled over, skidding on its hood over thirty feet and coming to a hard stop when it crashed against the median.

As soon as Saffron got her voice back she asked, "Are you okay?"

She pushed the airbag away. Her head was pressed against the top of the car, the seat belt had kept her from breaking her neck. Saffron couldn't turn enough to see Ranjan, but she could touch him. Shoving him back and forth just a little, she yelled, "Ranjan, are you okay?"

She forced her head toward the passenger seat. She saw blood, Ranjan's arm and part of his torso, but the deflated airbag covered his face. She rotated further, and screamed as an intense pain pierced through her.

Saffron twisted back to lessen the strain and froze. The Timberland boots near her face were worn out and dark, caked with old mud. The black jeans were too long, frayed in the back.

"Help us," Saffron said, not sure she wanted his help. The boots came closer, and the man moved a baseball bat from his right side to his left. He started swinging it, almost in slow motion.

"What are you doing?"

She struggled with the seat belt, ignoring the stings of pain that shot through her body with each movement. She tried to unlatch it, but couldn't find the clasp. The man dropped the bat. The sharp sound of aluminum hitting the pavement filled her ears.

He kneeled. His hands were covered by black leather gloves. His face was hidden by the car. Saffron held her breath.

"Please, don't. Don't hurt us." Her voice cracked, her mouth filled with imaginary cotton.

The dim light reflected on a large hunter's knife as he slashed the seat belt with a swift motion. Saffron fell against the car's roof, and bent her neck in an almost impossible position. He grabbed her forearm and pulled her out of the car with such force she thought he would dislocate her shoulder.

A flash of light distracted him for a second. A car's engine and the ding-ding sound of an open door flooded the air. A man's voice, about fifteen yards away, asked, "Are you guys okay?"

Before Saffron could yell for help, she heard the bat scraping against the asphalt and muffled steps running away. She looked in the direction of the fainting sound, but the upside-down car was blocking her view.

"Please help me," she yelled toward the newcomer.

"Some nasty accident. No surprise in this rain." He kneeled next to her. "Are you okay? Can you stand?"

"Please, help my boyfriend. He's hurt!"

CHAPTER 3

Wednesday

Detective Darcy Lynch rubbed his nose, trying to wipe away the Lysol-and-death smell of the hospital. A chill ran through his back. He pushed away the memory that triggered the shiver.

"Where can I find Saffron Meadows?" he asked the receptionist while he flashed his badge.

She locked eyes with him and continued talking on the phone, apparently giving directions to Good Samaritan Hospital.

Darcy stiffened but decided to wait. The clock on the wall showed 3:10 in the morning. He pulled his black notebook and reviewed the notes he wrote after talking to the deputies at the scene.

"Miss Meadows is with her boyfriend in Room 305," the receptionist said after hanging up the phone. "Down the hall, to the right."

"Thanks," he said over his shoulder, already walking away.

The hallway was long and flanked by closed doors. He moved around a few nurses, carts and gurneys with patients probably being transferred after treatment in the ER. Lynch knocked on the door of Room 305, and opened it without waiting for an invitation, finding an Indian man lying on the bed, asleep. He had an angular face, very short, black, almost blue hair, and a prominent five-o'clock shadow. The most noticeable thing, however, was a nasty bump on the right side of his forehead, large as an egg and already dark purple.

A woman was holding his hand. Her dark wavy hair covered part of her face. She looked tall and lanky, and her legs went on forever. Her eyes were closed. Her fingers kept stroking the man's hand.

He coughed, uncomfortable for intruding on such an intimate moment. She looked at him and stood, not letting go of the man's hand. "Yes?"

"Are you Miss Meadows?"

"Yes." She tucked a long strand of hair behind her ear that came loose almost immediately.

"I'm Detective Darcy Lynch, with the Santa Clara Sheriff's Office. I would like to ask you a few questions about the accident, if that's okay with you."

"Sure. Do we need to go outside?" She looked back at the bed. "I would like to be here in case Ranjan wakes up."

He motioned to the chair she'd been sitting on, then grabbed another one, moving it closer.

"Please tell me what happened last night with as much detail as you can remember."

"I'll try." She broke eye contact, as if she needed to look at the white sheets to remember what had happened just a couple hours earlier. "I was mad at Ranjan. We were driving back to San Jose from Santa Cruz, on 17. Well, you probably know all that."

She stopped and looked at him, her eyes pleading for something. He didn't know what she was asking of him, so he nodded for her to continue. When she didn't, he said, "Miss Meadows, don't worry. Just tell me what happened."

"Call me Saffron, please."

"Okay."

"I was going a bit faster than I should have, because I just wanted to get home."

"Why were you upset?"

She broke eye contact, blushing a little.

"It's personal, really, but whatever. Ranjan's Indian. Well, that's obvious." She turned away, looking embarrassed. "Sorry, I'm not being very eloquent. I'm not normally this way. I must have hit my head," she said with a shy grin.

Darcy smiled but didn't say anything.

"Ranjan had just told me that his family was pressuring him again to consider an arranged marriage." She moved both hands to her lap and rubbed them together. "I was mad, because we've been together almost a year and he's kept our relationship a secret from them all this time." She slouched in the chair and looked back at him. Her eyes were intense and a little red. "Anyway, that's not important. I saw this big car in the rearview mirror. He was coming fast at us, with his high beams on and the other lights, the ones on top of the roof, and then he started acting all weird. I tried to let him pass, but he didn't want to. He kept at my tail until he pulled up to my side of the car, and before I was able to slow down enough, he crashed into us on purpose." Her voice was high. Her words came out fast, as if floodgates had opened and she only had seconds to share all of the information.

"Did you recognize the car?"

"No. I don't think so. It was really dark. But I don't even think I know anybody who drives one of those cars. Well, it was a truck, not a car. Anyway, he pushed me off the road, I tried to get back, but I hit a fallen tree and ended up rolling over. I asked Ranjan if he was okay, but he wouldn't answer, and I couldn't turn around because of the seat belt. I was trying to move when I saw the bat."

"The bat?"

"Yes, I saw these Timberland boots—dark, dirty—and he was swinging a bat. I didn't understand anything, but then I heard the bat hit the ground and saw the big hunting knife shining as he was kneeling down. I swear to God I thought he was going to kill me."

She stopped and breathed. He waited for her.

"He got on his knees and cut my seat belt. At that moment I thought that maybe I was wrong, that maybe he just wanted to make sure I got out of the car before it exploded. But then he pulled me out so hard I thought he was going to rip my arm off. Then another man appeared and asked if we were okay, and the next thing I know the Bat Guy was running away toward the trees. By the time the other man came to my side, all I could think about was for him to save Ranjan."

"Did you have a chance to see the face of the man with the bat?"

"No."

"Was there anything you recognized about him? Or anything distinctive?"

"No."

"Do you have any idea why he wanted to harm you?"

"No."

"I talked to Mr. Simmons already, the man who stopped to help you and called 911. He did see the man run away as well, but he was too far for him to give us any details, with the exception of him being tall and stocky. He was also wearing a black baseball cap."

"What about the truck?" she asked.

"Stolen. The owner didn't even know. He was very upset when we woke him up to ask him where his car was. Even more so when he couldn't see it in his driveway."

Saffron smiled for a second. She was probably imagining the scene. A silence filled the room. Ranjan breathed but didn't move.

"This wasn't a hit-and-run," Saffron said.

Darcy nodded slightly. He hated giving any information victims could then misconstrue, but this was too obvious to interpret any other way.

"You really have no idea why anybody would want to harm you." It was more a statement than a question. "What about work? What do you do?"

"I'm a project manager for a tech company. Like everybody else in the Valley."

"Any company secrets? Patents?"

"No. I don't have access to any of that."

"How about Mr. Balasubramanian?" he said, not looking at his notebook.

"He's a senior manager, in sales, for the same company. But we don't work on anything that exciting. We do plug-ins for web browsers."

A nurse walked into the room and stopped. Her face was wrinkled and tired. Looking at Lynch and then Saffron, she said, "You have to leave now. Visiting hours were over a long time ago."

"I'm staying until he wakes up."

"Are you family?" she asked in a raspy, almost manly voice.

"I'm his girlfriend."

"Sorry. You have to leave. Only family members can spend the night."

Saffron remained seated. Detective Lynch stood but didn't head toward the door.

The nurse stopped reading her clipboard and rested it on her hip. She locked eyes with Saffron. Finally, she said, "You

18

can come back in four hours. If you don't leave, I'll call security."

"No need to do that," Darcy said, showing his badge. "Can't you see that she really wants to stay?"

"The rules." It was all she said before she brushed between them and started checking the drips and numbers displayed on the machine against her notes on the clipboard.

"Come on, I'll drive you home," Darcy said, gently placing a hand on Saffron's elbow, coaxing her toward the door.

She didn't resist. She exhaled silently and allowed him to pull her away from Ranjan.

The ride home was mostly silent. Darcy glanced at Saffron. She was looking out the window, gazing at empty streets and dark buildings. The sky was still pitch-black, and the streets glittered with the thin sheen of the earlier rain. It was all too bleak to help the mood.

"Thank you for the ride," she said when he killed the engine outside her building.

Lynch nodded and got out of the car. "I'd like to check your place. Just to make sure there's nothing weird going on."

"Do you think he knows where I *live*?" Her voice cracked on the last word.

"Better to be cautious."

Saffron used a fob to get through the gate and led him to the elevators.

"I normally take the stairs," she said, a little shy, "but it's been a long day." She pushed the button for the second floor.

He smiled, understanding. She returned the smile and stared into his eyes a little too long. He wondered if she noticed that his left eye was different from the right one.

The elevator opened to a large veranda overlooking trees and a large, lighted pool. They turned right into a hall with tall beige and terracotta walls, rough to the touch. Saffron stopped in front of a sage door displaying the number 202 right below a small, lit lantern. A moth fluttered away when they arrived. Saffron ducked, even though it flew at least a foot away from her face.

She opened the door. Without turning back, she asked, "Do you know if moths are only around in the fall?"

"I have no idea." The strangeness of the question surprised him.

Saffron shrugged. She stopped at the entrance. Darcy waited but when she didn't step inside he asked, "What's wrong?"

"My cat. She always welcomes me home."

A shuffling noise coming from inside the apartment made her jump, almost stepping on Darcy.

"Wait here," he whispered, walking past her.

He opened his jacket and released the snap on his gun holster. He moved slowly, letting his eyes adjust to the darkness of this unknown place. The streetlights helped him identify the edges of the furniture and the doorframes. There was another noise, a window sliding.

"Stop. Stop right there!" His voice was firm, authoritative.

Another sound followed, a thud that seemed further away. When Darcy reached the bedroom, the blinds were clanking against each other. He ran to the window and saw a man dressed in black running away from the building. Before he could make out anything distinctive, the figure turned the corner and was gone.

Detective Lynch ran back to the front door and said, "Go inside and lock the door. I'm going to see if I can find him." On his way out, he yelled, "I'll call for more help and will be back in a couple minutes. Don't open the door for anybody but me."

CHAPTER 4

Saffron stared at the empty hallway. She pushed the door closed and locked it. Her arms wrapped around her body, tight, as if they could protect her from harm. After a few minutes, she filled the kettle with water and realized she still hadn't seen Cat since they'd come in. She called out, "Hey, Cat, sweetie. Come here." Saffron waited, expecting the black cat to run to her as she always did. She called out again, a little louder, but Cat didn't come.

The high-pitch whistle of the kettle startled her. She poured the boiling water into the French press. This time she had doubled the amount of grounds she normally used. She swirled the coffee and pressed the plunger in. She called Cat again with the same result.

The knock on the door was firm. "Miss Meadows, it's Detective Lynch."

"Did you find him?" she asked before the door was fully open.

"No. By the time I got down, he was too far gone." Before she could voice her disappointment, he said, "I've called in a BOL with the description we have. The streets are empty, so if he's moving around, we'll find him before he gets too far."

The words didn't feel as reassuring as he probably meant them.

"Coffee?" she asked, guiding him to the kitchen.

"I'd love some. Thank you."

She poured two generous portions. "Milk? I don't have sugar."

"Black's perfect."

She walked past him toward the living room. "Please, sit," she invited.

Before she reached the rich leather sofa, Cat appeared, not sure whether she wanted to meow or purr but unable to do both concurrently.

"There you are," Saffron said, relieved. She picked up the skinny cat, squeezing her against her chest, and planted a loud kiss on her forehead. Instead of running away, Cat started to purr.

They sat at opposite sides of the couch, not quite looking at each other. After a few moments, Lynch said, "I've asked the San Jose PD to place a car outside, just in case."

"I thought you worked for the Sheriff's Office."

"Yes, but they have more manpower, so they help us sometimes. Besides, you're in their jurisdiction."

She nodded, not really sure what that all meant. "You think he'll come back?"

"I'd rather be prepared if he does. I can get them to follow you to work if you're thinking of going tomorrow."

Saffron was silent for a moment. She closed her eyes, then looked at her watch. "You mean today." Her smile felt tight.

"Yes."

"I haven't even thought about it yet." She took two sips of hot coffee.

"How are you holding up?" he asked.

She looked at him as she scratched Cat behind the ears. "I feel as if I'm in a bad movie. These things don't happen to regular people." She stared at him as she drank the rest of her coffee.

"You'd be surprised," he said, then shook his head slightly.

Her eyes widened and she shivered.

"I'm sorry, I didn't mean it that way." He finished his coffee and stood to carry the empty mug back to the kitchen.

"Please, have some more," she offered.

He brought back the press and filled both cups. "What I meant was that these types of awful things normally have explanations. We'll figure out what's going on in your case. The most important thing is to keep you safe until we do."

She looked at him. For some reason she found it endearing that he was trying so hard to make her feel better about the whole thing.

"Yeah, I know. Not quite the best save I've had after putting my foot in my mouth."

"Does this type of stuff happen often, then?"

"No. Actually, it doesn't. But what's true is that most crimes have rational explanations." His eyes lit up, as if he had just thought of something. "You mentioned that Ranjan's family wanted him to go through with an arranged marriage."

She nodded.

"Do you think they may have anything to do with this?" he asked.

"You're asking if they would've hired somebody to kill me?"

"Yes. Is it possible?"

"No," she protested, a little louder than she intended. Then she thought for a few seconds. "I honestly don't think they know I exist. That was the whole point of our argument. Well, that and the fact that he was going to go through with meeting prospective wives."

"Oh," Darcy said.

"Yeah, exactly. How screwed up is that?"

Darcy didn't answer. "But if they knew of you, do you think they're desperate enough to try something like this?"

"Long distance?" she asked. "I doubt it. The only family member who's here is his uncle, and as I said, I doubt he knows who I am." She took a sip of coffee. "Besides, Ranjan was eager enough to meet these women, so why risk killing me?" she added, bitterness in her voice. "All they need to do is find one that works."

Her cell phone rang. "It must be the hospital. It's not even six a.m. yet." She jumped off the sofa and almost ran to the kitchen to pick up her cell. "Hello?"

"Miss Meadows, we wanted to let you know that Mr. Balasub..." The nurse stalled, clearly struggling with the full name. "Well, we just got the results of his MRI."

CHAPTER 5

"Move it, asshole!" Sheila screamed at a septuagenarian taking too long to go through the four-way stop. She stepped on the accelerator a little too hard. The wheels screeched over the asphalt, damp from the night's rain. Her fingers never stopped scratching her left breast.

I got to stop this itching. She clenched her teeth. Pink nails left crimson marks on the skin, even though she scratched over the silk blouse.

Sheila steered with one hand through the quaint Willow Glen neighborhood while blurting insults to every person who slowed her down. In less than five minutes she pulled into her driveway, but she didn't open the garage door. She jumped out of the car, leaving her coat and purse behind.

There were sweat spots under her armpits, and the front of her blouse was fuzzy with a peach-like texture where she'd rubbed the silk. The peacock color of the blouse had lost its shine. Her nails continued scratching, but now her fingers were moving the breast mass from side to side, as if that would help calm the prickling.

She pulled her shirt open, ripping the buttons loose, and lifted the lacy, black bra. Streaks of blood had formed below the skin.

"What the hell's this?" she asked, looking down at her breast in the mirror. "Why won't you stop itching?"

Sheila opened the right cupboard under the sink and rummaged around. Nothing. She searched the left one but couldn't find what she was looking for. She saw a tube of topical ointment. She picked it up and stared at it. The word "itching" screamed at her as if it were bold and flashing. She squeezed half a tube in her hand and spread the cream over her breast. The momentary relief felt glorious. She breathed deeply and closed her eyes. A few seconds later, the itching started again.

With her free hand she pulled her auburn hair back, twisted and tied it into a loose knot, unwilling to stop scratching with the other.

She looked around, her eyes darting from the sink to the mirror to the towel hanger, trying to figure out if there was anything that would help her stop the itching. The sweat now stained her entire blouse. She pulled open the shower curtains so hard that one of the rings came loose from the bar.

"Ah, yes," she said. Her brow relaxed briefly. "This should work."

She grabbed the large tortoiseshell comb and began to scratch her breast with it, harder with each stroke, pushing past the raw nipple.

"Please, stop," Sheila begged, gritting her teeth. "I can't stand it anymore."

She descended the stairs, tripping on the last step and falling onto the floor. She got up, kicked her shoes loose and headed toward the kitchen, knowing what would finally help ease the itching much better than the comb.

Mocha walls covered the spacious living room. The timid morning sun entered through the east-side windows. She passed a large, dark dining table and headed straight to the state-of-the-art kitchen island. She circled around it and grabbed the Henckels stainless steel barbecue fork. The comb fell to the floor, but Sheila didn't hear it clink against the Spanish tile. All she could think about was the feel of the cold metal on her distressed skin.

"Ahh," she said, but the cool metal became less cold with every pass. The tips left red pathways as they moved over the dermis into the flesh, and blood started dripping down her ribs and stomach, soaking the waist of her herringbone pants. Sheila leaned against the marble countertop and rolled her eyes backwards, as if she were having an orgasm.

With the help of both hands, the fork continued to move, faster at first, deeper. Sheila's knees became weak and she slid, sitting down on the floor, without losing a stroke. Blood spurted out with each heartbeat, staining her slacks, overflowing to the floor. Small strips of flesh and fat hung from the open wound. She didn't feel pain, only the burning itching that wouldn't go away. She continued rubbing, digging. The fork punctured her lung and her hands slowed down until they didn't move anymore.

CHAPTER 6

Detective Lynch's desk was covered with files. When he moved to Silicon Valley from Seattle, he had expected the technology age to have reached the government agencies. It hadn't. He was happy to see that at least nobody used typewriters anymore, but many of his coworkers still pecked at their keyboards.

"Hey, Lynch, I heard you let the perp escape last night," Detective Sorensen said, passing by his desk too fast for his bulky frame.

Darcy ignored him, pretending to concentrate on the report he had to write about the incident but hadn't started yet.

"Seriously, dude, what happened? He sneaked out by moving past your bad eye?"

"Fuck you," Darcy murmured, not looking up. "Don't you have some parking tickets to write?"

Sorensen faked a laugh on his way to the kitchen. Everybody else pretended to work, but Darcy knew they were thinking the same thing.

He finished his coffee in one gulp and stretched. Sleeping only three hours never did him any good. He went to refill his cup, passing Sorensen on the way, and headed toward the boss's office.

"You have a sec?" he asked after knocking on Captain Virago's doorframe. He knew it would have been better to show her a finished report, but he didn't feel the literary inspiration necessary to write it.

The woman looked up over her narrow reading glasses and removed the tip of the pen from her lips. "Sure." Her tone was more annoyed than inviting, but he decided to ignore it. She claimed to have an open-door policy, but she always seemed irritated when you took her up on it.

Darcy sat on one of the chairs across her desk and tasted his fresh coffee. He grimaced when the flavor hit his mouth. He missed the coffee from Seattle. He placed his elbows on the armrests, but the right one slipped. He was glad he was holding the coffee in the other hand. He took another sip.

After a few seconds of silence, Captain Virago looked up again, sighed and put the pen on of the pile of papers.

"What's up?"

He sipped one more time, just to make a point. When he knew he had her full attention, he said, "You know I moved here because I wanted to do simple stuff, right?"

She stared. Not a single muscle in her face moved.

"I wanted to come to a warm place where an extra hand could be useful, but where there wasn't too much excitement going on."

"You should've moved to Europe, then."

"The point is," he said, ignoring her, "that you need to assign the Meadows case to somebody else."

"No can do." She shook her head violently.

Darcy thought she was overdoing it on purpose.

"There's something going on there. The worst thing is, I actually believe that she has no clue why somebody's trying to kill her."

"You checked the boyfriend's uncle angle?"

"I'm on it, but it's a stretch."

She looked down at the pile of files and picked her pen back up. Then, before she got back to work, she looked at him and said, "Lynch, if you wanted to retire by the beach, why did you come to work under my command?"

"Captain, I'm telling you, somebody's trying to kill this woman, and I'm not the man to figure out who or why. If you don't put somebody else on this case, she's going to die." Before she could protest, he added, "And your stats will go up."

Her eyes narrowed, but it was hard to feel the venom through eyes the color of honey. He managed to slip out of the office just in time to hear the pen hit the door as he closed it behind him.

CHAPTER 7

The alarm went off, but Saffron was already awake. She'd checked the visiting hours of the hospital before going to bed and wanted to be there as soon as she'd be allowed in. Her entire body ached with the stale adrenaline from the accident. After the fastest shower Saffron had ever taken, she dressed and headed to the hospital with her hair still wet.

She browsed through email while traffic moved at less than five miles per hour. There were several emails from Vincent, her boss, and over a hundred others she'd have to go through as soon as she got to the office, if she decided to go.

The visitor parking was full. She had to go around a few times before a spot opened. The hospital, however, was not as crowded as she had expected from the lack of parking spaces. A few nurses and doctors dotted the hallways, speaking in low voices as if they didn't want to wake the ill. Her heels clicked on the floor and she cringed with every step, swearing to wear flats the next time. The door of Room 305 was open, but before she got all the way inside, she stopped, almost too fast. An older Indian man was sitting by Ranjan, just where she'd been the night before. He looked up. His eyes were bloodshot and watery.

"Hello." She wished she hadn't come. "I'm Saffron Meadows." She wished Ranjan had told her uncle about them. She tucked a loose strand of hair behind her ear.

"I know who you are."

"Oh," she said, surprised, almost hopeful. She extended her hand. He never took it.

"How's he doing?" she asked, shoving her hand inside her jeans pocket.

"He's resting."

She took a few steps to get closer to the bed, dragging her feet so the heels wouldn't click.

"He'll wake up soon," Saffron said, reaching for Ranjan's foot.

"He already did," the old man said, but his voice was bitter.

"He has?"

She wanted to rush to Ranjan, hug him, hold him, kiss him and make him wake up in her arms. But before she could move, Manoj Balasubramanian said, "You need to leave now, Ms. Meadows. He needs to be with his family."

"Mr. Balasubramanian—"

"Miss Meadows, please," he said, pointing to the door with his open hand.

Ranjan stirred just as Saffron was fighting the urge to challenge the man. She got closer and put both hands on the cold metal bar at the end of the bed. Dr. Balasubramanian saw it and twitched but quickly turned to his nephew and grabbed his hand.

"How are you, Ranjan?"

"I have a really bad headache." He smiled at his own bad joke. "We were in an accident, right?" he asked, looking at Saffron.

"Yes." She shifted her weight from one foot to the other a couple times. She didn't know how much his uncle knew, or how much he blamed her for.

"When am I getting out of here?" he asked no one in particular.

"I talked to the doctor," Dr. Balasubramanian said. "You had a concussion and they want to monitor you for another twenty-four hours or so, but the MRI didn't come up with anything to worry us about." His Indian accent was more noticeable the more he spoke.

Ranjan looked at Saffron. His eyes were sweet, but his face offered an apology. She looked down, knowing exactly what he was asking her to do.

CHAPTER 8

There were no prints on the car. Nobody had observed anybody suspicious, and although many had seen plenty of men dressed in black around the stolen-car owner's neighborhood, most were either going to, or leaving, their homes. Darcy had gone back to Highway 17, now open to traffic, to try to find something, anything, CSU might have missed. But that was just wishful thinking. He knew there was nothing there that would break the case.

Before returning to the office, he decided to pay a visit to Ranjan's uncle. He was a professor of applied economics at Stanford. He called the university department, and a nice elderly voice told him that Professor Balasubramanian was at the hospital, visiting his nephew.

Darcy turned around and backtracked a couple miles toward Good Samaritan Hospital. This way, he would be able to talk to Ranjan and his uncle at the same time. He found parking right away and walked straight to the room. At least this time he knew where he was going.

He wondered if Saffron would be there. She seemed very eager to be with her boyfriend, even after the fight. But when he arrived, he only found two men engaged in a lively conversation about economic bubbles.

"Hello, I'm Detective Lynch, with the Santa Clara Sheriff's Office," he said, focusing his attention on Ranjan. "I would like to ask you a few questions about what you remember from last night."

"Can't this wait?" The older man turned toward him, squaring his shoulders.

"Mr...?" Lynch asked, even though he knew who he was.

"Dr. Manoj Balasubramanian. I'm Ranjan's uncle."

"Nice to meet you." Lynch extended his hand. The man took it, but his grip was weak. "As you can understand, we're trying to figure out what happened. We don't think this was an accident."

The old man's face showed surprise. It looked genuine. "You think somebody tried to hurt Ranjan?"

"Or Miss Meadows."

Dr. Balasubramanian winced. Lynch asked Ranjan to tell him what he remembered, and his account was very close to Saffron's, except he was already unconscious when the man came to take Saffron out of the car and wasn't able to provide any description of the perp.

"Do you have any idea why anybody would want to run you off the road?"

"No. No idea."

"Can you think of any?" Lynch now asked Dr. Balasubramanian.

"Me? No, of course not. But who knows what that woman may be involved in."

"Uncle, please," Ranjan said, his voice more tired than exasperated.

"Why would you say that?" Lynch pushed.

"Detective, please excuse my uncle. He doesn't mean anything by it." Ranjan shook his head but stopped almost immediately.

"I would like to hear what he has to say," Lynch said to Ranjan without breaking eye contact with the older man.

"I am sorry, Detective. I didn't really mean anything by it. I do not know that woman."

"You don't know her or you don't like her?"

The doctor in applied economics thought for a few seconds, probably weighing his possible answers. Finally, he said, "Both, Detective. I met her this morning for the first time in my life, but I do not like her, nor do we wish her to be involved with my nephew in any way outside of work."

"Who is 'we'?"

"Ranjan's family. We have better plans for him."

"How far would you go to ensure that Miss Meadows is out of Ranjan's life?" Lynch asked.

"Whoa, what are you implying?" Ranjan interrupted.

"I'm not implying anything. I'm simply asking your uncle a question." Lynch kept his eyes on the PhD.

"I am a professor at Stanford. I'm not a stupid man, Detective. I can have an intelligent conversation with my nephew and make him understand his erroneous ways. I do not need to run anybody off the road, especially not with him in the car. That would be incredibly senseless."

"Can you tell me what you were doing from ten to one in the morning last night?"

"I had a poker game with a group of professors. It is a monthly game, so you can check with them. I left a little past midnight. The game was in Palo Alto. So, as you can see, it would have been impossible for me to run Ranjan off the road close to Santa Cruz at the same time."

"Thank you. That should be easy enough to verify. Can you give me the names of the people you were playing with yesterday?"

The professor gave him four names. Darcy wrote them down in his black notebook.

"Any large sums of money leaving your bank accounts lately?" he pushed.

"Detective," Ranjan protested. "Seriously, my uncle didn't have anything to do with this."

Darcy ignored him and waited for Dr. Balasubramanian to respond. After a few more seconds of pregnant silence, he did.

"No. I will talk to my lawyer and give you access to my accounts if this is really necessary."

"That would be greatly appreciated." Darcy gave both men a business card and thanked them for their time. "I hope you recover soon," he said, looking at Ranjan's bump on the forehead, which was still dark purple.

About half an hour later he was back at the office, sitting at his desk. He'd been mulling over the conversation with Ranjan and his uncle during the drive. He'd check the alibi, but he was pretty sure the old man didn't have anything to do with the case.

It's not even my case, he thought. *I don't want it to be my case.*

Darcy turned the computer on, and Saffron's picture from LinkedIn stared back at him. Her faint smile encouraged him to keep looking, to help her, even if it was only until somebody else could step in.

He'd run through her entire background, trying to figure out why somebody would want to kill her. There was nothing. She had graduated from Berkeley with a business degree ten years ago and had hopped companies in the Valley every few years. Facebook had a few pictures from past vacations and a couple with ex-boyfriends, but there was nothing there that indicated animosity from anybody in her life.

Lynch had also checked out Ranjan and was surprised to find he was five years younger than Saffron. He wondered if the uncle's reticence toward her had more to do with her age than her race. Ranjan had come for college and lived with his uncle until he graduated. He hadn't quite fulfilled his family's expectations yet, as he had only managed to get his MS in computer science, not a doctorate. Besides two very typical profiles for the Valley, he came out as empty with LinkedIn and social media as he had with his search on ViCAP.

"It happened again," Sorensen said, bringing him out of his daze.

"I swear I started a new pot of coffee when I took the last cup," Jon said, the last intern they'd managed to get on board before the budget went dry for background checks.

"Not that, you idiot. We got another suicide."

"The boob thing?"

Sorensen's steel-blue eyes descended on Jon and stayed there until the young intern's cheeks turned red with heat. "I'm sorry, I didn't mean..."

Before he could finish his apology, Sorensen slapped his shoulder a little harder than needed. "Just remember this next time you have something clever to say about a case." He said and walked to the hallway.

Darcy followed him. Anything was better than staring at a computer screen and not knowing how to proceed. "Are you investigating, then?"

Sorensen stopped in front of the vending machine and got a Red Bull. "We got three. Too many for a coincidence."

Darcy filled his cup with black coffee and took a gulp, even though it was steaming. He squinted as he felt the hot liquid descend to his stomach. He didn't say anything.

"How's your hit-and-run-turned-attempted-murder going?"

"Nowhere. There seems to be absolutely no reason why somebody would want to kill this woman. Especially not bad enough to try on the highway and then again at her place."

Sorensen shook his head. His blond locks swung back and forth. "Man, the world's becoming a weird place."

"You're quite the existentialist," the captain said, a few feet away. "In my office. We need to talk about this," she said, tapping a set of files in her hand.

"You're going to write me up for bringing some quality philosophy into the workplace?"

"Bring Jon too. We can use his help."

"No, not Jon. He's too green."

"Sorensen, this is a suicide. There's probably nothing to investigate."

"Right. That's why we're going to your office."

Sorensen looked back at Darcy. "I'll trade you," he said.

CHAPTER 9

Virago sat behind her desk and set the files to the side. Sorensen and Jon took the chairs across from her and waited. She closed her eyes and exhaled audibly.

"It's the third suicide we've got. Same type of deal as the other two. I want to dedicate some real time to it. It's fishy, and I want to figure out what the hell's going on."

Sorensen nodded, a million questions forming in his head, but he didn't speak, because he knew she wasn't finished.

"I can't tell you what a PR cluster fuck this can be if the media starts making stories about this and we've got nothing."

That's what he was waiting for. Sorensen respected Virago but knew she was juggling too many balls. Several of them had to do with making her bosses look good in the eyes of the public, the politicians and other department heads.

"I want you to investigate it as a suspicious death"—she made quote marks with her fingers—"but talk about it as if it's a gruesome suicide so we don't generate panic, in case this starts showing up in the media, okay?"

"You got it. So far I've got nothing linking the first two vics, so we'll see if the third one brings any clarity," Sorensen updated.

"What can I do?" Jon asked, sounding eager.

"Follow Sorensen's lead. I'm counting on your contributions, Jon." She fixed her eyes on the intern and he shifted in his seat.

"Of course. I'll do everything I can."

She nodded. "That's all. Thanks." Virago put on her reading glasses, letting them know it was time to go.

Before Sorensen walked out, she reconsidered. "Sorensen, two minutes."

He did a one-eighty and sat back down in the chair. "Yes?"

"How's the search?"

"Still haven't found a new car. Why?"

Virago looked over her glasses. Her lips were pursed. "I don't have time for your games. You know what I mean."

"Captain, I'm okay. I don't need a partner. Besides, if I need moral support, I can always talk to Chu."

She raised a finger to admonish him. Her expression was stern, but her voice sounded too tired to be vicious. "Sorensen, I'm about to reach the limit. I've been asking you for over six months to find a new partner. I know it's hard to replace somebody like Chu, but you don't have a choice."

"I have Jon. He's actually helping a lot. I give him a hard time, but he's bright and gets shit done."

"And he's not a detective, so he's not a valid replacement."

"I can manage."

"What about Lynch?" she asked, ignoring his comment.

"No. I've told you many times. If I wanted a crippled partner, I already have one."

"Don't be an asshole. Chu retired with MS. He's not active, he doesn't want to work anymore, and he's happy spending quality time with his family, so leave it alone."

"He's happy? Spending quality time? He's happy not being able to make his own coffee or wipe his own ass? He's happy?

41

How is any of that quality time?" He raised his voice, and his right jugular pulsed with every heartbeat.

"I'm sorry. You know what I meant." She lowered her voice but met his eyes.

Sorensen shook his head, willing himself to calm down. He knew she didn't mean it the way it sounded.

"Chu retired. You have to move on—that's all I'm saying. Besides, you know I respect Chu a lot and he's one of the best detectives I've ever worked with, but he's gone, and you have to pick a new one or I'll assign one for you."

"Fine. Give me a couple weeks."

"These cases would go a lot faster if you worked with a partner."

" Okay, fine. Give me a week."

"I want three names no later than next Monday morning."

Sorensen nodded and left Virago's office.

CHAPTER 10

Tyler Warren eased his Tesla into a spot right outside the Los Altos Rod and Gun Club door. He had the best parking karma. He grabbed his large black duffle bag from the trunk and looked at the sky. Not a cloud and no wind. He opened the store's door after hearing the double beep of the car lock.

"Mr. Warren, how are you this morning?" Carmela asked from behind the counter. Two deep dimples framed her smile.

"Excellent, excellent," he said.

"I have row eight outdoors for you ready. The one at the very end, just as you requested."

"You always take good care of me, *chiquita.*"

When he saw her cringe, he winked and scribbled his signature on the form she'd pulled out when he came in.

Warren made a point of not using her real name, which was displayed on a tag pinned to her double-D chest. Ever since his first visit to the shooting range about two years earlier, he'd taken some guilty pleasure in seeing her face react when he called her *chiquita.* He didn't know why he did it, and he was amazed that it hadn't gotten old yet.

The store lighting reflected against the yellow walls. The large glass cases contained everything from vintage and antique guns, to revolvers and semiautomatic pistols of all sizes and calibers, and all the accessories a shooter could ever wish for. Shotguns and rifles occupied the wall space, and the shelves were filled with ammunition boxes.

"Excuse me," Warren said, passing behind a man drooling over a gun he probably would never be able to afford. His duffle bag brushed the man's shoulder, but he didn't protest.

He stopped before a pair of large double doors and fetched his 3M Peltor earmuffs. He eased them over his slick, gelled black hair and went inside. Warren passed by the rows of indoor shooting, surprised again that only three lanes were in use. He wondered briefly if it was the weak economy, but as soon as he went through the last set of doors, he understood that the perfect California weather had lured everyone to shoot outside.

His stride was strong, determined. He'd always walked as if he knew exactly where he was going. He reached row eight and started to settle in. He pulled his Sig P226 X-FIVE pistol and a box of ammo. He started loading the magazine.

A loud yet hesitant voice pulled him out of his concentration. "Mr. Warren."

"Ah, Harper, I'm glad you could join me." His smile was wide, almost genuine. He knew Harper wouldn't have refused.

Tyler pulled the slide back sharply. He turned his back on the visitor and aimed at the target. The shots from all the other lanes were muffled by the earmuffs and didn't distract him. His pulse was steady. The gun settled in his left hand, while the right cupped the grip. Warren pulled the trigger in rapid succession until the magazine was empty.

"That felt good," he said, turning back to Harper. "Would you like to shoot?" His hand extended, gun pointing downward as he ejected the magazine into his left hand.

"No, thank you. I do enough shooting back at the ranch."

Harper shoved his hands further into his pockets, as if to avoid temptation.

"Suit yourself, but it's a perfect day for it." He looked at the sky again. "I don't think I'll be able to claim a perfect score based on my ability alone," he said and laughed. It was a hearty laugh that came from the gut.

Harper shivered and kept quiet.

"I'm grateful for your progress," Tyler continued. "I think we're going to be okay." He began pushing new cartridges into the magazine.

Harper bowed his head. "You told me to be creative, so I'm making sure each one is different."

"Yes, and I hope you understand why."

Tyler now turned to look at him and placed the loaded gun on the shelf to his left, after inserting the freshly filled magazine. He dug through his bag and pulled out two more boxes of ammunition.

"Hold these for a sec," he said, handing them to Harper while he looked for something else. He finally found a few sheets of paper folded in half and held together by a silver paper clip on the left-hand corner. He handed them to Harper in exchange for the ammo. "These are the next ones."

Harper opened the folded papers and saw the new list. "How many more are there?" he asked under his breath. Sweat had begun to mist his forehead and create dark stains under his arms.

"Just a few more, Harper. Just a few more." He tried to sound reassuring, but his voice betrayed him, and sadness seeped through.

Before Tyler started shooting again, he turned again and locked eyes with Harper. With the words still lingering in the air, he smiled trying to lift the mood, showing perfectly aligned white teeth.

Tyler kneeled down again and grabbed a thick envelope from his bag. "Here's what we talked about for the latest work."

"You know that's not what I really want," Harper said, not taking the envelope.

"And I'm working on it, Harper. I told you already that you would be the first one to know when it's ready."

He placed the envelope on the shelf where the gun had been just moments ago. Tyler re-aimed the pistol at the target and started squeezing off shots in a deliberate cadence.

"Okay," Harper said, his voice muffled by the overwhelming noise. He took the envelope from the shelf. Tyler watched him walk away. His shoulders seemed too heavy for a man his age.

CHAPTER 11

Detective Darcy Lynch was tapping the floor of the squad room with his right foot. It was a tic that had driven more than one girlfriend to despair. He gnawed on the cap of a blue Bic pen while he listened to Lou.

"So basically, you've come up with absolutely nothing," he interrupted, holding the receiver harder than he needed to. His gaze was lost on a computer screen that had long ago gone black.

"What I'm telling you, Detective Lynch," Lou said, marking every word with a pause, "is that we've run about sixty percent of the items and have found no evidence so far." He took a deep breath and added, "We still have forty percent to go."

"You have the knife," Darcy said, feeling that he had to cling onto something.

"We have a possible match on the knife. I mean, at least we narrowed it to a particular kind of knife. It's sold in specialized hunting stores. The seat belt cut was really clean. That knife was extremely sharp."

Darcy closed his eyes. He pictured the head forensic scientist sitting in his office, his lab coat bursting around his huge stomach while his boyish haircut made him look at least ten years younger than he was.

"Thanks, Lou. I'm just frustrated. I have nothing. I don't think I've ever worked a case where I had so little to go on."

"We're working on it. I'll call you as soon as something comes up," Lou said and hung up.

Darcy put the phone down and clicked the mouse. The computer screen came alive. Before he was able to enter his password, Captain Virago caught his attention. She had come out of her office and was standing by the doorframe, as if waiting to be noticed.

He figured she'd been a knockout when she was younger, but juggling the job and three kids had done a number on her. Now she was a plump, middle-aged woman with good skin, beautiful eyes and graying roots that needed touch-ups more often than she took care of them.

"Yes?" he said, looking in her direction.

"I have an easy case for you."

Darcy lifted his left eyebrow and smirked. "I don't believe you."

"No, seriously," she said, walking toward his desk. She stopped on the other side, facing him, and explained. "A couple days ago there was a car accident."

"Oh, not again. The last one was supposed to be a hit-and-run, and look at me now, buried in a attempted murder." He rolled his eyes and slouched further in his chair.

"Stop the whining. Seriously, you're too manly to whine so much."

Darcy smiled.

"As I was saying, a car went off the road. It looked like the driver had fallen asleep at the wheel or something like that. But Lou's team worked its magic and found that the brakes had been tampered with." She handed him the case file.

"Oh, man. I wish they weren't so good at finding stuff sometimes," he said, pushing the folder away on his desk as if it were dirty. "You know this is going to be a shitter, like the one you just gave me yesterday."

"Lynch, you wanted easy, I'm here to oblige." She turned around and plugged her ears with her index fingers just in case he decided to whine some more.

He opened the file and read the report. It was a standard accident report until he got to the forensic notes. The brake lines had been punctured just enough for the fluid to leak out slowly.

Darcy hit the redial button on his desk phone and waited for Lou to answer. "Hey, is Rachel in the office?" he asked.

"Why? You want to ask her out?" Lou started laughing, but it sounded more like an asthmatic wheezing than a laugh. Darcy imagined Lou's belly lurching up and down like Jell-O and shook his head to push the image away. Lou ran out of air and almost choked. "Man, that was funny," he said once he finally caught his breath. "Can you imagine you with Rachel?" He started laughing again.

"Lou, really, stop it. She's a really nice lady. You shouldn't disrespect her like that." He waited until he made sure that Lou could hear him. "Virago just handed me the car accident she worked on. I wanted to ask her a few questions."

"Ah, that one. Are you specializing in car cases now?"

"Very funny. I'm surprised you are not cracking up at that one."

"She's doing some testing on the evidence we got from the latest suicide Sorensen's working on. She's very busy, so if you want to talk to her, I suggest you come over here and talk while she works."

Darcy walked to the forensic unit located a couple blocks away. The air was dry and the sky a beautiful deep blue with two parallel white stripes made by a plane flying high above. The structure was old—it could have been a courthouse or a post office in the past. The forensics lab and the morgue shared the entire building.

He figured Rachel would be in the lab, so he got into the large elevator and pushed *3*. He was alone. The doors closed after several seconds, and the elevator started going up with a whine, as if the effort were unbearable. After what seemed like a full minute, the doors opened and he walked into the lab's reception area.

"Mary, how are you?" Darcy asked, reaching the front desk. He didn't bother showing his badge.

"Doing great, handsome. When are you going to take me on that date you've been promising for months now?"

"As soon as you divorce that body-builder husband of yours. You know he scares me."

She patted his hand. "Who are you looking for?"

"Rachel. Is she around?"

"She is, actually. She was downstairs in the garage the whole morning, but she just came up. Do you want me to page her?" she asked, picking up the phone.

"No, I'll find her." He pointed to his left, toward a wide and short corridor that ended in large frosted doors, looking for confirmation.

Mary nodded. "I'll let you know as soon as I file those divorce papers," she called out behind him.

"And I'll make reservations," he replied without looking back.

Before he reached the doors, he heard a beep followed by the loud click that disengaged the lock. He pulled on the large handle, and the emptiness and silence of the lobby was suddenly replaced by the bustle of technicians working, walking and talking about their respective projects.

Darcy crossed paths with a few people he barely knew and nodded. He continued down the hall, peeking into each department, looking for Rachel. He finally found her in one of the last rooms. He opened the door and heard classical music coming out of Rachel's white headphones. She didn't notice him.

She stood barely five feet tall. Short silver curls, probably permed, framed her face. She didn't wear any makeup except for the brown kohl she used to carefully paint her almost nonexistent eyebrows. Her hands were small, but they moved efficiently through the evidence, even though they were twisted by arthritis. She had the most uncanny ability to do several things at once he'd ever seen.

A large metal table took up most of the room. Several pieces of evidence were spread on top of it, every single one tagged. He coughed, then again more loudly, but she still didn't hear him. He finally knocked on the table.

She jumped, clinching her lab coat around her chest. "Jesus Christ, Detective Lynch."

"But Rachel, with your adoration to heavy metal, there's no other way to get your attention."

"No, no. You just do it because you enjoy scaring the bejesus out of me." She pursed her lips but didn't keep that face for long. "Besides, I don't listen to heavy metal." Darcy winked, and she asked, "What can I do for you?"

"Jacqueline Pritchard's car," he said.

"Ah, yes. Just finished processing the brake lines about an hour ago."

She moved a few inches from the table and peeled off her latex gloves. Her nails were painted a Christmas red. Without looking at her notes, she said, "I checked the brake lines and I first was surprised to find brake fluid on the rubber hose going to each caliper in the front. So, I inspected the hoses and found one puncture in each. This would have caused the brake fluid to leak out."

"But wouldn't she have noticed the loss of brake pressure?"

"Probably, but with such an old car, the brakes were probably soft already and she may have not noticed until it was too late."

Darcy rubbed his temple. His eye was bothering him again. He nodded for her to continue.

"The pricks were very small."

"Have you narrowed it down? Do you have any ideas what could have been used to make them?"

She shook her head. "They may have been done with something as common as a pushpin. So no, there are too many things that could have been used to make such small holes." She reached for a set of color printouts she had taken from the microscope. "See this thing here?" She pointed at one of the holes.

"Yeah."

"Even when you blow it out to this size, you can see that there's nothing distinctive about it." Her shoulders hunched over, making her even tinier than she already was. "I'm sorry, Detective. I wish I had better news for you."

Darcy left Rachel and walked back to his office, wondering why somebody would have gone to the trouble to puncture the brakes lines of such an old car.

CHAPTER 12

Saffron grabbed the ceramic bowl from the floor and set it on the counter. It was pink and covered in colorful polka dots. In the center the words "Cat's Food" stood out in royal blue. She filled it with kibble, and Cat jumped onto the countertop, purring while circling and rubbing against Saffron's arms.

The bowl made her think about the time when she took her best friend's little girl to the Petroglyph Ceramic Lounge in Los Gatos several months earlier. Emma and her husband needed some time alone to discuss the different alternatives they faced. She'd noticed a lump in her left breast, and Dr. Leavenworth had strongly recommended doing a biopsy, or removal, rather than waiting another six months. They decided to go for the biopsy, and eight days later they got the results back. It was benign.

Saffron placed Cat's bowl back on the floor and remembered the day she had taken Sofia to the ceramic store. They had stopped first to get two big frozen yogurts, filled with sprinkles and hot fudge.

With dripping cups of halfway-melted yogurt, they entered the Petroglyph store and settled at a table. They almost took more time deciding which ceramic figure they wanted to decorate than actually painting it.

"I'm not going to tell you what I'm doing," Sofia said, sitting next to Saffron with a small bowl. She reached for her yogurt and finished it in a few big spoonfuls.

"Oh no? And why's that?" Saffron asked, putting some paints on the table.

"Ouch, ouch," Sofia complained, closing her eyes and pressing her hand against her forehead.

"You got a brain freeze? Press your tongue to the roof of your mouth," Saffron instructed.

The girl nodded and did, still holding her forehead with her tiny hands.

"So, why won't you tell me what you're going to make?" Saffron asked when the girl's pain was gone.

"Because I want it to be a surprise." Sofia was too young to have a smug smile, but she did.

Saffron moved a strand of light brown hair out of Sofia's face. The girl watched her with incredibly large eyes behind matching green-paste glasses. Saffron smiled and began to work. Sofia did the same.

After a few minutes of deep concentration, Sofia said, "I need some help."

"Sure, what is it?"

"I want to make sure I spell 'Cat' the right way."

"Okay. Do you want me to help you pick the letters?"

"Yes!" she said, pushing herself off the table so fast the chair almost fell to the floor. "Sorry," she apologized, looking embarrassed.

Saffron smiled, waving her hand, mouthed, "It's okay."

They huddled over the three buckets with letters. Checking one by one took too long, so Saffron grabbed a handful and set them on the table. They both searched.

"How would you spell 'Cat'?" Saffron asked.

"Here, I found a *C*." Sofia did a happy dance, holding the letter in her tiny hand.

"That's excellent. What do we need to find next?"

"An *A*. Right?"

"Absolutely." Saffron picked one and showed it to her. Sofia grabbed it and placed it carefully next to the *C*.

After going through a couple more handfuls of letters, they finally found the *T* and moved back to table. A few minutes later, Sofia asked for help again, this time to spell the word "food."

An extra letter made it back to the table later. The *S*. Saffron's heart got warm when she saw Sofia was actually using the possessive correctly.

"What do you think?" The girl asked once the last coat of paint was done.

"I love it." It was surprising that a six-year-old could make something so cute. "And what do you think of my mug?"

"I think you should give it to me for my birthday." That snooty smile framed her face again.

"But your birthday was a few months ago and you already got a lot of presents."

"No. For my next birthday."

"You think? I bet you'll forget all about this present when you turn seven next year."

"No, I won't!"

"Are you sure?"

"Absolutely," she said, mimicking Saffron from earlier.

"Okay, then. But you should know that I'm going to remind you if you forget."

Sofia took one of the few clean paper towels left on the table and, with a brush still full of pink paint, wrote, "Birthday present." After she inspected it to make sure all the words were spelled correctly, she handed the reminder to Saffron.

Two weeks later they went back to pick up the baked pieces. The pink bowl had turned out perky and girlie. Perfect for

Cat. The mug was bright blue and covered with orange sea creatures. Chocolate milk would probably look pretty gross in it, but Sofia seemed happily pleased.

The noise of Cat scratching the sofa brought Saffron back to the present. "Hey, Cat, stop that," she said.

Her entire body hurt as if she had done three hours of cross-training. The adrenaline from the car crash the night before was starting to take a toll.

She grabbed her jacket and purse and locked her front door on the way out. She headed back to the hospital, hoping Ranjan's uncle wouldn't be there, so she could spend some time alone with her boyfriend.

The afternoon rush hour hadn't started yet, so the drive was fast. When she walked into the hospital she noticed that her jaw hurt. She realized that it had nothing to do with the adrenaline. She'd been clenching her teeth during the entire drive in anticipation of running into Dr. Balasubramanian again. Saffron wondered how Ranjan could still be so close to a man so strict and narrow-minded when he was so open and interesting. But maybe it was the blood tie. "Who knows?" she asked out loud when she opened the door to Room 305.

What she saw when she walked in made her wished she'd never come.

CHAPTER 13

Sorensen turned up the volume on the radio, masking the engine's roar. "I love this song," he said when the raspy twang of Carrie Underwood came up. He started singing, completely out of tune.

Sorensen saw Jon trying to hide a smile by looking out the window. He still looked a little green from his first crime scene.

"What's so funny?" Sorensen tried to fluster the intern.

"I just find it funny that a Viking like you likes country music." Jon said, crossing his arms and not meeting Sorensen's eyes.

"Nothing wrong with that. I bet you like some hip-hop crap talking about beating the shit out of somebody's mother." He slammed on the brakes, launching both of their bodies against the seat belts. "Asshole!" he yelled at the car that had just cut them off. "I should give him a ticket for reckless driving."

"Can you do that?" Jon asked.

"I can do anything. I'm Erik the Viking Sorensen." He pounded his chest twice with a closed fist. "What do you make of these suicides?" he asked, changing the subject.

"What's the saying: 'Once is chance, twice is coincidence, third time is a pattern'?"

Sorensen nodded. "It's really strange that the three deaths occurred in pretty much the same exact way, but they're all suicides."

"Did you see anything suspicious at any of the crime scenes?" Jon asked. "I didn't notice anything from the reports."

"No."

"Do you think somebody may have tampered with them in any way?"

"It didn't seem that way, but anything's possible."

"Do you believe somebody could have killed these three women and left no evidence behind?" Jon pushed.

"That's hard to believe. But we don't have the final evidence report. Something may still come up," Sorensen said, sounding more hopeful than he felt. "The thing that keeps me awake, besides the images that won't go away, is why would somebody want to kill these women that way? There are many easier ways to kill somebody, even if you want to make it look like a suicide."

"Yeah," Jon echoed, "why do it this way? Why these women?" Then he added, "I haven't found any connection between them so far."

The GPS in Sorensen's car was broken. Jon checked his phone. "We're getting really close. In about two streets, turn right. It should be the second house on the right. The yellow one."

Sorensen turned to look at him for longer than was safe. "How the hell do you know the color of the house?"

"I checked Google's Street View."

He touched the screen of his phone a couple times and showed it to him. A one-story yellow house with white trim was staring back at him.

"Man, that's some creepy shit," Sorensen said and made the first right, still shaking his head.

"There, that's the one." Jon pointed to a modest house with a well-manicured lawn and colorful flowerbeds.

58

They walked toward the house. Sorensen took out his small black notebook to double-check the name. When they reached the porch, he put the notebook back in his pocket and stood there. Nobody rang the doorbell. They exchanged glances.

"What the hell are you waiting for, Jon?"

When he pressed the bell, musical chimes rang inside the house. They waited. After a couple seconds Jon pushed the button again.

"I don't think anybody's home."

"Really?" Sorensen rolled his eyes.

"Excuse me...?" a voice called from the street.

They turned toward a small elderly woman with a white poodle.

"Excuse me? Are you looking for Mrs. Robinson's daughter?" Before they could respond, she said, "You know that poor Taisha died, right?"

They walked toward the old lady, Sorensen taking the lead. "Good afternoon, ma'am. I'm Detective Erik Sorensen, and this is Jon Evans. Yes, we knew."

He extended his hand. Hers disappeared in his when she took it.

"Very nice to meet you. I'm Isobel. Isobel Lewis."

"Did you know Mrs. Robinson well?" Sorensen asked.

"Yes, we were best friends. I still cannot believe what she did." She shook her head, as if trying to push the thought away. "I live right next door. Would you like some tea?"

"If it's not too much trouble," Sorensen said.

Her house was as modest as Mrs. Robinson's. The entry walls were covered with flowery paper that was probably a hundred years old. At the end of the narrow hallway there was a tiny, lacquered wooden stand covered by a crochet tablecloth and five small porcelain figurines, all evenly placed.

"Coats?" Isobel asked, opening the entry closet. It was very full and it smelled musty, as if it stored old treasures that were in dire need of dusting.

"We're okay, thank you," Sorensen said.

She took off her own jacket and placed it on a hanger that held three other ones. Both men made a gesture to help hang it, but she swiftly inserted it in the crammed closet and closed the door with a soft thud.

"Cookie, come over here," Isobel called down the hallway. The dog trotted back wagging her tail. "You don't want to walk around on a leash all day, do you?" she asked, shaking her head. She removed the leash and hung it on a little hook by the closet door. She then led them to the living room. "Please sit. I'll make some tea."

The sofa was the same yellow as the victim's house. It was old but well kept. Sorensen and Jon watched Isobel fill the kettle in the open kitchen. Cookie settled down between the two men and started snoring almost immediately. Isobel took a box of biscuits from the cupboard. She placed three saucers, tiny porcelain cups and spoons on a tray, and brought it to the coffee table while the water began to boil. Jon helped her set the cups and then took the tray back to the kitchen.

"Can I help you with anything?" he asked.

"It would be lovely if you could bring the biscuits to the table, dear," she said, handing him a full plate of tea pastries. Jon took it and sat again on the sofa.

The old woman came back and served everybody tea without saying a word. Jon looked uncomfortable, and Sorensen wondered if Jon was the kind of person who didn't deal well with silence. He made a mental note to learn more about that. Jon was an extremely valuable researcher, but Erik knew there was more he could do.

"Isobel, I understand that you were the one who found Mrs. Robinson, right?"

The hand that was holding the saucer started to tremble, rattling the cup and the tiny spoon.

"Yes, I found her." She took a deep breath. "It was her turn to come to my house for tea. You see, we always have tea…had tea together. Mondays, Wednesdays and Fridays we met here. Tuesdays, Thursdays and Saturdays we went to her house. Sundays we always had tea after Mass at a tiny coffee place next to our church, down by First Street. You may know it."

The two men shook their heads, then Sorensen nodded for her to proceed. Jon nibbled on a chocolate cookie. Sorensen put a whole one in his mouth.

"It was a Wednesday, so she had to come over. But it was already ten minutes past three and she was never, ever late." She took a sip and closed her eyes, then shook her head. The plate started shaking again. She held it with both hands and put it back on the coffee table.

"So I went over to see why she was late. I knocked first, but there was no response. I knew she was home, so then I got scared and thought that maybe she had fallen or something. You know, at our age you never know…I have a key. She had one for my place too. I opened the door and called her. There was no reply. I went to the kitchen first, then her bedroom. She wasn't there. Then I saw that the door to the backyard was open. She had a little shed there. She was very proud of her roses. I thought maybe she'd gone there to do something and lost track of time."

Sorensen took another cookie. Isobel finished her tea before she continued.

"That's when I saw her. She was on the ground. Facedown. I rushed to her and saw the blood. I couldn't move her. She was quite bigger than me, so I ran back to the house and called 911. They didn't want me to stay, but I did anyway. When they came, I saw the big garden shears and all the blood. Then I found out she had hurt herself." She shook her head, her face still showing disbelief.

"Do you have any idea why she would've done that?" Sorensen asked.

"She had cancer. Breast cancer. I think it was her way to tell the world that the cancer didn't win."

"I'm so sorry for your loss," Jon said.

Sorensen stood. "Thank you very much for the tea, Isobel," he said, holding her hand softly in both of his.

She walked them to the door. Right before Isobel closed it, Jon turned.

"Mrs. Lewis, do you know who Mrs. Robinson's doctor was?" Jon asked before she closed the door.

"I do. I recommended her. Dr. Leavenworth, down at Good Samaritan Hospital."

CHAPTER 14

Detective Lynch clicked the cursor on his computer to display the next picture. Another large hunting knife appeared. The specs detailed overall length, blade length, width, material, handle thickness and composition. The knives all looked pretty much the same to him. Some were completely smooth, some were serrated. Others were both. Some were long, others short. Most were black or gray and made of stainless steel, with rubber, wood or nylon handles... He clicked faster and faster to the next images, frustrated that none of the details meant enough to him to make a connection to the case.

Two files were open on his desk, staring back at him. Two cases. Both involving cars. He doubted that Lou or Rachel would be able to narrow down the type of knife much more than they already had. After all, the fringes of a cut seat belt could only provide so much insight. Or maybe he was just feeling negative.

He clicked the mouse one more time and another knife appeared, but he didn't really look at it. He knew he was just wasting his time. He was trying to figure out what he could do that might be useful and knew that browsing knives on the Internet was not really it. He sighed, reached out for his coffee and took a sip. The liquid was dark, cold and stale.

"This is disgusting," he said to nobody in particular.

He headed to the kitchen and saw Jon coming toward him.

"When the hell are we going to get decent coffee in this joint?" Darcy spat his words at him, as if the responsibility of good coffee fell on the young man.

Jon stared at him but didn't engage.

"How was it?" Darcy asked the intern when he got back from the kitchen with a fresh, steaming cup.

"Which one?"

Darcy didn't answer but gave him a quizzical look.

"We just came from Mrs. Robinson's house. Ended up talking to the neighbor." He swallowed, Darcy noticed that his face was still ashen, as if Jon was suffering from a really bad ulcer. "We went first to Sheila Rothschild's house. It was awful."

"There was so much blood." Jon blinked a few times. "This woman carved her breast out and bled to death on her kitchen floor. What on earth could make a person do that to herself?"

"So, pretty much the same as the other two suicides, right? Just different suicide…tool?" Lynch asked, not quite sure how to phrase it.

"It looks like it."

Darcy turned toward the hallway, feeling Sorensen's presence the moment he walked out of the elevator. He was one of those men who could never sneak up on someone, and not only because of his size. There was something in the air that changed when he was present, as if his body heat was high enough to change the room temperature.

"Man, this is getting old. Have you reconsidered switching cases with me yet?" Sorensen asked Lynch when he came into the room.

"Anytime."

"You know the weirdest thing?" he asked. "These women don't seem to have a single thing in common. They are all

64

from different parts of town, with different incomes, social circles, ages. Jesus, I just have no idea what's going on."

"Remember that movie from M. Night Shyamalan?" Darcy asked. "The one where people start killing themselves and nobody knows why, and at the end it's because of something from the trees, or whatever?"

"*The Happening*," Jon said.

They both looked at him. Jon looked away.

"M. Night is one of my favorite directors. I have all of his movies." His face flushed.

"What about it?" Sorensen focused back on Darcy. He combed his hair smoothing out his blond curls.

Darcy smiled to himself, secretly hoping that one day Sorensen would lose his hair. He would look like a large egg if he ever shaved his head.

"Nothing. This case just reminds me of that movie. I bet at the end there'll be some supernatural explanation."

Jon looked at Darcy with piqued interest. When the detective winked at him, he saw Jon's excitement fade as he blushed a little. Sorensen stared at both.

"Yeah, thanks, man," he said and sat down, chugging the remainder of a Red Bull that had been sitting on his desk for hours. "If you come up with any more brilliant ideas about how to solve my cases, please make sure you share."

Darcy found it funny that Sorensen always wanted to have the last word. Without engaging back, he picked up the phone and dialed. "Miss Meadows, this is Detective Lynch," he said, leaving a voice mail. "I was wondering if you could come to the station for a little bit to take a look at some knives. I should be here for another hour or so. Please call me back when you get this." He hung up after leaving his office number in case she didn't have his card with her.

CHAPTER 15

Harper Johnson left the shooting range and headed home. Traffic was not too bad going toward the mountains. He took the Mount Hermon Road exit, and after a few miles he turned left into the McDonald's drive-through.

"Good afternoon, what can I get you?" a teenage voice asked through the machine.

"Two Big Macs, large fries, large Cherry Berry Chiller and extra ketchup."

"That'll be thirteen dollars sixty-eight cents."

He drove a few feet forward to the window, and a young girl with pink hair handed him a paper bag with the food. Harper set it on the passenger's seat, grabbed the drink out and drove the last few miles to his house. Slowing the car, he made a left on the private road and checked the mailbox, finding nothing in it. He drove a few more yards and parked right outside his house.

The brown paint was peeling and there were several places where it was gone altogether. The screen door screeched when he opened it. It was gloomy inside, but the place was tidy and clean. He put the food on the dining table and grabbed a beer from the fridge. While he ate, he stared at the new list Tyler Warren had given him.

There were three names. Each had a picture, a work and home address, daily schedules, activities and a list of likely places where they could be found. The second name grabbed his attention. David Jameson. He read the bio and then flipped to the page relating to activities and possible whereabouts. Halfway through he stopped and checked the date on the magnet calendar on the fridge's door and then his watch. He got up from the table, leaving half a burger uneaten on top of the paper bag but grabbed one last fry. If he rushed, he might be able to take care of him right away.

Harper moved the chairs out of the way, slid the table with the uneaten food toward the wall and lifted the rug. He then opened the trapdoor to the basement and descended. Only a couple steps squeaked in protest. He reached his gun safe underneath the stairs, punched in the code and stared at its contents. The safe held a lot less than it had a few years earlier. He went for the AR-15 rifle, leaving the Benelli 12-gauge shotgun behind. He grabbed a box of ammo and confirmed that there were enough rounds. After locking the safe he headed upstairs.

He replaced the rug and table and left, not bothering to lock his place up. He had already pawned everything of value, and nobody would ever guess there was a basement in the house. Before he started the car he saw Lasky running toward him. He opened the door and let the Lab mutt come up and lick his face.

"Where have you been, you crazy dog?" he said, smiling for the first time that day.

The dog continued to lick him while he rubbed her behind the ears. She got down on the ground and pounced, while her tail wagged the rest of her body.

"You want to come?" he asked.

The dog jumped into the cabin of the truck, leaving muddy paw prints on Harper's already dirty jeans. She sat down shotgun and stared happily at him, with her tongue sticking out to one side.

Johnson turned on the radio but only half listened to it. He got back onto Highway 17 and drove for a few minutes until he reached the Scotts Valley Wildlife Ranch. He had not been able to renew his hunting permit in the last few years but knew the area well. He parked the car on the side of the road in a somewhat hidden spot and got out, letting Lasky come with him. He followed the fence a few yards until he found the opening he had been using since he stopped being able to afford the hunting license.

He knew the wannabe hunters' routine. They started together, early, walking through the forest as if they knew what they were doing. A few hours into it, they started feeling cranky, their fancy coffees were gone, and their clothes started clinging to their bodies with sweat due to the increasing heat. He remembered being surprised when he took his first hunting party out as a guide. They had no stamina, no patience. After a few more tours, he wasn't surprised anymore. He knew exactly what to expect.

Lasky followed him, only increasing the distance between them by a few feet when she thought she could catch something. She stopped, smelled the air, pricked her ears and pounced. Then did it all over again. She was used to hunting for food, as it was rare that Harper got any for her. He always thought that she had some Bluetick in her. He had almost called her Blue back when he got her but then decided that naming her after a color was stupid.

He listened for voices. That was the other thing the city hunters were not so good at. The moment they got bored, they started yapping away. He thought he heard something. He stopped and patted his thigh for Lasky to come and sit by him. In complete stillness he listened. After a few moments he discerned voices coming from the east. The sounds were moving away, so he walked toward them to see if he could spot his target. Two men strolled between the trees as if they were in a park. Maybe that was all they could do, Harper thought, shaking his head. Unless Jameson had put on over a hundred pounds, he was looking at the wrong party.

He continued to wait. He was good at waiting. He sat, leaned against a tree trunk and cleaned his nails with the tip of his knife. The sun was still bright, but it had started its slow descent. Harper folded the knife and checked his watch. He decided to follow a few well-known trails heading toward the entrance of the hunting ground, expecting Jameson would have to come that way eventually, if he was still there.

After almost another hour of searching, he sensed movement. He watched until he could see the men well. There were three of them, getting closer to him but not heading directly toward his location on the trail.

Harper looked around and found a large tree about ten feet to his right. He reached it and rested his rifle against the gnarled oak. He checked to make sure it was loaded. He knew he had loaded it in the truck before leaving but wanted to double-check. He was not sure David Jameson was among the three men who were coming, but he wanted to be ready if he was.

He pulled the printout Tyler Warren had given him and studied the photo. He didn't want to kill the wrong guy. Harper concentrated on the sounds around him. The forest noises were increasingly displaced by the sounds of the approaching men, who started to come into view.

One was large, almost as tall as him, but probably beat him by fifty pounds. The one in the middle was David Jameson. He was the shortest of the three. His hair was gelled, just as Warren's always was. He shook his head. It always amazed him that these city slickers didn't know deer could smell that shit from miles away.

All of his hunting clothes were new. Harper was sure Jameson had just got them from the Cabela's catalog and removed the price tags that morning before he put them on. The last man was the eldest. Harper recognized him. His name was Sam Baker, and he was the guide. They had shared some beers in better times and laughed at the ineptitude of the city hunters.

He knew he would have to separate them. He looked around and found a nice wooden stick. He grabbed it and showed it to Lasky. He seized his rifle. When he was ready, he looked at his dog, tempted her with the stick, glanced at the men walking about sixty yards in front of him and then threw the branch as far as he could toward his ten o'clock.

Lasky sprinted away, rustling the vegetation as she went by. The noise got the attention of the three men. They stopped talking. Harper saw them stiffen a little in anticipation of catching a decent buck. Sam gestured for his clients to get in position on opposite sides of the ridge overlooking a clearing. David Jameson and the other man exchanged glances and began to move away from each other, communicating via hand motions as if they were in a military operation. It took him everything he had to not burst into laughter.

Harper lifted his rifle and aimed. He had a clear shot at Jameson's head. He pulled the trigger and felt the recoil in his shoulder. Before he could move his eyes away, the rifle slug entered Jameson's back. The man stood for a moment and then fell against the tree he'd been hiding behind. Harper lowered the rifle at the same time Lasky returned with the stick, wagging her tail. Nobody would believe a shot to the head to be a hunting accident.

CHAPTER 16

Saffron's first surprise was to find Ranjan's room empty. But that feeling was quickly replaced by disbelief, indignation and finally rage when she spotted a close-up picture of a beautiful Indian woman on the table by her boyfriend's bed. She walked closer and realized there were more. The photographs were professionally made. The women were all smiling, with nice white teeth and deep black eyes that tempted the camera. Not one was over twenty-five years old. Saffron wondered who were the engineers and who were the doctors.

She then noticed the other papers on the table. They were bios. She glanced through them. All from good families with great dowries. She was still leafing through the documents when she heard Ranjan down the hall, joking with somebody. She thought about putting the photos down and pretending she hadn't seen them, but she knew her face would tell Ranjan everything he needed to know.

He was pushed into the room in a wheelchair. His color was back and he looked happy. His smile faded fast the second he saw Saffron in the room, still holding the portraits. The male nurse awkwardly stopped in his tracks, without reaching the bed.

"I can manage from here," Ranjan said. "Thank you for pushing me around, Albert."

"Anytime," he said and nodded at Saffron, quickly leaving the room after that.

Saffron raised the photos. Her hands were shaking and she couldn't find the words she wanted to say.

"Saffron…" Ranjan started. "I told you in the restaurant that my whole family was insisting."

She raised the pictures higher, still unable to speak.

"They just want me to meet them. That doesn't mean I have to marry one of them."

Her jaw clenched. She put the photos back on the table and finally asked, "And you can't say no? Why do you have to meet them if you're not interested? Or are you?"

He tilted his head as she spoke, recoiling from the high pitch. "Why won't you understand that this is something very important to them?"

"Of course it is," Saffron scoffed.

"Don't do that." He shook his head slowly. "Please, let me appease my family. Once I tell them I don't like any of them, things can go back to normal."

"Ranjan, you do know you're lying to yourself, right? Your family is never going to give up."

"Please, Saffron, let me handle this."

"If you could win this argument, you would've done it already."

"Can you just let me handle this?"

She looked at him. Her cheeks were flushed and she felt a drop of sweat slide between her breasts. She crossed her arms and stared at him with daring green eyes.

"I think you're interested."

He shook his head, suddenly looking worn-out.

"I think you want to check them out, because you might find exactly what you want. And you know what? I hope you do, because once I walk out that door, you and I are over."

"Why are you doing this?"

"Because this is obviously what you want but you don't have the balls to do it yourself."

She waited for him to protest. When he didn't, she knew she was right. Saffron fought every urge she felt to beat the crap out of him. She wanted to but knew she would feel even worse having assaulted a man in a wheelchair. Her phone began to ring, but she ignored it. The noise filled the room, but she didn't feel any relief. After the third ring, it stopped.

"Good luck to you, Ranjan," she said and walked by him toward the door.

She hoped he would grab her hand, ask her to stop, but he didn't. Outside, she heard him get off the wheelchair and slide his feet toward the bed.

CHAPTER 17

Darcy watched Sorensen put up the new victim's photo on his case board. Below, he carefully wrote in block letters "NAME: Sheila Rothschild. DOB: 7-16-65. TOD: around 8:30 a.m." Then he paused and looked back at the file, searching. He wrote "Likes to BBQ?"

"Do you find that useful?" Darcy asked him.

"What? The board?" Sorensen put the file back on his desk.

"Yeah. We didn't do anything like that in Seattle."

"I do. Find it useful. It helps me think. I often add things that don't even seem relevant at the time, but that for some reason grab my attention. Sometimes they end up meaning something. Sometimes they don't."

Sorensen turned back to his board. "See this?" he said, pointing to the second victim, Taisha Robinson.

Darcy got up from his chair and walked closer to Sorensen's board. Leaning on the desk, he said, "Likes gardening."

"She had a shed and a very nice backyard. Beautiful flowers and bushes all well pruned. She was an old woman and yet she must have spent a lot of time in the yard."

"Okay..." Darcy said, not really understanding why that mattered. "So?"

"Well, the tool she used to mutilate herself was some gardening shears. See this one?" Sorensen pointed to his new victim.

"Yes. She liked to barbecue."

"She had a nice kitchen and a full set of Henckels barbecue tools. They are the best in the market. I wish I could afford a set like hers." He paused and looked at Lynch. "She carved her breast out with a barbecue fork."

Darcy nodded.

"Does it mean anything?" Sorensen asked, more in general than to Lynch. "I don't know yet. Maybe. But having it out on the board helps me keep it in the back of my mind. You never know when a brilliant idea is going to surprise you."

He smiled and hit Darcy on the shoulder. This was the first sign of camaraderie Darcy had felt coming from the huge detective.

"I think I'm going to try it," Darcy said, heading toward the supply closet.

A few minutes later he came back with a brand-new whiteboard a little smaller than Sorensen's. He placed it on the right side of his desk, close to his chair, so he could write while seated. He browsed through the first file, trying to figure out what he wanted to highlight. He picked Saffron's DMV picture and put it up. He stared at it for a few seconds. It didn't do her justice. He looked for a better photo, but there weren't any others. Darcy made a mental note to print the photo from her LinkedIn profile later. He rummaged some more and settled on a picture of the totaled car and a smaller one of Ranjan. He still hadn't ruled him out as the main victim yet, though he was almost sure this wasn't about him.

He looked over Sorensen's board to see what type of information he had written on it and copied it on his own. Instead of time of death, he wrote the time of both incidents, the hit and run on the road and the chase after the perp ran away from Saffron's place when they got there. Then he added everything else he could think of, but specially the first things that popped into his head: knife, Timberland boots, black leather gloves, stolen truck.

When he ran out of evidence, he wrote the biggest question of all in red marker: "Motive." He looked at the word and then added two question marks after it. He stared at the board for a few minutes, trying to take in all of the information and wondering if there was anything else he wanted to write or thought he should. Nothing came to mind. He felt green doing this exercise, as if he were back in school taking a test he hadn't prepared for. The initial feelings of enthusiasm he had felt by writing all of this down died instantly when he realized he still had nothing.

Darcy reread the entire file but didn't find anything else worth noting. He then moved on to Jacqueline Pritchard. He pinned her DMV picture. She hadn't been a very attractive woman, but she looked kind. Her wiry silver bob accentuated her round face and crooked teeth. There were smile lines around her eyes and mouth. She was an elementary school teacher. She lived alone and would have retired in a couple years. She had a cat.

"Saffron has a cat," he said to himself and wrote "Cat" toward the bottom of the board, under both names.

He focused on the CSU report. Based on the information from Rachel, the lines must have been punctured anywhere from a few minutes to several hours before the accident. He wrote "Pushpin?" as well.

He leafed through the file one more time to see if anything else caught his attention. Mrs. Pritchard was divorced, didn't have children but had a sister living in Arizona. She had been notified at the time of the accident and was making arrangements to come to California to claim the body. He decided to give her a call.

"Mrs. Hudson, my name is Detective Darcy Lynch. I'm very sorry for your loss," he said as soon as Jacqueline's sister answered the phone. "I would like to ask you a few questions about your sister if you have the time."

"Hello, Detective. I just arrived in San Jose. I was on my way to my sister's. Would you like to meet there?"

"Yes, I'll come by in thirty minutes."

He read the file one more time, just to make sure he had all of the information fresh in his mind, then headed for his car. He decided to take the surface streets to avoid the beginning of rush hour. The journey took him a little longer than he expected, but he managed to be late by only a few minutes. He parked on the street.

The house was modest but well kept. The grass looked recently mowed. The white trim was bright and contrasted nicely with the red door. Darcy had always liked red doors for some reason.

He rang the bell and set his sunglasses to the top of his head. The spitting image of Jacqueline Pritchard opened the door. He was surprised, and it must have shown.

"Yes, I know. People used to think we were twins," Michelle Hudson said, extending her hand. "I'm actually a year older than my sister." A shadow of sadness darkened her face. "Detective Lynch, I'm assuming?" When he nodded, she said, "Please, come in."

They walked in silence to the kitchen, where she poured two generous cups of tea without asking him if he wanted any. Then she motioned for them to go to the living room. It was spacious and bright. Two large bay windows faced the backyard. A young plum tree provided a bit of shade for the tomato bushes.

"We can go to the patio if you want. I always forget that it's often nicer outside than inside in California. That's rarely the case in Arizona. Too hot."

They went to the back and sat on two comfortable lounge chairs. The light breeze made the afternoon pleasant and fresh with fruit tree scents.

"Were you two close?" Darcy asked.

"Yes. We'd always been. It was a really hard decision for me to move to Arizona, but Jackie had just got married and my job offered me a good package if I relocated. We talked every week. I knew something was wrong when I called her last Sunday and I couldn't reach her. By Monday I was not surprised when the police called me to tell me that she had been in a fatal accident."

He nodded. "Did she have a good marriage?"

"For the most part. Ron was a nice man."

"Why did it end?" He took a sip of the tea. It was really strong. He wasn't expecting that, and it made him cough.

"Ah, sorry, I should have warned you," she said with a smile. "Old habit."

"It's good. The light color threw me off."

She closed her eyes and smelled the steaming cup. She had a serene expression, as if the scent had transported her to somewhere far away with good memories.

"She wanted children and he didn't. At the end, they were both too smart to realize that neither would change their mind, so they went their separate ways. That was over fifteen years ago."

"Did she get along with everybody at work? Did she belong to any clubs or groups? Do you think she had any enemies?"

Mrs. Hudson looked at him over the rim of the mug. She then focused on the yard and then back at him. "Detective Lynch, I thought my sister died in a car accident. Went over the railing at a curve or something like that. Why are you asking me all of these questions?"

"We have some reason to believe that somebody tampered with her brakes."

Her eyebrows rose. She set the cup down on the tiny table between them. "Why on earth would anybody do that?"

"That's what I was hoping you could help me figure out. Can you think of anybody who would want to hurt your sister?"

"No. But if there was somebody, all they had to do was wait a few months."

Darcy looked at her, uncomprehending.

"She had breast cancer. Terminal."

CHAPTER 18

Saffron decided she was done crying. Dozens of crumpled Kleenex covered her coffee table, some spilling over onto the floor. She picked them up in a quick, swift motion and threw them into the kitchen garbage can. She blew her nose one more time, avoided looking at herself in the mirror by the door and dialed to return the long-overdue phone call.

"Detective Lynch, I believe you wanted to talk to me about knives," she said. Her voice was raspy from all the crying.

"I'm on my way back to the station. Could you meet me there?"

"Actually, if it's not urgent, can we meet tomorrow?" She almost told him she had broken up with Ranjan but figured he wouldn't care about her personal business.

"Sure, no problem. Any time in the morning would work."

"Okay," she said and felt the tears come again.

"Are you okay?"

"Yes, yes. See you tomorrow." She hung up.

She called Emma, who promised to be there in less than an hour. Saffron opened a bottle of wine, but before pouring a glass she took a long, hot shower. Her hair was still wet when Emma showed up.

"Jesus, the taxi service is getting worse by the day in this town," Emma said as Saffron opened the door. As soon as she saw Saffron's face, she changed gears. "How are you?" she asked while they hugged.

"Not so well."

Saffron started crying again. Emma stroked her hair and told her everything was going to be okay, as if she were a little girl. After a few minutes, she calmed down and poured two generous glasses of Merlot. They moved to the balcony, and Saffron told her everything that had happened in excruciating detail.

"Wait, wait. What do you mean somebody tried to kill you? Shouldn't you be crying about that instead of this douchebag?"

Saffron laughed. "I guess you're right," she said. "To be honest, I was so worried about Ranjan in the hospital, then so upset about his dick uncle, that I really hadn't had any time to think about that."

"Girl, you better start. What do you think's going on?"

"Honestly? I think it's a misunderstanding. I mean, I've got no money, no company secrets, haven't pissed off anybody that badly..." She took a sip of wine and thought more about other possible options. "There's just no reason at all why anybody would want to kill me."

"And yet he's tried. Twice."

"But now I have—what do they call it in the movies?—my own personal police detail," she said and smiled, pointing at the car stationed on the other side of the street.

"I don't think you should be so flippant about it. This is serious." Emma refilled the glasses. "Why don't you come and stay with us for a while?"

"And lose my handsome cops out there watching over me? No way."

"Maybe you can bring them along."

They toasted to the idea. Emma's phone rang.

"Sorry, Sofia is with the baby-sitter, so I have to check."

Saffron nodded and started thinking about the man with the Timberland boots and the shiny knife. The weather was still hot for October, but she felt a shiver. Emma was right: she should take this more seriously.

"Crap, my baby-sitter has an emergency back home. I have to get back."

"Okay, no worries."

"I wanted to spend the evening with you, but I can't reach Bob. It went to voice mail, and I know he had back-to-back calls with Asia tonight."

She hung up and dialed the number for a taxi.

"Why don't you come?"

"No. I'm going to stay in, watch a sappy movie and catch up on email."

"Read them, but make sure you don't answer any."

Saffron gave her a puzzled look.

"I don't think you are in any state to do real work," she said, pointing to the empty glass in her hand.

"I think you're very right," Saffron poured another one.

"What?" Emma asked speaking into the phone. "The taxi's going to take twenty minutes. Can you believe that?" she said to Saffron, not covering the phone with her hand.

"What happened to your car?"

"It's in the shop. They told me it would just take a few hours but then called me to say they needed to change something or other and it had to be there overnight."

"Take my car if you are sober enough to drive."

"Are you sure? What are you going to do tomorrow?"

"I can always ask my new friends for a ride. I have some police business to take care of in the morning anyway," she said, trying to sound smug but already slurring the words a little.

"You are the best, thank you."

Emma kissed her on the head. They hugged, and she headed toward the door.

"Remember to lock up behind me," she shouted back and took Saffron's spare car keys before closing the door.

"I love you too, Emma," Saffron responded and smiled. "You are the best friend in the world," she said, even though she knew Emma wouldn't hear her.

CHAPTER 19

Tyler Warren opened the bottom drawer of his desk and pulled two new shirts. One was white with thin blue and burgundy stripes. The other was black with that sheen that only new shirts seem to have. He chose the black one. Without bothering to close the blinds in his office, he stripped from the waist up and put on the new shirt. Nobody bothered to look. This had become routine in the last few months.

He splashed on some cologne and headed for the bathroom. He thought of shaving but decided that the five-o'clock shadow gave him a more masculine look. His hair was still held in place by the morning's gel and his eyes were bright, even though he was tired. His tanned skin masked the dark circles but intensified his few crow's-feet. He grabbed his jacket and, satisfied with his look, left the office. His Omega said it was 7:30. He barely had thirty minutes to make it from Palo Alto to San Francisco. He was going to be late.

The Tesla weaved between traffic while Warren listened to a TED podcast on the potential of regenerative medicine. Thirty-five minutes later, Interstate 280 turned into King Street—he had finally reached the South of Market district. He took a left on Third Street and stopped by the W Hotel's front door. He handed the keys to the valet and headed directly for The Living Room bar and lounge.

The place was bathed in a soft blue light with brighter colors emanating from the shelves filled with designer alcohol bottles. The patterns projected on the walls changed in tune with the house-lounge music.

I'm getting too old for this place, he thought.

He looked around. The place was pretty full with good-looking people in their thirties with money to spend. At a first glance he didn't find her, so he decided to grab a place at the bar and text her. He put his jacket on the empty stool next to his to save her a seat.

"Vodka martini, please."

The alcohol soothed him. He felt the syrupy liquid fill his mouth and coat his throat. He savored it. He reached out and grabbed a couple honey-roasted peanuts. The sweet and salty flavor clashed with the vodka and ruined the soothing effect. He wiped his fingers on a paper napkin and took another sip.

He had no missed calls, voice mails or unread texts. *Maybe it's better this way*, he thought.

Tyler looked around him. There was a group of women a few feet away. He couldn't quite make out what they were saying, but they laughed often. The one facing him had really large teeth and was flat chested. The one next to her was much sexier. On the plump side, but her blond hair, blue eyes and double-Ds would be perfect for a good time. He finished his drink and ordered another one.

He wondered if he should text his date but decided not to waste his time. Tyler figured he was much better off picking somebody from the crowd, already knowing what they looked like. With online dating, it was always a surprise, and very often a bad one. He took another sip of his martini and felt a light tap on his shoulder. He turned and saw two huge brown eyes framed by incredibly long eyelashes smiling at him.

"Tyler?"

Her voice was soft but not timid. He nodded.

"I'm Eva. Nice to meet you."

She extended her hand. She was much more formal than he would have expected. He took it and shook it firmly.

"May I sit?" she asked, motioning toward the high stool next to his.

"Please," he said, standing up and removing his coat from the back of the chair.

She asked the bartender for a cosmopolitan. Her hair was much longer than in the pictures. It was very thick and shiny. He saw her taste her drink and smile, probably enjoying the combination of flavors. Her lips were full and shiny, forming a perfect heart shape.

Tyler realized that he was pleasantly surprised. He looked at her via the bar mirror and found her eyes looking back at him. They both smiled at the same time. She looked away first.

"I'm sorry I was late," she said.

"Not a problem. Gave me enough time to find a place to sit."

"How's the dating going?"

"I'll tell you tomorrow."

She smiled and raised her glass. They toasted silently, maybe wishing the same thing.

"You're much taller than I expected," she said.

"Six one, like it says in my profile."

"Yes, but most men lie about their height."

"I'm not 'most men.'"

"I've noticed." She touched his arm.

He was surprised to feel a strange surge of electricity shoot through his body. It took him a minute to realize what it was. He shifted in his chair, trying to relieve the pressure in his pants. She smiled, as if knowing the effect she had caused.

Her pink nail traced his arm all the way to the back of his hand. When she reached the cuff of his shirt, she pulled it up a little and checked the time. He figured she was also checking his watch and was glad he was wearing his better Omega.

"Don't you think it's too hot here?" she asked, almost whispering, leaning toward him as if she were confiding a great secret.

"Would you like to go somewhere else?" he asked, feeling the need to oblige.

"I have a better idea." She got up from her chair and grabbed his hand.

He pulled a hundred-dollar bill out of his money clip and left it under his drink, then followed her outside. He hoped they would be alone in the elevator, but at the last moment a well-dressed fifty-something man joined them.

He nodded and said, "Good evening. Beautiful night out there." His voice was deep. He had a southern drawl.

"Yes it is," Eva said, inching closer to Tyler. She wrapped her arm around his and kissed his neck, biting lightly and leaving a wet spot with her tongue.

They reached the seventeenth floor, and Eva took his hand and led him through a long, dark hallway to a burgundy door with the number 1709 in an Asian-style script.

"It's simpler to get a room when I come to the city. That way I don't have to drive back to the South Bay late at night," she explained when she saw his confused look.

She inserted the key card into the lock, the green light flashed three times, and the door clicked open. The light was on. The room was spacious. The bed was made, but one corner was turned down, and there was a tiny chocolate on the pillow. A small carry-on luggage rested against the sofa.

Eva turned the lights off but went to the windows and opened the heavy curtains. There was just enough light coming in from the city to make out the room. Tyler caught Eva's coy smile. He stood there just inside the door, watching her. She started walking toward him really slowly, watching him back.

She got close but not quite close enough to touch him. He could smell the sweet fragrance of petunias on her. She placed her hand on his chest, her pink nails wandering sensually toward his belt. His blood was pulsing. His pants tightened.

Eva pulled in closer to him. Her lips were slightly parted. She moistened them with the tip of her tongue. He shivered, and goose bumps covered his entire body. He grabbed her by the waist and pulled her toward him. He kissed her, not using his tongue but instead tasting her lip, biting it a little, without pain. She kissed him back, bit him harder. He felt a sting, but it also made him want her more.

He picked her up and carried her to the bed. The city lights reflected on her hair. Her eyes invited him to join her. But he just stood there, silently watching her from above. Eva's blouse had shifted, revealing the top of her lacy, black bra. Her skirt had hiked up enough to show the garter's clasp. He crawled on the bed, then on top of her, careful not to touch her body. She arched her back. Her eyes were locked on his while her hands unclasped his belt and then she begun to tease him.

Tyler touched her breasts over the blouse, and finally slid his hand under the bra. They weren't double Ds but fit perfectly in his large hand. He pinched the erect nipple roughly. She gasped. Eva hiked his shirt without undoing the buttons and kissed his toned chest, slowly moving downwards, leaving a wet trace behind. She rolled on top of him. Then she took his penis in her mouth and teased the tip with her tongue. She sucked, bobbing her head up and down. He was so hard he thought he would come, but then she stopped.

Eva looked at him, licking her lips, as if she had just enjoyed the most exquisite dessert. He almost came just watching her do that. She teased him again with her tongue. He propped the pillow underneath his head so he could watch her looking back at him. Then, instead of finishing him off with her mouth, Eva sat on top of his chest, bent forward and kissed him, long and hard, her tongue exploring every inch of his mouth. He felt his penis stiffen even more. She stopped kissing him as abruptly as she had started and before he knew what she was going to do next, she sat on his face. Eva was wearing no underwear.

He explored her. He licked up and down her labia, found her clitoris and bit it slightly. She twitched. She was really wet. He drank from her, sucked and penetrated her with his tongue as far as he could reach. She rocked slightly back and forth. He worked on her clit, licking around it, circling it faster and faster. Then he closed his lips and sucked, creating a vacuum, and rubbed the clitoris with his tongue. Her body tensed and her muscles shuddered until she came hard, grabbing the headboard and letting out a scream of release.

He fought hard against his own urge to come, hearing her and feeling her orgasm wetting his face. As soon as she was done, she took him in her mouth again and sucked for a couple of seconds until he came in her mouth. She swallowed and licked her lips again.

CHAPTER 20

"Hey, Lynch. Why do you have a girl's name?" Sorensen asked, lifting his eyes from his computer screen, looking at the only other detective still in the office.

"Jesus, Sorensen, what are you, in high school?"

"Sorry, man. I looked at you, and you seemed so depressed I thought giving you a hard time would pull you out of it."

"You have a strange way to show love."

Sorensen laughed. It was a hearty laugh. It felt genuine, which was a rare thing.

"Let's grab a beer. The missus is out with her friends and my kids always hope I'm pulling a double shift."

He grabbed his suit jacket and waited by Darcy's desk.

"Sure, what the hell. I got nothing. Staring at the files for another hour is not going to make the evidence appear from nowhere."

They walked a few blocks to Fibar McGee's. It was the closest to a cop bar you could find in Silicon Valley. The Irish bar was dark, grim, dirty and scarcely populated. There were about ten beers on tap, and *SportsCenter* played on the TV without sound.

"Howard, how have you been?" Sorensen asked a stocky man sitting at one of the side tables with an older guy.

"Great. You?"

They shook hands and Howard's head tilted toward Darcy, as if to get confirmation from Sorensen he was one of them.

"This is Detective Lynch. Import from Seattle. The biggest pain in the ass you've ever met."

He moved enough to let Darcy shake hands with the other detective.

"Do you remember Thomas?" Howard asked, gesturing toward his sitting partner.

Sorensen nodded. After considering it for a few more seconds he said, "How could I forget. You worked on that black widow case way back when."

Thomas looked away and finished his beer.

"Outstanding work." Sorensen's voice didn't hide his disdain. He didn't shake his hand.

Before Howard could protest, Darcy started walking toward the bar and said, "Great to meet you both, but I need a beer."

Sorensen followed him without saying good-bye. They sat on the short side of the L-shaped bar, both facing the door. Sorensen looked back at Howard and Thomas and, not caring much about whether they could hear him, said, "That fucking asshole got one of our biggest cases dismissed."

"What happened?"

Before he could respond, the owner appeared from the back and approached them. He was a large man with pockmarked skin from teenage acne. His hair was mostly white, in a short buzz cut.

"Long time no see, Detective."

He put a Stella in front of Sorensen.

"Been busy with the kids, Bernie. You know how it is."

He then introduced Lynch.

"What can I get you?" Bernie asked.

"I'll have the same."

Once Bernie left to polish some glasses, Sorensen answered Darcy's question. "Apparently the dick forgot all about the Fourth Amendment and those little details about illegal searches and seizures." He looked over to see if the other two detectives had heard him, but if they had, they were trying to ignore him. "A few years ago, this woman hired a dude to do her husband, but her thing was that she wanted to make sure it was done, no mistakes or half tries. So, one day she calls the assassin and tells him that her hubby is at a restaurant down in Los Gatos and that she wants to come with while he does it. After some persuasion, she wins. You know how women are.

"They wait until he leaves the restaurant and gets in his car. They drive by, the assassin pulls a gun and shoots the husband through the passenger window. Blood spatters all over the place, including her pretty blouse. She goes home and makes sure everything is washed. Mr. Asshole over there is sure she's done it, so he decides to break into her mansion the next day while she's shopping in Santana Row for new clothes or something. He's looking all over the place with no warrant and finally finds something that looks like blood on the side of the washing machine. He takes a sample, and before he's able to sneak out, the victim's brother comes into the house and catches him there. Long story short, by the time they got a warrant there's no more blood and nothing else to go after her."

"What about the shooter?"

"Probably basking in the sun on some Mexican beach somewhere. We never found him."

He munched on a few peanuts.

"Was it his blood?"

"Yep." Sorensen washed a mouthful with his beer.

"Have you ever done it?" Darcy asked, knowing he was stepping on quicksand.

Sorensen didn't respond. He stared straight through the bar and watched the door open. A couple, probably out-of-towners looking for a cool bar, peered in and then walked back out.

"This guy is an arrogant son of a bitch that screwed up the case and put the department in jeopardy. The brother almost sued the Sheriff's Office for breaking and entering. Can you believe that? And he didn't even like the widow."

They drank in silence for a few minutes. The TV now showed the weather. Another balmy week in the Valley.

"You never told me what happened to your eye."

"I don't like to talk about it," Darcy said and rubbed his left temple, more out of reflex than need.

"Fair enough."

Darcy was grateful Sorensen didn't push it. Maybe he was more decent than he let on.

"How long have you been married?" he asked, partly to change the subject and partly to try to establish that rapport he'd been unable to build since he joined Santa Clara Sheriff's Office a few months back.

"Too long, that's for sure." But he smiled. "Thirteen years."

"That's pretty impressive for a cop. You may be reaching a record."

Darcy lifted his glass.

"Yeah, no shit. You?"

"Nope. My last girlfriend got sick of me working under-cover. One day I came home and all of her things were gone, except the fish."

"She left you a dead fish? That's cold."

"No, actually, the frigging fish was alive. In fact it still is."

"You kept it?"

"What the hell was I supposed to do?"

"Let it swim down the toilet?"

"Harsh," he said, but they both laughed.

"Her name's Lola."

"Your ex?"

"No. The fish."

CHAPTER 21

Harper Johnson was tired of stealing cars. But he was smart enough to know that his beat-up pickup truck would stand out like a sore thumb in an affluent neighborhood like Los Altos. So he stole a nice Lexus ES that seemed to be well kept.

After tonight, there would be only one more name on his latest list to cross out. But he also needed to take care of Saffron Meadows, the woman who kept evading his grasp. After that, he hoped to be done, but with Tyler Warren, you never knew for sure.

He studied his crossword puzzle against the streetlight, but it was hard to see. He heard a car approaching. He checked the picture one more time and then watched the car get closer. It stopped a few yards away. A couple in their sixties got out of the car. He could hear them talk, but not what they were saying. The woman laughed. The trunk opened. They each took a Trader Joe's bag out. He hoped they didn't have to make a second trip.

He realized he was holding his breath. He forced himself to inhale deeply and exhale slowly. He had no idea when his victim was going to arrive, so there was no need to stress. He was not on a deadline. Not yet, anyway. So if it didn't happen today, there would be another chance some other day.

The porch light turned on as soon as the couple stepped inside the sensor area. The old man set the heavy bag on the floor and fetched the keys he had put back in his pocket. He opened the front door and held it for his wife to go in first. Harper saw the man pause on the other side of the translucent door and figured he was locking it.

He looked back at his crosswords puzzle. "Three-letter word for 'race the engine,'" he murmured. He often did better when he read it out loud.

Another car entered the cul-de-sac. He looked up. He grabbed the photo of the woman resting on the passenger seat and looked at it again. When he confirmed the match, he put it in his breast pocket without losing sight of the passing car.

Harper waited until she pulled into the driveway. He hoped she wouldn't go into the garage. She didn't. She parked the car in the driveway and shut down the engine. He got out of the car quietly and walked toward her. Then he waited behind a large bush that framed the side of the driveway. The woman was busy doing something, but she finally opened the door. He watched. He turned around and surveyed the neighborhood. There was no activity on the street.

He saw her step out of the car, switch the purse to her left hand and fiddle with the keys to lock it. Harper walked behind her and hit the back of her head as hard as he could with his fist. His knuckles hurt. Her head slammed forward with such force she broke her nose against the hood of the car. He thought she would drop to the ground, but she turned around and tried to hit him with her purse. Her eyes glared at him, wild with fear. Her mouth was open. She was trying to breathe through it without swallowing the blood that poured from her nose. She glanced to her right, and Harper knew she was weighing her chances of fleeing.

He reached for her purse and pulled as hard as he could, throwing her off-balance and drawing her much closer to him. He knew he had very little time before she realized she should be screaming. He turned her around and managed to cover her mouth with his large, gloved hand and pressed hard. With the other, he stabbed her with his hunting knife. He punctured her right kidney first, then stabbed her between the fifth and sixth ribs, perforating the right lung. She stopped resisting. He held her a moment longer and thrust the knife into her two more times to make sure she would die. Her strength faded, and once she stopped resisting him, he let her slide from his grip and fall to the ground, a large pool of blood forming beside her.

He pulled a large black garbage bag from one of his cargo pants' pockets, put her purse in it and jogged away from the scene, trying to not call attention to himself. A few streets away, he took his flannel shirt off and stuffed it into the bag. He checked his black T-shirt for blood, but in the moonlight he couldn't see any, so he left it on. He would probably stand out more walking around shirtless than with soiled clothing.

A few blocks further away, he pulled his slim jim out of another pocket and used it on a dark blue Acura RLX. He started driving away, but suddenly his body froze.

"Fuck," he said out loud. "Fuck, fuck!"

He hit the steering wheel with increasing force. Then he stepped on the accelerator and drove away from Hawthorne Court as fast as he could, wondering if he had chewed on the pen he was using for the crossword puzzle.

CHAPTER 22

Darcy motioned for Bernie to pour them two fresh beers.
Sorensen grabbed a handful of peanuts and shoved them all into his mouth. "This is why I'm fat. I have no self-control," he said once he finished chewing.

"I'll drink to that," Darcy said. "I swim a lot. You should try it."

Sorensen's phone rang. He pulled it out of his pocket. "Shit, it's the captain." He pressed the green button. "Yes, ma'am."

"There's been a mugging-turned-homicide. I need you to go to the scene." The volume on the phone was so loud, Darcy could hear everything she was saying even though it was not on speaker.

"Give it to the new guy. He always gets the easy ones."

"I'm sorry, you said something?"

"I already got a full plate with all those suicides."

"I'll text you the address. I want you there in ten."

"Captain, I can't. I've been drinking."

"Beer?"

"Yes." He made a face realizing fatal mistake. "I mean, beer backed with cheap scotch, neat."

"Better splash your face with some cold water before heading out. I want you there in ten minutes." She paused for a second, but before he could argue again, she added, "Make it eight now. You've been talking too long."

The line went dead.

"Call of duty?" Darcy asked, as if he had heard nothing.

Sorensen nodded. "I guess my kids will be happy I'm actually pulling a double and won't be home all night."

"I'll go with you. I have nothing else to do."

Sorensen remained silent while he put on his jacket. Finally he said, "Sure. But you know what they say about too many cooks..."

"Understood."

Darcy paid, and they both headed back to the station's parking garage, then went to the scene in separate cars. Darcy wondered if Sorensen would make a point of getting there faster than him. He decided to not push his luck and stopped at every yellow light.

When Darcy got to the crime scene, the area was already cordoned off. There were two Sheriff's cars with the lights still flashing, and the captain's black Mustang was behind them. Darcy parked, and as he approached the uniform holding the clipboard, he spotted Sorensen inside the yellow tape.

"Name, please."

"Detective Darcy Lynch." He showed his badge.

The deputy noted it, wrote down the time and nodded, indicating he was cleared to go through.

"I see that you brought reinforcements." Captain Virago's brow wrinkled. She didn't seem particularly happy Lynch was there.

They were standing by the trunk of the car, leaving enough space for the medical examiner to finish with his preliminary findings.

"I thought it would be easier for him to get up to speed once you transfer the case to him."

"Shut up, Sorensen, and get to work."

She shook her head and went to the victim's house. Sorensen circled the car and knelt down to check what the ME was doing.

Lynch looked around. The car door was open and seemed to be in Sorensen's way, because he pushed it closed.

"Detective, I had that open for a reason," the ME protested.

"Oh, the flood lights not bright enough for you?" Sorensen asked and handed him his extra large flashlight.

The ME's face twitched in disapproval. He went back to work without taking it.

Darcy pulled his own Maglite and aimed it at the ground. The car shaded the area he wanted to check out. He swept the flashlight left to right and then up and down, in layers.

He doubted anything he found would be of use, since the crime scene had been contaminated already by all of the people present. It always amazed him that if you didn't get there first, then secured the area yourself and monitored absolutely everything that happened from that point on, you could pretty much consider the evidence collection a joke. This usually excluded the body and its immediate proximity, for whatever reason.

He gave up his search when the ME stood up. He was a very tall man, with a slight hunch. Darcy wondered if he had developed it over the years by having to bend to everybody's eye level, or if he had been born with it. His pants were held in place by a tight belt in its tightest hole. His large hands came together on a soft clap, and then he rubbed them, as if they were cold.

"Four stab wounds. She died about half an hour ago. I'll give you more information in the morning." He grabbed his case and said goodbye to Darcy with a soft nod.

Two assistants came by and bagged the body. They put it on a stretcher and took it to the ambulance that had responded to the 911 call. Darcy stood in the road and watched the ambulance's taillights fade into the night.

CHAPTER 23

Thursday

Lynch didn't leave the crime scene until past midnight, even though the case wasn't his. He hadn't slept much and felt run down.

On the way to work he made Starbucks his first stop. The line was longer than normal. Darcy wondered if it was because he was there earlier than his usual nine-ish. The woman before him started ordering drinks for a full regiment. Then she decided she wanted food too. Darcy shifted the weight on his feet. He wasn't in a hurry but felt uneasy wasting time with coffee. His phone vibrated with a new voice mail. He was annoyed he hadn't heard it ring.

"Detective Lynch, I think I found something interesting. Come by the lab when you have a moment." Rachel's voice was vibrant. It almost gave him hope.

He was about to skip the coffee when the woman before him started to pay.

A few minutes later he arrived at the lab's reception area, where Mary greeted him from behind the desk.

"Ah, you truly are the man of my dreams."

"No, I'm not," Darcy said embarrassed. "I'm sorry. I brought this one for Rachel."

"You owe me one, then." She raised her steaming mug and

took a sip. When she saw Darcy's relived expression, she winked. "Rachel's in the garage."

"Thank you."

He turned around and headed back to the elevator. Once inside, he swiped his security badge by the electronic reader and pushed the button for the basement after the light turned green. When the doors opened, the temperature dropped at least ten degrees and the place was noisy, even though there weren't that many people working this early.

The garage looked exactly like a body shop. There were three frame racks, two of them occupied by different vehicles. There was a Kansas Jack Auto body-measuring machine on wheels, two pulling towers, chains and many tools worthy of any professional body shop. Between all the regular tools for vehicles, the wall shelves were also filled with typical CSI equipment: magnifiers, evidence bags, seals and labels, scales, luminol kits, and a couple serial-number restoration kits.

"Excuse me, where can I find Rachel?" Darcy asked a young man in a lab coat testing a piece of gray carpet for blood.

"She's under number two," he said, pointing to the left with his head.

"Thanks."

When he reached the second frame rack, Darcy saw two tiny feet in white tennis shoes sticking out from under the car.

"I got you a short caramel mocha with extra whipped cream."

Rachel rolled out from under the car, avoiding hitting him at the last second. "Yum."

She raised her arms so he could help her stand up. She had a grease smudge on her forehead and right cheek, and her lab coat was covered in soot.

"You've got some good news for me?" Darcy asked, wanting to brush the spots off her face but refraining from doing so.

"Well, I don't know about that. I wouldn't want to get your hopes up. But I did find something interesting."

She moved toward the table that stood by the frame rack and searched through the different evidence bags lying there. When she found what she was looking for, she handed it to Darcy.

"A really tiny black...piece of fabric?" he asked after inspecting the content.

"Rather, a plastic thread."

"I want my caramel mocha back," he said, trying to exchange the baggie for the coffee.

Rachel smiled. "I found it yesterday when I was inspecting the bottom of Pritchard's car. I thought it odd that it would be lodged on the tie-down bracket holding the brake line. So I tested it."

She placed the baggie on the table and had a long sip of coffee while she stared at Darcy.

"Rachel, you know you're my favorite mad scientist, but if you don't get to the point soon, I am taking my coffee back."

"This is not the type of thing that normally gets stuck to the bottom of cars, unless you drive over a Goodwill drop-off container full of clothes or something."

Darcy nodded, encouraging her to continue.

"It's pleather."

His face was blank.

"Plastic leather. Fake leather. The material used in fake leather gloves, for example."

His face lit up, and a smile started growing, lining his eyes with tiny creases.

"I'm not saying they're from fake leather gloves, but with the theory that the lines were punctured, maybe the perpetrator was wearing gloves to avoid leaving prints."

She grabbed the bag again and shook it in the air, as if to reiterate that she did have something important to share.

"You have an endless caramel mocha supply until Christmas," Darcy said, running toward the door. "Oh, and you're still my favorite," he shouted over his shoulder.

He walked the few blocks back to the station and went directly to his board. "Pleather gloves," he wrote in Jacqueline Pritchard's column. Under "Saffron Meadows" he added a dash from "black gloves" to the word "leather," followed by a question mark. He made a mental note to remember to ask Saffron if she could tell if the gloves her assailant wore were leather or fabric.

CHAPTER 24

Tyler Warren inserted two Eggo frozen waffles in the toaster. The kitchen was large, white and sunbathed by a large window. He placed the maple syrup and butter on the table and took the tea bag out of his steaming cup. He added a drop of milk and emptied a packet of Splenda.

"Lucas, you're going to be late," he said toward the stairs.

"Coming," Lucas yelled as he stomped down. "Sorry, Dad, I couldn't find my glove. We have practice after school." He raised the baseball mitt and placed it by the plate. His broad smile showed a missing tooth.

"You still liking it?" Tyler asked, ruffling his hair.

"Yeah. I think me and Simon are the best on the team."

The toaster ejected the waffles. Tyler put both on Lucas' plate and watched him drench them in syrup.

"I told you you were good," he said to his son.

"I know, I know. But parents always say stuff like that to their kids."

"What? I've never heard that before." He faked a shocked expression.

Lucas laughed, his mouth full of half-chewed waffles.

"That's disgusting," Tyler complained, covering his eyes with his hand. "Close that mouth immediately, Lucas Warren."

Lucas laughed more and had to run to the sink to spit out the food before choking on it.

"Smart move, little man."

The kid coughed a little and smiled back at his dad with bright blue eyes.

"Let's go," Tyler said.

Lucas grabbed his glove and headed out of the kitchen. He stopped by the stairs to pick up his backpack and the bag with his baseball gear and then held the door to the garage open for his dad to go through first.

Tyler got in the car and pressed the button to open the trunk of his Tesla.

"Dad, the trunk's full."

Tyler got out of the car and removed his gun bag.

"Wait in the car."

He left the garage and placed the full black canvas bag into the gun safe and locked it, making a mental note to clean the guns later.

A few minutes later he pulled by the entrance of Bowman International School and hugged his boy good-bye.

"Have a great day. Tell me tonight how practice went."

"I will, Dad. I love you."

"I love you too, Lucas."

They waved at each other, and Tyler sped away from the school. He checked the time. He had less than twenty minutes to make it to his staff meeting.

Traffic on 101 was worse than normal. He called his secretary to let her know he was going to be late and turned the radio on. He decided to listen to music, instead of the news, and relive his encounter with Eva while inching away on the crowded California Highway in rush hour. A few minutes later he got off the freeway and drove through every yellow light until he reached El Camino Real. He was still smiling.

The office was off of the main artery, in a technology park that had been built in 2005. When it opened, the entire building was occupied, even though a square foot was going for over $200. Now, when Tyler's company moved in, they were able to get the entire two floors of Building C for less than just the lab would have cost them back then.

"Good morning, Mr. Warren."

"Good morning, Sebastian," Tyler said to the security guard watching the entrance as he hurried past into the elevator.

Bright windows overlooking Silicon Valley greeted him when he got out. His secretary saw him walking down the hallway and opened the door to the largest conference room they had when he came closer. He'd missed the first quarter of the meeting.

When he stepped in, all heads turned.

"Nice of you to join us," Sheldon Michaels, the VP of sales, said, shaking his head. Everybody else avoided him.

Tyler nodded in response, silently moving toward the middle of the table, where he found a couple empty chairs.

Qiang Li, the VP of research, was in the middle of presenting her latest test results. She nodded at him and blinked several times as her bangs got into her eyes. She had called him the night before to tell him the news, so the grim expressions around the table did not surprise him.

"As I was saying, we're getting closer, but we're not there yet," Qiang said, tapping the table. When everybody was looking back at her, she moved on to the next slide.

Before she could start explaining the changes in the research, Sheldon interrupted her. "Qiang, isn't this the same information you presented in the last Exec meeting?"

Qiang sucked in her cheeks and blinked again.

"What am I missing?" he pushed.

"It's not the same. I just described the progress we've made—"

"All I see is more 'close but not quite,' and let me tell you, there's no way to sell this bullshit." Before she could respond, Sheldon turned to Tyler. "This is not good enough. I don't need to tell you that if we don't come up with something we can generate buzz about ASAP, we may as well start selling off our assets to pay the rent."

"We've assembled one of the most talented teams in the medical research industry," Tyler said. "You need to give them enough time to do their jobs."

"That may be the case," said Dolores Fabruko, VP of finance, "but Sheldon's right. We're running out of money fast." She pushed her Fendi glasses up the bridge of her nose. "If we don't get a viable product for trials soon, we woun't generate enough interest for a third round of VC funding." She looked around the room to make sure she had everybody's attention. "We'll go under."

They all started talking at the same time. Tyler just watched but didn't listen. He knew Qiang was really close to finding out what the issue with the first cure was. Once they solved that, and he managed to take care of the other glitch, they would have no problem finding VC backing.

CHAPTER 25

Captain Virago entered the room. Her stride was more determined than usual. She marched past Darcy's desk and stopped in front of his whiteboard. Darcy watched her but didn't disturb her concentration.

"I see that you're finally bonding with Sorensen," she said, her eyes still glued to the board.

"Nah. I'm just smart enough to know a good idea when I see one."

Virago looked at him. Her expression was unreadable, but her eyes were warm. "Call it what you wish." She sat on the corner of his desk after moving a few files out of the way. "What was that about you showing up at the crime scene yesterday?"

"I was at McGee's with Sorensen when your call came in. I had nothing better to do with my evening, so I offered to come along. He didn't object too loudly, so I went."

"So you're bonding." Only the left side of her mouth rose a little.

Darcy ignored her smirk. He wondered where she was going with the conversation. She passed her hand over her mouth as if she were trying to hide the smile.

"If what you're worrying about is me intruding in Sorensen's cases, there's no need to worry about that. Sorensen made the boundaries very clear last night."

She started saying something, paused, and moved on. "Tell me about your cases."

"I don't have a lot to go on with Pritchard's. The poor woman was going to die anyway in a few months, according to her sister. She had a very small savings account, no life insurance, a huge mortgage on her house and a very old car. There's no apparent reason why anybody would go through the trouble. The only possible evidence we've found so far is the punctures on the brake lines. The marks are not distinctive enough to narrow down what they were made with, but it may have been something as common as a pushpin. Rachel also found a bit of fabric that could be from the gloves the perp wore when he was tampering with the brake lines."

"Is there any way the holes could've been caused by degradation? You said it was a really old car." She stretched her back, forcing herself to a better posture. Darcy heard her spine crack twice.

"Rachel was positive they were man-made."

"Do you have anything more?" she asked without looking too hopeful.

"I wish."

Virago nodded.

"I'm going to go to the school where she taught and visit her doctor later today. Maybe they know more than her sister did."

She pointed back to the board and asked, "What about the Meadows case?"

"I've got nothing on that one. The woman seems to have a completely common Silicon Valley life. I have no idea where to go from here. She's coming this morning to go through some knives and see if she can spot the one used to cut the seat belt, but even if she does, I'm not counting on it leading us to the perpetrator."

"It would be better than nothing."

"Indeed."

Virago got off Darcy's desk. "By the way, your qualification's coming up. Let me know when you've done it."

"What? I got at least half a year."

"No, you don't if you are going to work on cases."

"But I'm not going to work on cases."

She turned and faced him. Without a word she pointed to the whiteboard with her index finger.

"I'm just doing this as a favor to you for taking me into your department. I'm not on active duty and will not be. I don't need to requalify for another six months to work desk duty."

"Get it done before the end of the week," she said over her shoulder. "I want the results on my desk before I go to Tahoe on Friday. I'm leaving at three p.m."

Darcy threw his pen hard. It hit the keyboard where it met the desk, and the weird angle sent it bouncing back, almost hitting his good eye.

CHAPTER 26

Saffron laid in bed without being able to move. Her eyes were locked on the white ceiling. She was staring at a small spider web that had come loose on one end. Cat purred while kneading Saffron's armpit with long, sharp claws. It hurt, but not more than the pounding in her head. She could hear the sounds of cars driving by and the faint rattle of blinds brushing against each other in the light morning breeze. She willed herself to move, but no muscle obeyed. She wondered if she should just stay there for the rest of the day. Her phone rang three times and it went to voice mail. The sound split her head in a million pieces.

Very slowly she grabbed Cat, pulled her close and kissed her forehead. She set her aside and, as if walking through molasses, managed to shuffle to the bathroom to take a shower.

About thirty minutes later, she was able to move around with intermittent nausea. She fed Cat and decided to go to Starbucks for coffee instead of making it at home. On her way to the garage she checked email and hit the key for the car door to open. When she heard no noise, she looked up and froze in place.

"What the hell?" she said out loud. A cold shiver ran through her back. "Where's my car?"

She walked around the garage, wondering if she had parked it somewhere else. She didn't remember doing that, but her head hurt too much for her to be totally sure. After going around twice, she decided to go up to the concierge to report the car stolen, then remembered she had lent it to Emma. On the way out of the garage, she called the hospital. Even if she wasn't seeing Ranjan anymore, she still felt responsible for the accident.

"Good Samaritan Hospital, how can I help you?"

"Can you transfer me to the Clinical Observation Unit?"

"Please hold."

Once she was connected, she said, "I'm Saffron Meadows. I was in a car accident with Ranjan Balasubramanian. I just wanted to check how he was doing."

"Kristina," Saffron heard the woman call out, covering the phone but not enough to mute it. "The girlfriend wants to know about the patient in Room 305."

Saffron heard a muffled voice, and then the woman spoke back into the phone. "Here's the head nurse."

"Hello, I'm Nurse Mitchell," she said. Before Saffron could say anything, she continued: "The concussion was light. I think most likely he'll be discharged sometime this afternoon. I think his uncle is in the room with him. Would you like me to transfer you?"

"No, that's okay. Thank you."

She hung up and had an incredible urge to call Ranjan on his cell. But she forced herself to put the phone back in her purse and move on with her day.

Once outside of the garage she approached the patrol car that was watching out for her. The two officers were engaged in a lively discussion about football. Saffron stood about a foot from the window, not wanting to interrupt. The younger one, in the driver's seat, saw her first and motioned for his partner to roll the window down.

"Good morning," she said.

"Good morning, Miss Meadows. Thanks for the pizza last night."

"Ah, sure. Of course. I'm glad you liked it." It took her a second to remember that she had come down to ask them if they wanted any food before she got hammered.

"What can we do for you?" the one closer to her asked when the silence started to feel uncomfortable.

"I feel really stupid asking for this. And I'm not even sure it's allowed." She paused, looking at the backseat of the car. It looked clean at least. "But my friend borrowed my car last night and I was wondering if you could take me back to the station." She blushed and put a strand of hair behind her ear. "I have an appointment with Detective Lynch this morning."

The two officers looked at each other and the more senior one said, "Yes, of course. Jump in."

There was a steel mesh partition separating the backseat from the front. It looked sturdy and closely knitted. She passed her fingers over it, wondering how many people had done so before her, then pulled her hand, as if stung by fire, and she wished she had Purell in her purse.

"The modern cars have Plexiglas," the older officer explained, seeing her curious expression, "but we haven't got the upgrade yet. I'm sorry about that."

"No worries. It'll give my neighbors something to talk about," Saffron said, sliding back on the hard plastic seat.

"We didn't see anything suspicious last night, Miss Meadows," the younger officer said, hoping to make her feel safer.

"Please, call me Saffron."

"I'm Sergeant Colin Russell and he's Officer George Bush. No relation," he said and chuckled, as if it were an inside joke.

Saffron smiled and, unable to shake their hands due to the partition, she waved.

"Very nice meeting you both. I feel bad you've been put on this job. What did you do to piss someone off so badly?" she said and regretted it immediately. She had probably just offended the two men who were trying to protect her. "I'm sorry, I didn't mean any disrespect," she said, feeling the heat burn her cheeks.

"None taken. Actually, this is overtime for both of us, so we do it gladly."

"Ah, cool." She looked out the window. Everything went by very slowly at less than twenty miles per hour. "You've been in the force long?"

"I'm going on my third year," Bush said.

"I was a detective for twelve years but started back on patrol because I needed a change of scenery." Russell shared.

Her cell phone rang. "Excuse me," she said to the officers. "Good morning, Detective Lynch. What can I do for you?"

"I just wanted to know when you think you'll be here."

She checked her watch. "We should be there in another five minutes at the most." She saw Sergeant Russell nod.

"Perfect. 'We' you said?"

"Yes, Sergeant Russell and Officer Bush are taking me to the station. I'm getting the full criminal experience, but without the handcuffs," she said and winked at Russell, who smiled back at her.

"Oh, okay."

"Detective?" she said before he could hang up. "I'm going to need some serious coffee. Is there somewhere we can go before we get to work?"

"There're a few options."

"Perfect. See you soon, then."

CHAPTER 27

Sorensen's eyes were bloodshot and felt like sandpaper every time he blinked. Four coffee stains decorated his light blue shirt. He had worked the crime scene with CSU until he was satisfied. He didn't expect to find anything significant, but he still liked to be thorough and made them go through everything with a fine-tooth comb.

He had met with Virago inside the house. "This is Detective Erik Sorensen," she said, introducing him to a large man and a teenage girl, who was holding a sleeping girl in her arms. "He's our lead investigator."

Sorensen shook hands with both and said, "I'm so sorry for your loss. I will do everything in my power to find out who did this."

They both nodded. Large tears fell on the man's face. He wiped them off with one hand.

"I think we have enough for tonight." Virago said. "I'll brief Detective Sorensen on what we've talked about. Would you mind coming to the station tomorrow if we have more questions?" Virago asked, trying to wrap up.

"Yes. Anything we can do," Mr. Hughes said and pulled out his wallet. "I don't think I'll be in the office, but you can contact me on my cell." He handed them both a card.

Sorensen looked at the card. The paper was thick and glossy, the letters raised in shiny gold: "Robert L. Hughes, Director of Mergers and Acquisitions, Norman and Smits."

"I'll see you tomorrow," Sorensen said before leaving.

When they got outside, Virago said, "The purse is missing. It looks like a mugging gone bad, but this is not the neighborhood for it. I want you to check the husband's alibi first thing tomorrow morning. His law firm is in downtown San Jose, on First Street, I think he said he had a few conference calls with Asia in the evening, so it should be easy enough to check."

Sorensen made a mental note to go to the law firm as soon as Clark Evans was done with the autopsy. "Any problems in the marriage?" he asked.

"Not that he would admit to. The baby-sitter seemed to agree. But check with friends and neighbors too."

Virago started heading toward her car.

"Any particular reason why you feel the need to tell me how to do my job?" Sorensen asked. The tone of his voice was cold. It didn't have the affable edge it normally did.

Virago stopped a few feet from him and turned. They locked eyes, and she exhaled slowly. Sorensen waited.

"You're right, Detective. Go and do what you do best."

He nodded and she went to her car.

Less than four hours later he opened the morgue's double doors and found the medical examiner halfway done with the autopsy. The air was stale and cold, but he welcomed the chill.

"How many times have I told you that I don't do autopsies first thing in the morning?" Sorensen asked. He turned around and swallowed hard. After he'd had a minute to compose himself he faced the body. "At least you could have warned me."

The woman's chest was open. The medical examiner removed the heart and placed it on the scale that hung from the ceiling. He checked the weight, pushed the foot switch of the recorder and said, "The heart is normal, weighs nine-point-one ounces and doesn't have any apparent signs of stress outside of what would be expected for a thirty-six-year-old female."

He turned the recorder off and placed the heart on the smaller table, on his right-hand side, so he could open it. While he explored the right ventricle, he said, "I'm glad you could make it. You know I started over an hour ago."

He stared at Sorensen through his face protector before he focused again on the heart.

"I know. I'm sorry. I got here as soon as I could. I worked the case until almost three a.m."

"And yet you had enough time to get coffee. Or are those from yesterday?" He pointed at the coffee stains on Sorensen's shirt.

"No. They're fresh. I would've brought you one, but you're such an asshole, I couldn't bring myself to do it."

Clark's face twitched. "Detective, you know I don't approve of such language in my lab."

"Apologies." Sorensen slurped his coffee. "Cause of death?"

"Asphyxiation."

"Excuse me? She was stabbed four times and she died of asphyxiation?"

"The second stab pierced her right lung, filling it with blood. The fourth did the same with the left one. She died in less than two minutes. There was nothing anybody could have done."

Sorensen pictured the attack. The mugger must have been pretty strong to hold her in place while he stabbed her four times in her driveway. And if all he wanted was the purse, why not just grab it and run?

"Could she have screamed?"

"Before the last stab, yes, but probably not very loud."

Clark put the inspected heart back on the larger table and started looking through some evidence bags. "Which reminds me of this," he said, handing him what looked like an empty baggie.

Sorensen took it and brought it so close to his face, his eyes crossed. "What am I looking at?"

"You tell me, but I found it between the eighth and ninth teeth."

"The top front teeth...She bit him?"

"Well, she bit something. It's not human," Clark said, looking down at the bag in Sorensen's hand.

"Do you mind if I bring it to Lou?"

"That's why I'm giving it to you."

"Anything else you think I should know?"

"Well, the only other thing that I've noticed so far is that Emma Hughes had stage two breast cancer."

CHAPTER 28

Harper Johnson built a fire outside his cabin. Lasky came wagging her tail and sat by his side. Once it began to roar, he walked into the house and grabbed all of the clothes he was wearing when he killed the woman last night. He'd checked and hadn't seen any blood on them, but they retained the smell of death.

"At this rate I'm going to run out of clothes soon," he said to Lasky as he threw his T-shirt into the flames.

The dog looked at him and cocked her head. Only one ear was raised. She stared back at the fire. He thought about the shirt he had put in the plastic bag with the woman's purse. He cursed himself for having thrown it into a garbage container instead of bringing it to the house. He was not smart enough to do this job, he thought.

"Damn you, Tyler Warren," he said out loud.

He threw his pants into the fire and thought about how, three years earlier, he had come to meet the man who would be the end of him.

He hadn't known what to expect. At the funeral, Father Dominique had taken him aside and told him about a group that might help him cope with his loss. He nodded but didn't really understand what the father was telling him. He walked outside. It was raining so hard it felt like an early evening rather than an afternoon in mid-February.

Father Dominique said a few words and motioned for Harper to speak. He looked up. He was surprised to see so many people had come in this weather. Marjorie Johnson was a loved woman.

Harper had prepared a little speech. He pulled a small piece of paper out of his pocket. It was immediately drenched, the words fading as the ink ran down the paper. He stared at it as if he couldn't comprehend what was happening. Then, lost, almost desperate, he looked up and saw several dozen eyes looking back at him patiently, encouragingly. Father Dominique put a hand on his shoulder and nodded for him to go on.

"My mother made the best banana nut muffins in the world," he said.

Everybody laughed. The tension dissipated and it even seemed as if the clouds broke a little, letting some sunlight in. A shy rainbow peeked between the trees to the west.

"My mother fought real hard, but she's now resting in peace. She was an incredible woman who loved everybody and was always happy to help people in need. I wish I was in heaven with her now."

He lowered his gaze to the empty hole in the ground. Father Dominique instructed the two undertakers to lower the casket. Once it settled in the grave, Harper knelt down and grabbed some mud. He threw it on the pine box, but half of it stuck to his hand. He wiped it on the side of his dress pants.

Mary Anne, his mom's best friend, provided food at her house, just a few miles from Harper's home. The entire town came, bringing more food, drinks and flowers. Everyone had something nice to say about Marjorie. After a few hours everybody left, except Mary Anne, Father Dominique and Harper.

"Harper?" the father asked.

"Yes?" He had been lost in thought, remembering one of the last hours of his mother's life. She had been very thin and her lips were cracked and blue.

"Here's the information for that group I told you about." He handed him a flyer.

"Thank you." Harper folded it and put it in his pant pocket without looking at it.

"Promise me you'll think about it," the father said.

Harper nodded and excused himself after giving Mary Anne an awkward hug.

He had forgotten all about the flyer until almost a month later, when he finally got around to sending the pants to the local dry cleaner to get rid of the grave's mud. He unfolded the piece of paper and stared at it. "Support group for family members of cancer victims." He almost threw it in the trash, but something prevented him from doing it. Harper left it on the counter and went into town to get the pants cleaned.

A few hours later he came back and saw the flyer staring back at him. "Wednesdays at 7 p.m. Sacred Heart Parish, Saratoga."

He checked the calendar. It was Wednesday. It would take him about forty-five minutes to get there. He decided to go.

The drive seemed longer than normal, and he considered turning back and going home a few times, but something, probably the void the death of his mother had left in his chest, made him continue.

The church was a small building with a large cross stuck in the middle of the tiny front lawn. The parking lot was half-full. He stood by his truck, locked and unlocked it, thinking of going back inside and driving off. He saw a middle-aged woman heading toward the church. She was holding a cotton bag. Two large knitting needles stuck out of it, and a string of fluffy red yarn trailed behind her as she walked.

Harper went in but stood by the door. The church was warm, the off-white walls had lost their original sheen, but the place had a homey and welcoming feel to it. The room had a large folding table with coffee and two large trays with cookies. There were two towers of paper cups and a few red stirring sticks. A single carton of half-and-half stood by the carafes.

Twelve metal chairs were arranged in a circle in the middle of the room. Only two were occupied. The woman he had seen in the parking lot was sitting on one of them. She was already hard at work, the knitting needles clicking and clacking as she passed the yarn from one to another. She was talking with a much younger woman, with bleached dreadlocks, wearing distressed jeans with holes in the knees.

A man in a suit sat across from them. A few others joined, and soon there were only two empty chairs left. Harper didn't move. A woman in a long wool sweater and a colorful scarf got out of her chair and came to greet him.

"Hello, my name is Elena. Would you like to join us today?" she asked in a barely noticeable Spanish accent.

"I'm...I'm not sure," Harper said.

"Please come. I bet you'll feel better after."

She put her hand on his elbow and led him gently to the group. She sat down and started the session.

"Good evening. I see that today we have some new and some old faces. Welcome to all of you."

Harper looked down at his hands and listened to everybody talk about their week. They were all in different stages of grief, some contributing more than others.

"Would you like to share something with us?" Elena asked Harper.

"No." He looked at her briefly, almost surprised to be addressed. "Not today. Thank you," he added, feeling his first response may have been rude. He looked back down at his hands. They were rough with calluses and a few scabs he got from picking up and cutting wood. His nails were dirty. He felt a flash of embarrassment and hid them in his jacket pockets.

The woman with the knitting project picked a blue yarn ball from her bag and started talking about her son in Iraq. Harper was surprised that they all seemed to have some history together, and they talked more about their regular days than the grief and the void in their lives caused by losing someone they loved. He was relieved and upset at the same time. He wanted to know that he was not alone in his suffering, that there were others who were going through the same thing, and yet he found that all of these people managed to go on, live on, without their loved one around. He wondered if the same thing would happen to him and then resented the thought.

"Okay, I think they're going to close the church with all of us inside if we don't end soon," Elena said with a broad smile that showed crooked teeth.

"Wait, I almost forgot," the man in the suit said a little louder than necessary. "Somebody brought a stray puppy to work today."

"Somebody abandoned a puppy?" the woman with the dreadlocks protested, emphasizing her indignity with a punch to her thigh.

"I took it in, but with Lucas being so young, I can't manage both by myself. But I promised I would find a good home for her. Is anybody interested?"

His eyes were bright, shining with hope as he looked from one person to the next in the group. Everybody diverted their eyes when his gaze met them and shook their heads slightly. His hope quickly faded.

"What breed is she?" Harper surprised himself and regretted it as soon as he asked the question.

"A mutt. But I think she has some Lab in her."

He walked closer to Harper but left enough space between them.

"She has big paws. I think she'll be quite big." There were faint wrinkles around his eyes when he smiled.

Harper nodded but still couldn't make himself commit.

"Why don't you come check her out. She's in my car."

He started walking toward the door, but before he got too far he looked back as if checking that Harper was following him. He wasn't.

"Come on, no pressure," he said and waved for him to join him.

Harper met him and they both walked out into a dark parking lot. The man in the suit stopped in front of a black Mercedes sedan. He unlocked the door, and the inside of the car lit up, startling a puppy that had been happily sleeping in the backseat. The dog stood up and started wagging her tail so hard the rest of her body moved with it.

"How old do you think she is?" Harper asked, standing a good few feet from the car.

"Probably eight or ten weeks. She's going to need some potty training."

"That's ok, my cabin has a trap door leading to the woods," Harper said.

"I'm Tyler, by the way. Tyler Warren." said the man in the suit said, extending his hand. "Nice to meet you."

CHAPTER 29

The ride to the station didn't take long. Saffron learned that Sergeant Russell and Officer Bush were both married. The sergeant had three daughters, one in law school, the middle one pursuing a career in dance, and the youngest one a senior in high school. Officer Bush had a four-year-old son and a daughter on the way.

"Here you are, safe and sound," Sergeant Russell said once they'd pulled into the station's parking lot.

"Thank you very much," Saffron said and shook their hands through the open window before going into the building.

At the front desk, she asked for Detective Lynch and waited in the lobby until he came down to fetch her. She was looking at the elevator, but he surprised her coming out from the stairwell. She lifted an eyebrow at him.

"This way, I can eat French fries with my burger," he said when he saw her expression.

Saffron laughed.

"We can either do Starbucks, walking distance, or take the car and go to Crema, on The Alameda. They have great coffee."

"Let's go there. I've always wanted to try it."

Once in the parking lot, Darcy guided her to his car, which was a few feet from the elevator.

"Whoa, a 1965 Shelby Cobra?" Saffron asked as soon as she saw his car.

Now it was his turn to show surprise. "You know about cars?"

"I know about this one. My dad's a fanatic. One of the very first Christmas stocking presents I can remember was a little Cobra toy car. But mine was blue with two white stripes."

She marveled at the candy-apple red with a light tint of gold and wondered if it was real or a visual effect caused by the parking lot lighting. The interior was black leather. He opened the door for her and closed it softly once she was inside. She leaned across the driver's seat and held the door open for him until he reached it.

"No woman has ever done that for me," he said and blushed, quickly adding, "I'm sorry, I didn't mean—"

"It's the least I can do. You gave me a protective detail, for God's sake. I bet you don't get to trail many bad guys in this baby."

He smiled and looked at her. "You'd be surprised."

"No way," she objected. "You'd be spotted miles away."

"Notice the gold tint?" he asked once they were out in daylight. "It has incognito powers."

"Whatever," she smiled and looked out the side window.

The top was down and the temperature was perfect. Her stomach felt better, and her headache was almost gone.

"Seriously." He winked when she turned to look back at him.

"Prove it," she dared.

"It'll have to be next time. We're already here."

"How convenient."

Saffron stuck her tongue out and regretted it immediately.

"I didn't see anything," he appeased her.

"There was nothing to be seen," she said and smiled again. Her face was flushed, as if sun-kissed and brightened by the wind during the ride.

They walked inside and ordered coffees. Darcy's black, Saffron recited her complicated drink, having to repeat parts of it a couple times.

"Let's sit outside," he said after paying.

The chairs were wicker and had arms. The stone tables were cold, even the ones under the sun. They picked one covered by a large red umbrella. Darcy took his sunglasses off and set them on the table. Saffron put hers on her head, to hold her hair away.

"You still have no idea who tried to kill you?"

"No. Do you?"

"No." He looked out into the road, as if he were reviewing something in his head. "Do you remember if the gloves were actual leather, or could they have been fake leather?"

"What do they call that, pleather?" She laughed. "It's such a stupid name."

Darcy nodded. "Do you?"

"I don't think I could tell the difference, to be honest. Besides, I didn't get to touch them, I just saw he was wearing gloves. I think besides the knife that was one of the things that freaked me out the most. It was way too warm to wear gloves. Of any kind."

"And the knife. You said it was serrated."

"Yeah, but not all the way."

"It was half-smooth and half-serrated?"

"Yes, I think so."

Detective Lynch pulled his phone, tapped at the screen a few times and handed it to Saffron.

"Was it something like this?" he asked, showing her a picture of a SOG Seal Team Knife.

She stared at it for several seconds. "Yeah, something like this, but not exactly. I think the serrated part was all the same, not like this one that has three tiny grooves and then a larger one." She gave the phone back. "But I'm not a hundred percent sure, though."

Saffron looked into Darcy's eyes, sharing a silent apology for not being better help. She saw again what she had seen that first night in her elevator. There was a difference between his eyes. One looked bluer.

"I have more photos at the station. Don't worry about it. I'm sure we'll find it." She watched him as he rubbed his left temple. "It's a fake eye," he blurted out and immediately looked away.

"Accident?"

"You could say that," he said and stopped rubbing.

CHAPTER 30

Tyler Warren stared at his computer without seeing anything on the screen. All he could think about was his evening with Eva. She was insatiable and he had barely got a couple hours of sleep. When he woke up, she was already gone. He knew it was silly, but he had been disappointed when he hadn't found a note. He had showered at the hotel, put on a clean shirt and made it home just in time to wake Lucas up and take him to school.

He surprised himself when he realized that he wanted to see her again. This was the first time he'd wanted to see a woman a second time since his wife died. He fought the urge to call her and settled for a text: "I want to see you tomorrow night." As soon as he sent it, he felt like a loser and wished he could recall the message.

A few minutes later the beep of an incoming text made his heart jump, but the message was from Lucas. "Hey, Dad, can I go to Simon's after school? His mom's making meatballs." He smiled and replied, "Yes, I'll ask your aunt to pick you up there. Love ya!"

His desk phone rang. "Qiang is here to see you," his secretary said.

"Send her in."

He put the phone back on the desk and watched his VP of R&D open the glass door and close it behind her. Her lab coat hung as if it was several sizes too big, even though he knew she had the only XS size they had in the company. Her hair was shiny and very dark. If she ever decided to put it up in a set of pigtails, she could pass for a teenager.

When Tyler first met her, he thought she was very insecure. Her accent was strong and she just blinked and blinked, trying to keep those overly long bangs from getting into her eyes. But after five minutes of conversation, he realized he was talking to the one of the most brilliant scientists he'd ever met.

"Tyler."

She sat across from him and moved the chair closer to his desk, as if she wanted to confide something to him, but the distance between them made it impossible.

"Yes, Qiang?"

He smiled. She was always so proper, so calm and demure.

She leaned forward and interlaced her thin fingers, resting her hands on his desk. She looked at him and started blinking again.

"Have you ever considered cutting your bangs shorter?" he asked.

"What?" She looked puzzled.

"Never mind. What's up?"

"I didn't want to say this at the staff meeting this morning..."

Tyler took a deep breath. He rubbed his chin, still smooth from the morning's shave.

"The latest trials failed too. We're going to need more time."

"We don't have more time," Tyler said under his breath. That was all he could do to not scream from the top of his lungs.

"Tyler, we're close. Very close, but we're not there yet. You need to sell our progress to the board."

"Qiang, there's no progress to sell to the board. You just said it. We're at the end of the rope and we're falling fast. You have to do better. You're our last hope to find a cure."

His eyes shined, but not from excitement. Tyler reached out across the table and opened his hand so Qiang would take it. She did. He squeezed hard enough to let her know they were in it together.

"I really need you to find the problem so we can save people."

She squeezed his hand back and got up. "I know, Tyler. I know." And she walked out, her head low, her stride slow and tired.

He followed Qiang out of his office to speak to his secretary.

"Nancy, I need some time. No interruptions until I tell you, okay?" he said to his secretary.

"Got it," she said, looking at him briefly.

He closed the door behind him. When he sat back in his chair he looked for the prepaid phone in his briefcase. There was only one number in the call log. He hit redial and waited.

"How's the progress?" he asked as soon as Harper answered.

"Only one left from the last list."

"All different?"

"As you wanted."

"Very good. How come I haven't seen anything in the news?"

"Maybe check the obituaries," Harper said.

"I have a new list. It's a bit longer. We need to speed things up."

Harper was silent for a long time. Finally, he said, "I still have the one left from the previous list."

"Oh?"

"I ran into problems with her."

"I trust that you'll take care of it. You've done a remarkable job so far."

"About that..." Harper paused. "Things are getting worse on my end."

Tyler bit his fist, almost breaking the skin. After a few seconds he said, "I have your back, Harper, I promise. I just need you to get this done. See you tomorrow, same time and place, okay?"

"Okay," Harper said and hung up.

Tyler put the phone back in his briefcase and logged into his computer. The screen came alive, and he opened an encrypted document. He stared at the list. Twenty-four names stared back at him. Sixteen were crossed out already. They had a long way to go and very little time.

CHAPTER 31

Sorensen headed directly to see Lou. He guarded the evidence bag, fully sealed with the tiny piece of glove, in his pocket. The day was already hot and he was sweating profusely under his jacket. He entered the building, hoping to feel a rush of cold air, but there was nothing.

The elevator doors opened, and he walked into the reception area, waving his hand in front of his face, trying to cool down.

"The AC's broken," Mary said behind her desk. "They're supposed to fix it tomorrow, but who knows."

"This is terrible. How can you stand it?"

"I'm used to it. It seems that it's broken more often than not."

He plunked an elbow on the high desk and said, "I think I got something." He pulled out the evidence bag and waved it in the air. "Straight from the ME's office."

"Right on."

He arched an eyebrow and stared at her, watching her face the whole time.

She didn't even flinch. "Sorry. Teenage boys. You end up speaking like them. You'll see soon enough," she said and pushed her chair away from him. Mary pulled a couple flyers she had on the counter and used them as a fan.

"Ah, no. Mine are girls." Sorensen said.

"Same difference."

"Don't spoil it for me. I like to live in ignorance as long as I can." He wiped the sweat from his forehead. "Lou in?"

"You're lucky. He just came back from a meeting. He's in his office."

"Thanks," he said, already walking away.

Sorensen liked coming to the lab. There was always the hope that they would find something that would help him break a case. Sometimes that was true. Sometimes it wasn't.

"Mr. Lou, how are we doing today?"

"I fucking hate bureaucrats. Have I told you that before? I hate them. They're the scum of the earth, and I'm fed up. I'm going to quit this thankless job and send them all to hell."

"Okay. Should I come back?" Sorensen asked, but he sat down instead.

Lou was walking back and forth behind his desk, his large body moving slowly and his wobbly stomach dancing up and down.

Darcy wasn't joking when he said it looks like Jell-O, Sorensen thought, making a mental note to avoid eating it ever again.

"I think it just turned noon somewhere. Want to go for a drink?" Sorensen asked. It was going to take a lot more than pacing to calm Lou down.

"I'm fine. I'll be better when I quit."

He sat down. His eyes were bloodshot. His dark chocolate skin was peppered by even darker freckles. He passed both beefy hands over his bald head.

"You haven't come here to listen to me bitch. What do you want?"

"I'm actually enjoying this. I've never heard you cuss this much." Sorensen leaned back and rocked on the chair, watching his friend.

136

"Oh shut up. You've gone to enough Raiders games with me to know that's not true."

"Fair enough. So, what did the bureaucrat sons of bitches do to you this time?"

"Same shit, different day. I got a nice pep talk last week about how the department's doing awesome and blah, blah, blah. So, I go in there today, asking to buy the LTQ XL Linear Ion Trap Mass Spectrometer, which would help in so many ways, and do you know what they tell me?"

It was a rhetorical question, but Sorensen played along. "No, what?"

"The motherfuckers told me no. No. Can you believe that?"

Sorensen shook his head, trying really hard not to laugh.

"They said no. They said no to a machine that could solve cases in half the time than with the piece of crap we have now."

Lou looked up and saw Sorensen's face.

"Oh fuck you too. Why are you even here?"

"Lou, you go through this every single time you find a new toy. I'm amazed that in the seventeen years you've been working here you haven't learnt that if you want something, you have to get it yourself."

"This is a $35,000 machine!"

"Well then. Kid's college fund you can dip into?"

Lou shook his head in frustration. "The reason the bad guys always win is because we don't have the best tools to solve crimes."

"Hey, hey, the bad guys don't always win. And that's why you have people like me, to pound the pavement."

Lou brushed him off with his hand. "You know what I mean."

"Anyway, I brought you something interesting."

He pulled the evidence bag out of his pocket. Lou looked at the tiny contents.

"From the mugging victim last night. The husband's coming over this afternoon. I'd like to be able to tell him something."

"This afternoon? Are you joking?"

"No."

"Fine. I'll have Mauricio work on it." Before Sorensen left his office, Lou said, "But just so you know, if we had the mass spectrometer I could have this for you in less than an hour."

"Make sure you get it, then," Sorensen said, only looking back quickly enough to see his friend's face flush with fury.

CHAPTER 32

Saffron felt cold even though it was hot at the station. She felt as if she were an observer of her new life, as if everything that was going on happened to somebody else and she got to see it from the outside. She clicked the mouse and saw a new image appear on the screen. This knife was larger, looked meaner than the previous one, but she couldn't tell whether it was the same one the man had used to cut her seat belt.

"I'm sorry, but I think this is pointless," she said to Detective Lynch.

He was sitting on the chair normally used by visitors.

"I know it seems that way, but it would really help if we could narrow it down somewhat. Please, just a few more."

She nodded and clicked the mouse again. Nothing. She did this for another ten minutes without getting any closer than she had been an hour earlier. Finally, she leaned against the chair's back and sighed. "I need a break."

"Okay. I understand."

"Is it okay if I go to the gym? I think I need to clear my head."

"Are you sure that's the best idea?"

"I can't go home. I'm getting cabin fever," she explained. She looked away. She tied her hair into a knot that came loose as soon as she had made it. "Detective, there's no reason why somebody would want to kill me. I really think it's not me who you should be worrying about."

"Saffron, he was at your house."

A shiver ran through her back. "It may have been unrelated. We've had some break-ins in my building before."

"It may have been." His face showed he didn't believe it.

"Yeah, okay, I don't believe it either, but it just doesn't make any sense."

"Okay, I tell you what, go to the gym and I'll call you later to see how you're doing."

"Sounds good." She grabbed her purse and walked toward the door before she remembered something. "Oh, my friend has my car...Do I still get to enjoy my police detail?"

"You know that neither San Jose, nor the county of Santa Clara, has a town car service, right?"

"No? Ah, that explains why there was no booze at the back of the patrol car, and why the seat was made of plastic." She stayed there for a second, but when Lynch didn't go on, she said, "Okay, no worries. I'll take a cab."

"I'll drive you. But only this one time. I have some leads to follow up on anyway."

He grabbed his jacket, and they both headed out back to the red candy-apple Cobra. After a small detour for Saffron to grab her gym bag, they finally got to 24 Hour Fitness. It was a large building with an even bigger parking lot, which was fairly full, more than she would have expected for the middle of a workday.

"You okay getting back on your own?" Lynch asked before she got out of the car.

"Oh yeah. I'll call my friend and see what's up with my car. If not, I'll catch a cab back home."

"I think you should go somewhere else. Maybe stay with somebody until this is over."

"I know. I'll think about it."

She closed the car's door but before leaving she said, "Detective, thank you for all you're doing. I know it seems that I'm very flippant about this whole thing, but I'm not. I'm really freaking out." She looked down and then looked up, locking eyes with Darcy.

"I know. I'm going to do all I can to find this creep. I promise."

Saffron nodded and went into the gym. The music was loud and welcome. She headed for the locker room to change. When she got out, she scanned the cardio machines and chose a treadmill in the middle of the room with nobody around it. She picked the Pandora dance station saved in her phone and started running. As the machine kept increasing the pace, she pounded on it with each stride, and sweat began to mist her body.

After a few minutes, Saffron took a sip of water from her bottle. Her eyes rose and rested on the mirror in front of her. She almost tripped when she saw a man staring at her reflection. He diverted his gaze as soon as he saw her looking at him. She put her water in the cup-holder, grabbed the handles and turned around, looking for the man.

She spotted him pretending to read a magazine or a book propped on a StairMaster. He was very tall, probably six foot four, and trim. His muscles were well defined. He looked like one of those middle-age men who spent a lot of time at the gym in hopes of attracting twenty-year-old chicks.

"I must be getting paranoid," she said to herself and sped up the run.

Saffron looked up into the mirror a few more times, checking the man, who was only a few machines away from her. She caught him looking back at her on several occasions, each increased her uneasiness. Before her twenty minutes were up, she moved to the machine area, taking the longer route just to avoid him.

CHAPTER 33

Sorensen was back at his desk, updating the whiteboard. He had to rearrange the information he had on the three suicide victims to make space for the Hughes case.

"At this rate I'm going to need a second board," he mumbled to himself. He was writing about the evidence they found between her teeth when Jon startled him.

"I got it!" he said, raising both fists as if he had just scored a goal.

"If you do that again, I'm going to beat the shit out of you." Sorensen took the eraser and wiped off the scribble he'd just made.

"Sorensen, I found a stolen car."

"Good for you."

"By the victim's house last night."

"What?" Sorensen put his black marker down on the whiteboard's base. He walked to Jon's desk and stood behind him, staring at the information on the screen.

"All of the cars on the street are accounted for except this Acura." He pointed at the entry on his list describing a black Acura with California plates, 6NJH183.

"Is it confirmed stolen? Maybe somebody was visiting," Sorensen said, wanting to confirm that Jon had thought of all the possible angles.

"I checked all of the stolen car reports and, wait for it, wait for it—"

"Oh, Jon, cut the crap. I'm this close to punching you." He put his thumb and index fingers together, right in front of Jon's face.

"You really spoil everybody's fun, you know?" Jon's voice lost its excitement. "The report just came in."

Sorensen focused on the computer, double-checking the list of cars, and when all the information matched, he said, "Jon, this is really great work. You definitely deserve every penny you get at this job."

Jon's face lit up. "Can I follow up with the owner?" After Sorensen's crack sank in, he protested, "Hey, you know I don't get paid, right?"

The detective patted him on the shoulder and said, "Let me know everything you find out."

Then he went back to his desk and saw Jon pick up the phone. He reached out for his own and called Lou.

"Have you calmed down yet?"

"Some. What do you want?"

"Jon, the super intern, found a stolen car by Emma Hughes' house. I need somebody to go there immediately and check it out before somebody screws up the evidence."

"Do you want that more than the results on the fibers you gave me earlier?"

"Can't I have both?"

"No. I'm sending Mauricio. If there's anything, he'll find it."

"Keep me posted."

After hanging up, he went back to Jon's desk to listen in on the conversation, but Jon was also wrapping up.

"Okay, Mrs. Chopra, thank you for your help and we'll call you as soon as you can come to pick up your car."

"So?" Sorensen asked.

"Yes, the car's registered to Ketki Chopra. She reported the car stolen an hour or so ago when she was going to use it to go to the store."

"Where does she live?"

"Campbell. She doesn't know the victim, and doesn't have any friends or family who live in that neighborhood."

"Great work. Let's see if they find anything."

CHAPTER 34

"Darcy, it's Mary at the lab. I have a package for you. Should I send it over or do you want to come and say hallo?"

"Why did it go there?"

"It looks like a bunch of DVDs. Want me to send them over?"

"No need. I'll be right there."

Detective Lynch left the office without grabbing his jacket. It was hot and the lab was only a few blocks away. When he got outside he realized his gun was in plain view. He walked faster and started to sweat. At the lab's reception area, Mary was on the phone. She lifted her index finger, asking for a second, but Darcy didn't have the time to spare.

"This?" he mouthed without making a sound, pointing at a bag with five DVDs.

She nodded. Darcy took the bag and waved goodbye.

A few minutes later he was back in the office.

"Where can I watch these?" he said to the open room. In the four months he'd been in the department, he hadn't had to watch any DVDs.

"What are they?" asked Detective Ramirez, a short Hispanic man with a Fu Manchu mustache everybody made fun of.

"DVDs from ATMs."

"You can watch them in the small conference room at the end of the hall. The one that looks like a closet with no windows," Ramirez said, pointing toward the other side of the building.

Darcy grabbed the bag, went to the kitchen for a fresh cup of coffee and headed in the direction he was given. Ramirez was not kidding. The room barely fit two people. There was quite a lot of equipment, though some of it was already obsolete. Darcy looked through the DVDs. He picked the one from the bank located closest to Saffron's place. The screen came to life with twitchy images of an empty street. The time was 2:04 a.m. That was too early.

He fast-forwarded until a couple filled the screen when they came up to the ATM. They were talking and laughing, and Darcy wished he could listen to what made them so carefree. They took some money out, kissed and walked away, leaving Darcy alone again. The time was 2:27.

He fast-forwarded the DVD again. The minutes passed with empty streets. He reached out for the coffee mug. Without looking he put it to his lips, but the cup was already empty. He returned it to the table. At 4:39 a.m., the image changed again. He was staring at the grainy footage of a man dressed in dark colors running toward First Street on Santa Clara. He was only on the screen for a little more than a second. Darcy rewound the video and watched it again. And again.

He walked into the main office area and from the entrance said, "Jon, I need you to do something for me."

The intern jumped off his desk, frazzled, more than in a rush. "Sure. What?"

Darcy took him to the video room and showed him the still image of the man.

"Can you get me footage from all the cameras in a two-mile radius of this location?"

Darcy pushed the print button on the screen.

"Is this your guy?"

"Best lead I've got so far." Darcy grabbed the picture of the man and looked at it closely. It was grainy, and it would be nearly impossible to make an ID. "I already have some of the DVDs, so make sure you don't ask for the same ones."

"Are they all here?" Jon asked, digging into the bag on the table.

"Yes. Can you start watching through them while we wait for the other ones? I want you to check between 3:00 a.m. and 6:30 a.m. for anybody who looks like this, and anybody else who looks suspicious at all."

"You mean if they're running or something?"

"Yes, that, and you'll know it when you see it. Most people are pretty generic. Log the time of every single thing you find that seems out of the ordinary. I'll check them when I'm back."

"You got it."

"Thanks, Jon."

Darcy folded the photo and went back to his desk to grab his jacket. He pulled out his phone and dialed.

"Where are you now?"

"Just got home," Saffron responded.

"I'll be there in twenty. There's something I want to show you."

CHAPTER 35

It took Detective Lynch half that time to make it to Saffron's condo.

"How was the workout?" he asked when Saffron opened the door.

"I attacked a guy who I thought was the killer," she said, now dressed in jeans and a bright red peasant blouse.

"You did what?" Darcy almost choked on his own saliva. "Why did you think that?"

"He kept staring at me, kept going everywhere I was going, but staying just far enough away, you know?"

Darcy just looked at her, the initial worry fading and the beginning of a grin forming on his tanned face.

"Don't look at me that way. It was a very legitimate thought, given what I've been through the last few days."

"So, what happened?"

"Well, when I got fed up, I took a barbell—it was only two and a half pounds, because I didn't want him to know I took it—and I lured the creep into the hallway that leads to the pool. It zigzags a few times, so I thought I could surprise him. I hid there, the barbell raised, and when he turned the corner to kill me, I screamed and hit him."

"No, you didn't," Darcy hoped.

"Actually, I missed. The weight of the barbell propelled me forward, and I ended up on the floor. I turned around and he faced me. I got up really fast and was going to charge at him again, but without the element of surprise, he grabbed my arm."

"I'd have paid anything to see this."

"Oh, shut up. Where were you when I needed you, huh?" She turned around and grabbed a Vitamin Water from the fridge. "Want one?" she offered.

Darcy nodded, and she gave him a pink one.

"Anyway, so I kicked him. He yelled at me."

"What did he say?"

"He said something like, 'What the hell are you doing, crazy bitch?' To which I responded, 'You're not going to kill me, you creep!'"

Darcy started laughing.

"By that time some people started coming up to check out what was happening. He told them that I tried to attack him, and they kicked me out of the gym."

"This is priceless," Darcy said, still laughing.

"No, it isn't. I almost got the guy for you, and here you are, laughing. We need to go back to the gym and find out who he is."

"The most I could charge him with is having a horrible pickup style."

"What do you mean?"

"Saffron, the guy was trying to pick you up."

"Oh no he wasn't. Don't be ridiculous."

Darcy stared at her, the smirk still filling his face.

"Whatever. Why are you here anyway?" she said and sat on the sofa, crossing both legs under her.

Detective Lynch sat across from her and pulled the printout from his pocket. "Does this guy look familiar?"

"No. Hard to tell, but no, I don't think so."

"You sure it's not the guy from the gym?" he joked.

She smiled, and gave him the finger.

"Seriously, doesn't ring any bells?"

She stared at the photo for a few seconds. "Oh my God, the boots." She tapped the picture. They were lighter than the rest of his outfit. "They look like Timberlands. The guy who tried to kill me wore Timberlands. I never saw his face when he pulled me out of the car. Do you think this is the guy?"

"This picture was taken from an ATM machine around the time he ran from your place." He saw a shadow pass her face. "I'm having somebody at the station check other cameras and see if we can get a better shot."

Saffron hugged herself, then rubbed her arms as if trying to warm them.

"Did you get your car yet?" he said, changing the subject.

"No. I can't get a hold of my friend, which isn't normal. Maybe you can take me to her place?" She batted her eyelashes at him.

"No way."

"Please." She pouted her lips.

"That's not a good look for you," he lied.

"Seriously? Surprising. It's worked every time in the past."

"Okay, I'll take you, but only because you made me laugh. Not because you look cute when you pout."

"You just said it wasn't a good look for me."

"Don't push it," he said and stood. "No time for you to change. I actually have a job catching bad guys."

He headed for the door.

"You should consider a career change. You're a much better driver," she said.

He closed the door behind him, leaving her inside.

"Hey, I was joking."

"The bus stop is a few streets over. Good luck to you." He said and squinted his blue eye in the bright sunlight.

CHAPTER 36

Sorensen opened his notes and perused them for leads to follow up. There was so much legwork he needed to do, and he didn't know where to start.

"Boss, we need more people," he yelled toward Virago's office.

"You got Jon," she shouted back.

"We need more people besides Jon."

"Do you have a couple mil to donate to the department?"

"Yeah, I've been saving my yearly bonuses just for this."

"If you didn't waste so much time complaining, you'd be halfway done by now, and you wouldn't need more people to help you."

"Yeah, right," he said under his breath, knowing the conversation was over.

Sorensen started typing yesterday's notes into the case file before he forgot them. He tapped at the keyboard harder than he needed to, making the keystrokes resonate throughout the office. When the phone rang, he picked it up, thankful for the break.

"Sorensen," he said without looking at the caller ID.

"Guess what?" Mauricio said in his high-pitched voice.

Sorensen checked his watch. Mauricio was fast but not that fast. "You can't possibly have the results already."

"No."

Sorensen pictured him waving his hand in dismissal.

"I just got done collecting all the evidence from the car."

"Great. Anything interesting?"

"Everything's interesting."

Sorensen rephrased. "Anything that will help me solve this case?"

"Maybe. That's up to you, detective. I just sent a messenger over to you with all the bags." He went on: "I'll start working on the evidence you gave Lou earlier as soon as I get back to the office. If I find anything, I'll let you know."

"Thanks, Mauricio. Work fast."

"Always do."

Sorensen hung up and looked for the Post-it note with Mrs. Chopra's number. When she answered, he asked her to come by the office to identify some items found in her stolen car. Before he was done giving her directions, the box with the evidence showed up.

He started looking through it. Everything was bagged and sealed. There weren't that many things—a couple pens, a baby juice bottle, a couple toys, a small blanket, a phone charger and a book with crossword puzzles open somewhere in the middle, with a puzzle halfway done. Sorensen put everything back into the box and returned to writing his notes.

Almost an hour later, his concentration was broken by another call.

"Sorensen, a Mrs. Chopra is here to see you," the receptionist told him.

"Send her up, please."

He saved his notes so a system crash wouldn't lose the entire hour's worth of progress and grabbed the box. When the elevator doors opened, he was there to greet her.

"Mrs. Chopra?" he asked even though she was the only woman in the elevator.

"Yes," Still inside, she moved the child she was holding from one hip to the other.

Sorensen introduced himself and led her to an interview room. Once there, he took out all of the items from the box, placing them carefully in front of her, equidistant from each other.

"Mrs. Chopra, do you see anything here you do not recognize?"

She took the sippy cup and, smiling, said, "This is definitely mine. Well, Sudhir's." She patted the head of the small boy, who sat peacefully on her lap.

Methodically, she picked one bag after another, and without spending too much time looking at the item, moved it to the end of the table, saying "Mine" each time. Finally, there was only one item left. She reached for the crossword puzzle booklet.

"Can I open this?" she said, extending her arm, pushing the bag closer to Sorensen's face as if he couldn't see it otherwise.

"Is it yours?"

"I don't recognize it."

Chopra looked at it again. Her son moved a little. "No, I don't think it's mine."

"Do you think maybe somebody who's been in your car recently forgot it there?"

She thought for a few seconds. "No, I doubt it. Everybody has the games on their smartphones."

"Can you double check that everything else is yours?"

She looked back at all of the bags she had already checked. She shook her head but hesitated for a second.

"Mrs. Chopra, it's really important to figure out what is yours and what isn't so we can catch the person who stole your car. If there's something you're not sure about, let me know."

She vacillated, looked again and discarded the obvious items, but finally picked the bag containing a white pen with a chewed blue cap. "I don't think this is mine."

"Why don't you think so?"

"Neither I nor my husband chew on pens. It's bad for the teeth."

After reconfirming there wasn't anything else that looked out of place, Sorensen walked her out.

"Can I take my car now?" she said after they shook hands.

"No, we still need to run a few more tests. Somebody will call you as soon as you can pick it up."

"But I thought that's why I was called to come here," she said, switching her son from one hip to the other.

"I'm sorry. We needed to identify the items we found in the car so we could rush the investigation. Your help today was invaluable. And I promise you, it won't be that long before your car is ready."

She nodded and left. Sorensen continued on to the lab to give the two evidence bags to Mauricio in person.

"Do you have the results yet?" he asked the moment he was within earshot of the lab technician.

"No. And I won't get them faster by you asking me every five minutes."

"I got two more for you. Super top priority."

"Isn't everything?"

CHAPTER 37

Traffic was slow and it wasn't even three thirty in the afternoon yet. Darcy cursed himself for not having taken surface streets, and now they were stuck in bumper-to-bumper traffic on 101. The Cobra's top was down and the sun was blazing.

"I should have grabbed the sunscreen," Saffron said.

Before Darcy could reply, his phone rang.

"Lynch."

"You have to come back to the station," Mauricio said, using the tone of a confidant. "I found something peculiar."

"Can't you tell me over the phone? I'm in the middle of something."

"No. I think you need to come."

"Okay." Darcy looked at his watch and said, "I'll be there in ten."

Saffron looked at him.

"Change of plans. We have to go back to the office for a minute." He said when he hung up.

"But we were so close," she said, whining a little.

"Not close enough. Besides, this way you get to spend more time with me." He turned his face to see her expression.

"And that's a plus... how?"

Back at the station they stopped at the reception area, and he signed for Saffron's clearance. Darcy offered her the spare chair next to his desk, and phoned Mauricio.

"I'm here. Where are you?"

"Close." Mauricio appeared through the door a minute later. "Where's Sorensen?" he asked, looking around.

Jon looked up. "He was here a minute ago."

"He needs to be here too. Can you call him?"

Before Jon had the time to punch in all the numbers, Sorensen came into the large room, stuffing his shirt into his pants. All eyes fell on him.

"What?" He turnerd his back to them and finished adjusting his pants. "Man, there is no privacy in this place."

Mauricio sat across from them and pulled two bags of evidence from his satchel.

"Is it okay to talk?" He looked at Lynch, but nodded toward Saffron.

"Yes, she's a victim/witness in one of my cases."

"Which one?"

"The hit and run on Highway 17."

Saffron looked up, her interest was piqued.

"Oh, okay. This isn't about that one."

She grabbed her phone and it slid from her hand, crashing to the floor. They all looked at her. She blushed and moved to pick it up.

"Sorry. I've been meaning to get a case so it's not so slippery."

Sorensen and Lynch focused back on Mauricio, who had set the evidence on the table. When he was sure he had the detectives' full attention, he said, "Darcy, remember that piece of fabric Rachel found under Pritchard's car?"

Darcy nodded.

"Sorensen, remember that piece of fabric you gave me just a few hours ago to check from Hughes?"

"Jesus, Mauricio, get to the frigging point," Sorensen said, rolling his eyes.

"Okay, okay, spoil the fun, will you?" Mauricio protested, but he grabbed both bags, one in each hand. Lifting them up, he said, "Well, they are the exact same material."

"They come from the same place?" Darcy asked, more confused than excited.

"I can't tell you that without having the piece they come from, but they are exactly the same composition."

Sorensen and Darcy exchanged glances.

"What's even more interesting is that the Hughes sample contains a glycol ethers."

His smug faced beamed.

"Are you sure you didn't get them mixed up?" Lynch asked.

Before Mauricio could protest, Sorensen asked, "What's glycol ethers?"

"Brake fluid," Darcy said, not wanting them to get sidetracked. "It makes no sense at all. You're a hundred percent sure you have the right sample?"

"Please, don't offend me, Detective Lynch. This is why I wanted both of you in this room together before I shared the news."

"This is crazy," Sorensen said, shaking his head. "What you're saying is that the piece you found in Hughes' teeth has brake fluid, and not the one that came from under the car?"

"You win the prize, Sherlock."

"Oh, fuck you." Looking at Lynch, he added, "What the hell's going on?"

"I have no clue."

"Any info on the pen and the crossword puzzle yet?" Sorensen asked Mauricio.

"Working on it. Rachel's helping, so I should have something for you very soon."

He got to his feet and grabbed both evidence bags. "Okay, I'm taking these back with me."

He left the room, moving in short little hops like a sparrow.

Darcy stared at the desk where the evidence had been, wondering how the pieces fit together. Normally things were much more straightforward, like making a puzzle with a lot of sky. You had to try each piece to see if it fit, and most didn't. But eventually you found one that did and then another and another, until you were done. In this case, it seemed that as you tried to find a piece that fit, you eventually discovered it actually belonged to a different puzzle. It made no sense.

He turned around to ask Sorensen what he made of the whole thing, but he was on the phone.

"Bring him up. Thanks," he said.

"What do you think?" Darcy asked after Sorensen hung up.

"I think it means you get to have my mugging, as I told you you would."

"Whatever. Seriously. Could it be a coincidence?"

"I don't know, but we're going to have to talk about this later, because the husband of the mugging victim is just about to come up."

Darcy went back to his desk and turned on the computer. He typed "glycol ethers" in the browser and scanned through the results. There were many different uses for it. Maybe it was just a weird coincidence.

"Detective Sorensen?" a man said from the doorway.

Saffron looked up and jumped from her chair. "Bob?" She walked toward her best friend's husband and asked, "What are you doing here?"

"Saffron?"

His eyes were bloodshot, his demeanor uncharacteristically shy. He stood by the door, as if he needed a formal invitation to cross the threshold.

CHAPTER 38

After talking to Harper, Tyler made a few calls to catch up with some of his closest investors. Sheldon Michaels was right. Their tone was curt and they were losing patience. He went to the lab to check the work for himself.

The place was buzzing with PhDs testing, formulating, computing, talking and arguing about details that mostly escaped him. Nobody noticed him, and he liked that. He knew it was better not to disrupt their flow, and what he really needed was to have them all at their best.

After walking around awhile, he headed toward Qiang's office at the end of the lab. She wasn't there, but he entered anyway. He sat on her chair and for the first time, he got to see her world with his own eyes. He could feel the energy of the lab, even though the door was closed. He no longer wondered why she wanted to work there, in that room, with no outside windows and a light hum coming from the air conditioning, rather than in her other beautiful office, next to his on the second floor, where all the upper management offices were located.

His chest puffed a little. He was so proud of his team, of the company he'd built. He knew deep down they would come up with the cure for breast cancer. They would all be famous one day. They would save lives—hell, maybe even win the Nobel Prize. He then noticed he had been clenching the armrests of Qiang's chair. He let go and decided to leave the office. There was nothing else he could do to help out today. When he got back to his desk, he shut down his laptop, put it in his briefcase and left, leaving the door open.

"Your dinner with Rox and Tory from Arcadia Ventures has been rescheduled to tomorrow, but breakfast instead," his secretary said when she saw his jacket trailing behind him.

"Okay," he said over his shoulder without slowing down his pace. One more clue that his investors were pulling away.

"Where are you going?" she asked behind him, a little louder.

"I'm getting out of here. My cell phone works everywhere."

He turned the corner and didn't hear anything else from her. The left side of his mouth tilted upwards, even though he wasn't really sure why he was smiling.

Tyler knew he should go to his sister's to pick Lucas up. But he needed to do something else first. He got in his car, but before he started the engine, he pulled his phone from his pocket and dialed.

"Hey, buddy, how's aunty Julia treating you?"

"We're building a hospital."

Tyler pulled the handset away from his ear a little.

"That's a big project. Do you have that many Legos?"

"We stopped at the store and got more on the way home."

"Don't tell him that," he heard Julia whisper on the other side of the line.

"Oops, sorry," he whispered back, but he was still talking into the phone.

Tyler smiled. He breathed in deeply and could almost smell his son's scent.

"Okay, buddy, make me proud."

"It's going to be really big and we even have three ambulances."

"That's impressive. I'll see it tonight when I pick you up."

When Lucas gave the phone to Julia, Tyler told her he would be a few hours late. After hanging up, he dialed a different number.

"Where are you?" he asked when Eva picked up.

"I'm busy," she said, but her voice rolled over her tongue like a purr.

"I want to see you."

"I thought we made plans for tomorrow."

After a few seconds, he said, "I want to see you now."

"I want to see you too, but I can't today. I'm busy."

"Get un-busy."

Another moment passed.

"Will have to be tomorrow." Her voice was colder, a little more distant, as if she were entering a tunnel.

"Don't play games with me. I want to see you now. Meet me at the W in thirty minutes."

"I can't today. I just told you."

"Stop playing," he yelled and punched the wheel with his open hand. A sharp bolt of pain shot up his arm.

She hung up, and he hit the wheel again, but this time not as hard. He started the car and sped away, scraping the bottom of his Tesla on a speed bump.

CHAPTER 39

Darcy knocked on the door of the second interview room. He balanced a cup of coffee in each hand while he opened the door with his elbow. He found Saffron and Bob trying to console each other. They turned and looked back at him as if he were an intruder.

"I'm sorry to interrupt, but I thought you could both use some coffee." He set the cups on the table. Steam swirled upwards.

"Thank you," Saffron said, taking one in both hands as if she were trying to warm her fingers.

"Detective Sorensen will be at his desk when you're ready," he told Bob and closed the door behind him.

Darcy now understood the grave danger Saffron was in. He had told Virago it was just a matter of time until the killer got her, that she needed to put a real detective on the case, but she refused. The brake fluid-tainted piece of fabric in Emma's teeth didn't make any sense, but he had a nagging feeling the two cases were connected somehow. Even though some people think a coincidence is just that, he really didn't believe in coincidences.

He walked back to the bullpen. It was bustling with noise and activity. It was the end of the day and everybody was at their desks working on their case notes so they could go home. He knew that wasn't going to be his fate.

He saw Virago come out of her office from the corner of his eye. She walked toward the space that separated his desk from Sorensen's and put both hands on her hips, hoping her silent presence would draw the desired attention from her detective. Darcy sat on his desk facing her, but Sorensen kept working, oblivious of the captain's visit.

"Sorensen," she said louder than she needed to.

"Yes, boss?" He turned around at once.

"In my office."

As soon as they started moving away, Darcy realized that whatever the captain wanted didn't have anything to do with him.

But before he had time to start his computer, Virago turned from her office door and said, "You too."

"*Moi*?" he asked, imitating a bad French accent.

She ignored him and headed in but held the door open until Darcy entered. Virago followed him and leaned against her desk while the two detectives stood kitty-corner from her.

"Lynch, tell me what you think about the new developments."

Darcy thought for a second. He wished he'd had more time to try to make sense of everything they'd learned in the last half hour.

"I think the perp that's after Saffron Meadows killed Emma Hughes. I think he followed Saffron's car..." Darcy saw Virago raised an eyebrow when he mentioned the victim by her first name, and rephrased: "I think he thought he was following Meadows and in the dark killed Hughes, thinking it was her."

"But they don't look alike at all," Virago argued.

"She was wearing a scarf. Maybe she covered her hair and the killer didn't see that she was blond."

"Sorensen, anything to add?"

165

"I told you this case was going to be Lynch's."

"Anything of value to add?"

"I talked to Clark. He's finished the autopsy and he told me that the last stab wound, the one to the right lung, was less deep, as is if it was done with less force. Maybe he realized then that he had made a mistake and didn't push the knife all the way in."

They fell silent for a few seconds. There was still a lot of movement outside of Virago's office, and the noise seeped into the room. The captain moved around her desk and sat down. She brushed her hair back with both hands, closed her eyes and sighed loudly.

"Have you gone to the range yet?" she asked Lynch.

"No."

"I told you that you had until the end of the week. What day is today?"

"I'm done here, right?" Sorensen interrupted.

"No," she said and paused for a second. "I want Darcy to take the Hughes case since it's probably related to the Meadows case. You busy enough with the suicides?"

"I told you that you should have given it to him from the start."

"Get the hell out of here and get me some progress on those suicides."

Sorensen left, mumbling something. Darcy had to force himself to stop grinding his teeth. He sat and looked straight at Virago.

"I can't have you working cases and not be qualified. You have to get this done tonight or tomorrow."

"I won't pass. I took this job because it was mostly a desk job, with some menial cases that nobody else wanted. This is a serious case, with one victim already dead and another one who attacked a guy who was trying to pick her up at the gym, because she thought he was the guy who's trying to kill her." He paused, trying to maintain his voice level.

"What?" she asked.

He looked at her, not knowing what Virago was referring to.

"What was that about attacks at a gym?"

Darcy glossed over Saffron's little assault as fast as he could, regretting having mentioned it. Virago's expression told him she didn't really want to know more either. He moved on.

"And based on what Mauricio said, I think the car accident is also connected to these other two."

"Because of the glycol?"

"Yeah. I don't know. It's just a feeling." He rubbed his left temple and looked back at Virago. "If you really care about solving these cases, and possibly not having any more deaths, you need to assign them to somebody else. I'm not your man for this."

The captain stood up and put both hands on the table. She leaned forward and looked at him. There was an intensity in her honey eyes he'd never seen before.

"I don't have anybody else. Get qualified in the next twenty-four hours and do your fucking job."

Darcy stared back at her, wondering how long he could keep his good eye from blinking.

Almost a minute later, she said, "You used to be one of the best detectives in Seattle. What the hell happened to you that made you such a pussy?"

His body tensed up and he jumped from the chair. Heading toward the door, he said through clenched teeth, "You know exactly what happened in Seattle."

When he reached the door, he opened it and, loud enough so everybody could hear, he said, "I quit. This way you won't have to fire me when I don't pass the qualification."

"Don't be an asshole," she yelled back, but he was already out of the bullpen, heading to the elevator.

CHAPTER 40

Sorensen tapped at his computer with two fingers. Searching the ViCAP database was better than it had been in the old days, but the system still had its handicaps. From the corner of his eye he saw Lynch storm out. Then he saw Bob Hughes' and Saffron's shocked expressions as the detective walked by.

"The interview room is in the other direction," he yelled behind him, but Lynch was already gone. Sorensen turned 180 degrees and saw Virago walk toward him. She looked as if she had just sucked on a lemon.

"Uh-oh." He mumbled under his breath.

As soon as she reached his desk, she whispered, "You're back on," motioning toward Hughes with a tilt of her head.

He refrained from complaining even though he really wanted to, then approached Hughes and apologized for the scene they*d just witnessed.

"What happened?" Saffron asked.

"You know as much as I do," Sorensen said. "Please follow me," he said to Bob Hughes.

Saffron and Bob hugged.

"I'll help you with all the arrangements," she said, squeezing her best friend's widower's arm.

Bob nodded and mouthed a silent "Thank you."

Sorensen walked Bob back to the interview room. Sitting across from Hughes, he covered the standard preliminary questions. Bob had an alibi and no, he couldn't think of anybody who would want to kill his wife.

"Do you know of anybody who would want to kill Saffron Meadows?" Sorensen asked.

"Saffron? No. Nobody." He paused, trying to make sense of his new reality. "Saffron told me somebody had tried to kill her on Highway 17. I can't believe it."

"Was your wife pretty close to Ms. Meadows?"

"Yes, they worked together a few years back. They've been best friends since." He interlaced his fingers on top of the table and leaned forward a few inches. "Yesterday you said it looked like somebody was trying to rob my wife and they killed her in the process. Why are you asking me about Saffron?"

"Mr. Hughes, your wife was driving Ms. Meadows' car."

"You think he was trying to kill Saffron and killed my wife instead?"

"We don't know enough to make that assumption. I'm trying to collect all the information I can as part of the investigation. Please understand that even questions that seem irrelevant to you have a purpose for us."

Bob nodded. He rubbed his eyes and exhaled, leaning back into the chair again. "I understand. I'm sorry."

Sorensen continued asking questions, some routine, some more specific. What did Emma do? Any uncharacteristic behavior lately—late meetings, new friends, weird calls at odd hours? Nothing. After almost an hour of throwing darts in the dark, he said, "I think we're done for today, but I may have more questions tomorrow. Is it okay if I call you?"

"Of course. I may go to Marin to leave Sofia with my parents, but you can reach me on my cell at any time."

Sorensen walked Bob to the elevator and after they shook hands he said, "I'm going to do everything I can to find who did this."

Bob thanked him and left, looking older than he had when he walked in a few hours earlier.

Sorensen went back to his desk and turned the whiteboard around so he could look at the evidence. He then went to Darcy's board and brought it over to his, so he could look at all of the cases together. But he didn't get any brilliant ideas.

He decided to go back to do some research on ViCAP. Nothing jumped out. He grabbed the stress toy that looked like a soccer ball and squeezed it with his left hand while he typed different keywords in the search bar.

"Jon, any luck with the DVDs?" He needed a different angle to look at things from.

"Unfortunately not. I looked through all of them."

"Shit. Okay, thanks."

He stared at the boards and saw three women staring back at him. Three women who had supposedly killed themselves in horrible ways. Sorensen convinced himself Lynch would come back and decided to check one more thing on the database before going home.

He searched for suspicious deaths having to do with self-breast-mutilation and waited for the results. After a few minutes Sorensen got three possible matches.

The first one was a prostitute who had jumped, or had been pushed, from an overpass, fell on a fence and bled to death. Sorensen had no idea why the computer thought this was a good match, and after carefully reviewing all of the data, he concluded that the case was not remotely related and moved on.

The second one was a woman from Fremont, California, who had carved her own breast with a number four Phillips screwdriver her ex-husband had left behind in the garage. It took over a week for anybody to find her. Sorensen printed the case details and made a mental note to call the detective who worked on the case before he headed home.

The third one was also a woman, living in Seattle, who had cut her breast out in the master bathroom while her family was eating pizza downstairs. The husband went to look for her, found her bleeding on the floor and called 911. She was pronounced DOA at the hospital. Sorensen also printed her ViCAP notes.

He picked up both printouts and knocked on Virago's door. Before she answered he went in.

"You know my suicides?"

She looked up over the rim of her glasses.

"I found two more."

"Where?"

"One in Fremont. I'm calling the detective on my way home. One in Seattle. You need to get pretty boy back and have him reach out to his old buddies."

CHAPTER 41

Saffron realized her mouth had been open since Darcy made his grand exit. She forced it closed and headed toward the elevator to get the scoop directly from him. She wiped her already-dried tears with the back of her hand and hit the elevator button several times to make it come faster. When it didn't, she ran down the stairs, hoping to still find him before he reached the parking lot. But she didn't see him, so she walked into the structure and looked for the spot where he had parked before. When she heard the Cobra's engine roar she knew she had to hurry. Her heels clicked loudly on the pavement and she prayed not to sprain her ankle on the run.

Lynch was beginning to pull out when she reached him. She placed herself behind the car, put both hands on her hips and looked directly at him through the rearview mirror.

She saw his head shake, and she almost smiled.

"You need to talk to Detective Sorensen," he said to her, not turning his head. "He's handling your case now."

"I thought you were doing it."

"Not anymore."

She still didn't move. "Why?" she asked.

"Please move. I have somewhere to be."

"Are you working on another case?" From his exit, she figured he wasn't, but she didn't want to say what she thought she'd heard, as if saying it out loud would make it true.

"No, I quit," he said, making it real. "Didn't you hear it?"

"You can't do that," she said, now moving to the passenger side and getting in before he had a chance to react.

"I just did, Saffron."

"You can't quit my case. Why would you do that?"

"Please get out of the car. I have to leave."

She turned slightly, but instead of opening the door, she grabbed the seat belt and clicked it. She saw Darcy shake his head again.

"I still don't have a car. The least you can do is take me home."

Before he could protest, she crossed her arms and faced him. He ignored her and put the car back in reverse.

"You should buckle up. It's the law," she looked at him and saw him clench his teeth and knew she had won another argument.

"Saffron, I quit the job. It's got nothing to do with your case. I'm no longer a detective."

"Semantics, don't you think?" She looked down as he snapped the buckle. "If you quit, why do you still have your gun?"

He reached to his hip and felt the gun inside the holster. "Fuck!"

Saffron started laughing, then he followed.

"Well, so much for my dramatic exit. Now I'll have to go back and return my badge and my gun."

"You seriously left high and all mighty and forgot to leave the company goods?" She punched him on the shoulder as she said the words between more laughs. "I would pay anything if you let me go with you when you give them back."

"Hey, at least I didn't attack a guy who was trying to pick me up," he countered.

She looked at him, showing him the comparison didn't even come close.

Before reaching the exit, Darcy stopped.

"Oh, you can't go back now," she said, reading his mind.

He didn't move but nodded. He started moving again, heading toward the exit.

"Let me buy you a drink. For all the driving you've done. Then you can come back. At least by then there should be less people in the office to watch your walk of shame."

He passed his hand over his face and agreed. "Okay, fine. But don't even think you're going to convince me to change my mind."

"I promise. I was actually going to offer you a job."

His eyebrows lifted when he looked at her. The outside air was getting colder. It was starting to get dark, but the orange streetlights were still too dim.

"I would like you to be my personal chauffeur."

She grinned and shoved both hands into her jacket pocket.

"You can't afford me."

He tried to remain serious but the corners of his mouth lifted upwards.

He drove to Santana Row. She wondered if he wanted to go there because he needed the distraction of people walking around, laughing, trying to hook up, drinking, or because that was his regular hangout spot. She decided not to ask. They settled for Straits. It was dark, the music was loud, and it was pretty crowded. They found a place by the bar, in a comfortable white leather love seat. They sat with enough distance between them to avoid touching, but close enough so they could hear each other without having to yell.

A young girl in a very short and tight teal dress came with menus. Saffron ordered a lychee martini, and Darcy asked for a Macallan 25 scotch, neat.

Before she could ask the question, he said, "One drink, no work talk, okay?"

She nodded, disappointed she hadn't spoken first. "So, what do you want to talk about, then?"

"How's Ranjan?"

"I don't know."

A pang of guilt hit her gut. She hadn't even tried calling him to see how he was recuperating.

"You don't know?" He put the glass to his lips and observed her over the brim.

"We broke up yesterday."

His stare was fixed on her. His good eye shined a little.

"The arranged marriage thing?"

Saffron nodded and looked away, put the glass down on the low table and crossed her arms. Darcy moved back a little.

Before she replied, he said, "I went back to the hospital and his uncle was there. I also saw a bunch of pictures of different women. I just put two and two together because of what you told me about your fight before the hit and run."

"Yeah. Honestly, I've known for a long time that it wasn't going anywhere. What was I thinking robbing the cradle? You just get into a routine and don't see what's what until things get shaken."

"I understand."

"Anyway, I cried for a second. I'm over it." She raised her glass. "For new beginnings. You, a job as my driver, and me, as a single woman."

Before their glasses touched, he moved his away. "I'm not toasting about my new job."

"Okay then, for my singlehood."

The second round of drinks arrived. Saffron knew it wasn't appropriate to ask, but she felt that having been on the verge

176

of being killed twice in that many days probably gave her some leeway to ask whatever she wanted.

"What happened to your eye?"

Darcy immediately started rubbing his temple He looked away. And after a second he stopped.

"I'm sorry. You don't have to tell me."

He sighed loudly and looked at her. "Do you want to know the truth or the story I tell girls when I want them to think I'm super interesting?"

Saffron looked away and took a sip of her martini so she had a little time to think.

"Whichever one you want to give me, Detective Darcy Lynch." Her voice was lower, graver, but not quite a whisper.

She stared at him, searching for something. Was he flirting with her? She didn't know. Darcy leaned toward her, so close that his musky, masculine scent filled her nostrils. His breath was warm on her lips. She opened them just a little, and she saw him do the same. Her heart was pounding so hard she thought it would leap out of her chest. She closed her eyes.

He brushed her lips with his but then Saffron felt the air get cold between them and opened her eyes. He was pulling away from her. She felt lost, rejected, disappointed. Then she tried to smile to dissipate the awkwardness between them, but the muscles on her face felt tight, forced. She leaned toward the table, grabbed her drink and finished it in three gulps. When she leaned back on the sofa, her back was straighter. She crossed her arms.

"I'm sorry—" Darcy said.

She put a hand up in the air to make him stop. Her eyes blinked a couple times, fighting away the tears of embarrassment.

"Just tell me about your eye," she said, trying to refocus the conversation.

"Let me make a pit stop. I'll tell you the whole story when I get back."

"Sounds good."

As soon as he was out of sight, she grabbed her purse and jacket and left the restaurant. She cursed herself again for not having rented a car. As she walked toward Stevens Creek, she searched in her contacts for a San Jose cab service. The dispatcher told her that number 4238 would be there in two minutes. She waited by the Best Buy store, hoping that Darcy, if he even went after her, wouldn't find her before the taxi arrived.

As promised, the green-and-white car with number 4238 on the hood showed up, and she headed home. She felt tears of humiliation burn her eyes. She started singing a song in her head to stop thinking about the evening. Then her mind wondered to Emma and how much fun they had the last time they went to karaoke and sang that song. Saffron started to cry. Her whole body heaved while she wiped away the tears that wouldn't stop.

CHAPTER 42

It was almost eight thirty, and Sorensen's eyes were beginning to glaze over. He shut down the computer and annotated the detective's name in charge of the case in Fremont before he got up from the chair. He looked around. Virago's light was still on in her office. Jon was also staring at his monitor. Sorensen wondered if he was doing work or posting shit on Facebook.

"Go home. Don't you have a girl to take on a date or something?" Sorensen said over the empty tables.

Jon took a second to realize the comment was directed at him. "Huh? No, I have no plans."

"What are you working on?"

"I've been doing all kinds of searches on ViCAP. I started with the chemical composition of the gloves to see if there were more cases, and I found a few, but they didn't seem related, like a burglary in Tampa and a motorcycle gang fight in North Dakota."

"Okay," Sorensen said, coming closer to Jon's desk.

"Then I started looking for cases with tampered brake lines, I even looked for different things related to the suicides. But I haven't found anything that stands out."

"Well, call me if you do. Go home soon, though." He patted the intern's shoulder and headed home.

In the car, he put on his Bluetooth headset and grabbed the Post-It note where he had jotted the Fremont detective's number. He dialed when he stopped at a red light.

"Detective McArthur," a tired voice said, almost muffled by loud sports announcers in the background.

Sorensen introduced himself and gave the detective the necessary context for the call. Then he asked, "Was your case regarding Miss Juliette Davis ruled a suicide by the ME?"

"Yes. That's why we stopped investigating. Though I gotta tell you, I've seldom seen anything more gruesome."

"Do you know if the victim had breast cancer?"

"What?" McArthur paused. "Give me a sec. Let me go outside." After a few seconds, Sorensen heard a door open and then the music stopped. "Ah, much better. This place is noisy, or maybe in my old days I just can't hear so well."

"Do you know if the victim had breast cancer?" Sorensen asked again.

"Yes, as a matter of fact, she did."

"Do you know who was her doctor?"

"I'll have to check my notes. But you'll have to wait until Monday. I'll have to find the file."

"I need you to tell me today. I have three victims who have died the same way and at least one of them had breast cancer."

"Shit happens, man. I don't know what knowing her doctor tonight is going to do to solve your case. Besides, you don't have a case. They're suicides. Case closed."

Sorensen gripped the steering wheel so hard his knuckles started hurting. He let go a little and took a very deep breath. He could find this information on his own, but it would take more legwork than if this asshole gave it to him.

"Could you email or fax me your case notes? This way, you can go back to the bar and I don't have to wait for Monday."

"Asshole," McArthur said before he hung up.

Sorensen cursed and dialed Virago, who was still in the office. Just before he got home, he saw an email notification pop up in his phone. Somebody in the Fremont Police Department had understood the value of collaboration and scanned the file for him.

He opened his front door, and Melissa came to greet him. She hugged him for a long time and buried her face in his large neck.

"What's going on?"

"I love you," she said without moving.

Now he was sure there was something he was going to regret coming home to. "What happened?"

"Why can't you accept that sometimes I just hug you and kiss you because you are the greatest man in the world and I'm happy to see you home safe and sound?" she said, pulling away from him but now holding both of his hands. "And to show you how much I love you, I made meatloaf."

"Oh, crap. How long is your mother staying this time?"

"You're going to love this meatloaf. She comes on Sunday. Only three weeks."

"Woman! Why do you do this to me?"

After Sorensen had his well-deserved double serving of meatloaf with extra mashed potatoes, he kissed his wife and checked on the kids. He then went to his small office, turned the computer on and started reading the file from the Fremont suicide. All the details of the case were pretty much a carbon copy of any in his three files. McArthur didn't have a lot of notes, so it didn't take him long to find the name of the doctor: Leavenworth. The same doctor his second victim had.

CHAPTER 43

"I have to go back to the office," Sorensen said to his wife as he put his jacket on.

"At this hour?" she said, pausing the TiVo. An image of Charlie Sheen from *Two and a Half Men* was frozen on the TV.

"Yeah, I didn't take my notes and I have to check on a few things."

He kissed his wife softly on the lips and headed for the door. "Don't wait up."

Driving in California was mostly a pain in the ass. There were always cars, even outside of rush hour. However, the night was fairly light, and he made it back in half the time it usually took him.

"Captain," Sorensen said when he arrived.

Virago was immersed in paperwork and her eyes were crossed. "I swear to God I'd have never signed up for this job if I knew half my existence would be spent on budgets."

"Yeah, fun. Listen, I think I have a lead on my suicides."

She leaned back on her chair, welcoming the distraction and focused her attention on him. "Do tell."

He explained the doctor connection between his second victim and the case in Fremont. "By the way, thanks for getting me the file."

"Don't mention it," she said, waving her hand back and forth. "I hate it when people don't do their jobs." She crossed her arms. "What's next?"

"That's why I'm here. I'm going to check if the other victims share the same doctor. If they do, I guess I'll be paying her a visit first thing in the morning."

"Sounds good."

"I need your help with something."

"Sure. What is it?"

"I want Lynch back."

She started shaking her head to protest.

"Listen, there's something going on here. I think we have something much bigger with the multiple suicides than we could've ever imagined." He got up, but before leaving he added, "Besides, it would help if he called Seattle."

"What do you need, a formal introduction?"

"No, but I'm sure he can get more from his old buddies than I can."

"Okay, you ask him about making the call, and I'll try to figure out a way to convince him to come back, but I'm not making any promises."

Back at his desk Sorensen dialed Lynch. He didn't pick up, so he left a voice mail. "Lynch, I need a favor. There was a suicide in Seattle, carbon copy of my three here. Can you reach out to…" He paused to look back at the detective's name. "Detective James Danielson and find out if the victim ever lived in California and if so, if she was a patient of Dr. Leavenworth?"

He hung up and added the two new victims to his board, then wrote "Dr. Leavenworth" in the center, circled it and drew an arrow from Juliette Davis, the victim in Fremont, to the circle, and another one from his second victim, Taisha Robinson.

Sorensen checked the time. It was past nine thirty. "Not too late," he said under his breath and decided to make some calls to find out who else was connected to this doctor. In between, he left new messages for Lynch.

Finally, his phone vibrated on top of his desk.

"Stop stalking me," Darcy said.

"Have you called your buddy?"

"No. You do it."

"Then why are you calling me?"

"To tell you to stop bothering me. I quit. I'm not your friend. I don't owe you or the department anything, so leave me the fuck alone."

"Wait," Sorensen said before Darcy hung up. "I don't give a shit if you don't care about anything at all, but there are at least five women dead, and four of them were seeing the same doctor. I can call your friend and get the answer, or you can be a fucking cop and help me find out who's killing these women."

Darcy didn't say anything but he also didn't hang up. Then Sorensen heard him sigh and mutter something about his mother under his breath.

"I know Danielson. I'll give him a call now. Then you leave me alone."

"Fine."

Sorensen drew new arrows from his victims to Dr. Leavenworth's circled name. There was no way that was a coincidence. He was about to shut down his computer and head back home when he got a hunch. He sat back down and looked at his notes to make a final call.

"Mr. Hughes, sorry for calling so late. This is Detective Sorensen."

"Did you find who killed my wife?"

The hope in his voice almost made him choke.

"No. I'm sorry, we're still working on it. I wanted to check something with you."

After a long silence, Bob said, "Yes, of course. Anything."

"Do you know the name of the doctor who was treating your wife's cancer?"

"My wife didn't have cancer."

Sorensen cradled the phone between his shoulder and ear while he browsed through the ME's report.

"I'm sorry, but the ME found that she had stage two cancer."

"That's not possible. She had a lump that was checked, they did a biopsy, and they said it was benign. You can check with her doctor if you want to."

"Okay, can you give me the doctor's name?"

"Dr. Leavenworth."

CHAPTER 44

Darcy grabbed another beer from the fridge and sat on the large chocolate leather sofa, putting his feet up on the coffee table. The living room was spacious, but he felt suffocated by it. He got up and opened the deck door but left the screen closed. Before reaching out to Detective Danielson in Seattle, he tried calling Saffron one more time. He'd left three messages already. When the call went to voice mail he hung up, just as he had done the last few times he'd called. At least he knew she was home, and the security detail had a visual on her.

He took a deep breath and made the call Sorensen wanted.

"Coming back from the dead?" Danielson asked.

"Pretty much."

"How're you liking warm and overpriced California?"

"Depends on the day."

Darcy asked about Danielson's family and caught up on his old colleagues at the Seattle PD. New people on board, some common friends retired, a few new babies, and no deaths on active duty. It seemed that life went on for everybody but Darcy Lynch, he thought, feeling sorry for himself. He brushed his hair with his hand and shook the feeling. He didn't need to make himself feel worse than he already did.

"But anyway, I'm sure you didn't call to find out if Richard Lee has finally reached three hundred pounds, which by the way he hasn't. He actually hooked up with this health nut and lost a bunch of weight. You wouldn't recognize him if you saw him."

"No fucking way. I was so sure I would win that bet."

"You and half the department."

"True." Darcy said almost laughing. Then he went right to the meat of the call: "You have a suspicious death case about a woman, who carved her breast out and bled to death, right?"

"Yeah, Sonia McCarthy. Terrible thing. Was ruled a suicide, though, so we closed it."

"We have four similar cases here. Can you email me your case notes?"

"You have four? What the hell? Yeah, sure thing. I'll open the case again too. Do you have anything on it?"

"No, not much. Same type of deal with all four."

"All suicides?" Danielson asked.

"Yes. You won't happen to remember if the victim had breast cancer, do you?"

"Yeah, she did. Everybody thought she killed herself to avoid the agony."

"Same story here. All our victims had cancer."

They both felt silent for a moment. Danielson finally said, "Man, it must be the air in California."

"What do you mean?"

"My vic moved from California three weeks before she killed herself."

"Bay Area?"

"I think so. I'll have to double-check, though."

"Do you remember her doctor's name?"

After a short pause, Danielson said, "No. It was something long. It reminded me of one of those air freshener scents—you know, like lavender."

"Leavenworth?" Darcy asked, his voice excited for the first time that evening.

"Yeah, that's it."

"Shit, I think we have something."

"I'll send you everything I have, but keep me posted. It would be nice to close this one the right way. Nobody deserves to go like that."

Darcy called Sorensen back and told him everything he had found out. Then Sorensen shared the latest news. "Hughes went to the same doctor."

Darcy fell silent, his head working fast trying to make any connection that made sense. He failed.

"But isn't Hughes related to Saffron's case?" he asked.

"At this point, man. I brought your whiteboard next to mine so they can cozy up."

After a few seconds, Darcy said, "I want to go with you to visit the famous doctor tomorrow."

"I thought you quit," Sorensen said, but his voice was good humored.

"I can quit again tomorrow night. Who has my cases?"

"You do. Virago hasn't given them to anybody. She knew you'd be back."

"That's pretty arrogant. I'm not coming back. I just want to return the favor to Danielson. His case's still open in Seattle."

"Sure. Bright and early at the station. I want to be this bitch's first appointment."

"I'll meet you outside at eight."

"Suit yourself."

As soon as he hung up he called Saffron again.

"Saffron, I know you don't want to talk to me, but I have a very important question for you about the case. Please call me back and let me know if you see a Dr. Leavenworth." He wanted to say something more, but he would be repeating himself, so after a pause he added, "This is really important. Please call me as soon as you get this message."

He got another beer from the fridge and walked out to his patio. There were several lounge chairs surrounding the pool. He sat on one. It was really dark and a bit chilly. Darcy took a long sip of his drink and looked up, seeing more stars than he'd seen since he moved to California.

His phone vibrated with a message. He opened it and saw a text from Saffron: "Yes, she's my doctor."

A chill ran through his body.

CHAPTER 45

Friday

Darcy woke up to the sound of the alarm clock but soon realized it wasn't the alarm at all.

"What the hell are you doing?" said an intense female voice over the phone.

"I love you too, Kate," he responded, combing his short hair with his hand.

"Do you know how hard it was to get you into that desk job you wanted so much?"

"And I'll owe you forever."

"Quit the sarcasm. It doesn't suit you. All I want to know is why you're fucking it up."

"Oh wait, I got another call. It's work. I'll drop by later and we can discuss then, okay?"

Without waiting for a response, he hung up and went for a long swim. The cold water woke him up, but he still felt like shit. While he swam, he thought about his sister. Kate was almost ten years older than he was. He'd always known that he was "The accident" child, as his parents weren't expecting, nor really wanted, more children. She had always taken special care of him. When she moved to Washington DC to go to law school, he'd been devastated. She never made it back to Seattle. Kate met Mr. Perfect, and they both moved to the Bay Area.

Now, almost twenty years later, she was an important figure in Bay Area society—if there was such a thing in Northern California. She was one of the most successful divorce attorneys in Silicon Valley and was married to the deputy sheriff of Santa Clara County. Damon hadn't had to pull many strings to get him the desk job but liked to make sure Darcy thought he had. Kate only rode his ass when her husband was being whiny.

An hour later, he waited on the corner of Younger Avenue and North First Street with two cups of coffee. Both black. It was hot even though it was early, and he was burning his hands holding the scalding drinks. Finally Sorensen came down.

"I'd have invited you to more interviews if I knew you would bring coffee," he said, taking one of the cups.

"Meadows had the same freaking doctor," he said, ignoring his snooty comment.

"Your hit-and-run victim?"

"Yeah. The same one who let Hughes borrow her car the night she was killed."

Sorensen stopped walking three feet from the shade of the building. Darcy took shelter and then turned to face him.

"All of these women are connected somehow through this doctor. But what's the story?" Sorensen asked without moving but was now covered in glossy sweat.

"Can we go over and find out?" Darcy said, wanting to get moving.

They both got into Sorensen's Jeep and headed toward Good Samaritan Hospital complex.

The reception area of the building was empty. They checked the directory and found that Dr. Leavenworth's office was on the second floor. They took the elevator, closed their jackets to conceal their weapons and found the office, which had large glass doors and a pink horizontal band painted across them.

The receptionist pointed at a clipboard, put out a pen with a large flower on one end and said, "Please sign in. First time?"

Sorensen blushed and Darcy grinned. He decided to let him do all the talking.

"No. We're here to see Dr. Leavenworth."

"You need to sign in," she insisted.

Sorensen's brow tightened. He seemed confused. Darcy took a step back so Sorensen couldn't see how much he was enjoying this.

Sorensen took the pen and looked at the sign-in sheet, but right before he started writing, the receptionist said, "What time was your appointment?"

Her eyes were focused on the computer screen. She was probably checking the names of the patients and not finding anybody male was as confused as Sorensen.

"We don't have an appointment. We need to talk to Dr. Leavenworth."

The woman lifted her black eyes, a full mouth with red lipstick opened, and with a sour tone she said, "I'm sorry, but she's booked all day. You need to make an appointment."

"This is police business," Darcy said, showing his badge, having enjoyed enough of the show.

Her expression changed and her lips became two very thin red lines. "What is this regarding?"

"We need to talk to the doctor, and now would be a good time." Sorensen had regained his composure.

"One moment."

She left the front desk and exited through a door at the back. Darcy turned. The office was warm, with earthy and burgundy tones, and paintings of women in flowery dresses. There was a coffee carafe at the corner and paper cups. He walked toward it, opened the lid of his empty cup and refilled it. A woman sitting a few chairs away watched his every move, even though she pretended to read a fashion magazine.

The door opened and a petite woman with long, wavy black hair appeared.

"Good morning. I'm Dr. Leavenworth. How can I help you?"

"We would like to ask you a few questions. Can we go somewhere where we can talk in private?"

Darcy saw the fashion magazine slip from the woman's hand. In a reflex, she slapped it to stop it from reaching the floor. The noise filled the otherwise quiet room, and all eyes fell on her. She turned beet red. Darcy spotted a large headline about *Ten things you can do to drive your man wild* and met her eyes with a mischievous smile.

"My office," the doctor said.

In silence they followed her through a wide hallway the color of café au lait. She stopped at the last door on the left and opened it, letting them go in first. The office was fairly large, square and lit a little dimmer than Lynch imagined a doctor's office would be. She took the chair behind a dark wooden desk and leaned back.

Darcy pondered how many people might have sat where he was and heard bad news. How many people cried, and how many partners held their hands, offering their love and support.

"What can I do for you?" Her voice was soft, almost milky, but her eyes were hard, annoyed, steadily moving from Lynch to Sorensen, evaluating them with each stare.

"Do you treat Sheila Rothschild?" Sorensen asked.

"You know I can't answer that question."

"Do you treat Jacqueline Pritchard?"

193

"Detective, you know—"

"Do you treat Taisha Robinson? How about Emma Hughes?"

Dr. Leavenworth shook her head and looked down at her desk.

"And Juliette Davis? Do you treat her?"

"Detective, please, tell me what—"

"How about Saffron Meadows? Do you treat her?"

She shook her head again. "You know I can't disclose this information." She crossed her arms. "Can you tell me what this is about?"

"Could you disclose it if these women were dead?"

Darcy felt a pang of fear wondering if Saffron was dead or Sorensen was just saying that to make a point. He knew it was the latter, so he kept his poker face and observed the doctor.

"What are you saying?" she asked, now staring back at them again.

"Because they are. All of them. So, can you now tell us? Were they your patients?"

"Yes, they were," she said, showing surprise. "How did it happen?"

"Did they all have cancer?"

"No. Not all of them."

"Right. That's not true now, is it?" Sorensen pushed.

"I can't show you my files, but I can tell you that not all of them had cancer. Can you tell me what happened?"

"We need your help to find out what happened to these women," Lynch jumped in, trying to soften the dialogue.

"Yes, of course. How can I help?" Her voice was sincere, the annoyance now completely gone.

"You can start by telling us who didn't have cancer," Sorensen said.

She was silent for a moment, as if she were reviewing her case files in her head. She turned her computer on and clicked on the keyboard several times.

"All of them but Emma Hughes and Saffron Meadows had cancer."

Darcy sighed with relief.

"Are you sure?" Sorensen asked.

"Positive. Both came in to see me because they had found lumps. We performed a biopsy in both cases, and the results were negative for cancer."

"Somebody made a mistake," Sorensen said. "Hughes had stage two cancer."

Dr. Leavenworth arched her perfectly shaped eyebrows. "Is that confirmed?"

"Directly from the ME."

She shook her head, her long hair dancing as if moved by a slight breeze. "That's too bad. Lab results are not one hundred percent reliable."

"The other three victims, were they terminal?"

"No. Only Taisha Robinson."

Darcy felt his phone vibrate. He excused himself and moved to a corner.

"Yes?" The lab's number showed in his caller ID.

"Mauricio here. Sorensen told me that you'd taken over the Hughes case..."

Before Darcy could correct him, he went on. His voice was high pitched again, indicating that some news was about to rock Darcy's world.

"We matched the DNA on the pen we found in the stolen Acura by the crime scene."

"No shit. To whom?"

"A guy named Harper Johnson."

CHAPTER 46

Darcy's voice was louder than he wanted it to be. Full of excitement and urgency, he spat orders back to Mauricio: "Text me his address and his photo. Give all the information to Jon and ask him to find out everything he can about this guy. Tell him I'll call to get more details when I'm on my way. " Then, to Sorensen he said, "Give me your keys."

"Excuse me?"

"Mauricio found something. I need your car." Seeing Sorensen's hesitation, he said, "I'll come pick you up when I'm done, or I'll send a car for you. Give me your keys now."

Sorensen mumbled something that made Dr. Leavenworth smirk but finally handed the keys to Lynch.

By the time he got into Sorensen's car, he had Harper Johnson's address and photo on his phone. He tapped the app to get directions to Harper's place, but before he moved, he stared at the picture to make sure he memorized the suspect's face. Darcy tried to picture Johnson running away from Saffron's condo or cutting her seat belt with that hunting knife. He pulled the ATM photo and tried to compare the grainy black-and-white picture with the DMV color headshot. *It could be the same person*, he thought.

The man stared back at him with dark brown eyes. They looked tired, almost a little dead, like the eyes of a fish that has been out of the water for too long and knows the end is near. His crew cut was peppered with gray, but the man still had a full head of hair. Too many weather creases lined his face, but not too many were around his mouth. He seemed the type of man who didn't have very much to smile about.

As he drove toward Highway 85, Darcy got three texts from Jon. Instead of reading them, he speed-dialed him.

"Tell me everything you've found," he said when Jon picked up.

"Harper Johnson's prints are in the system, not because he has a criminal record, but because he's tried to become a cop a bunch of times."

"Where?"

Jon took a second to respond. Darcy exited Highway 85 and merged into Highway 17. He heard Jon shuffle through his notes.

"Mountain View and Sunnyvale in 1992, then San Jose in '93, and Fremont and Oakland in '95. Then he tried for the Santa Clara Sheriff's Office in '96. He failed the psych test every time due to anger management issues."

"Any connection to Dr. Leavenworth?"

"Not that I could find but I'll keep checking."

"Any connection to cancer?"

"His mother died of liver cancer about three years ago."

"Any connection to the vics?"

"None yet."

"What car does he drive?"

"A truck. A Chevy Silverado, light blue, license plates BA-NANAM."

"What?"

"Yeah, it's registered to his mother."

"Text me that."

"Already done," Jon said.

"Anything else?"

"I couldn't find if he has a full time job yet, but he does a few hours here and there at a gun range."

"Of course he does. Send me the details on that too."

"That's all I've been able to find so far."

"Great job. Call me as soon as you have more."

He hung up and checked the map in his phone. He was close to the Summit Road Exit. He merged to the right and slowed down behind a semi. Darcy continued following the directions on his phone, getting deeper into the Santa Cruz Mountains. The high trees covered the road, and the morning sun disappeared over the luxurious leaves.

Lynch slowed down to thirty miles per hour and looked at every private road to see if he could find Lomas Lane. The phone told him it was less than half a mile out, and he wanted to make sure he didn't miss it.

Finally, he saw the road and took a right turn. It was narrow and wound upward. Each turn was flanked by trees. He was crawling, not knowing what he would find around the next bend. After a few minutes of nothing but trees, a run-down house appeared at the end of the road. It was made of wood, and he could smell the rot even inside the car.

He checked his gun and opened the holster snap. There was no light blue truck in sight, only a rusty 1982 Oldsmobile with no tires and a missing left back door. He stopped the car a few yards from the house and got out.

Lynch walked slowly toward the front door, moving his head from left to right, scanning the empty space. He couldn't hear the road, only birds and leaves swaying in the wind. As he got closer to the porch, a Lab mutt came running from behind the house. The dog didn't bark, just ran and wagged its tail.

"Come here, buddy," Darcy said, extending his hand to let the dog smell him before he petted it. "Is anybody home?"

The dog licked his hand but didn't answer. Darcy could feel each rib, there was nothing but skin and bones.

Darcy continued to move forward. He reached the door and knocked. There was no answer. He could hear no movement coming from within it. He knocked again.

"Mr. Harper?" he called out.

The dog rubbed his body against his legs. Lynch scratched him behind the ears and started to walk around the house. He caught a movement with his good eye, and his hand quickly settled on his holster.

"Who are you?" asked an old man half-hidden by the trees. His right hand held a rifle with its bolt open.

"Santa Clara Deputy Sheriff. Drop your weapon." Darcy pulled his gun but didn't point it at him. With the other hand, he pulled out his wallet and showed him his badge.

"I was just hunting squirrels."

Darcy got close. He could see the weapon was a .22. The old man set it on the ground and put both hands on his knees to help straighten back up.

"What're you doing here?" he asked, almost out of breath.

"Are you Harper Johnson?" He didn't look like the person in the picture he'd memorized.

"I'm his neighbor. I saw you drive up and was curious. He never gets any visitors."

"Do you know him well?"

"No. When I first moved here a couple years ago, I ran into him at the bar sometimes, but he was never very social. My property extends all the way to here." He pointed at the end of the trees. "I like to take walks."

I'm sure you do, Darcy thought.

"I'm Alton Lane," he said, walking toward Lynch, leaving the rifle behind and extending his hand.

Darcy shook it. It was strong and calloused. They walked toward the firearm, and Darcy picked it up for him. The dog came and licked Alton's hands.

"Yours?" Darcy asked.

"Harper's. I'd never let a bitch of mine get that skinny. I just made a fresh pot of coffee. You want a cup?"

Darcy nodded, and they both started walking through the trees toward Alton's house.

"You said Johnson doesn't have many friends. Girlfriend maybe?"

"I've never seen a woman come by. I've seen him drive by Sporty's, so I think that's where he gets his rocks off."

Darcy responded with a quizzical look.

"Sporty's Bikini Bar," Lane said, as if that explained it all.

Darcy didn't ask how Lane was acquainted with the titi-bar. He knew a nosy Mr. Lane would shed more light on his neighbor than hours of legwork would ever do.

CHAPTER 47

Sorensen tried to steer Doctor Leavenworth back to his questions after Darcy left in a rush. He looked back at the physician. Her face was stern, there was nothing welcoming. He wondered if she seemed this cold to her patients.

"How many years have you practiced medicine?" he asked, just to get back into the groove.

"Almost twelve."

"How many in this office?"

"Five."

"How many of your patients have died of cancer?"

"I don't know off the top of my head. Cancer is the second biggest cause of death in America."

"I can tell you how many unsolved homicides I've had in my career."

Her eyes closed and she rubbed the bridge of her nose. "Detective, I'm not trying to hide anything. If there's information that I can, by law, tell you, I will. If there's information I can't tell you because I don't know, I won't make it up just to satisfy you. Besides, if you give me a couple hours, I can find the exact numbers for you and let you know. There's no reason for you to attack me."

"Very well."

He turned the page on his notebook and rested it back onto his knee. Staring at the blank page he said, "Do you have any idea why these women would want to kill them-selves?"

"They committed suicide?" Dr. Leavenworth asked, show-ing genuine surprise.

"Yes."

She took a minute to think. "Besides the obvious reason, no." Then she added, "Specially Emma Hughes. We got the re-sults from the lab, and they were negative for cancer. She and her husband were ecstatic with the news, especially because she had a long family history of breast cancer."

"What's the probability of false negative?"

"They happen, but it's very small. That's why we always recommend that the patient comes back in six months for a follow-up so we can see if there've been any changes."

"And there were none in Hughes' case?"

Sorensen saw her move the mouse and hit a few letters on the keyboard. After a few moments, she said, "She was due to come back in a couple weeks."

"What about Meadows?"

"She also did a biopsy about six months ago."

"Any chance she also has cancer?"

"I thought you said they were all dead."

"Just humor me, Doctor."

"Not a laughing matter, Detective."

Sorensen nodded. She was right, and he was being an as-shole.

"She's the only one who's still alive," he conceded. "So, could she also have a false negative?"

"I guess. The same chance as Hughes," she said and set her eyes back on his.

After a few more questions that didn't give him a lot more insight into the case, Sorensen walked out of Dr. Leavenworth's office. He felt like there was more to the story than what she'd shared, but he needed more time to research the doctor. He shook his head, knowing he should have done that before coming to see her.

He walked toward the parking lot, trying to figure out if he had a case for a warrant to get the names of all of her patients with cancer, but he knew he needed much more than what he had. He considered going up the stairs to the second floor, where his car was parked, but opted for the elevator. He looked for his Jeep, and when he had walked almost the entire length of the row, he said out loud, "Son of a bitch." He shook his head and checked his phone to see if Lynch had sent him a patrol to get picked up. There was nothing.

I'm going to beat the crap out of that asshole, he thought, punching the numbers for the station.

The deputy on the line promised him that somebody would be there to get him in less than five minutes.

While he waited he thought about the victims. The suicide victims not only had the good doctor as a connection, but they also shared the cause and method of death. Then there was Pritchard, the woman who died in the car accident, and Meadows, with two attempts on her life and no cancer. Maybe the connection of the last two was a mere coincidence. But he had been on the job too long to believe that. He also had a weird feeling about the doctor, but he couldn't figure out why.

When the patrol car showed up, he sighed with relief.

"Thank God. I thought I would have to ride in the back if you came with a partner," Sorensen said to Martinez as he got in the passenger seat.

"No, today I'm alone."

"What happened to Wong? Claiming to be sick again?"

Martinez laughed. "Man, that guy always has something.

But at least I don't have to ride with him when he's sniffling and sneezing all over me."

"What, you get that cozy?" Sorensen said, hitting Martinez's shoulder and laughing.

"Yeah, you wish." He smiled and took the exit for Highway 87 North.

A few minutes later Sorensen thanked him and walked into the station. When he got out of the elevator he bought a Red Bull from the machine and walked into the bullpen.

"Jon, have you worked any of your magic yet?" he asked, seeing the intern focused on his computer monitor.

Jon grunted, but didn't reply. Sorensen came around and stood behind him so Jon could feel his body heat warm up his personal space.

"What are you working on?" Sorensen asked when he realized it didn't have anything to do with what he wanted.

"Finding what I can about Harper Johnson."

"Who the fuck's that?"

"Detective Lynch didn't tell you?" He turned to face Sorensen. "His DNA was on the pen in the stolen car found by Emma Hughes' crime scene," he said, beaming as he shared the good news.

"Why the hell am I finding this out now?"

Jon's face darkened. "You said this wasn't your case anymore, that it was Detective Lynch's." His voice was low and quavered a little.

"Never mind that. You should've told me."

Sorensen walked to his desk like a kid asked to take the bench because no team wanted him.

"I'm sorry, I just..." Jon tried to explain.

CHAPTER 48

Saffron wondered if she should go to work. She didn't feel like it. She lay in bed petting Cat, who was lying on her chest and purring. She wondered if Darcy had gone back to the office and officially quit. She also wondered if Ranjan had finally picked his wife.

Her cell rang, pulling her out of the self-pity spiral she was embarking on. She answered, even though the number was blocked.

"Hello, Miss Meadows. We were wondering if you were going to make your appointment today." It was more a statement than a question.

"Oh, what time is it?"

She didn't remember having anything on her calendar.

"Right now. With Doctor Leavenworth."

"Oh, right. I'm so sorry, I got the time wrong. I'll be there in thirty minutes. Would that work?"

Saffron looked at her watch. It was barely past nine in the morning. She got out of the bed, and Cat protested.

"Yes, we'll fit you in."

While she figured out what she was going to wear, Saffron called a cab and made a mental note to rent a car later that day. After a flash shower, she got in the taxi, which maneuvered through dying rush hour traffic and let her off by the hospital entrance with three minutes to spare. She walked to the elevator at the end of the hall and went up two floors to the doctor's office.

"Hello, Lydia. I'm so sorry I'm late."

Saffron contemplated telling her about the car accident but decided not to. She didn't want to talk about it.

"Don't worry. These things happen. Why do you think we keep patients' numbers handy?" The receptionist smiled, showing a large gap between her two front teeth framed by red lipstick. "How are you doing anyway?"

"We'll see, I guess," Saffron said, pointing at the door to the ultrasound lab. "Do you need the insurance info again?"

"Nope if nothing's changed."

Saffron put her wallet back in her purse and sat down next to the endless supply of lukewarm coffee and powdered milk. She poured a generous cup and winced at the disgusting taste the combination left in her mouth as she swallowed.

She checked her work email. There were too many new messages already. She put the phone away, grabbed an *InStyle* magazine, browsed through it and when done, grabbed another one. After she finished leafing through it, she checked her phone. It was almost ten o'clock. Saffron wondered what was taking so long but then remembered it had been her fault for being late, so she couldn't really complain about the wait. Besides, she had nothing better to do or a better place to be at.

About fifteen minutes later the door opened and Julia called her name.

"Please, remove everything from the top, and leave the opening of the gown on the front," she said after they exchanged pleasantries.

Finally, Saffron lay down on the examination table, and Julia asked her to expose her right breast.

"You know this is just routine," Julia said, spreading warm goo all over the bare area. "They did the biopsy and it was negative for cancer, but the doctors always want to do a follow-up in six months."

"I know, I know. But..." She stopped talking and began to breathe slowly. Not just talking affected the ultrasound machine, but also heavy breathing or even sighing could alter the reading.

Julia worked through the different images, and Saffron saw her selecting screen shots to save.

"I'm going to call the doctor now."

Saffron took a deep breath. Her rib cage hurt. Even though she had walked out of the accident without a scratch, she was still sore with adrenaline.

Dr. Leavenworth walked in the room and asked her how she was doing, but Saffron could tell she wasn't paying attention. The doctor was a million miles away. She grabbed the transducer and rubbed it over Saffron's skin, focusing on the monitor.

"Hummm, I don't see it," the doctor mumbled.

"The lump? Is it gone?" Saffron said, flooding the monitor with red and green streaks.

"No. Do you remember when we did the biopsy we put in a little titanium marker?"

"Yes."

"It's used to mark the lump, so if another one ever shows up, they can be easily distinguishable from each other."

"Right."

"Well, I can't seem to find it now."

"Oh?"

Dr. Leavenworth moved the handle up and down, right and left, as if following an invisible grid. Her eyes concentrated on the images portrayed on the monitor. She grabbed the lubricant, added another generous dollop and tried again.

"I wouldn't worry. It probably moved behind the lump and that's why we can't see it." She saved a few more images. "It's not altogether uncommon. In fact, we've seen it a couple times before."

"Okay..." Saffron said, not as confident as the doctor obviously wanted her to feel.

"Julia, can you pull the images from six months ago?"

After she studied each one and compared them to the new ones, she said, "We're done."

The lab technician took over the machine, and after clicking on several buttons and turning a few knobs, she handed a tiny towel to Saffron. Dr. Leavenworth stood at the foot of the examining table waiting to get her patient's full attention.

"Your lump has not changed, so that's good news." She paused a few seconds while Saffron absorbed the information. "And as I said, I wouldn't worry at all about the marker. Sometimes they move around a little."

"Okay. I'm just happy about the good news."

"Absolutely. We would like to see you in another six months, but after that, if everything remains the same, we can extend the checkups to every year."

"Very well," Saffron said, shaking the doctor's hand.

CHAPTER 49

Saffron came out of the examination room and changed back into her clothes. She placed the used robe into the basket outside the changing room and headed back to the reception area. Lydia was busy giving instructions to somebody on the phone, so Saffron waited.

"All good," Saffron said when the receptionist hung up.

"Congratulations." Her broad smile had very little red lipstick left, but it was genuine and warm.

"Thank you. Have a great weekend."

She waved and left the doctor's office craving a latte.

The line at the hospital's coffee cart was too long, and the coffee was usually burnt, so she decided to go across the street to Mochas & Lattes coffee shop. It took her ten minutes to get there. Half the time was wasted waiting for the light to change at the crosswalk.

She removed her sunglasses as soon as she was inside. The contrast with the bright sun made her temporarily blind. There were a few people seated at tables, and at least ten others in line before her. Not much different than back at the hospital, but at least the coffee was better. The door opened again, and a heavyset man walked toward her, stopping right behind her a little too close for comfort. She moved a few inches forward.

"No matter when you come, this place's always packed," the man said, reeking of onions.

She didn't turn to face him but thought it would be too rude not to respond. "Yep."

"Did you know that there are a hundred million daily coffee drinkers in America, and about thirty million drink specialty coffees?"

"No. I didn't know."

Saffron sucked her teeth and advanced another few inches, breathing through her mouth.

Her phone vibrated in her pocket with a new text, saving her from further small talk. She pulled it out but slid from her hand and fell on the floor, sliding a few inches until it hit the stand showcasing bags of the latest coffee blends and a few new mug designs. The queue moved forward, creating space in front of her. She leaned down to pick up the phone. Another text from Detective Lynch.

Before she could stand up, the loud sound of fireworks, followed by glass shattering, filled the coffee shop. She dropped to the floor and laid as flat as she could. She saw the fat man right behind her get hit and realized they were being shot at. The impact was so severe that his body twisted to the left. The second bullet went through his side. It never exited. He started falling, while a third bullet entered his lower jaw, and left through the right cheek. She heard screams, blood splattered everywhere, and she saw people dropping all around her. Some moaned, while others, already dead, fell on the floor with their eyes open and expressions of disbelief.

The man fell on top of Saffron and gurgled, trying to say something that she couldn't understand. She felt his warm blood soaking her clothes. The overwhelming smell of copper mixed with onions wrenched her stomach. The screams around her filled her head, and the man's weight crushed her to the point that she wondered how much longer she would be able to breathe if she couldn't get out from under him. He kept saying unintelligible words while copious amounts of blood fell on Saffron with each breath.

The firing ceased, the screams stopped, but the moans and cries were still loud. She tried to crawl out from under the man, but he moved with her. With her left hand, the one holding on to the phone, she tried to push herself up to see if she could roll him to the side, but he was too heavy. The door opened.

The glass was shattered, so the only thing left preventing the shooter from just walking in was the horizontal bar that had held the two windowpanes in place. Saffron could see the image of the man entering the store reflected on the pastry display. She could hear him. Each step was slow and methodical. The sound of glass being crushed underneath heavy boots seemed louder than the groans of pain that surrounded her.

"Why?" a woman's voice asked a few feet away from Saffron.

The boots stopped. Glass screeched under him as he turned a few degrees to face the woman who had spoken. He didn't say anything. Everybody stopped making noises, and an eerie silence filled the coffee shop. Saffron watched the man's reflection, distorted on the convex glass casing the pastries. After a few more seconds, he raised his rifle.

"No," the woman pleaded, extending her hand in front of her for protection.

He pulled the trigger. The muzzle blast filled the room, and the bullet shattered the woman's hand before it crushed her skull. Then the man turned again, focusing his attention on the other patrons, his feet finding empty spaces and avoiding the limbs and bodies, as if he were playing a macabre version of Twister.

Over the sobs, Saffron heard his footsteps on the shattered glass getting closer. She knew this was the same man who had tried to kill her just two days ago. She tried to relax every muscle and play dead. She was grateful most of her face was hidden by her hair and the Onion Man would probably hide her breathing.

He stopped by her side. She could feel him staring down at her, as if he wanted to make sure she was the one he'd been looking for. Then she felt the muzzle of his rifle against her cheek, but only for a few seconds. He stopped pressing and used it to brush the hair away from her face. Blood dripped from her neck onto the floor, turning it crimson. She didn't move. The pool of blood continued to expand, sneaking into the tread of his Timberland boots.

He pushed the Onion Man off of her with one violent kick that left a deep, bloody boot impression on the man's beige corduroy jacket. The body rolled off her, and his arm hit the floor like a chunk of fat, but the only sound he made was another incomprehensible gargle.

Saffron wanted to inhale but didn't. Her body was so tense she thought her tendons would snap. The man pressed her shoulder a couple times with his rifle again, as if he were testing whether a still snake was really dead. When she didn't move, he pressed harder and for so long that Saffron wondered if he would ever stop.

She didn't know how many other people were alive, or if there would be anybody brave enough to save her. After the man shot the lady who asked "Why?" she hadn't heard other sobs or cries. She thought about opening her eyes, wondering whether it would be better to die seeing the face of the man who killed you, or die in oblivion. She didn't know, so she didn't open them. Her only hope was that he would take her for dead and leave her alone.

The pressure on her shoulder subsided, the barrel lifted, and she fought an urge to rub the area where he had pushed. She waited, expecting him to do something else to her, but he didn't. She imagined him scanning the room, looking for somebody else to hurt, someone else to finish off. But he didn't move. His boots didn't go away. She felt the barrel of the gun on her cheek again and the pressure sent rays of pain to the back of her skull.

Saffron tightened her hidden hand around the phone, wishing she could claw her palm, instead, with the recently manicured burgundy nails. Just when she thought her head would shatter from the pain of the metal against her face, she heard a police siren. Then another. The man stopped pushing. Her pain decreased, but she still willed herself to not move any muscles in her face.

A couple seconds later, the man took two steps back and turned around, facing the shattered windows. The noise from the police and ambulance sirens was almost deafening. He just stood there, looking out.

Saffron opened her eyes a sliver, but all she saw were the heels of the yellow boots she already knew so well. She heard cars approaching, stopping, some screeching, some skidding a little on the gravel, but all far enough away in the street to be safe. She wondered if she had a chance to get up and run away now that his focus was somewhere else. But she was too scared. Her muscles were locked, her heartbeat pumping against her ears almost louder than the sirens. She knew she didn't have the strength to move. She knew she didn't have the courage to risk it.

"We don't want any more casualties," a man's voice came loud and clear from a megaphone. "Please let people go and we can talk about what's going on."

Saffron saw the barrel of the rifle move out of her line of vision. She strained her neck, wanting to see what the man was doing. He was looking through the shattered windows, watching the police. Then he turned and looked back at her. He faced her, seeing she was alive. They locked eyes. He lowered the gun and placed it right between her left shoulder blade and the spine. He didn't push hard this time, just enough to keep her in place. She closed her eyes and cursed below her breath. She didn't even think of begging.

The man pulled the trigger and fired.

The sound of an empty chamber filled her ears.

"Jesus, why won't you die?" he asked her. His voice was low, raspy and sounded tired rather than mad.

He was checking his pockets for extra bullets when she opened her eyes and looked at him. He found none.

"Sir, talk to me. I'm sure we can work this out," the voice on the other side of the megaphone said.

Saffron watched the killer. She wondered if, like in the movies, the police would crouch behind their cars, aiming their guns at the man standing next to her. He dropped the rifle on the floor, the stock hitting Saffron's shoulder. He then reached down and pulled a five-inch combat knife from the left pocket of his black cargo pants.

Saffron recoiled, more in her mind than physically, recognizing the knife that had come so close to killing her two nights ago. She scooted a little and tried to move sideways, sure that the man would finally kill her. But the body of the onion man was too heavy behind her and she barely moved an inch or two away. She looked up and saw the killer was not focused on her anymore. He had the knife by his side and was staring at the cops outside.

"Sir, drop your weapon. We don't want anyone else to get hurt today."

The man stayed there as if in a trance, not moving a muscle. Then he switched the knife to his right hand and curled his left fist. Saffron saw his knuckles turn from red to white. After another second, he started raising his arm, as if he were going to surrender.

"Great. Both hands in the air please."

His right hand didn't move. Then, with the trained move of a hunter who kills a deer badly shot, he slit his own throat, cutting the left jugular with such force that he almost severed his head from his body before he dropped to the floor. Saffron tried to move away again, but the spray of blood bathed her as the man fell on his knees and then face down on the floor with a loud thud.

"Holy shit," the man with the megaphone said before he had moved it far enough from his mouth.

Saffron crawled backwards, climbing over the Onion Man and away from the blood still sputtering from the assassin's body. After a few feet, she was stopped again by something. She looked down. A skinny woman with red hair covered in shattered glass was gasping for air, her eyes pleading as her hand stretched toward Saffron. She took it and sat next to her. Saffron started stroking the woman's hair while she held her hand as hard as she could.

"It's going to be okay. It's going to be okay," she kept saying, trying to calm her down.

Before she was able to say it another time, she felt the woman's strength slip away.

Saffron looked down at her. Two deep blue eyes, half-closed, stared back at her, lifeless. Saffron started to cry.

"No, you can't leave . It's going to be okay," she said and continued to smooth the woman's hair. "You can't leave me."

Her body rocked slightly back and forth while she cried and pleaded.

CHAPTER 50

Right before Darcy and Mr. Lane reached the man's house, Darcy's phone vibrated in his pocket. He fished it out and looked at the caller ID. It was Virago. He didn't answer and put it back, but then it rang again. And a third time. He finally said, "Excuse me" to Lane and answered the phone. "What?"

"Where are you?" The connection was not great, and her voice came up a little broken.

"Far."

"Stop being an asshole. I need all hands on deck. You better be here in two minutes."

She hung up.

When he was about to put the phone back in his pocket, he saw the emergency BOLO pop up. "Multiple shots fired. All units to 18755 Burton Boulevard. Exercise extreme caution."

Detective Lynch excused himself without giving Mr. Lane any details and rushed back to Sorensen's car. He reached Highway 17 while he looked for the red-and-blue lights inside the glove compartment. They weren't there. He searched underneath the passenger seat and, feeling something there, pulled until they came out. He turned them on while pushing the old Jeep to take the curves at a much faster speed than such a high car should. He took the Bascom exit and found several police cars already parked outside the coffee shop. Every officer was taking cover behind patrol cars or anything else that could act as protection. Each had a weapon drawn, aiming at the thrashed storefront.

"Can anybody see if he's still alive?" he heard Sergeant McNally say addressing his colleagues.

Lynch grabbed a bulletproof vest from the back of the car and put in on while he crouched behind the cars. He spotted Sorensen and ran toward him.

"What the hell's going on?"

"Glad you could make it." His voice was dry. "Lone gunman from what we can tell. The guy's 1055."

"He killed himself?" Darcy asked, wondering if he had heard right.

"Better offing yourself than getting caught, I guess," Sorensen said, still looking straight ahead.

"Are there any survivors?" McNally asked through the megaphone.

"Do we know who he is? Why he did this?" Darcy asked.

Sorensen shook his head. Lynch spotted Virago next to McNally, assessing the situation.

"Roger, Smits, Ramirez, go in," Virago said, pointing toward the shattered door.

They each straightened their bulletproof vests, and with their weapons drawn and pointing forward, they started moving in.

"Please help," a woman's voice came from within the coffee shop. "I need somebody to help me." Her voice was strained, high pitched, almost hysterical.

Darcy felt a shiver run through his back and cold sweat form under his arms. He knew the voice. He stood behind the patrol car, removed the snap in his holster and took his gun out. He maneuvered around the cars in front of him, avoiding going straight by Virago, and started running toward the entrance as soon as he got past the captain.

"Lynch, get the hell back here!" she yelled the moment she saw him.

He ignored her and reached the entrance. The three officers were already inside, looking at the devastation the man had caused.

"We need medics now," Ramirez yelled hard enough to be heard outside, while Smits went directly toward the man with the knife.

Darcy's eyes darted from person to person, trying to find who he was looking for. Everybody was on the floor. Most tables and chairs were on their side, some with holes, some intact. Shattered glass covered the floor as if it were hail. A lot of it was covered in blood.

There were probably fifteen victims, some already dead, while others wouldn't even make it across the street to the hospital. Darcy scanned the room but couldn't see her. He heard the killer's rifle slide across the room and saw Smits pushing the knife out of reach too. He then bent to check the killer's pulse, but it was more out of habit than necessity.

"Clear," Smits yelled.

Four paramedics came through the door and started working on the victims who were alive. Roger moved, and that's when Darcy saw Saffron. He was paralyzed for a split second. She was covered in blood but still alive. He ran to her and kneeled on the floor by her side.

"Where are you hurt?" His voice was tense, his hands checking her body for wounds.

Her eyes didn't focus on him. They seemed lost and she kept whispering, "I need help. She's dying, I need help." Her hands smoothed the woman's hair.

Darcy checked the woman. She was dead. He grabbed Saffron's hands and tried to get her to snap out of her shock.

"Saffron, listen to me. Where are you hurt?" he yelled at her.

He shook her by the shoulders, but not too hard. She looked up at him, but there was no sign of recognition.

"I'm okay. But she needs help." She tried to get her hands free, but Darcy wouldn't let them go. "He had come here to kill me, but I'm the only one who survived," she said, looking into his eyes, shifting from one to the other.

"What did you just say?"

He wondered if it was the shock, but then she looked at the killer lying in a pool of his own blood and she said it again.

Darcy got up and ran toward the man, crunching glass with each step. He looked down and saw the face of Harper Johnson, the same face he'd memorized just a couple hours earlier.

CHAPTER 51

Detective Lynch checked the pockets of the man on the floor. He found a wallet and opened it. Sorensen walked into the scene and headed toward him.

"ID?" he said when he reached his side.

Lynch pulled out the driver's license and read out loud: "Harper Johnson. Forty-three years old. 28856 Lomas Lane, Santa Cruz, CA." He put it back into the wallet. "Not an organ donor."

"Pity," Sorensen said.

Darcy searched through the wallet. There was sixty-eight dollars in cash, no credit cards, and a photo of an older woman on a porch.

"She looks too old to be his wife."

Lynch recognized the porch. It was the same one he'd seen that morning, but the paint was in much better shape when the picture was taken.

"Mother maybe?" Sorensen picked the photo from Darcy's hand and took a closer look. "This picture is at least ten years old. Anything else?"

Darcy shook his head. Sorensen bent down to pat the man's pockets, but there was nothing in them.

"Wait," Darcy pulled a small piece of paper from the coin pocket of the wallet. "Sacred Heart Parish, Saratoga."

The paper was old, fringed at the borders and faded, as if it had been frequently touched, or even rubbed.

"This is weird. He lives in the Santa Cruz Mountains. Why would he go to a church in Saratoga?"

Sorensen shrugged his shoulders. "He did quite a number here," he said, for the first time focusing on what else was happening around him. All of the live victims had been taken out already, except one.

Darcy saw Saffron refuse the help of a paramedic. She stood up and walked toward them. "All of these people...All this because of me."

"Do you know him?" Sorensen asked.

"No. But he's the one who tried to kill me on Tuesday."

"Are you sure?" Sorensen turned to face her.

Saffron nodded and looked at the man's boots. "I recognize the Timberlands."

"Did he say anything to you?" Lynch asked.

"Yes. When he pulled the trigger"—she took a moment to swallow—"and there were no more bullets, he asked 'Why won't you die?' That is when he took the knife from his pocket."

Both men watched her in silence. A paramedic came and stood a few feet away, too shy to interrupt them.

"Yes?" Sorensen asked.

"She needs to come with me. We have to check her out." He told him.

She recoiled, moving slightly behind Darcy.

"I'm okay. I'm not hurt."

Darcy put a hand on her shoulder and said, "Saffron, it's okay."

"No."

Sorensen gave him a look and walked away.

"Give us a minute," Lynch said to the paramedic, who nodded and took a few steps back.

Darcy faced Saffron. He put both hands on her shoulders and waited until she looked up at him.

"Saffron, I need you to go with the paramedic to the hospital. I need to make sure you're okay, and I need to ensure you're safe."

She stared at him. After a few seconds of silence she blinked, but he knew she wasn't buying it.

"I'm going to go to this man's house, and I'm going to find out why he was after you. But in the meantime, I want you to stay in the hospital until I come back for you. Give me a couple hours."

She looked down but finally nodded. "Do you think I'm safe now..." She looked at Harper but focused on his back, not his head. "Now that he's dead?"

"I don't know." He squeezed her shoulder a little. "That's why I want you to stay in the hospital until I come back to get you."

"Okay," she said but didn't move.

He walked with her toward the paramedic. When they reached him, Darcy said, "I want you to take her to the hospital and get her checked in. Then I want her to stay there until I get back. Do you understand me?"

"Yes."

"I'm holding you personally responsible for her well-being"—Lynch looked at the man's name tag sewed onto his uniform—"Matsen."

"Understood."

Darcy looked back at Saffron and said, "Just a couple hours, I promise," and nodded for Matsen to take her out of the destroyed coffee shop.

He watched them leave as Virago walked through the door.

"What the hell was that hero bullshit you just pulled?" Her brow was creased, and her fists were clenched, ready for a punch.

He ignored her question. "I told you somebody was trying to kill her."

"You should've found out who instead of quitting."

She brushed past him and headed toward Sorensen.

Darcy saw them talking, looking around, pointing at different things on the ground. The scene was completely compromised already, but it probably didn't matter, as they already had their man. They just needed to figure out why he'd done this.

He turned around and headed for the door. He saw the news vans already parked outside the perimeter, the journalists pushing to get as much footage as they could.

"Where the hell do you think you're going?" Virago asked him before he was able to step outside.

"I'm going back to his house," Darcy replied over his shoulder.

"You've been to his house?" Sorensen and Virago asked in unison.

"Where do you think I went with your car?" Darcy replied to Sorensen.

"You're not taking my car again."

"You both go," Virago said, addressing Sorensen. "*Now,*" she added when neither moved.

CHAPTER 52

A flurry of movement outside of his office captured Tyler's attention. He had been focusing on the latest report Sheldon Michaels sent him, just an hour ago, on the VC-backing projections based on the revised lab results. Even the best-case scenario didn't look so good.

"Tyler, have you heard?" his secretary asked, poking her head inside his office without knocking.

"No. What's going on?"

"Somebody just went into a coffee shop and killed a bunch of people right by Good Samaritan Hospital." She came inside, closing the door behind her, as if she were going to confide something to him. "I know your sister works around that area."

"Yes," he said, already dialing her number.

After confirming that Julia was okay, he met everybody in the cafeteria, where the latest developments were being blasted on the large TV. Rose Walters, the news anchor at Channel 7 News, spoke confidently into her microphone, making eye contact with each viewer.

"The only thing we know about the man who committed this atrocious crime is that he's killed himself. The police won't make a statement at this time, but we know that at least five people are dead and there are at least as many injured. They are being transported across the street, to Good

Samaritan Hospital." She paused for a second, as if to ensure she had everybody's attention. "This is the biggest massacre the South Bay has ever seen."

She stopped talking again and looked down, putting one hand over her right ear. Tyler watched his coworkers hold their breath, waiting for her to get back to them.

"We just got the latest update," she said, looking back into the camera with her deep black eyes. Her second of silence felt like minutes, but she made them all wait, as if she expected a drum roll. "The name of the man who's believed to have committed this crime is Harper Johnson—"

Tyler choked on his own saliva and had to walk out of the kitchen while he coughed. Once he had managed to calm down, he walked back in, just as Rose Walters said, "We expect the chief of police to address the public soon, and we'll provide you more information as soon as we know more. Back to you, Jeffrey." Her face disappeared from the large HD TV screen.

Tyler loosened his tie. It was suddenly too close to his Adam's apple and it was making him feel short of breath. The kitchen was hot—too hot—and he felt damp with sweat. He walked back into his office, straight to the only window that would open. The five inches of fresh air didn't make as much difference as he had hoped. He powered his computer back on to check the latest news online. There was nothing newer or different than what the TV anchor had shared. His eyes got lost on the gray words and his thoughts turned to a past not so long ago.

He had fidgeted in his seat and lost his concentration several times during the support group session. He was tired of hearing the same stories and wanted to stop attending, but every week, when the meeting approached, he felt a pull to go that was harder to push away than to give in to. So he kept going. But lately his mind had been wandering, focusing on work and not on the stories these suffering people were sharing. All of them had lost a loved one to cancer. Hearing them had given him strength, even hope, and a mission, sometimes even more so than the loss of his own wife had.

But maybe he was having a hard time facing his group's members because the results of the trials weren't as positive as he'd expected. They weren't nearly as good as Qiang had promised after the animal trials. And he was having issues convincing the investors to hold on for just a little longer.

Tyler thought about Hippocrates and wondered if it was true that "Desperate times call for desperate measures." He knew he was running out of time and wondered if his insane idea would work. Wondered if he could do it. He'd thought really carefully about all of his options but knew he only had one left.

The session ended. They all held hands and prayed to a higher power to help them through the hard times and shared a thank-you for the support they were able to provide each other. Then everybody said their good-byes, and some people stayed behind to help clean up. Tyler watched Harper leave. After a few seconds, he followed him.

As he tailed Johnson, he wondered what he would do if he decided to go home rather than to some bar to have a drink, as he'd mentioned he did sometimes after the sessions.

But that night was his lucky night. Tyler smiled when he saw Harper pull into the Black Door parking lot. He followed him and parked in the first empty spot he found. He waited a few minutes. He checked his email, the stock market—down again—and then the *Times'* headlines before he went in. The bar was a dive. He hated bars like this one. There were always peanut shells on the ground and drunks falling off of stools. The music from the jukebox always competed with the game on one or two TVs mounted somewhere on top of the bar. He opened the wooden door and his nostrils filled with the smell of stale beer. He almost sneezed.

He looked around and found the man he wanted to talk to sitting at the end of the bar. Alone, nursing a whiskey, neat, and a beer back. Tyler took the stool next to him.

"I'm glad I found you here," he said.

Harper Johnson just nodded. Tyler wondered if he knew he had followed him there. Since they'd met almost two years ago, they'd seen each other weekly at the meeting and often at the shooting range Harper worked at, but they hadn't exchanged more than a few pleasantries.

Tyler called the bartender and ordered another round for Harper and a Sam Adams for himself. He took a small sip of his beer and waited until the silence between them became almost unbearable.

"Harper, I'm very sorry you have cancer."

Johnson lifted his drink as if he were toasting.

Tyler didn't know what to do, so he just nodded. "I think I may be able to help," he said.

Harper continued to stare at something undefined in front of him. Tyler wished he got some cues from this man, something to let him know whether he actually cared to live or not. But he got nothing.

"Harper, I think I can help you," he said again.

"I don't have insurance."

Tyler took a deep breath. He was either going to plunge into the deep end and do it, go all the way, or he needed to get off the stool and walk out of that bar and never talk to Harper Johnson again.

There was silence. Some basketball highlights filled the TVs. There was no music coming from the jukebox. Tyler wished there was. He passed his hand over his hair. It was hard with gel.

"My company is working on a cure for cancer."

Harper looked at Tyler for the first time. There was a sliver of hope in his eyes. He blinked and then looked away again.

"We're very close, Harper, and I can ensure that you're one of the first ones to get the cure."

"What's the price?"

Tyler paused again. There was no turning back after this. He took another sip to buy time. He then exhaled deeply, but in silence.

"There is no monetary cost, but I need you to do something for me."

CHAPTER 53

Lynch walked out ahead of Sorensen. Before they left, both turned and looked back at the coffee shop. A bomb could've exploded there and the mayhem would have been similar.

"I'll take care of things here. Can you guys just go and do your jobs?" Virago's voice was hoarse, strained. She tied her hair in a knot and kneeled down to check on a casing.

"My car," Sorensen said.

"Sure." Darcy hid a grin.

"Oh, damn, you don't have your car here, do you?"

"Nope."

"Fucking A."

Longish blond strands moved from side to side when he shook his head. Sorensen passed his hand over his hair and mumbled that he needed a haircut.

Lynch gave him directions as they merged onto Highway 17. He had a strange sense of déjà vu. They drove in silence. Darcy thought about what had just happened, about the victims, wondering if the massacre was the end of it, or if there was more they needed to unearth. Darcy shifted in his seat, pushing away the trepidation he felt at the prospect of never solving the case.

"Man, don't you know that when you borrow somebody's car, you have to return it with a full tank?" Sorensen complained, seeing the gas tank dial way below the red mark.

"It wasn't the most leisurely drive back I've ever done," Darcy said, wondering what Sorensen would say if he knew how fast he had driven to the crime scene.

They took the next exit and turned into a run down gas station.

"Want anything?" Lynch asked, walking toward the convenience store.

"Red Bull. Make it two."

The store was empty. It was small, but the selection of drinks was rather impressive. He grabbed the drinks for Sorensen and poured himself a large cup of coffee. When he was about to pay, he said, "One more thing." He found what he was looking for and left the store at the same time Sorensen was capping the gas tank.

"Here." He put the cold drinks on the cup holders.

"I never would have pegged you as a beef jerky type of guy," Sorensen said, eyeing the large bag of dried meat Darcy had placed by his feet.

"There're a lot of things you don't know about me."

Sorensen turned the radio on, rotating the dial a few times. Every station was covering the massacre. Each had a different theory.

As they got closer, Darcy gave him directions to the private road. Sorensen stopped the car almost exactly on the same spot Darcy had done that morning. As soon as they got out of the car, the dog came running, wagging her tail.

"Jesus, does he bite?" Sorensen asked, obviously uncomfortable with such a large dog running toward him.

Darcy ignored him. He opened the bag of beef jerky and got down on one knee. The ground was muddy and soft.

"Here you go, girl. Are you hungry?" he asked and gave her a piece.

The dog licked him first, then took the meat from his hand, careful not to bite his fingers. He scratched her behind the ears as she chewed. Sorensen came around the car and rubbed the dog's lower back. The dog chewed and wagged her tail. When she was done she sat and raised her paw, asking for more.

"I don't think she's been this happy in a long time," Darcy said.

"I don't think she's had any food in a long time," Sorensen said, staring at her protruding ribs.

Darcy dumped the rest of the beef on the ground and headed toward the house. Sorensen opened the back door of the car and grabbed several evidence bags and a few sets of latex gloves. He handed a couple to Lynch when he caught up with him.

Trees surrounded the dirt pathway leading to the front of the house. Some birds chirped, and a squirrel ran in front of them, leaving one tree and climbing another. It was almost a peaceful place. The house stood one story and moss grew, protected by the nearby foliage, on the roof.

Sorensen walked up to the porch. The old wooden stairs creaked under his weight. He knocked on the door. There was no response. He checked the knob. It twisted and the door open with no resistance.

"Is there anybody home?" Sorensen yelled.

"He lives alone. His mother died a few years ago," Darcy said, and pulled his gun out of his holster before going in.

They walked inside the house and let their eyes adjust to the gloom of the room. There was no hallway. Sorensen opened the closet by the front door and found only an old coat and a pair of rain boots. There was a sofa to the left, no TV, no bookshelves. They both walked through the living room toward the kitchen, and Sorensen tripped on an old rug under the table. The garbage by the sink had a couple McDonald's bags crunched into balls, and the fairly empty fridge mainly hosted a single case of Red Stripe.

"Interesting beer," Darcy said.

Sorensen took a look. "Yeah, I would have pictured him for a Bud Light kind of guy."

Darcy pointed to the left, indicating that he was going to check that part of the house. Sorensen went in the opposite direction. Lynch walked into the small bathroom. The bathtub didn't have a shower curtain. The medicine cabinet was empty, except for a dirty glass and a toothbrush. There was no toothpaste. He walked into the master bedroom and was about to check the closet when Sorensen almost gave him a heart attack.

"Drop your weapon! Hands above your head."

Lynch ran out of the room with his gun drawn and saw Sorensen pointing the Glock at a man standing by the front door.

"Mr. Lane, didn't I tell you to stay away from this house?"

Sorensen didn't lower his gun but looked at Lynch, fighting to not lose sight of the intruder at the same time. "You know this guy?"

"We met this morning. Meet Alton Lane, Harper's neighbor."

Only after Alton placed his firearm on the floor did the two detectives holster their weapons.

"I saw you came back." The old man explained. "I figured we could finish the conversation we started this morning."

Sorensen gave Darcy a quizzical look. Darcy ignored it and picked up Alton's rifle from the floor. "We do. Let us come by your place when we're done here, all right?"

He walked him to the door and handed him the weapon.

"I could wait here, in case you can't find your way to my place through the woods." Alton said, turning back to face them before leaving the porch.

Sorensen rolled his eyes.

Darcy said, "Thanks, but no need. My partner here used to be a park ranger. We'll come by in a bit."

Lane nodded, eyeing Sorensen. "I'll put on a fresh pot of coffee."

Darcy closed the door as soon as Alton left.

"He's the nosy neighbor," he explained. "Let's do a sweep and then have a chat with him."

Sorensen nodded and walked back into the guest room. "I've never been a park ranger."

"I know."

After they cleared the whole house, they met up in the kitchen area.

"I didn't see anything too weird for a guy living by himself in the boonies," Sorensen said.

"Me neither."

Lynch pulled out his phone and dialed Virago. "We need CSU here."

"You found something?"

"No. That's why we need CSU."

"Cute." She exhaled. "I'll send one shortly, but make sure you do a thorough pass before they arrive." She hung up.

They started the thorough search, going over everything methodically, looking for something, anything. Some clue that would tell them why Harper Johnson had decided to not only kill all of those people, but also end his own life.

Sorensen checked the sofa, removed all the cushions, and found a few coins. He then turned it upside-down to see if there was anything taped to the bottom. There wasn't.

"Why is it that people never vacuum under their sofas?" he asked.

"Do you have any large evidence bags?" Lynch asked.

"No, why?" He put the sofa back to normal and walked toward him.

"I think he was trying to burn something."

Darcy was kneeling in front of a metal garbage can with what looked like some carbonized pieces of paper. He didn't dare touch them, in case they disintegrated.

"I don't even know if this would make it all the way to the lab. You better start taking pictures," Sorensen said, staring past him.

"It looks like…Damn, I can't really make it out."

Darcy squinted his good eye and moved his head in a couple different directions, trying to get a good angle.

"Me neither, but it may be something, since he tried to get rid of it," Sorensen said, losing interest and moving toward the entry closet. Finding nothing new there, he moved to the laundry room. "If there was anything on his clothes, it's now long gone. He's done all the laundry," he yelled too loud for the small distance that separated them. He closed the dryer's door with too much force.

Darcy checked all the drawers in the kitchen, even inside the oven and the freezer, but found nothing else as interesting as the burnt papers. Remembering what Rachel had told him, he went back to the silverware drawer and pulled out all of the knives that looked remotely sharp enough to cause some damage. There were only five.

He then went to the master bedroom and checked under the bed first. Besides dust bunnies and a few spiders, there was nothing there. He focused on the closet and the small gun safe he had seen a few minutes earlier during the quick sweep. It probably held three handguns at most. He pulled on the handle, expecting it to resist, but it didn't. It caught him by surprise, and the whole box moved with his arm.

There was only one firearm, a Ruger Redhawk. He photographed it and then bagged it. He did the same with the two boxes of ammunition and the hunting knife. Before Lynch placed the knife into an evidence bag, he took a picture and sent it to the ME, asking, "Could this knife be Hughes' murder weapon?"

He placed the evidence bags on the floor and searched the drawers by the bed stand. Nothing. No Bible. No condoms. No book. Nothing. He checked under the pillows and lifted the mattress to see if there was anything under it. Also nothing.

"What's up with this guy?" he asked out loud.

"I got no idea. It's so weird. You can tell he lives here, and yet it feels as if he's a ghost."

"I say we've done enough here. Let's see if Mr. Lane has anything to say."

Darcy grabbed the evidence bags and headed for the door.

"Sounds like a plan."

CHAPTER 54

After locking everything they found in Sorensen's trunk, they cut across the trees. Darcy's slick leather-sole shoes were slippery over the moss and fallen leaves.

Alton Lane's house was at least double the size of Harper's and displayed a fresh coat of paint. One of the curtains in a second-story window moved. Somebody was peeping at the newcomers. The curtain moved back. Not even a minute later the front door opened.

"Found what you were looking for?" Mr. Lane asked. This time there was no rifle in his hand.

"What do you think we were looking for?" Sorensen asked.

Darcy cringed. He didn't want to alienate the only person who may shed some light on Harper Johnson.

"Mr. Lane, we could really use your help," Darcy said before Sorensen could dig a deeper hole.

"What has he done?"

"We're not at liberty to discuss an ongoing investigation, but we could use your help," Sorensen said, following Darcy's lead.

"Yes, of course," he said, visibly disappointed. "As I said earlier, anything you need. Come on in. The coffee should still be fresh."

The hallway was ample and opened to a large living room with forest-green walls, hosting a stone mantel fireplace with eight-point antlers above it. Darcy looked around, half expecting to find a set of skis by the back door.

Lane led them to the kitchen. A large skylight filled the room with natural light. He took out three mugs from the cupboard and poured coffee. They all sat around a table made of a tree trunk. It was so varnished and shiny that Darcy wasn't surprised they didn't need coasters to protect it from the hot drinks.

"I don't have milk or sugar, sorry."

"This is good." Darcy lifted the cup in appreciation.

Sorensen nodded and, after taking the first sip, said, "Whoa."

"Blue Mountain. I have it shipped monthly from Jamaica."

"When we met this morning, you said you didn't know Mr. Johnson very well," Darcy said.

"That's correct. Not a social man. I do a monthly poker game. He came once. I think he felt obligated. We just bet quarters. The man couldn't play to save his life. He never came again." He drank in silence for a few seconds, as if he were recollecting something. But then he shook his head and remained quiet.

"Do you know what he did for a living?" Sorensen asked.

"He told me he was a retired cop."

Both detectives exchanged a glance.

"He wasn't?" Lane looked from one man to the other. "Well, that makes more sense. I had a feeling he was a dirty cop. Not sure why. Maybe because he wasn't very chatty, and he never wanted to talk about his job or his past."

"Can you remember anything else?"

"Well, a few weeks ago he gave me a key."

He stood up and left the kitchen. When he returned, he had a small key in his hand. He dropped it on the table. Sorensen picked it up using a latex glove without putting it on.

"Why did he do that?" Darcy asked.

"I think he just didn't know anybody else to give it to. He told me to keep it for him and if anything were to happen to him, to give it to a woman name Elena."

"Do you know her?"

"No. He gave me her number and told me to call her and tell her that I had something for her from Harper. That she would know what to do with it." He poured more coffee, took another sip and continued: "A few days later he asked me for the key, then the next day returned it. He did that two more times. In fact, he just gave it back to me again yesterday."

"Can you give me this woman's number?"

"Sure."

He stood again and disappeared.

Sorensen and Darcy looked at each other but waited in silence. Sorensen took out an evidence bag from his jacket pocket and put the key inside.

"It looks like a locker key."

"You impress me, Sherlock," Sorensen said.

Alton Lane came back and gave them the piece of paper with the woman's name and phone number. They thanked him and got up to leave.

Darcy asked, "You told me that you'd seen Johnson go to Sporty's Bikini Bar looking for company."

"Yes."

"Was this something new, or had he been doing this since you met him?"

Alton thought for a while. "He's definitely been going there much more frequently in the last month or so."

"Thank you. You've been a lot of help."

"Are you going to arrest him because of the hookers?"

"We're not vice," Sorensen said with a sly smile.

"I can call you as soon as I see his car drive up."

"Thanks, and if you think of anything else, please give us a call," Lynch said.

Both detectives handed him cards.

"I'll never forget that coffee," Sorensen added, shaking Alton's hand.

Once they were back in the woods, Sorensen asked, "What was that about the pros?"

"This guy only works a few hours a week, has no money, his house is about to collapse with rot, and lately he's been going to hookers on a regular basis?"

He slipped and grabbed Sorensen's arm to not fall.

"I told you to not wear heels on the job."

"I think this guy got some money lately, and we need to figure out from whom."

They reached Johnson's property, and the dog was waiting by the car, where Darcy had dumped the beef jerky. She wagged her tail when she saw them but didn't move.

"We have to take her with us."

"No way in hell that mutt's going in my car."

"I'll pay for full detailing."

"And a full tank of gas."

"Deal."

The dog jumped in the backseat, leaving muddy paw prints everywhere. The smell of wet dog filled the car.

"Man, you may have to make it two detailings. I doubt that smell's going to come out with just one." He wrinkled his nose. "Open the damn windows," he said, rolling his down first.

CHAPTER 55

Both detectives arrived back at the station with a few evidence bags, including the tin can with the burnt papers. Darcy spread them across his desk, and Sorensen called Jon over.

"Can you get these to the lab?"

"Sure. I could use some fresh air. I've been staring at my computer all day."

Darcy walked to Virago's office. The dog followed him. There were a few stares, but nobody said anything. He let the dog in and then closed the door. The captain was immersed in the massacre's paperwork and didn't even notice that Lynch had walked in. She jumped when the dog sniffed her leg.

"What the hell is that?"

Darcy stared back with his typical smug expression.

"Dogs are not allowed in the office."

"Well, you're not supposed to let detectives in the field if they haven't passed their qualification, so I guess we are both breaking the rules."

She pursed her lips and took off her reading glasses. "What do you want?"

"We got a potential lead. I just came to tell you that I'm going to follow it. Then I'm going to pick up Meadows from the hospital and see what else we can get from her."

"I thought she wasn't hurt."

"She wasn't."

"What's the lead?"

Lynch gave her a quick rundown of what they found in the house, as well as the conversation with Alton Lane.

"I'm not sure it's going to be anything, but we've got nothing better."

"Keep me posted with anything you find. Call me." She went back to her computer screen, but before her fingers started typing, she said, "And take the dog with you."

Lynch patted his leg, and the dog rushed to his side. He wondered how a semi-wild dog could be so well trained.

They both went to the garage, and Darcy opened the passenger door so the dog could jump in his car. Before he was able to go around, the dog moved to the driver's seat.

"No driving today, girl. Move over."

The dog obeyed and sat shotgun.

On the road, the air flapped the dog's ears and jowls, and her eyes were closed to thin slivers. Darcy laughed and scratched her neck.

"You need a name." The dog licked his hand. "And we need to get you some serious food and a bath."

Darcy decided to go home. On his way, he stopped at a Petco and got a large bag of dog food. At the register, while he was waiting to pay, he added a Kong. He wasn't sure what toys his new dog would like but it felt wrong to take her home with nothing to play with, except his shoes.

His house was of new construction. The second story had a large balcony with views of the Santa Clara Valley. A tall wooden fence shielded bystanders from a large backyard with a heated pool and a hot tub built into the ground.

Darcy went straight to the pool, took off his clothes, jumped in and started swimming. His body ached with each stroke. Before he got through half a lap, the dog jumped in and followed him.

"Oh no you didn't. That's disgusting."

He was more amused than pissed. He got out of the water and watched the dog swim to the opposite side and walk up the stairs to get out of the pool. She shook her body a few times, sending beads of water a few feet away.

Darcy dried himself and then used the same towel for the dog. He left behind the dirty clothes but grabbed his gun and badge and went into the house.

"Hey, Lola, how are you today?"

The Betta fish seemed a little less vibrant than normal.

"Okay, I'll change your water."

Darcy filled a half-gallon bowl and counted thirty drops of the pH controller.

"I'll feed you in the new tank."

The dog watched his every move. Darcy got a bowl out and filled it with food.

He left the kitchen and ran a hot shower that turned his golden skin a weird tone of pink. He then put on dark blue jeans, a black shirt and a pair Donald J. Pliner shoes. The gunk to keep his hair in place was sticky, but it smelled good. That was the main reason he kept using it.

"Oh, shit, it looks like I'm going on a date," he said out loud when he spotted himself in the mirror.

Back in the closet, Darcy changed into a dark gray suit and a white shirt, but kept the Pliner shoes. He knew the jacket would make him sweat, but he was still on the job.

When he returned to the kitchen fifteen minutes later, he scooped Lola out of the old tank and moved her to the one with fresh water. Her blue and red colors started coming back immediately. He pinched some food flakes and dropped them close to her. With a quick kick of the tail, she changed course and started eating.

CHAPTER 56

Detective Lynch left his house after giving his new dog a directive to not chew on anything. He left the sliding doors to the backyard open and hoped she wouldn't jump in the pool again. From the car, he called Elena, the woman Alton Lane said would get the mysterious key, should Harper Johnson die.

"Hello?" Her voice was sweet and welcoming.

"Good morning. I'm Detective Darcy Lynch, with the Santa Clara Sheriff's Office. I'd like ask you a few questions."

"What is this regarding?" Her Spanish accent was barely noticeable.

"I would rather do this in person."

"Very well. Can you meet me at the Big Basin Cafe in Saratoga?"

"I'll see you there in a half hour."

She agreed and hung up.

He checked his watch and sped up. Rush hour was starting and parking was an issue around the main strip of the little town. He managed to walk into the diner right on time.

The place was quaint. Only three tables were occupied, one with a family—they looked from out of town—one with an elderly couple, and one with a good-looking middle-age Hispanic woman.

"Elena?" he asked.

She nodded and extended her hand. He took it and sat down. The waitress came, and he asked for black coffee.

"You should have the apple crumb pie. It's really good here," Elena said.

"Let's have it then," he said, adding it to the order.

When they were alone again, she looked at him but waited for him to speak first.

"Do you know Harper Johnson?"

Surprise filled her face. She leaned back into her chair and interlaced her fingers on top of the table.

Darcy pulled Harper's DMV photo and showed it to her. She nodded in acknowledgment.

"I know Harper. I didn't know his last name."

"AA?"

She shook her head. "I run a support group for people who've lost a loved one to cancer."

"His mother."

"Right."

The waitress brought the pie and topped off both of their cups.

"He came to the meeting for the first time a few years ago. Very shy man. I never thought he would come back, but he did. Every week. He rarely talked. Just listened. His eyes were half-cast, his arms always crossed, but he kept coming."

Lynch took out the key inside the evidence bag. "Do you know what this is?"

She inspected it from across the table, then took it and checked the number inscribed on the key holder.

"Yes. Well, sort of. About a month ago he stayed behind to help me clean up. He did this on and off. I noticed that he kept looking around, as if checking to see if there were still people around. He was fidgety, but in this job you learn not to push, to just let people open up if and when they want to."

She took a tiny piece of pie and savored it before continuing. Darcy mirrored her and was surprised by the warm, sweet and also slightly tart taste of the pie.

"This is really good," he couldn't help commenting.

"I told you." She smiled and continued: "After everybody had left, he asked me if we could sit for a few moments. We did, and he told me that one day a man named Alton Lane would come and give me a key with the number 6213 on it. It was a key for the local storage unit. You know, the one up the street. He told me that he had there a little money he wanted me to donate to some nonprofit organization related to cancer."

"He told you this only a few weeks ago?"

"Yes, about three or four."

"Did he have any friends or anybody he was more social with at the group?"

"No, not really. We have a fairly steady group. Most people come every week. There are a few who come every once in a while and then we have a few first-timers who never come back. But the core group is pretty steady. But no, Harper just came, listened and left. He didn't even talk that much to me. That's why I was so surprised when he entrusted me to do this for him."

"Did you ask him what cancer organization he wanted you to donate the money to?"

"I did ask him, but he said I could choose."

"Did he say what he expected would happen to him?"

"No. And as I said, we tend to not ask a lot of questions in this job. I assumed he was probably diagnosed with cancer but didn't want to tell anybody. Many people decide not to fight it. I remember thinking that the police probably has great medical insurance, and that he could probably beat it, but I didn't say anything, since he didn't share."

"The police?"

"Yeah. One of the few things he ever shared was being a retired police officer."

Darcy didn't correct her.

"You do these meetings at the Sacred Heart Parish?" he asked, recalling the worn piece of paper in Johnson's wallet.

"Yes. Every Wednesday at seven."

"Can I get the list of names of the regulars?"

She hesitated. "I only have the first names."

"That's better than what I've got."

He smiled, inviting her to relax. He noticed how comfortable it felt to talk to this woman. She was a natural.

"You never told me why you're so interested in Harper," she said, pulling a notebook out of her huge purse and scribbling a list of first names on it. "Why aren't you asking him all of these questions?"

"Harper Johnson went into a coffee shop this morning and shot at everybody who was there."

Elena stopped writing. Her face drained of color. She put the pen down and covered her mouth with both hands.

"He killed and injured several people."

"Somebody mentioned this at work, but not the name. He was a kind man. I don't know why he would've done this. Are you sure it was him?"

"After he shot all those people, he killed himself."

She gasped. Her eyes showing disbelief.

Darcy gave her a few moments to process the information. He finished his pie and asked a few more routine questions, more as a distraction than anything else.

"What do you do for a living?"

"I'm a family therapist."

"I never asked you for your last name."

"Fernandez." Her smile trembled. Darcy could see that she was still processing the news. He wished he hadn't told her.

CHAPTER 57

The storage unit was less than three miles away. Lynch got in his car and turned left on Saratoga Sunnyvale Road. As he drove, he thought about Harper Johnson, the man who had massacred a dozen people, who had probably killed Emma Hughes in cold blood and who had tried to kill Saffron several times. The same man who had entrusted an acquaintance to donate his probably tiny savings to a cancer organization.

The thing that nagged him the most was that he still didn't know what could have possessed this otherwise ordinary man to do these horrible things to these specific people.

In less than five minutes, he saw the bright green sign for the storage facility and made a left into the parking lot. The office was a small building with large windows and a green stripe painted right below the shingles. The place was empty and well air-conditioned. A short, stocky man with salt-and-pepper hair sat behind the counter, playing with his phone.

"How can I help you?" he asked when Darcy reached the counter. He put the phone back in his pants pocket.

"Can you tell me how to get to unit 6213?"

The man eyed him for a second, probably trying to decide whether he cared enough to ask questions or not. He shook his head almost imperceptibly and then asked, "Is it your unit?"

Lynch had hoped to avoid the formalities, but he wasn't so lucky. He pulled his badge and introduced himself.

"Don't you need a warrant or something?" the clerk asked. His eyes were shining a little, now suddenly interested.

"No."

"Are you sure?"

Lynch almost found it funny. People watched too much TV these days and thought they knew everything.

"The owner is deceased. Now please direct me to where the unit is."

The man seemed disappointed with the simple explanation.

"I'll take you there," he said opening the partition on the counter and headed toward the side door.

They walked in silence by a long row of green doors. Then they turned right, passed two more identical rows and turned right again on the third one. The fourth door was the one they were looking for. This row contained narrower storage units.

"This is where our five-foot-by-five-foot units are," the clerk explained. "They're the smallest ones we offer. Surprisingly enough, they're one of our most popular."

Lynch nodded. Then he asked, "Have you seen anybody coming around to use this unit?"

"No. The patrons can just walk in directly, so most of the time they don't even stop at the office."

"Okay, thank you for your help. I can take it from here," Lynch said, facing the closed unit.

The stocky man took three or four steps back but didn't leave. Lynch waited, but when there was no further movement, he turned.

"Please go back to the office. I'll come and get you if I need anything else."

The man puffed in disappointment but left, dragging his feet a little, like a small child, and looking back every other step. After he turned the corner, Darcy put on latex gloves, tore open the evidence bag and took the key out. He got down on one knee and inserted it in the padlock. It opened after a couple jiggles.

The storage unit was empty except for a large black garbage bag tied in a loose knot. He opened it and found three three-by-seven-inch yellow envelopes. Darcy grabbed one. It was about two inches thick. The front had written in blue ink "S.D." Then underneath, "T.N." and below that, "B.D." The envelope was open. He peeked inside and found a bundle of money. He leafed through it. There was probably about $30,000 in $100 bills. He placed back the envelope and took the one that was next to it. This one only had two sets of letters, "H.I." and "E.S." It was thinner. It also had money, but he eyeballed it to be around $20,000.

He heard a car get closer and turn into his row. He put the envelopes back into the garbage bag and took a few steps out of the storage unit into the middle of the lane. A heavy-set woman approached him in a rusty brown Oldsmobile. Darcy pulled his badge out and stepped in front of the car. The woman slammed on the brakes, startling the toddler in the back seat, who dropped his sippy cup.

"Police business. Please come back later," Lynch said, walking toward the driver's side.

The woman stared at the badge, and nodded. She looked toward the storage unit, then put the car in reverse and left without saying a word.

Once she was out of sight, Darcy walked back inside and checked the remaining envelope. It was the same as the first one but had a different set of letters. He took a few pictures with his phone, then placed the envelope back into the garbage bag and put that into a large evidence bag, sealing it and labeling it before he closed and locked the storage unit, taking the bag with him.

He called Lou Davis, who promised to send somebody in the next few minutes. Then he called Virago.

"I've got loads of cash in a storage unit. I'm sending you a picture right now."

"Whose is it?"

"From what it looks like, Harper Johnson's."

"Holy shit." She paused for a few seconds. "Get CSU there ASAP."

"Already on their way. I need to secure the area and I'm heading back..."

"Anything else?" she asked.

"No. See you in a few."

He hung up and headed out to find the help he needed. He walked back into the office and found the clerk glued to his phone again. He looked up from behind the counter.

"I need to talk to your supervisor," Lynch said.

"Actually, he's on vacation. I'm the person in charge."

Darcy didn't believe him, but didn't have time to argue.

"Very well. I need you to close all access to storage units on that row. CSU is on its way and I'm going to put some tape on both entrances to the row, but I'm making you responsible that nobody enters that area."

"What did you find?" His face was twitching a little, as if he couldn't figure out whether to be excited or scared.

"You know I can't discuss an active investigation, but what I can tell you is that what we found is very important evidence in an ongoing case," Darcy explained, attempting to make this man feel a part of the action.

He took out Johnson's picture from his jacket pocket.

"Have you seen this man around here?"

The man took the picture. After a few seconds, he nodded. "Yes, I think I've seen him a few times in the last several weeks." He returned the photo as if it were impregnated with poison.

Darcy nodded. "When was the last time you saw him?"

The man thought about it for a while. "I'm not sure. The days kind of run together, you know? Has he done something?"

Darcy looked at him, and the man said, "Right. You can't discuss."

"Can I count on you to make sure nobody enters that row?"

"Yes, of course." He nodded his head violently up and down, then stopped suddenly and said, "Do you want me to call you if he comes back?"

"Sure," Lynch said, knowing that any other answer would generate many more questions. "I'll be right back."

He left the air-conditioned office and headed back to his car. He grabbed some yellow "Do not cross" tape and went back into the office.

"Can you come with me?" Darcy asked.

The man left his post and met Lynch on the other side of the counter. They both walked back to the storage unit. Darcy taped the entrance to the row, taped the door of the unit, put some tape around the lock and finally walked to the other end. When he was done, he said, "Please, stay here until CSU arrives. Remember, I'm counting on you: no one in or out." He extended his hand, as if he were making a pact. "What's your name?"

"Raul. Raul Sanchez."

"A pleasure having you on the team, Raul," Darcy said and saw the man stand a little taller before he walked out.

CHAPTER 58

Sorensen leaned back in his chair and watched the activity around him. The station hadn't been this busy since they had that series of bank robberies the year before. Virago had demanded all hands on deck and told everybody she wanted the entire team ready to provide valuable information by eight p.m.

Saffron Meadows appeared at the door, next to a uniform.

"Thank you for bringing me over here. I was going insane at the hospital with nothing to do," she said as soon as she reached Sorensen.

"No problem. I was hoping that you could help us, actually." He pointed at the chair by his desk for her to sit. "Can I get you anything?"

She thought for a while. She placed her purse on the chair and, still standing, said, "Coffee. I would kill for a coffee." Then she realized what she'd said. "Sorry. Poor choice of words." She blushed and passed a hand over her face. "I would love some coffee, please."

Sorensen smiled to make her feel more at ease. "After you've tried our coffee, you'll never want a cup again in your life."

She returned the smile and followed him into the kitchen. He poured two generous cups. "Do you have milk?" Saffron asked heading towards the fridge.

"No. Only half-and-half." Sorensen apologized. She emptied four of them into her cup.

On their way back to his desk, Darcy walked in holding a large evidence bag and stopped in mid-track when he saw her there.

"Saffron," he said. "I was going to get you as soon as I dropped this off."

She nodded, looked at the empty chair by Darcy's desk, but ended up settling by Sorensen, where she had left her purse. Darcy took the chair he used for guests and set it closer to where she was. Sorensen sat behind his desk.

"Would you rather go to an interview room?" Sorensen asked, worried she would be overwhelmed with all the activity.

"No. If it's okay, I'd rather stay. It feels better to be surrounded by people."

"We know who tried to kill you," Sorensen said, focusing the conversation on what they needed to get done. "We just don't know why, and we need your help."

Sorensen told Saffron what they knew about Harper Johnson. Every once in a while, he stopped and asked if she had been in the same places or knew the same people. But she didn't.

Darcy changed angles to see if they could get luckier. "How long have you known Emma Hughes?"

She smiled, "I remember the first day we met. She was my boss, about ten years ago. It was my first job out of college. Emma was only a few years older than me, and she was the best boss I've ever had. And my best friend." A somber shadow covered her face.

"You both saw Dr. Leavenworth, right?"

She flinched at the sudden change of subject but didn't comment on it. "Yes."

"Do you know Juliette Davis?"

She shook her head and did so again every time Lynch mentioned another name from a long list of victims.

"Would you mind if I ask you why you were seeing Dr. Leavenworth?"

"I discovered a lump in my breast half a year ago."

She explained that they gave her options for having it checked, and she decided to have a needle biopsy. The results came back negative.

"That's why I was at that coffee shop. I had just gotten my follow-up done and I wanted some coffee."

"How about Emma Hughes?" Darcy asked.

"Same thing. We actually went out to celebrate when we both got our negative results."

"Was there anything peculiar about the doctor or the procedure?"

"No." She stopped for a second, then added, "Actually, yes. They told me it was nothing, but apparently they put a little titanium marker where the lump is when they do a needle biopsy. This is done so they can easily identify the lumps they've checked already, in case there are more in the future. Anyway, they couldn't find mine."

Sorensen and Lynch exchanged glances.

"And the same thing happened to Emma?"

"I don't think so. At least she never mentioned it."

Sorensen went through the files on his desk until he found Hughes'. He searched through the ME report. When he found what he was looking for, he met Darcy's eyes and nodded.

"What? You guys know you're terrible at hiding things, right?"

"Sorry." Darcy swallowed. "The ME couldn't find the marker either but did find the lump."

She stared into empty space. "Why is this important?" she asked, not comprehending.

"We don't know yet," Sorensen said.

While he collected his files, Darcy and Saffron got refills on their coffees. They came back and she took a Red Vine from a box sitting on top of Darcy's desk.

"I bet that's all you've eaten today," Darcy said.

"Haven't been hungry."

He pulled a Clif Bar from his drawer and handed it to her. She devoured it in silence in less than a minute. She declined when Darcy offered her another one.

Sorensen excused himself and went into one of the interview rooms to make some phone calls. He walked back into the bullpen a few minutes later, beaming. He was unsure of whether he should talk about his findings in front of Saffron but not able to keep it quiet any longer, he blurted out, "Out of the five vics we have, three relatives confirmed that they had commented on the same thing happening to them. Another one couldn't remember but was going to check around to see if she had told anybody else."

"What's going on? What does this have to do with this asshole killing all of these people?" Saffron asked, her voice strained with frustration.

Lynch got out of his chair and turned the whiteboards around so they faced her. She looked at the photos of the dead women and Dr. Leavenworth's name circled in the middle with arrows from each victim pointing to it.

"I don't know what the connection between Harper Johnson and Dr. Leavenworth is," Darcy said, "but I can guarantee you that there is one and it isn't good."

CHAPTER 59

For the first time since the hit and run on Saffron, Darcy felt that the puzzle pieces may be coming together. "You know what comes next?" He asked Sorensen.

"You better believe I do," he said and headed to Virago's office to get the court order to force the doctor to give the names of her patients.

From the corner of his eye, Darcy saw Rachel walk into the office with a couple large photographs in her hand. She didn't have her white lab coat on. She was wearing a burgundy skirt and matching jacket that made her look more like a lawyer than a scientist. She reached Darcy's desk but didn't say anything.

"Rachel," Darcy said, happy to see her, "meet Saffron Meadows."

Saffron stood, towering almost a foot over Rachel, and shook her hand. "Pleased to meet you."

"Likewise." Addressing Darcy, she said, "Can we talk?"

He didn't move but nodded.

"The burnt papers you found in Johnson's house?" She phrased it as a question, as if she needed him to acknowledge he knew what she was talking about. "They were in pretty bad shape, so I wasn't able to get anything from the other pages."

Darcy sighed and slouched back in his chair. He had really hoped to find a link to the initials on the envelopes.

"I was able to get a list of names on the first page, though."

Her face didn't show as much satisfaction as it normally did when she carried her findings in person. She offered the photos she had brought.

Darcy took them and looked at the first one. It was really hard to see anything. It just looked like a picture of a burnt piece of paper. He changed the angle to see if a different light reflection helped. There were three names printed on the paper. The first name was unreadable, the second was David Jameson, the third Emma Hughes.

Before Darcy could say anything, Sorensen came out of Virago's office and, waving a couple sheets of paper announced to the world, "We got the court order. I'm going to get that bitch."

"You may want to look at this before you go," Darcy said, pointing at the pictures.

Sorensen stared at them for a few seconds. "This is what we got from the tin can?"

"Yep."

"Holy shit."

"Exactly what I was thinking."

Saffron ping-ponged from one to the other, "What?" she finally asked.

"It looks like Harper Johnson didn't kill Emma because he thought she was you," Darcy said. "He had a hit on her."

"But that doesn't make any sense."

"You kids work this out. I'm going to get some answers."

Sorensen grabbed his jacket, stuffed the paperwork in the inside pocket and left with some spring in his step.

"I know. We still don't know what the connection is, but there're too many things going on that can't be mere coincidences."

"Okay, I'm going back to the lab," Rachel said. "If I find anything else, I'll let you know ASAP."

"Thank you, Rachel."

"Add another caramel macchiato to that long list you already owe me," she said over her shoulder.

Darcy took the photo where the three names were most visible and went to see Jon.

"Can you run this guy's name and let me know what you find?"

"On it."

Before Darcy had time to walk back to his desk, Jon said, "Holy crap!"

A few heads turned to look at him.

"Sorry." His face turned beet red. "It's just that I typed David Jameson's name in ViCAP, and I get a report that he was killed on Wednesday."

"How?" Darcy asked, standing in the middle of the room.

Jon scanned the computer screen. "Hunting accident."

"Hunting accident, my ass." Darcy said. "What happened?"

"The notes are scarce, but apparently he was hunting with a guide and another guy and was shot in the back."

Darcy looked at Saffron. Her eyes were intense and a brilliant green.

"Who's the detective on the case? What jurisdiction?"

"Santa Cruz police. A guy name Peppernickel."

Jon gave him the number as Darcy dialed.

CHAPTER 60

Sorensen decided that catching Dr. Leavenworth while she was still at work was more important than abusing his power. So he pulled the red and blue lights from under the passenger seat and ran them with the sirens all the way from the station to Good Samaritan Hospital. Traffic was insane, but most people pulled to the side to let him pass without much nudging. Part of the road was still blocked because of the shooting at the coffee shop but, after showing his credentials, they let him drive through.

The receptionist had red lipstick on again. It looked freshly applied, as if she were ready to close the shop and head out. Her face showed disappointment when he walked in.

"I'm Detective Erik Sorensen," he said, showing his badge just in case she didn't remember him. "I have a court order to get the names of all of Dr. Leavenworth's patients."

The woman refused to take the paper and just stared at him, as if she didn't know what to do. Sorensen snapped his fingers in front of her face, which startled her into motion. She picked up the phone and dialed extension thirty-two.

"Dr. Leavenworth, I'm so sorry to bother you, but I think you need to come to the front desk."

Sorensen couldn't hear what the doctor was saying on the other side. The receptionist nodded a few times and tried to interrupt the doctor, with no success. She then looked at the phone and hung up.

"You are going to have to wait until she's done with her patient."

"I don't have to wait for anything. You need to pull these records now, or I'm going to arrest you for obstruction." He was bluffing, but he knew she couldn't tell.

She started typing some commands in the computer but was so rattled that she kept making mistakes. She stopped, wiped the nascent sweat from her forehead and picked up the phone again.

"Doctor, please, you have to come here. It's the police."

Less than a minute later Dr. Leavenworth appeared inside the reception area.

"What is it this time?" Her face was sour and her voice curt.

"I have a court order to get your entire list of patients and what they are being seen or treated for."

Dr. Leavenworth grabbed the ruling and scanned it for a few seconds. Then she pushed the receptionist out of the way and typed a few words into the computer. The printer started hissing and spitting papers out. Nobody said anything. When the printer stopped, Dr. Leavenworth picked up the sheets and slammed them on the counter. Sorensen wondered if she'd hurt her hand and wished she at least felt a little pang of pain. He grabbed the pages and skimmed through them to make sure they had all the information he needed. When satisfied, he said to the doctor, "Make sure you don't leave town. We may need to have you visit us at the station."

The receptionist looked away, as if she were afraid he was going to summon her as well.

Neither said anything as he left. When he got into the car, he turned the inside light on and took pictures of the sheets of papers with the names. He then emailed them to Jon. After the photos were sent, he called him.

"Did you get my emails?"

"Coming in now."

"I want you to check on our victims first. Write on the board what they were being seen for."

"Okay."

"Then I need you to check all the other names on the list."

"You want just a database check?"

"For now that'll be enough. If there's anybody who's died in the last two months, write them up on the board, regardless of cause of death. Don't forget to write what the doctor was seeing them for."

"You got it."

"I want it done before I get there." Sorensen said.

"Any pit stops?"

"No, and I'm driving with the sirens."

"Shit," Jon said before Sorensen hung up the phone.

CHAPTER 61

Sorensen walked out of the elevator and got a Red Bull from the vending machine on his way to the bullpen. He drank half of it before he reached his desk.

"What do you have for me, Jon?" He placed his jacket on the back of his chair. He had sweat marks under his armpits.

"Well, right after you left we found out that David Jameson was dead. He was also a patient of the doctor and funny enough, he was seeing her for breast cancer."

"Was he a transgender?"

"Huh?"

Sorensen looked at Darcy to get some support, but caught him exchanging glances with Saffron. "David's a dude's name," he said, as if trying to explain something hard to a small child.

"Right."

"About one percent of all breast cancer patients are men," Darcy interrupted.

"You're shitting me," he said, suddenly uncomfortable with his own man boobs.

Jon went on, "I talked to the detective in Santa Cruz who had the case. He closed it as a hunting accident. He interviewed everybody who had been at the hunting grounds. Apparently nobody was around the area at the time of the shooting and since nothing looked too suspicious, and 'These things happen'—his words—that was all he did."

"You're kidding me. This guy gave up after a couple interviews?" Sorensen finished his Red Bull.

"He couldn't find any evidence. It was a through and through and"—Jon made quotation marks with his fingers—"'You know how hard it is to find a bullet in the forest.' Since the evidence trail went cold, he just closed the case."

"This guy needs to be written up. What's his name again?"

Sorensen crunched the Red Bull can into a ball and threw it into the wastebasket, missing it.

"Shit," he grunted as he moved his body out of his chair to pick up the metal ball.

"Peppernickel," Jon said.

"Oh fuck. With a name like that, what can you expect?" He shook his head and asked, "Okay, next?"

"All of our victims were patients. All of them were seeing her for breast cancer or some type of breast lumps," Jon said, sneaking a peek at Saffron for confirmation, who nodded back at him. "All of them had a needle biopsy done in the last six or seven months."

"How many people outside of our list have had needle biopsies?" Darcy asked.

Jon checked his notes. "Seventy-three."

"Out of those seventy-three, how many are still alive?"

"Sixty-eight."

"There are five additional dead bodies out there?" Sorensen asked, raising his voice.

"In addition to our victims, yes," Jon confirmed, recoiling from Sorensen's intensity.

CHAPTER 62

Darcy was going to say something when he saw Virago come out of her office. Her eyes were bloodshot, and her hair was tied into a tight ponytail.

"I know it's not eight yet, but I want to know where we are," she announced to the room.

Her eyes rested on Saffron for a second, but she didn't say anything.

About a dozen detectives gathered closer to Sorensen and Lynch, who used the whiteboards to center everybody's attention. Jon stood by them, but about a step or two behind. Nobody wanted to start. Virago set eyes on Lynch, her patience running thin.

"Care to illuminate us with anything worthwhile, Detective?"

"Harper Johnson has been identified as the person who tried to kill Saffron Meadows on Tuesday."

"I thought you never saw his face," the captain said, addressing Saffron directly.

"I didn't. But I became very well acquainted with his Timberland boots. The left boot had an inverted V-type scratch on the tip, toward the inside. I saw it on Tuesday when he dropped the bat on the floor, before he cut the seat belt, and then I saw it again at coffee shop. It was the same boot."

"On it," Jon said before Virago could say anything. He pulled his phone and quietly instructed Rachel to check for the scratch on the boot.

Lynch continued. "When we went to his house, we didn't find anything except a Ruger Redhawk gun in the safe and a hunting knife, which could have been used to cut the seat belt, but we've found no evidence that it was actually the same one. The ME's checking to see if it was the murder weapon used on Emma Hughes."

"This guy didn't have much. He didn't even have a TV. Well, he'd had one. There was discoloration and a hole in the wall where one had been mounted but—" Sorensen started.

"This is important because…?" Virago interrupted.

"The point is that this guy had no money. There were discarded McDonald's bags in the trash."

"Hey, I eat Big Macs. What's wrong with that?" Detective Ramirez said, stroking his Fu Manchu. Everybody laughed, and the tension subsided a little.

"Jesus. The house was Spartan, that's all I'm trying to say. We didn't find anything there except the trash can with the burnt papers." When he had everybody's attention back, he continued: "Rachel was able to pull two out of the three names. Emma Hughes and David Jameson. Both dead and killed with different MOs."

"Which throws away the initial theory we had about Hughes being killed because Johnson thought she was Meadows," Darcy went on and looked at Saffron. She had lifted her feet onto the chair and was hugging her legs, resting her chin on her knees. She seemed to be concentrating on what she was hearing more than on being sad or scared.

"The neighbor, Alton Lane, told us Johnson gave him a key that he should give to Elena Fernandez if anything happen to him," Darcy continued. "Fernandez runs a support group for people who have lost a loved one to cancer. Johnson started going several years ago, after his mother died of liver cancer. The key opened a public storage unit in Saratoga that contained three envelopes with money totaling seventy-nine thousand five hundred dollars."

Somebody whistled.

"Not so poor after all," Ramirez said, as if they were talking about himself.

A few detectives laughed, but their laughter was mostly forced.

"Two envelopes had three sets of initials, one had two. Jon matched them to victims we had and new ones we're just learning about."

Virago nodded for him to continue.

"Meadows' initials were not there. We believe these were payoffs for hits. Since he never completed the hit on Meadows, he never got paid for it."

Saffron looked at Darcy as he said this. Her face was blank, stern, but her eyes shined with fear mixed with relief.

"We also cross-checked all of Dr. Leavenworth's patients with our known victims. All of our victims, including Meadows, are patients. Additionally, there are another five people dead under suspicious circumstance from that list that we didn't know about because the deaths occurred in other jurisdictions. And we're still cross-referencing some of the other names with the initials."

"Why the hits? What's the connection with the doctor?" Virago asked.

"We have no clue," Lynch said.

"Any theories?"

"We don't have any evidence that it was the doctor who ordered the hits."

"Get a court order for her bank records. Make sure to check everything." She was talking to Sorensen. "You have a good relationship with Judge Fox, and I believe he still owes you a favor. Hit him as soon as we're done here." She paused and checked her watch. "Okay, no, wait until tomorrow. He's finicky about late-night work."

"You got it," he said.

"Anything else?" she asked the room.

Detective Carmichael started talking about the shell casings found at the coffee shop and the state of the surviving victims. Only one died at the hospital. The others looked like they would make it.

"Has anybody wondered why he shot the coffee shop from the outside?" Virago asked.

Nobody answered.

"If I wanted to kill someone, or even a lot of people, I would have opened the door and started shooting with a good view of what I was doing." She looked at her detectives, almost one by one. "Instead, he started shooting from the outside, hitting the windows, then the glass door. Only after he had shattered them he went inside."

"The other thing that doesn't make sense is that he must have known that at least some of the cars driving by would figure what he was doing. It's not that he was using a silencer." Darcy added.

"Death by cop?" Jon suggested.

Nobody said anything, but they all exchanged glances.

"Let's try to find out what was going on in this man's mind." Virago shook her head. "Good work, people. Keep it up," she said, wrapping up.

When she walked by Sorensen, she added, "Don't wait for the court order. Go and talk to the doctor tonight."

CHAPTER 63

Darcy picked up his jacket from the chair and put it on. He was just about to talk to Saffron when Virago said, "Sorensen, I want you to take Jon."

Lynch stopped in his tracks and looked back at the captain. He felt a rush of heat and sensed all eyes on him. He met Saffron's. She asked what that was about in silence. He shook his head and took his jacket off and put it back on the chair.

Darcy watched Sorensen leave the room. He was always surprised at the man's agility, given his bulk. He walked with the spring in his step he always got when heading out to get a bad guy. After Sorensen disappeared, Darcy looked back at the captain. He passed a hand over his face and kept his eyes closed for a second.

"Lynch, a word."

He looked at her but was slow to move.

"Now," she said, heading for her office.

Darcy glanced at Saffron for a second, seeking some support. Her smile was warm, and she winked when she said, "Let me know if I need to go with you to the principal's office."

A few lines formed around his eyes as he sneered back. "Yes, Mom." He winked.

Virago was waiting for him inside her office.

"What's up?"

He closed the door behind him but didn't sit. She pointed to the chair and remained silent until he took it. He sighed, knowing what was coming.

"I appreciate you coming back to work on this case."

He nodded.

"You said it was bigger than it seemed, and you were right. I don't think we could've ever imagined it was going to be a case of this magnitude."

She grabbed her reading glasses but didn't put them on. She started playing with them. He waited for her to continue. He knew there was no point protesting before she said what she wanted to say.

"I need you here, Lynch. You need to be full-on in this case. I need you qualified."

He shook his head and got up from the chair.

"Detective Lynch, sit down."

He did and stared back at her. He rubbed his left temple and clenched his jaw, the muscles tight, grinding his molars back and forth.

"When I got the word from the assistant sheriff that you were joining my department, I was not happy. I've always prided myself on getting the best people because of their merits. I have a lot of personalities here, but they are the best of the best."

Lynch didn't say anything, didn't move a muscle, except for the grinding.

She continued: "I then checked you out. Everybody said you were a rising star in Seattle until—"

"What's your point?" He interrupted in a low voice.

Virago paused for a few seconds. "I need another good detective in my department. You are too good to be on desk duty or doing hit and runs."

"I told you many times I'm not interested. That's the job I want. If it's not available, I'll find another one."

"What's your problem?" She slapped a pile of files on her desk. The thump passed through the office walls, and Darcy saw some heads turning their way to see what was going on. "Is it just the fucking qualification?" she yelled. "Is that it? You think you won't pass?"

"Yes, that's exactly right," he shouted. "How the hell do you expect me to pass with one eye? I don't need the humiliation. Not from you, not from anybody." He stood but didn't walk out. "I'm not asking you for any favors or special treatment. There's either a job for me here or there isn't."

"The only job for you here is the job of a homicide detective."

"Then I'll officially quit as soon as this case is solved."

He walked out of her office without waiting for a response.

CHAPTER 64

Lynch walked to his desk and saw Saffron looking at him. He stopped. He wanted to leave, to not care, but he couldn't. He knew she wasn't his responsibility and he couldn't make it so. None of this was. And yet he felt it. He wished he could just go, but instead he said, "I've had enough. I'm going home."

"Without me?"

A few heads turned to look at them, and Saffron blushed.

"I can arrange for a safe house for you until things clear up."

She stood and put her hand on his arm to stop him from moving. "A safe house?" Her voice was grave, the look in her eyes so intense, so full of fear, that he understood she was his responsibility.

"I know. We'll think of something else. Come on."

They walked toward the elevators.

"What happened in there?" she asked when they got to his car.

"Nothing."

"Right."

The night was cool, he saw her shiver when they left the parking lot.

He drove in silence. She didn't speak either. They were driving on surface streets. They stopped at a few red lights, but it was mostly smooth and light with traffic. There was no radio or music, just the roaring of the engine and the night sounds.

"I have some good wine at home. Feel like having some?" he finally asked.

He wasn't sure it was even a good idea, but he didn't feel like driving all night without getting anywhere.

"Can we order pizza, or maybe Chinese? I'm starving."

He smiled for the first time in hours. "Sure. Actually, let's order now so we can pick it up on the way."

He searched through his contacts and handed her the phone.

A little later, they arrived at his house with two full bags of square cartons containing almost everything on the menu. It was too cold to sit by the pool, so Darcy set everything up on the kitchen table.

"Whoa, this is a nice house for a bachelor," Saffron said, looking around. "Oh, wait, maybe you are not. I'm sorry."

He smiled but didn't respond. He took a bottle of Shafer and poured two generous glasses.

"Do you want real chopsticks?"

"Absolutely."

She took the wooden ones inside the bag and threw them into the garbage.

"Plates?"

"Not if you don't mind sharing containers."

He nodded and sat on the table across from her. A loud bark came from the backyard. They both looked at the patio door and saw a snout pasted to the window for a split second. Then there was another bark, sadder than the first.

"You have a dog?" she asked.

He opened the door, wondering why the cleaning crew locked the dog outside. She pounced, wagged her tail and licked his hands.

"I just got her yesterday."

"Rescue? She looks neglected."

"She sure was."

"What's her name?"

"I don't know."

The dog came to check Saffron. She kneeled and petted her rubbing her tummy as the mutt rolled back and forth, loving every minute of it.

"You need to pick a nice name. This dog's great."

"Maybe I'll name her Dog," he said and looked back at Saffron playing down on her knees.

"No, you can't," she said, still concentrating on the dog.

"Your cat's name is Cat."

"That's different."

"Oh yeah? How so?"

"I came up with it first."

She stood and punched him on the shoulder.

"That's how you treat somebody who feeds you?"

She punched him again and sat down on the table. Chopsticks in hand and with her mouth full of chow mein, she said, looking around the room, "I thought cops didn't make a lot of money." She choked. "Jesus. You would think the trauma has made me lose all my manners. I'm so sorry. I didn't mean—"

He interrupted her, first with a dismissive wave of his hand. Once he swallowed, he said, "I inherited some money from my crazy uncle, and I got a nice settlement for what happened to my eye."

"Was it an accident? At the end, you never told me."

"And whose fault was that?" he joked.

"Yeah, exactly," she said, pointing at him with finely crafted black wooden chopsticks.

"It wasn't an accident." He fought the urge to rub his temple.

She chewed slowly and looked at him as if she were trying to decipher what he was trying to hide from her.

"Do you really want to know?"

"Yes."

He poured more wine and leaned back on the chair.

"Okay. But if it gives you nightmares, don't come crawling in my bed because you're scared."

"Yeah, you wish. I'm only here because of the food."

CHAPTER 65

Sorensen and Jon walked in silence to the parking lot. Most of the spots were still occupied, even though it was past nine in the evening.

"That was awkward," Jon said, getting into Sorensen's Jeep.

"Yep."

He put the keys in the ignition. The car sputtered a little. After a few tries, it started, and they headed to Dr. Leavenworth's house.

"I thought you guys would end up partnering up."

"No way in hell." Sorensen looked at him sideways. "Don't get me wrong, Lynch seems an okay guy, but he's not..." He scratched his temple, hoping Jon would see it and he wouldn't have to say it."

"He's not what?"

Damn it, this guy's dense, Sorensen thought. "He's on desk duty," he finally said.

"Because of the eye?"

"No, because he's from Seattle. What the hell's wrong with you? Of course because of his frigging eye." He accelerated without even noticing he was doing it.

"What happened to him? Do you know?"

"Nope. I asked him once, but he didn't want to talk about it. I didn't push."

"So you don't think he can be out in the field?"

"How could he? Have you ever tried driving with one eye closed?" He closed his left eye and opened it immediately, not wanting to risk their lives at night. "It's hard."

"Yeah, but he drives. He has the coolest car. So maybe it's okay."

Sorensen stopped talking. He wanted to think about the case. It still made no sense. Too many deaths connected by cancer and the lunatic Harper Johnson. Before he could get too far into his own thoughts, they arrived.

The house was an old Victorian. Even in the dark, the light blue paint with the darker trim looked fresh, well maintained. It had a decent-size front yard. No evidence of kids. The bushes were perfectly manicured, and the grass was short. The house grew as they approached.

"I hope she has a big family, with a house like this," Sorensen said, reaching the front door.

Jon rang the bell. After a few seconds, a man probably in his late fifties, with salt-and-pepper hair and a very thin mustache opened the door. His dark gray pinstripe suit shined with the glare of cashmere, and the tiny dots in his silk tie matched perfectly his light blue starched shirt.

"Detectives," the man said even before they had a chance to introduce themselves. "Please come in."

Sorensen and Jon exchanged glances and followed him to the large living room. A fire chirped, probably more for ambiance than warmth. The décor was the perfect mixture of functionality and class. There was a large, thick wooden coffee table framed by a gigantic burgundy sofa and matching chairs. Two cut-crystal glasses held amber-colored liquid. Sorensen could smell the high-end scotch from where he was standing.

Dr. Leavenworth sat in one corner of the large sofa. She seemed smaller in plain clothes. Her back was really straight. She stood and extended her hand.

"Detective Sorensen."

"Doctor." Her grip was strong for such tiny hands. "Jon Evans," Sorensen added.

She nodded and shook hands with him too. "Please sit."

She grabbed her glass and didn't offer the detectives anything to drink. The man who had opened the door sat next to her.

"This is Theodor Wilmore, my attorney."

Sorensen nodded and said, "We would like to ask you to come to the station with us."

"I'm sure this can wait until tomorrow," Wilmore protested. "It's almost nine."

"I wish it could," Sorensen said.

"Can you ask your most pressing questions now, and if that doesn't clear your concerns, we can meet you first thing in the morning for anything additional?"

Wilmore's intonation let him know this wasn't a question. Sorensen wondered how much of an asshole he wanted to be so late at night.

"This is not ideal, as you can understand. But okay, we can see how it works."

He locked eyes with Wilmore, ensuring he knew he was letting him win. The lawyer nodded almost imperceptibly and crossed his left leg over the right, resting both forearms on his knee. Sorensen wondered if Wilmore had been a classmate with George W.

The doctor leaned backwards, resting against the sofa. Sorensen wondered if they were sleeping together, even though Wilmore was probably fifteen years older than Leavenworth.

He dismissed the thought and asked about Harper Johnson. The doctor said she didn't know him.

"Why would he want to kill your patients?"

Before she could answer, the lawyer stepped in. "How would she know that?"

"Any idea why anybody would want to kill your patients?" Sorensen looked sideways at Jon instead of rolling his eyes.

"No, Detective. Some of my patients are already walking dead."

The thought lingered in the air. Sorensen wondered if Jon was also thinking of that TV show about the zombies.

"Why do you say that?"

"It's obvious, don't you think? Some of my patients have cancer, Detective. That's still one of highest causes of death in this country."

Wilmore patted her knee. She barely recoiled, but just enough for Sorensen to notice.

"I still don't understand why you think these horrible deaths have anything to do with me."

"From your list of patients, half a dozen have died in suspicious circumstances. Another few have killed themselves. You are the only common link between all of them."

Wilmore swallowed, and Doctor Leavenworth finished her scotch but nursed the empty glass in her hands.

"Now, is there anything you want to tell me that can help us rule you out?" Sorensen asked.

"What I can tell you is that I don't know what happened to these people. I don't know Mr. Johnson, and I have no idea why he would want to hurt any of my patients."

She stood up and Wilmore followed. "Now, if you excuse me, I've had a very long day, and I would like to go to bed."

"Just one more thing," Sorensen said before getting up. "Can you confirm if all of these people had cancer?" Before she could respond, he started naming all of the victims who had committed suicide.

"Yes," she said after hearing the last name.

"Is it common for cancer patients to kill themselves?"

"It happens. I'm not familiar with the exact statistics."

Sorensen observed the doctor. She was calm and composed, but her right eyelid had a tiny tic.

CHAPTER 66

Darcy grabbed his wine glass and pointed to the living room. Saffron followed him and sat on the large leather sofa, hugging her legs. The dog followed them and lay down on the floor between them. Darcy thought about what he wanted to tell her. How much he wanted to tell her. And then he began.

"I was a detective in Seattle. You knew that."

She nodded.

"About a year and half ago, I got involved in a pretty big assignment. It was a joint agency cooperation to take down an underground organization smuggling illegal arms. The ATF had tracked down the flow: the weapons were being stolen from the Fourth Marines Embark Logistics Base in San Jose by a couple marines and were exiting the country via Seattle's port and through Canada.

"They'd been watching the two marines for a while but hadn't been able to get close to any of the bigwigs. I was working vice at the time, not involved in any of this, when I got an interesting tip from one of my confidential informants."

As Darcy shared the story with Saffron, the whole event came back to him in vivid detail:

Pike Place Market had been crowded, even for a Thursday morning. The fish stand, behind the copper pig and below the red Public Market Center sign, amazed tourists even that early. A burly man behind the counter picked up a good-size salmon and threw it a few feet away to another employee standing in between tourists. Darcy watched a little girl open her mouth, cover it with her tiny hand and then laugh and clap in amazement when he caught it. He rarely got bored watching people.

He saw Gigi come down Pike Street. Her bleached blond hair was in bad need of a root touch-up. Her lips were bright red, and her thin figure sashayed over the brick ground as if she were figure-skating in an ice rink.

"Good morning, gorgeous," she said in her husky voice. It was deep and sensual, as if she'd had a two-pack-a-day habit for the last forty years, even though she wasn't even thirty yet.

"What flower would you like today?" he asked.

"We'll see what inspires me."

She smiled at him. There was a hint of lipstick on her front tooth. She saw him looking and passed her tongue over it, licking it away. She smiled back at him, and he nodded. They started walking down the market.

"You said you had something for me."

"I don't even have a flower yet and you're already pumping me for information? I thought you were a gentleman," she protested but put her arm around his.

Since they started working together several months prior, she had always insisted on meeting at Pike Place Market and for him to buy her a single flower. Always different, almost always exotic.

They got to the flower stand, and she scanned through her options. The vibrant colors clashed with the gray sky and misty air outside.

"What is this?" Gigi asked, pointing to a prickly flower with bright orange petals.

The florist smiled, pleased with Gigi's interest. "That's a *Calathea crocata*. It's also known as the 'Eternal flame.'"

Gigi eyed Darcy, as if expecting some reaction from him. "Well then, that must be the one." She turned to him glowing almost as much as the flower.

The florist wrapped it in bright blue paper peppered with golden specs and finished it with a gold bow.

"Enjoy it," she said, handing it to Gigi.

Darcy paid, and they strolled a few yards to the original Starbucks. The store was more brown than green and didn't feel like a Starbucks. There were no comfortable leather sofas, only a counter to get the coffee to go. Gigi ordered a skinny vanilla latte, and they walked outside again.

Finally, when they reached the end of the market, she stopped by the little park and, staring down at the water, she said, "I was at this party last night, at The Vixen. It was pretty wild, you know. Loads of drugs, free alcohol in the VIP section, many girls, most of them pros."

Darcy tensed but knew better than to interrupt her flow.

"I was working on this guy, buff, hard body, about a foot taller than me, five-o'clock shadow just because he thinks it makes him look cool. You know the type." She looked at him briefly. "He said he had something he wanted to share with me. I figured it was coke, so I just followed him. We headed toward the bathrooms. There's nobody there. He takes me into a stall and lifts me against the wall. He's strong. He hikes my skirt and kisses me on the mouth. He's a good kisser."

"Gigi, is there a point to all this?"

"I'm getting there, okay? I need to give you context. Isn't that what you used to tell me when I started?"

"Yeah, context for the information you give me, not of your particular remunerated encounters."

She waved a hand at him.

"So, as I was saying, he's holding me up in the air against the stall while he kisses me and with the other hand he unzips his fly. My skirt's already around my waist. And right before he enters me, the door opens. He stops to listen, like he's enjoying that we're there and somebody's on the other side of the stall door."

Darcy wondered if she went into all the details just to push his buttons. It always bothered him, because 99 percent of what she did was illegal. And dangerous. But she was the best CIs he'd ever had.

"He's hard against me. I can feel his dick pushing against my stomach."

"Gigi, please. Get to the point."

"Okay, okay. So, we're there, in silence. He's looking at me but doesn't say anything. The guy outside starts peeing. The door opens again and the guy peeing says, 'Get the fuck out of here.' I look at the buff guy, and he puts his index finger against my lips. I kiss it but he doesn't notice. He's listening to what's going on outside.

"The guy peeing stops. The new guy walks closer—he had leather soles or something, because you could hear each step. 'Where's my money?' he says. The other dude says, 'You'll see your fucking money when you bring me the guns I asked for.'"

Darcy stiffened. She went on.

"Buff Guy drops me on the floor and gets out of the stall, his dick still out of his pants. He rushes to Peeing Guy and gets in his face. He's taller than him by a good five inches. When he's really close, Buff Guy punches him in the face and says, 'Shut your fucking trap. Never—and I mean *never*—talk about this shit in a public place.' He turns and walks past New Guy. He brushes by him hard, almost making him lose his balance, but he doesn't protest. Before he leaves, he turns around and looks at me. He puts his index finger now on his lips and winks before he goes through the door."

"Anything else?"

"Isn't that enough?" she says, finishing up her latte.

"What was his name?"

"He said it was Stepan."

"Did you recognize the other guys?"

"No. I'd never seen them before."

"Did you see Stepan again when you got out of the bathroom?"

"No. I looked for him but he was gone."

"This is great, Gigi. I need you to come to the station and see some mug shots."

"Only if I can ride in your car with the top down, gorgeous."

She didn't like going to the station, but she loved the Cobra.

After she wasn't able to identify anybody from the photos, Darcy went to talk to his captain. He told him he thought he might have something related to the arms-smuggling case and that his CI could probably help. Darcy shared everything Gigi had told him, only skipping the unnecessary details. Captain Carpello thought about it and agreed to have him involved. When he got all of the necessary clearance from the other departments, Darcy was in.

A few days later, Gigi called him to let him know that Stepan had invited her and a couple other girls to another party. This was a private one, some rave or something at a warehouse in West Seattle. She didn't have the address, but he was going to pick her up and take her there.

The day of the rave, Darcy showed up at Gigi's place. He pulled an ear bug and said, "You have to put this in."

"No way. If he finds out, I'm dead."

"He won't. Just cover it with your hair."

"I was going to wear it up."

"Gigi…"

"Okay, fine, but if he finds out, you better be there to save me."

"That's why I want you to wear it. I'll be able to hear everything that goes on. I can't talk to you, but if anything goes wrong, just say 'Wednesday' in a sentence and I'll be there before you can blink."

She wasn't convinced. She held the piece between her thumb and index fingers and looked at it.

"Seriously," Darcy said. "Just say 'Wednesday.'"

"Okay, gorgeous. Just for you."

She fit it inside her ear.

"One more thing," he said, pulling a GPS tracker out of his pocket. "I want to put this in your shoe."

"What? You're not ruining my heels," she protested.

He ignored her and pulled the heel cap off with a kitchen knife. Before he had hammered the little screws back into the shoe the doorbell rang and they both jumped.

"Fuck, I think he's early," she said, suddenly nervous.

"Just tell him I'm your cousin."

"You're not that good looking," she joked and tried to relax, but her smile was forced.

She went to the door. He finished fixing the shoe and hoped the device worked, since he wouldn't be able to test it before Gigi left.

He then sat on the sofa, pulled his T-shirt out of his jeans and turned the TV on. There was nothing playing, so he started channel-surfing until he found a game. He was glad there was an empty beer can on the coffee table. He wanted to look as comfortable there as if it were his home.

She walked into the small living room holding the man's hand.

"Handsome, why don't you wait for me here while I change into something more appropriate? I wasn't expecting you this early."

He nodded and sat to Darcy's left, on the ample leopard-print chair.

"Hey," Darcy said.

"Who are you?" Stepan asked with a trace of a Russian accent.

"I'm Roger. Gigi's cousin from LA." He took the empty can and pretended to drink. "Shit. Empty. Want one?" he asked, getting up and heading to the open kitchen.

"I don't drink and drive."

"Suit yourself."

Darcy got back and opened the new can. Gulped a third of it, then belched. "And you are?" he said after wiping his mouth with the back of his hand.

Stepan didn't answer. Before the silence became too awkward Gigi walked into the room. Her hair was down, with shiny blond ringlets framing her face. She was wearing a really tight cocktail dress. The red matched her lipstick perfectly.

"Ready?" she asked.

Stepan got up from the chair and followed her out of the house. Darcy ran to the second story and peeked out the window. Stepan opened the passenger door of a silver BMW M5 and waited for Gigi to get in. When the car left, Darcy tried to get the license plate, but it was too far away for him to see it.

He called Carpello and told him that the action had just started. The captain confirmed that the backup team would be on standby and that the GPS was tracking.

Darcy listened to the chitchat in the car. Gigi talked about everything, while Stepan didn't say a lot.

"I've always liked Elliot Bay. Is this place we're going close to Alki Beach?" she asked.

Lynch ran to his car and headed down to West Seattle. Detective Starr gave him a play-by-play on where Gigi was going.

"If you want to end up in Alki, I'll take you there later," Stepan said.

She teased him and probably kissed him. Darcy couldn't quite make out what that particular noise was.

"They've stopped. They are in Harbor Island, at the corner of Thirteenth Avenue and Lander Street," Starr said.

Darcy remembered some old buildings there, but nothing too suitable for a party for thirty- and fortysomethings.

"Are we the first ones to arrive?" Gigi's voice was playful, but Darcy could detect some uneasiness.

"Yes, sweetie, I wanted to have a party for just the two of us."

Darcy's neck hairs rose. "This is not good. I think he made her," he yelled on the radio. "I'm going in."

"Do not go in," Carpello instructed. "We have units on alert and they'll be close but on standby. She's not said she's in danger. I repeat, do not go in." Darcy hit the steering wheel as hard as he could while trying to not lose control of the car over the West Seattle Bridge. As soon as he crossed East Marginal Way, he slowed down, finally pulling off the road on Eleventh Avenue, not wanting to get too close. He listened to Gigi's every word. She was trying to flirt, but what she was saying sounded more and more fake as the seconds passed.

"Where do you want to do it? Here?" she asked. "Or here, on the table?"

Stepan wasn't saying anything.

"Oh baby, you don't need a knife to get me hot."

"He's pulled a knife on her, I'm going in," Darcy yelled on the intercom.

He didn't wait for a response from the command center and started moving again but told himself to not burst in until Gigi said "Wednesday." For a second he feared she might have forgotten, but he let the thought go. She was way too experienced for that.

"You really want to play with knives?" he heard her ask.

Darcy parked about a hundred yards from the building and run toward it. His heart was beating so hard it felt as if it would leap out of his chest. He was short of breath, not from the run, but from hyperventilating. He forced himself to calm down so he could think better, act better.

"Can we play without the knife?" she asked. Her voice quivered. "I only do knives on Wednesdays," she said, almost under her breath.

"She's in danger, I'm going in. I need backup now!" he yelled into the radio.

He finally reached the building and had to jump to look into it from a broken window. The space was huge and dirty. It was also empty. He moved to the next window and the next one—no luck.

Then a scream filled the empty air. The cry didn't have words, but he knew Gigi's entire world had started to crumble. Darcy ran, peeking into every window he went by, still seeing nothing inside. Then he rounded the building and spotted the BMW and finally a door a few yards away.

Before he could reach it, there was another scream and then another. "Please, stop! Wednesday, Wednesday!" she shouted, and then there was silence.

Darcy reached the door and rushed in, his Glock ready and straight in front of him. He went through another empty room, opened a door and walked into a large space. He saw Gigi. She was on the floor, facedown. The trail of blood matching the color of her dress. She'd tried crawling away from Stepan. Darcy did a swift check around the room and, not seeing anybody, he ran to her. He got on his knees and checked her vitals. They were barely there but she was still alive.

"I got you. I got you," he said and turned her around.

She had several stab wounds and they were all squirting blood as her heart pumped. He took his jacket off and tried to apply pressure, but there were too many gashes to cover with just two hands.

"We need a bus right now," he yelled on the radio right before something hit his head so hard everything went white in front of him.

He flung over Gigi's body and fell sideways on the floor. He shook his head to force himself to focus. Stepan walked over the girl and kicked him again, this time in the stomach. Darcy felt his gut split in two and reached for his gun but only found an empty holster. He froze. Looking back at Gigi he saw his Glock lying next to her. It was too far away for him to reach or even do a run for.

Stepan kicked him again, but Darcy saw it coming and moved away, making his attacker lose his balance. Darcy returned the kick, hitting Stepan's knee. He grunted and fell but quickly moved on top of Darcy and punched him in the face. Darcy tried to throw him off, but Stepan outweighed him by at least thirty pounds.

Darcy threw an uppercut. It wasn't as strong as it would have been if he had been standing, but it produced enough of a sting for Darcy to slide away from under him. Before he could get up, Stepan stabbed him in the thigh. Darcy screamed. Still on his knees, he kicked Stepan with the other leg, but the impact was weak, as his stabbed leg was hurting too much to be used as an anchor.

Stepan rolled to his side, kicking Darcy back to the ground as he moved. Darcy landed on his back and before he could move, Stepan crawled on top of him again. Darcy threw a hook, trying to hit the arm with the knife. There was contact and the arm flew backward, but Stepan was able to recover quickly enough and thrust his elbow into Darcy's sternum. Darcy stopped breathing for several seconds. His eyes bulged and stared at a knife that was over him, about to end his life.

Darcy heard cars and sirens closing in. "Lynch, you there?" he heard somebody ask from outside. Finally the noise of many more bodies coming into the warehouse overpowered the sound of his own thumping heart. He locked eyes with Stepan. There was rage in them, but there was also indifference. He was still on top of Darcy.

"Drop your weapon!" Somebody shouted.

He started lowering the knife as if he was going to put it down. Then, with the fastest move Darcy had ever seen, Stepan lowered the knife to his face and stabbed his left eye.

As soon as the blade punctured it, he pulled it out, dropping the knife on the floor as a bullet entered his shoulder pushing him off of Darcy.

At first Darcy didn't feel any pain. He just stopped seeing. His good eye had closed, as if trying to protect itself. His now-empty eye socket flooded with blood. Then the pain started. It was an acute sting that grew more severe with each second, until the agony almost made him pass out. He felt somebody come by his side. Darcy started to scream as he rolled over in a fetal position pressing his hands where the eye had been. He never heard what they asked him. All he could think about was how the blood seeping through his fingers was nothing compared with the blood leaving Gigi's body.

CHAPTER 67

Saffron realized she was holding her knees so hard that her arms were starting to hurt and her legs were going numb. She let go and put her feet back on the floor in front of her. Darcy seemed to be in a trance, his good eye staring into empty space, recalling the past. He rubbed his left temple up and down slowly. He was silent for a few seconds. Saffron poured more wine.

"What happened next?"

He looked at her as if she had asked something in a foreign language.

"They did shoot Stepan right after he took my eye out, but they didn't kill him."

"Pity."

"Yeah. His full name is Stepan Kozlov. He'll be in prison for a while. He ended up being convicted in relation to the arms-trafficking ring also, so that was a good break in that case. He gave up a bunch of information in exchange for a lesser charge and a reduced sentence."

Darcy didn't say anything, but she could tell he felt betrayed.

"Is that why you left Seattle?"

"No. I was just tired of the rain." His smile was a little forced. Then his facial muscles relaxed and he continued: "Yeah, that's partially why I left. I was out a few weeks, then

I had to do some physical therapy to recover from the leg wound and even more to be able to partially function with just one eye. They wanted to give me early retirement, but I couldn't take it." He shook his head. "I probably should have."

Saffron raised her glass and toasted: "For being alive after a close call."

He clinked her glass. "I'll definitely toast to that."

She was not sure she should ask, but she had to know. "What happened to Gigi?"

His eye darkened and his stare got lost somewhere inside his wine glass.

"She never made it to the hospital. He'd stabbed her seventeen times."

"Did he ever say why?"

"The asshole planned on killing her all along. When they were in the bathroom at the club she heard that douche bag talk about the weapons and then saw his face. The only reason he didn't do it earlier was because he wanted to 'play with her first,' as he put it." He spat the words. "He never even suspected her of collaborating with the police."

"I'm so sorry," she said and put her hand on his forearm. His skin was warm. She left her hand there.

He looked up at her and moved a strand of hair behind her ear. She felt butterflies flutter in her stomach. Darcy passed his hand over her long hair. She closed her eyes, a sense of peace overcoming her body.

She sighed, slowly, silently, and opened her eyes. He was looking intently at her, his lips full and slightly parted. Her heart started thumping inside her rib cage, but she fought the urge to leap over the few inches that separated them.

But he did. He leaned closer and kissed her. The kiss was soft and inviting. She teased his upper lip with the tip of her tongue. He pulled her closer to him.

The phone rang. She ignored it. He did too. They kissed again, teasing each other's tongues. As soon as the rings ceased, it started again.

"I think it's work." He said.

"I don't hear anything." She breathed onto his neck.

"I don't either," he said, leaning on top of her.

She scratched his back over the shirt and pushed herself up onto him. She could feel how hard he was against her.

The phone rang again.

"Shit. Let me just take it," he said, almost breathless. "It could be a break in the case."

She moaned in disappointment but let him go.

"This better be good," he said into the handset.

"Detective Lynch, Officer Bush here." After a few seconds of silence he continued, "We wanted to confirm that Ms. Meadows is with you."

"She is. Why?"

"We drove by her apartment, just to check, and there's somebody in there. We saw a light come on."

"Okay. I'm on my way."

Saffron's eyes opened wide.

"What?" she asked, knowing the evening was over.

"Somebody's in your apartment. I'm going to check it out."

"I'm going with you."

"Absolutely not."

"You said you're not going to leave me alone tonight. I can't be alone."

"But you are here, and you have Dog."

"Don't call her that. I'm coming."

She got off the sofa and was halfway to the door by the time he managed to adjust his pants and tuck his shirt back in.

He drove in silence, and she was too self-conscious to talk about what had just happened but also upset it had ended so quickly. Saffron tried to avoid thinking about who might be in her place. She thought her nightmare was over when Harper Johnson killed himself, but thinking that was surely naïve.

She fought an urge to put her hand on Darcy's thigh. She wanted—needed—some human contact, some sense of feeling protected. Instead, she hugged herself.

"Do you think the person in my house is there to kill me too?"

"I'm not going to let that happen."

"But do you think somebody's still out there trying to kill me?"

"We don't know. There are still too many open questions."

When they got to her complex, they found the patrol car parked to the side of the main building, outside the line of vision from Saffron's apartment. Sergeant Russell and Officer Bush were standing watching Saffron's lit window. They told Lynch that they hadn't seen any more activity but the light was still on. He thanked them and asked if they could stay a little longer for backup. They agreed.

"Stay here," he said to Saffron.

"No way. I need to see this asshole's face."

He shook his head. "Fine, but you stay behind me the whole time. And when I go into your place, you do *not* enter until I tell you it's okay to do so."

"Deal."

They went up via the stairs. Saffron's heart was beating so hard she could hear it. About ten feet from her front door, he paused and pulled his Glock from his holster and pointed it to the ground. When they reached the front door, he opened his free hand, as if waiting for her to drop something in it. She gave him the keys, and he unlocked the door as silently as he could. He raised the gun and opened the door in one hard push. The door slammed against the entry closet with a loud thump.

There was a man sitting on the sofa.

"Freeze! Put your hands where I can see them!" Darcy yelled.

The man dropped the popcorn bowl on the floor, Cat jumped from his lap, and Saffron asked, "Ranjan?"

CHAPTER 68

Saffron pushed through the door, passed Darcy and put her hands on her hips. Before she could say anything, Darcy holstered his gun and asked, "You live together?"

"No," she said, blushing a little and not looking back at him. "But he has a key."

"What the hell's going on?" Ranjan asked, walking toward them.

Darcy called in the patrol officers to tell them everything was okay and they could leave the premises. Saffron wasn't saying a word or moving from where she stood.

"Who are you?" Ranjan said to Darcy. He looked as if he had been sucked into the Twilight Zone.

"I'm Detective Lynch. We've met. I interviewed you and your uncle after your accident."

"Oh. Right." He showed recognition for a second and then looked confused again. "Why is he here?" he asked Saffron.

She crossed her arms and took a step backwards. Then she sighed loudly and said, "Somebody's been trying to kill me."

"What? Why?" He now looked more confused than ever.

"Detective Lynch has been trying to find that out."

"Saffron, I think we need to go."

"Go where? Where are you trying to take her?" Ranjan moved past Saffron and faced Lynch.

Saffron turned around. Nobody spoke for a few seconds. The two men stared at each other. Saffron thought about walking by Ranjan and leaving with Darcy, but her feet were planted on the floor.

"Saffron?"

She heard Darcy's voice. It was deep, raspy, as if he had been talking a long time. She wanted to go back to his place. Go back to half an hour ago, when she had been in his arms, kissing him. Ranjan turned and took her hand. She almost jumped. She shook it off and shoved both hands in her jeans pockets.

"I can take care of her," Ranjan said to Darcy. "You can go now."

He scoffed audibly. Saffron almost smiled. She saw Ranjan's chest fill up as if he were a peacock ready to fight.

"It's okay," she finally said to Darcy. "I'll call you later."

He hesitated. "You want to stay?"

She nodded. He turned around and left without looking back.

"I'll call you in a little bit," she repeated.

She regretted not leaving with him, but she needed to stay.

Ranjan closed the door, as if he were severing a tie between Saffron and Darcy he didn't want to think about.

"I love you, Saffron." He hugged her. "I've missed you so much."

Her hands were still deep in her pockets. She pushed herself away from him and walked to the sofa, stepping on the popcorn salting the floor. Cat jumped on her lap and purred and sniffed her hands, probably smelling Darcy's new dog. Ranjan sat by her, a little too close. She moved further away. He noticed and put a hand on her shoulder, as if trying to regain some of the intimacy they'd lost.

"Please don't," she said and twisted her body enough for his hand to slip away. "Why aren't you with your uncle? Why aren't you with one of those women?"

"They don't mean anything to me, can't you see that?"

He tried touching her but once again she moved away.

"We're done, Ranjan. You had your chance and you chose to make your family happy."

"Saffron, do you remember when your brother invited us to dinner a few months ago?"

She nodded, grossed out already that he could even compare that situation to his. He went on, ignoring her facial expression.

"He was nervous through the entire meal and finally, when we got dessert, he blurted out that he was going to go through the sex change."

"What the hell does this have to do with anything?"

She set Cat to the side, turned to face him and crossed her legs to create some extra distance between them.

"He was really worried that you would judge him."

"I'd never do that."

"But he was still worried. And then he wanted you to break it to your parents, because he couldn't do it, even though he's your older brother."

"Sean's my younger brother," she said, shaking her head, disappointed he couldn't even remember that. "What's your point, Ranjan?"

"All I'm trying to say is that it's really hard to tell something to a parent who expects something different from you. I know your parents weren't happy about Sean's decision, but they're still supportive."

"Of course they were."

"Well, that's the difference between you and me. My family can't imagine how I could be in love with somebody who's not from our culture, who doesn't understand or follow our conventions. They don't understand how it could ever work with somebody who is not Hindu."

She didn't look at him. Her face was frozen, with tight jaw muscles.

"I had to make my uncle believe that I was trying. Once I did, I could then talk to my family and convince them that you are the one I love."

He grabbed her left foot and pulled it toward him. Once she stopped fighting him, he started massaging it.

CHAPTER 69

Saturday

Tyler Warren tossed one more time in his huge bed. The Tempur-Pedic mattress followed his body, making him feel as if he hadn't moved at all. His eyes were dry. He hadn't been able to sleep, even though he had taken a large dose of Ambien.

Harper Johnson was dead. Tyler traced all of his steps, all of his meetings with him in his mind one more time. The pre-paid phones. The only two places they had normally interacted were the support group and the shooting range. Both inconsequential enough, he thought. He decided to not worry about anybody remembering him at the dive bar, where he had made Harper the proposition.

The money he'd given him couldn't be traced to any of his accounts, as he'd used the cash he'd withdrawn from his account in the Caymans months before this whole thing had started. He didn't know how much the police knew. He wished he knew somebody in the department or at least the news would share more.

He turned around one more time and heard the phone rang.

"What's up, sis?" His voice was hoarse. He swallowed hard. He didn't want to deal with her but knew it would be worse to avoid her.

"Tell me you didn't have anything to do with that." she yelled into the phone.

He almost dropped it, startled by her intensity.

"With what exactly?"

He sat on the bed, suddenly feeling the heat of the morning sun coming in through the blinds.

"The massacre at coffee shop!" Her shouts pierced his eardrum.

"Please calm down."

He got out of bed and put on a pair of black light wool pants.

"You told me you were dealing with a guy named Harper. The asshole who killed all those people is also a Harper. Is it the same guy?" she asked, but her voice had lost its force.

Tyler figured she probably didn't want to know. "Yes."

"Oh my god, Tyler. What have you done?"

"Nothing has changed. Do you understand me? We're working really hard to find the cure for cancer. We're very close and nothing can stop that, or many more people are going to die." He paused but realized he needed to hammer the point home. "Remember how much Anne struggled? Think of everybody you see coming through your office every day, how much they suffer, how much their loved ones suffer because of this disease." He heard her cry on the other side. "Sis, we're going to find the cure, I swear to you. We just need a little bit more time. And I need your help."

She still didn't say anything.

"Let me come over. I'll make you grandma's blueberry pancakes."

She didn't say no.

CHAPTER 70

Darcy woke up to the sound of the alarm clock. He had fallen asleep with the phone by the pillow in case Saffron called asking for a ride back to his place. But she hadn't called. Not once since he left her with that loser ex-boyfriend. *Or maybe boyfriend again*, he thought.

After the shower and a strong cup of coffee, Darcy headed to the office and was surprised to find both Jon and Sorensen already there, even though it wasn't eight in the morning yet.

"Did you guys work all night?"

"No. Dr. Leavenworth is coming this morning to answer more questions," Jon said, not raising his eyes from the computer screen.

"That easy?" Darcy asked, surprised.

"With her lawyer," Sorensen added.

"Ah." Darcy sat on Sorensen's visitor's chair. "Is she good for this?" he asked, looking at the whiteboard.

"She's the best we've got so far."

"But that doesn't make her guilty," Darcy said.

"I know," Sorensen conceded, and Jon looked up and watched both detectives.

They all fell silent.

"So this is where the party is, then?" Rachel said, leaning on the doorframe.

A few other detectives walked in behind her. It was going to be a busy Saturday.

"Always." Sorensen's voice was flat. "Give us some good news," he pleaded.

"I have confirmation that Harper Johnson's DNA matches the DNA on the gloves you found in his car, and the pleather pieces we found under the car of Jacqueline Pritchard and between Emma Hughes' teeth seem consistent with pieces missing on the gloves."

"Yes." Darcy punched the desk with his fist.

"Consistent?" Sorensen asked, pooping the party.

"That's the best I can do. They look very close, but I can't be a hundred percent sure, as there is a small section that is missing from the Hughes' piece, and the gloves have more wear, so the edges of the missing pieces on the gloves have softened a little." She pulled out the photographs she'd brought to show them.

"They look close enough to me," Sorensen said, pushing away the photos. "We still don't know why he did it," he added.

"I have something else," Rachel said.

"This good?" Darcy asked.

"Maybe." She flashed a coy smile. "Mauricio confirmed that the rifle our guys found in Johnson's car had been fired in the last twenty-four to forty-eight hours, and the caliber is consistent to what was used to kill David Jameson at the hunting park."

"No fucking way," Sorensen said. "So you've now closed all of your cases?"

He slouched in his chair, defeated.

Darcy looked at his board. "Yep," he said, satisfied. To hammer the pointe, he said, "I keep telling you, Rachel, you're the best."

306

She beamed.

"Do you have anything for me?" Pouting as a little kid who didn't get picked to play dodge ball, Sorensen squeezed his stress ball and looked at her.

"Unfortunately, that's all I've got today." She looked down at her hands, then added, "You know, Detective Sorensen, there's little I can do with your suicides, because there's no evidence of foul play."

When she walked out of the room, her shoulders were a little hunched over, making her smaller than she already was.

CHAPTER 71

"You know what?" Sorensen told Darcy after Rachel left. "You can keep that smug face all you want, but you still don't have motive. You're not done."

"Why are you so bitter? You should be happy for me."

"Prick," Sorensen said under his breath.

"Now I have extra time to help you with yours," Darcy teased.

"I thought you quit. Shouldn't you be leaving your badge and your gun with the captain?"

Jon watched them banter from behind his computer screen. Then stood as soon as Dr. Leavenworth and her lawyer walk into the room. Sorensen got up and escorted them to the closest interview room.

Darcy and Jon followed and entered the adjacent room so they could watch Sorensen in action.

"Would you like something to drink?" he asked.

They both said no.

"I appreciate you coming back this morning." His sarcasm was only barely noticeable.

Dr. Leavenworth rolled her eyes, and Wilmore patted her hand before he said, "Detective, let's get to the point."

"Mr. Wilmore, there are already thirteen victims in this case, and every hour we seem to find more. They're all dead but one, and that one's only alive because of pure luck. I would imagine that you'd want your client to help us solve this case." The intensity of his blue eyes burnt. "Especially when they are all connected to her."

"Only because they are, were, my patients," she protested.

"So what were you doing to them?"

"Nothing." She raised her voice and her body stiffened. "How many times do I have to tell you?"

"Where did you meet Harper Johnson?" Sorensen said, changing the subject.

"I don't know this man."

"Don't lie to me. I know you do. He's personally responsible for killing Jacqueline Pritchard, Emma Hughes and David Jameson and for trying to kill Saffron Meadows. And we are close to connecting him to a few other homicides."

"I'm very sorry they are dead, Detective, but I don't know why they are dead, and I certainly don't know who Harper Johnson is." Her voice was low now, almost apologetic.

"Why did you want these people dead?"

"Detective, please stop. Either you treat my client with the respect she deserves, or we walk out of here until you have an arrest warrant."

Sorensen pushed his chair away from the table, then said, "I'll be right back. I need some coffee."

He left the room and walked next door to see Darcy and Jon.

"I need something to rattle this woman." He passed his large sweaty hand over his face, and left.

With a full, steaming cup, he came back to check. "Anything?"

Darcy shook his head.

Jon, with his typical shy voice, said, "I'm not sure this would help, but I've been reading a lot about doctors."

Both detectives stared at him.

"Maybe she was volunteering her patients to some start-up with an experimental drug? Not sure how that connects the murder victims, but maybe you can push something on that end for the suicides?"

Darcy looked up at Sorensen and saw his face light up.

Jon took the cue and continued: "Doctors enticing patients to participate in experimental drugs is quite common."

"Maybe she was getting kickbacks from a start-up?" Darcy suggested.

Sorensen walked toward Jon, who was the only one sitting down and seemed very small against him, then punched his shoulder.

"Dude, you're truly brilliant."

He turned to get back to his interview. Before he left the room, he said, looking over his shoulder, "So, what are you doing still here? Go dig into it."

Jon leaped out of his chair and sneaked through the small opening left between the doorframe and Sorensen's body.

"You're going to have to hire that kid full-time," Darcy said once Jon was out of earshot.

"First thing on Monday, I'll sit in Virago's office until she signs the papers."

Back in the interview room, Sorensen set the cup on the table but didn't sit. He paced the length of the room without looking at the doctor or his lawyer. Then he stopped right in front of Leavenworth and placed his massive hands on the table, closer to her than to himself. Leaning forward, he asked, "How much are they paying you?"

Doctor Leavenworth looked at her attorney.

"What are you talking about?" he asked for her.

"How much are you getting for using your patients as guinea pigs?"

"I have never!" she said, standing up and crossing her arms, as if that would make her bigger against Sorensen.

"Let me tell you what I know." He sat down, his eye level with hers. "I know that you convinced Juliette Davis, Taisha Robinson, Sheila Rothschild and Sonia McCarthy to participate in a fucked-up human trial."

"Detective," Wilmore objected, raising his hand, as if that would protect his client from foul language.

"You should advise your client that things will go much better for her if she cooperates and tells us what the company she's in cahoots with is," he said to the lawyer, never breaking eye contact with Leavenworth.

"I don't know what you're talking about," she said, still standing up. "This is ridiculous."

"Doctor, they're all your patients. You need to stop lying to us." When she didn't respond but pursed her lips tighter, he went on: "I know the trial went wrong somewhere, because they're all dead and they all died the same way. And I know it was easy to convince them to participate in the experimental trial, because they needed a sliver of hope because they all had cancer."

"You're wrong, Detective. Sonia McCarthy didn't have cancer."

CHAPTER 72

Darcy called Jon and asked him to bring him the McCarthy file. Less than a minute later he came with it and settled beside Lynch. He continued his research while the detective skimmed through the ME's report. Darcy couldn't find anything indicating the victim had cancer, so he called Madison putting the phone on speaker.

"If you do an autopsy on a suicide victim, is it standard procedure to note any findings of cancer?"

"Good morning to you too, Detective Lynch."

Darcy exchanged glances with Jon.

"Good morning, Dr. Madison. How's your morning so far?" Darcy asked, trying to hide his frustration.

"Busy, very busy."

"I have a question for you. We're in the middle of interrogating a person of interest in the multiple suicide case, and I would really appreciate your help."

Jon smiled back at Darcy.

"MEs should note everything they find. Including cancer." Dr. Madison said. "Sometimes it's easy to miss because it may be really small, but the complete physical state of the victim should be thoroughly described."

Darcy thought for a few seconds. "But there were no entries about cancer in any of the suicide victims' reports." He tried to not sound accusatory.

"That's because every one of them had essentially performed a self-mastectomy, removing the affected section of the tissue. You have to remember that some of these lumps might only be a few millimeters in diameter. Even if they were a few centimeters in size, if CSU didn't collect all of the tissue, there would be no way for us to find it."

"Makes sense. Thank you, Doctor. This is very helpful."

He hung up the phone and dialed again.

"Hey, Danielson, Lynch here."

"Whoa, two calls in one week," the Seattle detective said. "I never knew you missed me so much."

"You have no idea. You heard of the coffee shop massacre?"

"That you?"

"Yep."

"I don't envy your captain. That was some ugly shit there. Anyway, what's up?"

"Do you remember if Sonia McCarthy had cancer? There's nothing on the ME report."

Silence filled the room. Darcy looked at Jon and crossed his fingers.

"It never came up," Danielson responded.

"Do you think your ME could have missed it?"

"Gabriella Campellini? Are you kidding?"

"She's still around? Jesus, what is she, about a hundred years old now?" He laughed, remembering his old ME.

"I think she's probably closer to a hundred fifty. But yep, she's still around."

"That woman will never retire," Darcy said, still smiling.

"Let me double-check with her and make a few calls to the victim's family, and I'll get back to you later today."

"We're interviewing a person of interest as we speak."

"Got it. I'll get back to you in less than thirty."

"I owe you."

"You always say that. About time you start paying up," he said, and Darcy could feel the smile on the other end.

Darcy called Sorensen out of the interview room. Sorensen excused himself.

"Are we close to done, Detective?" Wilmore asked before he left.

"No, we're not."

"My client has been cooperating from the very beginning. This is getting really close to harassment," Wilmore protested.

Darcy watched Sorensen wave a hand in dismissal. The attorney sat back and looked as if he'd been punched in the gut. Dr. Leavenworth whispered something to him when Sorensen turned and closed the door behind him.

"It better be good," he said, still hoping for a Hail Mary.

Lynch shared his conversations with the ME and the Seattle detective.

"How does this help me?" Sorensen passed a beefy hand over his tired face. Blond strands came lose and dropped back into his eyes as his hand moved backwards. "I really need a haircut."

Nobody responded. The only noises were the faint humming of the air conditioning and Jon's fingers tapping the laptop's keyboard.

CHAPTER 73

Saffron woke up from a deep sleep. She felt a smile grow as soon as she remembered the kiss. It had been soft, yet full of hunger. She'd felt his pull, his energy and his desire. She closed her eyes and rolled to her side, wanting to relive the moment. Just when she was about to feel his lips on hers, her memory screeched to a halt.

"Wakey-wakey. I made coffee," Ranjan said.

"What the hell?" she murmured to herself. She had totally forgotten he'd spent the night.

"Your sofa is really comfortable," he said, sitting beside her on the bed. "But of course I would've preferred to have slept here with you."

He patted the sheets. She didn't move, her back to him.

"Are you still mad at me?"

"You're a rocket scientist," she said just loud enough for him to hear.

"Sweetie, I love you. I made you coffee. I slept on the sofa. I'm doing everything you want me to do, and I'll continue doing so until you forgive me."

She got out of bed, self-conscious for wearing shorts that showed her long legs. She pulled her hair into a knot and walked by him toward the bathroom. She felt him watching her as she walked away, and it almost crept her out. Saffron started the shower and locked the door. She didn't want him sneaking in thinking he had an invitation.

She thought about Ranjan, how he had talked nonstop about how good they were together and how his family would understand. The conversation lasted hours, and she had been exhausted by the time she managed to make him shut up. It had been past three in the morning. Too late to call Darcy, so she had let Ranjan sleep on the sofa, mostly because she was too afraid to be alone. Now, she regretted the whole thing and just wished she had left him there, with the popcorn and a bad movie, and gone back to Darcy's place.

When Saffron got out of the shower she heard the TV. Ranjan was watching the news.

"Your coffee's getting cold," he yelled from the other room.

She put on some jeans, a T-shirt and was zipping a hoodie when she entered the living room.

"Ranjan, it's over. I'm sorry, but it is."

He placed his mug on the coffee table and turned the TV off. He stood up and walked toward her, then grabbed her hands. She met his eyes. They were sad. His lips were turned downward. She looked away. He led her back to the sofa and she sat down. He did the same, facing her.

"Saffron, I know you're hurt." He shook his head and re-phrased: "No, I know I hurt you. This arranged marriage thing is something really important to my family. But, when I saw your face in the hospital room after you'd seen those photos...You looked so wounded."

She listened, even though she'd heard everything last night.

"I just needed time to make things right with my uncle. Convince him that I love you so he can help me with my family back home."

"It's too late, Ranjan. I'm sorry."

"But why? It's only been a couple days. I can't believe we can't work this out."

"We've had this fight one too many times." She met his eyes, but he looked away. "Ranjan, too many things have happened in the last couple days. I can't be with you anymore."

"But all of those incredible times we've had together, they have to count for something. We can go back to that, I promise."

She shook her head, but before she could say anything, he pleaded again. She crossed her arms.

"I'm sorry," Saffron said before she stood and walked to the door.

He pleaded one more time, probably knowing it was futile. He then went through the door and left without another word. She closed it and then saw his jacket.

"Ranjan," she yelled after him.

He turned, an expression of hope on his face, a little shine in his eyes that darkened the minute he saw the jacket hanging from her hand.

He murmured "Thank you" when he grabbed it and turned back toward the elevator.

Saffron wondered if she would regret her decision. She shook her head and decided she wouldn't.

After she dried her hair, she left to get some real coffee from Starbucks at the corner of San Pedro and Santa Clara. She always enjoyed the walk. It was only a few blocks away, but just long enough to get the blood flowing. The air was crisp but not quite cold. Saffron pulled out her phone and started dialing Darcy's number. She figured he would be up by now. Before she managed to enter the last couple digits, the screen turned black, the shutdown spinner rotated a few times and the phone went dead.

317

"Crap, forgot to charge it," she said out loud, shoving her cellphone into her back pocket.

The line was rather long at Starbucks. A shiver ran through her back and she forced herself to shake the memories of the last time she had been in a queue waiting to get a decent latte. She looked down at her shoes and then decided the mugs and trinkets they had on the shelves next to her were the most interesting thing she'd ever seen. She grabbed a few, inspected them, checked the price of each, put it back, grabbed the next one. The line moved forward, and she took a step closer to the cashier.

"Saffron?" a woman's voice asked from behind.

She looked but didn't recognize her.

"It's Julia, Dr. Leavenworth's assistant."

She had beautiful large black eyes and short, unruly hair. Large silver hoops dangled from her ears.

"Yes, of course. Sorry about that." Saffron let the man standing between them go before her.

"I totally understand. It's hard to recognize people out of context."

"You live around here?"

"Yes, a few blocks north, actually."

"Me too. How funny that we're neighbors and we never knew," Saffron said.

They chatted about the neighborhood while they inched toward the beginning of the line. Once they got their drinks, they started walking in the same direction.

"I'm just amazed at how well they've fixed up San Pedro Square," Saffron said.

"And I'm still bitter that they do the farmers' market on Fridays. Who has time to go on a weekday?"

Saffron agreed.

"By the way, I would love to ask your opinion on something," Julia said. "Girl to girl."

"Sure."

"Do you mind walking with me to my car? It's parked in the garage, on the second floor."

Saffron nodded, and they headed up the stairs like two new friends catching up on life.

"I bought this necklace for a fund-raiser I'm going to next weekend, and I'm not really sure I like it. I could use a second opinion."

"Absolutely. Glad to help."

The second level of the parking was almost empty. There was a red Mini Cooper close to the elevator and a couple other cars spread out throughout the floor. Julia led the way toward a bluish SUV parked closer to the stairs. They walked around the car to the passenger door. Julia reached into the console between the two seats, found the jewelry box, and handed it to Saffron.

She took it and started opening it, but from the corner of her eye she saw something shine in Julia's other hand. Saffron opened the box but instead of looking inside, she raised her eyes. Before she could react, her new friend pushed her against the car with her forearm and pricked her neck with a needle.

"What are you…?" Saffron asked before she lost consciousness.

CHAPTER 74

Lynch got a call back from Detective Danielson. The doctor had lied again. Sonia McCarthy did have cancer and had been scheduled to have it removed a month after she died. Sorensen scratched his head and looked over to the doctor and her lawyer on the other side of the one-way mirror. They seemed composed, almost bored, though the doctor's right leg twitched under the table.

"I wonder if she lied because she's hiding something or because she's a bad doctor who can't get the right diagnosis," Sorensen said, still looking at them.

Darcy remained silent.

"False negatives do happen," Jon offered without looking up from his computer screen. "It wouldn't be her fault. It would be the lab's."

Sorensen exchanged a look with Darcy. Then they both got sidetracked by movement in the other room. The doctor said something and then she and her lawyer got up.

"You're about to lose them," Darcy said.

Sorensen jumped from his chair and went to meet them.

"We're not done here," he said, opening the door.

"Yes we are. We've been here for over an hour. If you need to reach Dr. Leavenworth, please make sure you give me a call and we'll be happy to oblige. In the meantime we're leaving."

He pointed to the door for Dr. Leavenworth to go first. Sorensen blocked the exit.

"Detective," Wilmore said.

Sorensen tried to hide his disappointment with a silent sigh and moved out of the way. He looked into the mirror, trying to find Darcy's eyes, even though he couldn't see anything but his own reflection in a now-empty room.

Sorensen and Darcy met in the hallway and walked together to the bullpen.

"I damn well hope the kid finds something," Sorensen said.

"Me too. Because I don't want to be the only one stuck doing paperwork all weekend."

"Stop rubbing in that you've closed your cases."

Sorensen shook his head and left to get some snacks. A minute later he came back beaming.

"Can you believe we got Twinkies back in the vending machine? It's been ages since we've had them."

He waved the package around as if expecting the smell to seep through the plastic wrapper.

"You're going to have a heart attack one of these days," Darcy murmured loud enough for him to hear.

"Whatever." He gulfed a half Twinkie in one bite.

Darcy sat and started working on his final report on Harper Johnson's case. He put his phone on the table and noticed that he had a voice mail. He didn't recognize the number. He pressed the Play button and listened. "Detective Lynch, Alton Lane here," the message started. "I was on one of my walks yesterday and I saw a car go into Harper Johnson's property. I wouldn't have thought too much about it, but then I saw it come back this morning again. I'm sure...anything, but... know...the car...H4."

Darcy listened to the message again to see if he could pick up more pieces, but the coverage by Lane's property had been too poor. He made a note to call him later. Harper Johnson didn't have family or friends, let alone visitors.

"Jon?" Darcy heard Sorensen say.

Jon ignored him and ran to the printer to pick up several pieces of paper. Then he waved them in the air to get their attention. A couple other detectives looked up, semi-curious, but went back to what they were doing before Jon started to talk. Lynch and Sorensen pulled their chairs closer to Jon.

"Well, I should do more research, because you never know, but this could be a start," Jon said, facing the two detectives. "I was able to find seventeen start-ups in Silicon Valley that are doing some type of work with cancer. Out of those, four are related to breast cancer specifically. Two of them are still in stealth mode. That leaves us two."

"Why wouldn't we look into the stealth ones?" Darcy asked.

"Too early," Jon explained. "They are too young to be doing human trials. They probably haven't even started working on animals yet. Besides, they're in complete secrecy, so they won't share anything with us unless we have a legal order."

"Tell us about the other two," Sorensen said.

Jon looked through his printed notes until he found what he was looking for. Reading from the page, he said, "One is Nodal Labs. They are investigating the spread of cancer into the lymph nodes." He looked up and saw the two detectives exchange glances. "About a month ago, they announced a huge cash injection due to receiving the FDA approval to proceed to human trials."

"Doesn't sound too promising." Darcy said.

Sorensen leaned back in his chair and crossed his arms over his large torso. "I shouldn't have let the doctor leave." He cursed.

"The other one, Curarent Tech, is a bit more tricky. They came out of stealth mode barely a year ago. They've completed the first set of animal trials with very successful results, but I can't find any else about them. Not sure if that's good or bad."

"What do you mean?" Darcy asked.

"Well, if the trials were so successful, why haven't they got more funding, like Nodal Labs did? Why aren't they on the news or in medical journals bragging about how they're doing?"

"Maybe they want to keep it quiet?" Darcy asked.

"No. That's someting they would want to adverise."

He looked through the papers as if he had missed something that would answer his questions.

"Feel like a field trip?" Sorensen asked Lynch.

"You expect to find anybody in the office? It's Saturday," Lynch said, shutting down his computer.

"In Silicon Valley everybody works 24-7, don't you know that?"

"I thought that was only true for law enforcement," Darcy said, looking around at the full office.

"Now you know better."

"Jon," Darcy said, "send us as much dirt as you can on these two companies. Investors, board of directors, employees, where they went to school, whether they are married, have debt, where they vacation, whatever you can find."

"Which one should I start on? This will take a while."

"The second one," Lynch and Sorensen said in unison.

CHAPTER 75

Saffron opened her eyes. She was disoriented, and it took her a few seconds to focus. Julia was standing to her right.

She felt a hand slap her cheek. "C'mon, wake up. I don't have time for this," Julia said, hitting Saffron's face again.

Then she remembered the needle prick and screamed. But nothing more than a low grunt came out. Her mouth was taped. Saffron tried to move, but she was tightly secured by the seat belt. Her hands were tied behind her back. Both arms were almost asleep all the way to her shoulders. Her feet were restrained with silver duct tape, but they were at least half a foot apart. She tried kicking, but all she managed to do was bruise her shins against the dashboard.

"Saffron, I need you to listen to me," Julia said once Saffron had stopped kicking.

Saffron started squirming inside the car, trying to free herself.

"I don't have a lot of time and you're pissing me off, so quit that shit and listen to me."

Julia took a few steps back and pointed a gun at her. Saffron stopped, her eyes fixed on the muzzle, were wild with fear. Her nostrils flared with every exhalation.

"You're going to twist toward me and use your hands to click the seat belt open."

Saffron tried and succeeded on the fourth attempt.

"Now you're going to get out of the car." She stopped. Saffron didn't move. "Let me say this again: you're going to get out of the car. *Now*," she yelled, inciting the first move.

Saffron pushed herself to the edge of the seat and then swung her feet out of the car. The SUV was a little too high, and she almost fell from the car when she was trying to reach the ground. She managed to recover some balance and finally stood, shaking, in front of Julia.

"Good girl. Now you're going to head toward the house."

She took her first step. The tape only allowed her to advance half a foot at a time. Julia turned, following her movement with the barrel of her gun. Once Julia was behind her, Saffron couldn't stop herself from looking back, challenging her balance one more time. She finally reached the stairs of the house. She tried to climb the first stair, but the duct tape was too short. She planted her foot back on the ground and waited for further instructions.

Julia came closer.

"Turn around and sit on the landing. Swing your legs around and then get up."

Saffron looked at her as if she were crazy. She shook her head and shrieked, trying to make a noise that would translate to something like "Just cut the dumb tape and let me walk up like a normal person." But Julia didn't budge. After a few seconds of deadlock, Saffron knew she wasn't going to win. She turned around and did as she was told.

Saffron had a hard time getting up again without the help of her hands. Julia just watched and puffed as if annoyed that she wasn't doing it faster. Once she was standing, Julia passed by her and opened the door.

"Come on, go in." She said waiving the gun.

The place was sparse and tidy. Saffron stood by the door, wondering if she had a sliver of a chance to escape, but with her feet tied she knew she didn't. Julia walked to the dining table and moved it, not bothering to pull the chairs out of the way first. Then she hauled an old dusty rug to the side, and Saffron saw a trapdoor.

Julia opened it and said, "What are you waiting for?"

Saffron stood where she was. Only darkness came from inside the hole.

"I have ten bullets in this gun. I would only shoot your leg, though, and let you bleed out. So don't piss me off and go down."

Julia had moved into the open kitchen. She leaned on the stove. Saffron walked forward and saw a set of wooden stairs leading to a black abyss. Before she descended, she looked back at Julia, begging her to cut the tape on her ankles.

"Hop down. You'll be fine."

Saffron stared back at the woman who'd been so kind and gentle in every one of her visits to Dr. Leavenworth's office. She'd held her hand and told her she would be okay, that the lump she had in her breast was not cancer and that she would be okay.

"Go on!" Julia yelled.

Saffron faced the stairs straight on and got closer to the edge, then she tried reaching the first step, but Julia was right, her foot didn't quite make it. She brought it back and jumped. The wood creaked. She feared it would break under her weight, but it didn't. After she managed to regain some composure and her heartbeat slowed down a little, she took another hop. Then another. She jumped a little too far forward, so when she landed on the third step. She lost her balance. She moved forward and almost fell, but then forced herself to lean backwards, pushing all of her weight on her heels. After a few more swings, she managed to stand still. She was breathing so fast she thought she might hyperventilate.

Saffron looked back at Julia, but the woman's eyes only returned a heartless glare. She stared down, trying to make out how many more stairs were waiting for her, but she couldn't see the end. There was too much light coming through the windows, and her eyes couldn't adjust to the dimness of the basement.

She hopped the next step few steps without incident. Gaining confidence, she jumped a little faster. But then, she hit a step that was a little narrower than the rest, and slid when her heels didn't manage to ground themselves on it. She flew over it. Her feet banging into the steps as she slid down crushing her arms and hands, tied to her back, until she reached the ground.

Saffron didn't get up. She felt sore and everything hurt, including her head. She was sure she'd broken at least a couple fingers. She started to cry. *Why not kill me right away? Why make me go through this misery?* she asked herself.

"Oh, for God's sakes." Julia said and started going down the stairs. Each step was heavy, as if she were making a point to land with all of her weight on each one.

There was a click, and her eyes went blind. Julia had turned the basement light on. Saffron blinked a few times, trying to adjust to the new brightness. When she finally managed to keep her eyes open for a few seconds, what she saw made her heart stop.

CHAPTER 76

Darcy drove north on 101 toward Palo Alto. All they had was the address of the cancer research start-up. As Jon found out information, he texted it to Sorensen's phone.

"You know my cases are related to yours, right?" Darcy asked, passing a silver BMW in the left lane driving at the speed limit.

"Yep," Sorensen said, refreshing the phone one more time. "I don't know how, I don't know why, but I do know they are."

"It still bothers me that I can't figure out how Harper Johnson is the glue to all of this," Darcy accelerated. "Why would he kill all of these people?"

"Weren't you the one who found the eighty grand?"

Darcy gave him a quick glance. "This guy's a loner. Has no friends, no family, nothing to really need or want eighty thousand dollars for."

"Except greed," Sorensen said. A new text popped up. "Okay, when we get there, we should talk to the CEO, Tyler Warren, or ask for the lead researcher. Somebody named Qiang Li."

"What did you say the name of the CEO was?"

Sorensen repeated it. Darcy pulled his black notebook and opened the piece of paper Elena had given him. Handing it to Sorensen, he said, "Isn't there a Tyler in that list?"

Sorensen read through it. "Yep. What's this?"

"The list of regulars who go to Harper's support group. It may be a coincidence, but Tyler is not a very common name."

A few minutes later they pulled into the parking lot in front of a two-story building. It had large windows and was painted white. The logo of the company was pasted on the façade on the top floor. The full name was also engraved on the entrance glass doors: "Curarent Tech."

The parking lot was almost full.

"You were right. It looks like a lot of dedicated people work here," Darcy said, looking around.

"I told you. If you work in a start-up in the Valley, your home is your office."

Darcy looked at him. "You mean, it's like us but with the potential of becoming millionaires?"

"Exactly."

Darcy felt suddenly depressed thinking of all of his colleagues who worked around the clock, risking their lives on a daily basis, and all they could aspire to was retiring with a pension of only a percentage of their salary. He shook the thought and followed Sorensen toward the big glass doors. They were locked. Sorensen found a bell and pressed it. There was a buzz followed by a click, and the door unlocked. They went to the front desk, where a bored security guard waited for them. Sorensen pulled out his badge and showed it to him.

"Good morning, Sebastian," he said, reading the guard's name tag. "Detective Sorensen and Detective Lynch here to see Tyler Warren."

Sebastian typed several commands on the computer and after a few seconds said, "Mr. Warren's not in the office today."

"Can you tell us where he is?" Sorensen pressed.

The security guard looked at him as if he were crazy. He then rolled his eyes and looked at Lynch, expecting some understanding.

"Is Qiang Li here?" Sorensen asked after rechecking Jon's text for the exact name.

The guard repeated the same operation he had done before, then said, "Yes, she is."

Darcy stared at the security guard, expecting him to pick up the phone, but he didn't move.

Sorensen murmured "For God's sakes." Then, louder, "We need to talk to her. Where can we find her?"

"You cannot walk in without an invitation from somebody who works for Curarent Tech. The research they're doing is very important and very secret."

"I'm sorry, you didn't see the badge?" Sorensen asked. "It's a real badge, not like yours. So tell me where she is, or I'll go find her myself."

Darcy hid a smirk, though he was mostly embarrassed. He watched Sebastian taking a long look at Sorensen. This was his turf. He had power in this place, and he wanted the cops to know it.

"Sebastian, this is an urgent matter," Darcy explained. "Please page Miss Li or tell us where we can find her."

The guard snapped out of his feud with Sorensen and picked up the phone. He murmured into it and then hung up.

"Take the elevator to the second floor. She'll meet you there."

They did as instructed, but Sorensen couldn't help but look back.

Lynch said, "Quit it. How old are you, ten?"

"No respect for the brass, man."

The doors opened, and they exchanged a look. A child in a lab coat extended her hand toward nobody in particular and said, "Dr. Qiang Li."

Her bangs were long and pricked her eyes, making her blink constantly. Darcy moved in front of her first and shook a limp hand while he introduced himself, then Sorensen did the same.

"How can I help you, Detectives?" Her accent was strong. She didn't move but blinked almost uncontrollably.

Darcy had to fight the urge to move her bangs away from her eyes.

"Could we go to your office? It may be a better place to talk than the elevator hall."

"Yes, of course."

She turned and started walking away. Sorensen threw another look at Lynch and followed her. After a few feet, she stopped in front of a door with the name of the company etched into the metal door and a badge reader by its side. She swiped her name tag, and the reader cracked open. A fingerprint detector appeared. She pushed her index finger toward the smooth surface until the light turned from red to green. The door opened to a large reception area with a nice view of Silicon Valley.

"These doors are normally open during business hours, but not on the weekends," Qiang Li explained.

They passed the reception area, and Darcy and Sorensen trailed the woman through a set of sterile, white hallways with beige doors on each side. Finally, she stopped in front of one with a tag bearing her name. She swiped her badge again, no fingerprint this time, and they all walked into a spacious office overlooking a construction site. Her desk was glass, and two large computer monitors stood side by side to the left. She pointed at the black leather chairs as she sat opposite them.

"What can I help you with?" she said and blinked numerous times.

"We understand that you're doing cancer research, right?" Lynch asked.

"Yes."

"What kind?"

"Activation immunotherapy."

She finally moved the bangs to the side, but they moved right back into her eyes.

"Are you focusing on any specific type of cancer?"

Sorensen shifted in his chair. The leather squeaked.

"Ductal carcinoma."

Darcy wondered if she was a woman of a few words because she was shy of her accent or because she thought they were both too stupid to understand what she was working on.

"Are you close?" Sorensen asked.

Qiang Li blushed and looked out the window. Was she trying to hide that they were close to finding something life altering? It felt more like they weren't close at all, and that was a secret worthy of keeping away from investors.

"We've had very positive results so far," she said, now looking from one detective to the other.

"So I heard," Darcy cut in. "But not for a while, right?"

She was silent, staring back out the window.

"Any human trials yet?" Sorensen asked.

Her little frame stiffened on the large chair. She closed her eyes and took a deep breath.

"Detectives, I find it surprising that you're here because you are curious about my research. Can you tell me why you wanted to talk to me?"

"Routine, really." Sorensen leaned back on his chair, letting her know they weren't going anywhere. "We're investigating a set of deaths related to cancer."

Qiang Li fell quiet again. Darcy could see her brain work at incredible speed.

Finally, blinking again, she said, "Unfortunately, I can't tell you much about our research, because even though we're not in stealth mode anymore, we're still held under extreme secrecy rules, both internal and for our investors." She locked eyes with Lynch. "But you can ask me anything you want and if I can answer, I will."

"Have you started human trials yet?"

"No."

"Will you be ready soon?" Sorensen pushed.

She stared at him, hesitating again. "Maybe." She finally said, as honestly as she could.

"Is the company doing well financially?" Darcy asked.

"You'll need to talk to Mr. Warren or Miss Fabruko about that. I don't get involved with those things."

"Are they here?"

"I'm not sure. You can ask the security guard downstairs to page them for you."

"Can you try their office from here?" Sorensen insisted.

She exhaled nosily but picked up the phone. Neither answered.

"Cell phones?" Sorensen pressed.

She made the first call.

"Tyler, I've got two detectives here who'd like to speak with you. Are you coming to the office today?"

Neither detective could hear what the CEO was saying.

"I don't know," she said into the phone. A few seconds later she ended the call after saying, "Okay, I will."

Darcy and Sorensen looked at her expectantly.

She blinked and said, "He told me to give you his number. He's unavailable for most of the day, but you can leave a message, and he'll call back when he can."

Sorensen smirked. She saw it.

Fabruko didn't answer the phone, so she left her a voice mail. Both detectives asked her a few more questions, but they didn't lead to anything. Shortly after, she walked them out.

Back in the car, Darcy called Jon.

"Hey, quick question. Can you check what Mr. Tyler likes to do with his free time? Call me back as soon as you've found out."

Sorensen stared at Lynch.

"Well, if he's too busy to be at the office like most of his employees, he may be playing golf or something. Or what? You rather wait until he calls us back?

Sorensen fastened his seat belt and looked straight out the front window of Darcy's car.

"I was really hoping to get something here. What next? The other company?" he asked, his voice dull and lower than normal.

Before Darcy had a chance to get out of the parking lot, Jon called.

"Thanks, dude, you're the man," Darcy said and hung up. "Nope, it looks like we just found an interesting coincidence. Wanna do some shooting?"

CHAPTER 77

Tyler was trying not to speed down Highway 17. He was waiting for the phone to ring again and kept watching it, as if that would make it ring faster, keeping only one eye on the road. When it finally did, he clicked his earpiece on.

"What the hell was that about?" he asked.

"Excuse me?" a voice he didn't recognize asked.

"Shit," he said under his breath when he saw the caller ID. "Mrs. Gunther, I'm so sorry. I was expecting a call from work."

"I understand. Anyway, I was wondering when you were going to come and pick Lucas up." She coughed a few times. "He's a great boy, but we need to get going. We are driving to Sacramento to celebrate Simon's grandmother's birthday."

"Yes, of course. I'll be there as soon as I can."

"Very well. And when do you think that will be?"

He couldn't think of this right now. He didn't even know when he was going to be able to get free. When he was running out of time for a response, Qiang Li's call finally came.

"Listen, Mrs. Gunther, I have to take this other call right now. I promise you I'll arrange for Lucas to be picked up shortly."

Before she could protest, he hung up.

"What's going on?" he asked Qiang Li.

"That's exactly what I wanted to ask you. What the hell, Tyler?" Her voice came through like a shriek of a wounded animal. She spoke so fast he could hardly understand her.

"Tell me exactly what they asked you and what you said."

She did, and he concentrated on every word more than on the road. He veered too much into the lane next to him, and a car honked as it passed him on the left. He centered his car and slowed down further.

"You did well, Qiang. You've got nothing to worry about."

"To hell with you," she yelled again. "You swore we would never even get this far. You promised nobody would ever know what we were doing."

He knew she was squeezing her stress ball as she screamed at him.

"And they don't. They have no idea. They're probably asking a lot of different companies a lot of questions. That doesn't mean they're onto us." He tried to sound more reassuring than he really felt. "Trust me, we're fine."

"Next time they come, you talk to them. I don't ever want to be put in that situation again. You hear me? Never again!" she screamed into her phone again and hung up before he could respond.

He felt his blood pressure skyrocket. He forced himself to control his breathing to calm down. Things were definitely not going according to plan. He was close to the cabin but decided to make the call anyway.

"Julia, how are things?"

"Jesus."

Fuck, he thought. *Things are not going according to the plan at all.*

"What's wrong?"

"Well, this is just much harder than it looks, Tyler."

Before she could go on complaining, he said, "I'll be there shortly, but you have to get on it. We are running out of time."

With his full attention back on the road, he sped up for a few miles until he reached the Summit Road exit. He took it a bit faster than he should have and his wheels screeched on the turn. Tyler's head was spinning. He couldn't believe how his well-thought-out plan had gone so wrong. He had to fix it—and soon—or everything would have been in vain. Before he had time to dwell more on it, he saw a gas station, and he came up with a new plan.

Back in the car, he decided to push away the dread and think about Eva. Her skin, her mouth, her scent invaded his senses. He missed her. He was still disappointed she hadn't canceled her other plans, but he knew exactly what he would do to get her attention back. She was so sensuous, so sexy... Yeah, he needed to wrap this up so he could take her to the Caribbean for a few days. The sun, the clear blue water and infinite sex with Eva would make everything that had happened seem like a bad dream.

His thoughts were suddenly halted when he turned into the cabin's private road and spotted somebody walking toward the house. Tyler backed the car out of sight and killed the engine. Reaching into the glove compartment he grabbed his Sig P226 X-FIVE handgun. He got out of the car and walked slowly trying to not make a sound.

The man had gray hair and was wearing a black and red shirt under a brown vest. He was carrying a rifle, but it was open. He reached the house and peeked into the window furthest from the entrance. After a few seconds, he passed the next window and finally got to the door. Tyler wondered if the man would dare to go inside and if he'd have enough time to stop him, as he was still several yards away from the house.

The man searched for something, finally pulling out a phone. Tyler panicked and sped up. He'd no idea what Julia had done to the house, and he didn't want anybody wondering either. So he ran, and as soon as he was close enough, he yelled, "Hang up the phone and put the gun down now."

The man turned toward Tyler but didn't hang up.

"I said hang up *now.*"

Tyler kept getting closer with his gun raised. The man saw the muzzle pointed at his chest and raised both hands. One had the phone, the other the rifle, still open. Tyler reached the intruder and took the phone from him. Stepping back a few feet, he looked down to see whom he was talking to, but it was just a number.

He said, "Who is this?"

There was nobody on the other end. The man had been leaving a message. Tyler threw the phone on the ground and stepped on it, breaking it into several pieces. The man never uttered a word.

"Put the rifle down very slowly," Tyler said.

The man did.

"Kick it toward me."

The kick was weak, the rifle only moved a few feet. Tyler walked to it and picked it up. He then threw it almost thirty feet toward the trees.

"Who are you?"

"My name's Alton Lane. I live next door."

"What the hell are you doing here?"

"I knew Harper. He wasn't one for visitors, so when I saw the car on the driveway, I came to see if it was a family member or something. I wanted to pay my respects."

"Why are you carrying a gun?"

"I always do. I hunt on my property."

"Who were you calling?"

"My daughter."

Tyler eyed the man. He knew this was a lie. Nobody dialed a loved one's full number anymore. The numbers were all preprogrammed, even on old flip phones. He walked toward the old man slowly, still pointing the gun at him. Alton Lane retreated, but soon his back hit the wall of the house. Tyler wondered if the old man felt like prey being on the other side of the barrel. But there was no fear in his eyes, only curiosity, as if he were daring him in some twisted way.

The door to the cabin opened, and Julia came out. She got startled, jumped and let out a little cry of surprise. Alton looked in her direction. This gave Tyler the perfect chance to strike him. He hit him on the side of his forehead with the butt of his gun. Alton fell on the floor, unconscious. A bump appeared of about an inch that didn't quite open but turned blue almost immediately.

"What the hell are you doing?" Julia asked, fighting hard not to scream again.

"He was snooping. Who knows who he called." He pointed at the destroyed phone on the floor. "We need to take care of him."

Julia started to sweat. Tyler met her eyes. They were bloodshot but looked dead inside.

CHAPTER 78

The sun started to prick his skin. Darcy enjoyed driving with the top down but saw that Sorensen was having some issues trying to keep his hair out of his eyes. Darcy knew exactly where the Los Altos Rod and Gun Club was, and it was not too far from the Curarent Tech office.

"I swear to God, the first minute I get, I'm shaving my head."

Darcy laughed. "I dare you."

"Twenty bucks."

"Man, you're cheap. Deal," he said, extending his hand out for a shake.

Sorensen took it.

Darcy slowed down, turned right and pulled into the parking lot, taking a spot not too far from the main door. The place was much bigger than it looked from the outside. Darcy saw a cute woman with huge boobs and approached her.

"Good afternoon, Carmela," he said, reading her name from the tag conveniently placed on her chest. "Can we speak with the manager?"

"He's out back. Can I help you with something?" she asked after she popped her pink bubble gum.

"We're detectives with the Santa Clara Sheriff's Office," Lynch said, showing his badge.

340

She nodded and headed to a door at the back of the store. She knocked and then said, "Jimmy, you need to come out."

Before the door opened, she was back, standing where she'd been a few seconds earlier, popping gum.

"Gentlemen?"

Jimmy looked forty, but his voice put him in his late sixties.

Lynch made the introductions and went straight to the point. "I understand that Harper Johnson worked here."

"Oh man," Jimmy said, shaking his head. "Jesus, I knew sooner or later—"

"We're not here for that," Darcy said.

"You're not? I swear we run checks on all of our employees. There was no record of mental illness."

"We just want to know a little more about him. For example, did he socialize with anybody from the store?"

Jimmy thought about it for a while. Then, giving up, he turned to Carmela. "You worked with him on some shifts. Do you know?"

"Yeah, he didn't socialize much. Actually, didn't even talk much. Real quiet that one was."

"Was he good with customers?" Sorensen asked.

"Harper knew his shit." She covered her mouth with her hand, suddenly embarrassed. "Pardon my French."

Darcy smiled and waved his hand. "You should hear *this* guy speak," he said, pointing to Sorensen, who grunted in protest.

Carmela giggled and went on: "If a customer had a question, Harper always knew the answer. I liked working when he was in the store because of that. He knew everything about guns."

"Did he have any friends that came to the store or the range?" Sorensen leaned against the counter.

"No, I don't think he ever brought any friends here."

"How about customers? Did he seem friendlier with some customers or talk more with anybody?" Darcy added.

"I don't know about friendlier...There's this guy—a real dick, you know? He's all rich and puffy. He has a nice ride, like one of those fancy cars that don't run on gas, but not like a Prius. Looks more like a Camaro, you know? Anyway, about two years ago, this guy started coming, and they seemed to know each other from before. I wouldn't call it 'friends,' you know?" She quoted with her fingers and popped gum again. "Maybe acquaintances. About a month ago I saw the douche bag out in one of the outdoor lanes, talking to Harper. Then I saw them together a couple more times. They would talk for a few minutes and then Harper would come back to work. He always looked gloomier than normal when this guy showed up."

"Always, or lately?" Sorensen pushed his blond curls out of his eyes.

Another pop. "Lately," she said after she thought about it. "I also noticed that the rich guy only came when Harper was working, which was only once a week."

"Do you know his name?"

"I try to forget, because he can never remember mine, but it's not good for business, so I do remember."

Jimmy patted her on the shoulder, as if he was proud.

"His name is Warren. Tyler, I think, is his first name."

"Did Harper ever tell you what they talked about when they met at the lanes?"

"No. As I said, Harper never talked much."

"Did you ever see Warren give anything to Harper, like a piece of paper, or an envelope?"

She thought about it. She popped more gum.

"Carmela," Jimmy admonished her, somewhat embarrassed.

"Sorry, boss."

She took a few steps away from the men and threw the gum into a garbage can hidden underneath the counter.

"No, well, maybe. About a week or two ago I remember Harper came back from talking to Mr. Asshole and had a folder with him—you know, one of those yellow ones lawyers always use in the movies."

"Did he say what was in it?"

"No. I teased him about it, though. But he just ignored me and went to the break room. I never saw the folder again."

"Did you ever see if Mr. Warren gave Harper money?" Darcy new he was hoping for a miracle.

"Well, yeah, for the store, when he bought something."

"I mean outside of regular business."

"No, I don't think so."

Darcy thought about what he knew about Harper. Was there anything else he needed to ask? He felt satisfied.

"Thank you, Carmela," he said and extended his hand to shake hers. She took it and giggled. He then extended it to Jimmy. "Thank you, Jimmy." He was a bone crusher. Darcy fought hard for the pain to not show on his face. Jimmy had a subtle smirk when he shook Sorensen's hand too.

Before they reached the store door, Darcy thought of something else: "Is Warren a good shot?"

"See for yourself," she said, pointing to a target on the wall with twelve holes in the bull's-eye.

343

CHAPTER 79

Saffron thought about all the movies where somebody kidnapped and tied to a chair manages to come loose, beat the shit out of the kidnapper and escape. She had tried wiggling her hands out of the tape tying her to the armrests. But no luck. Then she tried loosening her ankles, but that didn't work either. The duct tape on her mouth was getting really old too. She had never been really good at fully breathing through her nose and much less now when she was completely freaked out.

To her left sat an older woman with bleached blond hair, cut in a bob. The hair looked coarse, as if it had been treated way too many times with harsh chemicals. She had been heavily made up, but now most of her mascara had dripped from her eyelashes down her cheeks. Saffron wondered if the woman's lipstick was smeared underneath the tape covering her mouth. She was shaking and whimpering like a cold, wet, abandoned Chihuahua.

Next to that woman was another one, probably about ten years older than Saffron. Her skin was dark chocolate, and her hair was short and spiky. She was not shaking. Her back was straight, and her nostrils flared every time she breathed. Every few seconds her fingers wrapped around the end of the armrest, and Saffron could see her tendons stretch and the knuckles turn white. Saffron stared at her, trying to grab her attention, but the woman was fully focused on the stairs.

The basement was damp and smelled of mold. Every once in a while she heard rustling sounds around the walls and figured some rodent was making its way from one end to another. It made her want to lift her feet on the chair and she shivered every time she realized she couldn't.

After Julia came down the stairs and tied her up, she left them there but didn't turn the light off. Saffron didn't know if it was because she was coming back or because she forgot. A few minutes later the door opened again. The older woman shrieked and even managed to move her chair back an inch or two. She began to cry again. Saffron stared up the stairs, wondering what was going to happen next.

A man in nice Italian shoes started descending. His black pants were virgin wool and had a perfect crease running down from the waist to the cuff. He was carrying an older man on his shoulder. She noticed the black-and-red-checkered shirt and brown hunting vest. She had no idea people actually wore such things in real life. The man in the expensive clothes dropped his cargo on the floor with less care than needed.

"Can you bring down another chair?" he asked up the stairs.

"We're running out," Julia yelled from above.

The man looked around and then said, "We only need a few more."

Saffron looked at the woman with the short hair, and their eyes finally met. She didn't need words to communicate what she was thinking: *We're in deep shit.* The woman's tendon's flexed again and she focused her attention back on the well-dressed man.

Saffron started kicking her heels on the ground and moving her hands to draw his attention. When the man looked at her, she tried telling him with her eyes to remove the duct tape over her mouth. He walked to her and started to pick

345

at a corner of the tape. When there was enough material to grab, he pulled as hard and fast as he could. Saffron felt cold, then heat, and then as if the tape had taken half her skin with it. It stung so bad all she could think about was rubbing her face with her hands. But she couldn't.

"That hurt," she protested, still shaking her head to cool down the stinging skin.

"Fast is better," he said in lieu of an apology. "What do you want?" His voice was level, but there was an undertone of urgency.

"I need to go to the bathroom."

"Hold it." He rolled his eyes and walked away from her.

"I've been holding it for a few hours already. I really need to go. Please."

"Julia, come down here," he yelled up the stairs.

Julia appeared, carrying a chair. She placed it in on the floor, next to the woman with spiky hair. Her face was flushed. She looked at the man with a sour expression.

"Take her to the bathroom."

"What? What if she tries to escape?"

"Shoot her."

Julia walked toward Saffron and stopped a good two feet away.

"If you kick me or something, you'll regret it."

Saffron nodded. Julia pulled a box cutter and sliced the tape on her feet first. Saffron rotated her ankles a few times, letting the flow of blood reach her toes. Then Julia freed her hands. Saffron stood but lost her balance. She fell on the chair again.

"Come on, let's go." Julia said. "I don't have all day."

Saffron used her hands to pull herself out of the chair. Intense pricks of pain shot up her arms. Her wrists were sore from her fall down the stairs and half-asleep from the binding. She wiggled her fingers. They weren't broken. At least something was not as bad as it could have been.

Julia walked upstairs first.

"Tyler, make sure she comes up nice and steady," she said to the man.

Saffron saw him turn around and point the gun at her as she walked up. When she reached the top, she stopped, waiting to hear further directions from Julia.

"The bathroom's straight ahead, then on your left."

Saffron walked forward until she found it. She went in and closed the door, but Julia opened it immediately.

"Don't even think about it," she said.

Saffron looked around for anything she could use to hit her, but the bathroom was bare. When she was drying her hands, she tried the towel rod to see if it could be easily removed, but it was securely attached to the wall.

As she walked back toward the basement, Julia stepped to the side to let Saffron go by her. In that split second, Saffron made up her mind.

She turned as if she were going to ask Julia a question, but instead she pushed her as hard as she could against the kitchen counter. Julia tripped over her own feet and fell backwards, hitting her head against the oven. The gun fell from her hand, but Saffron didn't stop to pick it up. She ran toward the door as fast as she could.

"Bitch, get back here!" Julia screamed after her, rustling back to her feet.

Saffron opened the door, took two steps on the deck and jumped to the ground. She ran as fast as she could. For a second, she looked backwards to see if Julia was behind her, but she wasn't. Instead, the man with the gelled hair named Tyler came out of the door and yelled, "Stop right now or I will shoot you."

Saffron ran faster. Then a thunder filled the air and a she knew he had fired at her.

CHAPTER 80

Darcy checked his phone for voice mails or messages from Saffron, but there were none. He told himself that it was for the better. He shook the feeling of disappointment as if it were a shiver and checked the message he did have.

It was another voice mail from Alton Lane. "Detective... Car again...Checking...hung up...gun..." Then it ended with a screech.

"Hey, can you listen to this and see if you can figure out what he's saying?" He pushed Play again and handed the phone to Sorensen.

He hiked the sound all the way up. "Something about a car and a gun?"

Darcy looked at him. "Really? That's all you can get out of it?"

"Sorry, dude," he said. "Maybe if we were in the office or a in a car that actually had a roof..." He pointed upwards at the sky, where the top of the car would have been.

"You wanted to ride in my car."

"Yeah, yeah." Sorensen waved his hand. "Not what it's all cracked up to be, I have to say."

"Whatever. This is the most powerful car you've ever been in."

"Nope." Sorensen's chest puffed up a little.

"For sure."

"Nineteen-seventy Plymouth Superbird."

Darcy cursed. "Damn it," he said, admitting defeat. "That's an amazing car."

"I told you."

"When did you ride it? At a car show?"

"My dad had one."

"And now you drive a Jeep? What's wrong with you, man?"

"I've got nothing to prove." Sorensen looked straight out in front of him, but his smug smile was friendly.

They drove in silence for a few minutes.

"We need to find this Warren guy," Sorensen said.

"I know." Darcy stepped on the gas, toward Palo Alto. "Can you call him? If we don't find him there, I want to head back to talk to the support group counselor again."

Tyler Warren didn't answer any of his phones. They arrived at his house, a modern two-story home painted white, with large windows and a Japanese–style lawn. They knocked on the door, and a Hispanic middle-age woman opened it, dressed in a pink dress with large white flowers.

"Can I help you?" she said in a strong Spanish accent.

"Is Mr. Warren home?" Lynch asked.

Before she could answer, a kid came running down the hallway and peeked out the door beside her.

"No. Mr. Warren is not home. Can I give him a message?"

"Please, tell him that Detectives Sorensen and Lynch need to talk to him immediately," Darcy said, giving her a card.

"Are you from the police?" the blond kid asked, looking from one to the other.

"From the Sheriff's Office," Sorensen said, getting on one knee and showing him his shiny badge. "And who are you?"

"My name is Lucas. Can I touch it?"

350

Sorensen held it flat on his palm. The kid passed a shy finger over it, as if he were afraid it would bite him.

"Do you have a gun?" Lucas asked with his finger still tracing the badge.

Sorensen opened his jacket so the kid could see the gun in his holster. Lucas took a step forward, index finger extended. The detective closed his jacket before the kid could touch the gun.

"When you're a little older, you can. Right now you need a few more years under your belt."

"But you don't even know how old I am," he protested.

"You are seven."

The kid's eyes opened wide, and his mouth formed a perfect circle.

"I'm a detective. I know everything," Sorensen said, standing up and ruffling the kid's hair.

"When I grow up I want to be a detective too," he said, lifting his arms above his head as if to indicate how tall he would grow up to be.

Sorensen laughed. "And it would be my honor to work with you then," he said, shaking the boy's little hand.

They both thanked the woman and asked her again to relay the message to Warren.

"Bye, Detectives," Lucas said, waving them away.

When they were back in the car, Darcy said, "Cool kid." He put the car in gear and headed toward Saratoga to talk to Elena.

"He won't be if he ends up in foster care." Sorensen's voice was grave. He was looking out the side window and shook his head.

"Maybe he has some relatives," Darcy offered.

They both fell silent for the rest of the ride.

CHAPTER 81

"The next one will go through your heart," the man had told her after the bullet passed a foot away from her head.

Saffron had stopped, then walked back toward the house and into the basement. She now sat on the same chair, hands and feet tied, and mouth taped again. She wondered what time it was. Her stomach rumbled. The woman with the blond bob looked at her, and Saffron blushed, ashamed for feeling hungry, given their dire circumstances.

At least an hour went by with nothing happening. They couldn't talk to each other, they couldn't move, but at least the light was still on. She had looked back at the man on the floor a few times to see if he moved at all, but he hadn't.

The door opened. A man in his late forties walked down the stairs but stopped midway when he saw the rest of them there.

"Keep moving," Tyler said, walking behind him with the gun pointing at the man's back. "Sit there."

He sat on the chair Julia had brought down earlier. His shirt was wet around the neck and below his armpits and large man boobs. He breathed with difficulty, as if he'd just run a marathon. Beads of sweat dripped down his face onto his large stomach.

He had to wiggle to fit his body between the armrests, but he finally managed. Tyler tied his feet first. Saffron wondered if he would be brave enough to punch him before his hands were also bound but figured he wouldn't.

When Tyler stood to work on the arms, the man said, "Please don't. I'm asthmatic, and I need my inhaler. If you tie me, I won't be able to use it."

Tyler passed his hand over his gelled hair and looked down to the floor, thinking about his options, then asked, "Where is it?"

"In my pocket."

Tyler pulled out the inhaler and placed it on his lap.

"I'm going to believe you, but I want you to know that if you try to free yourself, or anybody else here, I will kill you. If you don't believe me, ask that one over there." He pointed to Saffron.

Saffron and the new man exchanged glances. Her first thought was to give him an expression that said *He's telling the truth*. But then she thought she should better try one that said *He's just talk* in hopes that once they were alone, he would help everybody escape. At the end, the expression that came out was one of utter confusion.

"Thank you," the newcomer said to the man who had just kidnapped and tied him to a chair in a moldy basement.

Tyler nodded and headed toward the stairs, then paused for a second, as if these two words of kindness had gotten through to him. Before he continued up, he said, "You're welcome."

"Can you tell us why we are here? I'm not rich, so it can't be for ransom." His voice was low and level, even though he had to breathe between the words.

"For the greater good," Tyler said and walked up the stairs two at a time.

The door to the basement closed, and silence inundated the room. Saffron watched the man. He first inspected the hellhole they were in. Breathing in the mold caused him to wheeze, and he rapidly grabbed his inhaler and used it a few times. Feeling better, he checked every one of the people who were there with him, nodding sadly to each of them. He finally said, "My name's Keith."

Everybody else had tape over their mouths, so nobody could respond in kind. Saffron inched a little toward him and moaned, trying to tell him to at least take the tape off of her mouth. He looked at her. "I can't. He said he will kill me."

She said *He's going to kill us all* with her eyes, but saw that he didn't want to understand her.

He looked away and used his arm to scratch his right boob discretely. After a few moments, he used his fingers. Saffron saw his hand move up and down and side to side. Keith was averting her stare intentionally, probably embarrassed by what he was doing but seemingly unable to stop.

Saffron watched him, still hoping to get his attention back. But he wasn't looking at her. He was now using the inhaler to scratch his breast, leaving creases on the cotton T-shirt with each pass. She wondered if it was a tic, something he did when he was nervous, because he seemed to be completely absorbed by what he was doing. His eyes were lost, his brow lined. He stopped the rubbing for a second and started working on the tape that tied his other hand. He focused his eyes now on it and looked for the edge so he could peel it off.

Saffron exhaled through her nose, a shred of hope filling her chest.

He scratched his boob again, then worked on the tape, then scratched again. The movements became monotonous, almost as if dictated by some silent metronome in his head. The switch from one to the other quickened, as if he couldn't keep his hand from scratching his breast long enough to work on the tape. He finally got enough peeled off so he could grab it between his fingers, and pulled on it. The ripping noise filled the quiet basement.

Saffron watched the other two women, who were now looking at him too. The blond wailed harder. The one with short hair moved her body forward and stretched her neck to see the progress. Their eyes met. For the first time, they shared a little optimism.

Keith managed to free his hand, but instead of using it to work on the tape on his feet, he now had both hands on the inhaler, pushing it with force against his body, moving it in erratic motions over his breast. The woman with the short hair looked back at Saffron. Saffron shrugged. They both stared back at Keith.

He tried standing up, but the chair moved with him. He sat back down. Then he pushed the armrest toward the floor with one hand and pulled his body out, while the other hand continued to scratch his chest. He finally stood and, with his feet still tied to the chair, he started moving around, a few inches with each step, dragging the chair with him.

Saffron made some guttural noises to grab his attention, but Keith ignored her. His eyes focused on the room, which was pretty bare. He walked toward a pile of wood, knelt down and grabbed a log. He tried using one end to scratch that itch that wouldn't go away, but it was too large and heavy, so he discarded it. Saffron flinched at the noise of the wood falling flat on the cement floor.

Keith kept moving, following the perimeter of the basement, looking for something that would help him with the itch. He kept scratching and scratching, each time a little harder. He walked to the man on the floor. When he reached him, he stopped and looked at him for a few moments, then he bent over and started going through the man's pockets with one hand, still scratching with the other. He found a switchblade.

Saffron smiled underneath the tape. There was hope for them.

Keith stared at the knife in his hand. He opened it. The blade was smooth and shiny. He turned the knife a few times, as if he were inspecting the craftsmanship. Sometimes the light hit the blade in a way that projected a ray across the room. It was almost mesmerizing. Then Keith stopped rotating the knife and stopped scratching his breast. With his free hand, he grabbed his man boob, pulled on it and with a rushed movement, he cut through the flesh with the knife.

The three women pushed their chairs backwards at the same time in horror and squealed, but Keith didn't stop.

A gush of blood sprayed the wall in front of him. He still pulled on his breast, blood filling his hands, soaking his T-shirt, and continued slashing until it came loose from his body. He stared at the flesh in his hand, then at the knife. Without a need for it anymore, he let the knife slip through his fingers, and fell on the man on the floor with a soft thud. He then lowered his other hand, letting the loose flesh also fall in front of him. He stared at his bloody hands and for the first time his face showed recognition of what he had just done. His eyes rolled into the back of his head and he lost consciousness, collapsing on top of the man, with the chair up in the air, still tied to his ankles.

CHAPTER 82

Darcy called Elena while they drove south toward Saratoga. She was going to go lead a group, covering for somebody who had called in sick, but she could meet them at the diner after the session. The detectives decided to grab some food while they waited for her.

They both ordered a burger. Sorensen asked for it well done, no lettuce or tomato, but extra cheese. Darcy added avocado and asked for it rare. When the food came, Sorensen bathed the French fries in ketchup.

"Anything new from Jon?" Darcy asked.

Sorensen looked at his phone. "Nope."

"Maybe we should call him?"

"Don't be needy," Sorensen teased.

"I'm getting desperate."

Without realizing it, he pulled his own phone out and checked for anything from Saffron. There was nothing. He washed away another pang of dejection with a big bite of burger.

After a few seconds of silence, feeling better with something in his stomach, Darcy turned one of the paper placemats over and asked the waitress for a pen. He wrote down Dr. Leavenworth's name and circled it. Then he added Curarent Tech and Harper Johnson's name, circling each. Then he wrote "Murder victims," and separately he wrote "Suicide victims." He paused and took another bite of his burger. He saw Sorensen's eyes dart between the circles on the paper.

Without a word of explanation, Darcy pulled his phone and called Jon.

"Hey, can you check something on Harper Johnson's ME report?"

"Sure, give me a sec." Jon put the line on hold.

Darcy set the phone on the table and put it on speaker.

"What am I looking for?"

"Check for cancer."

"Shouldn't you talk to Madison directly?" Sorensen asked.

"I thought about it, but it's Saturday and I would never hear the end of it if I interrupt his game of golf."

"Good point."

"I got it," Jon said. "Yes, liver cancer, stage three, apparently."

"In English?" Sorensen asked.

"Give me a sec. I'll look it up."

They could hear the keyboard as he typed.

"I found this website that says that Stage Three is when the tumor has spread to the fatty tissue around the kidney, and maybe, but not necessarily, into a large vein leading from the kidney to the heart, but it hasn't reached the lymph nodes or other organs yet."

They all felt silent. Sorensen finished his food and took a big gulp of his Coke.

"One more thing. Can you check Dr. Leavenworth's phone records and see if she's had any contact with anybody from Curarent Tech?"

"Everybody?" Jon asked, a little dread in his voice.

"Start with the *C* letters, but make sure you also cover the lead researcher, Qiang Li," Darcy said.

"Last name starting with *C*, or first names too?"

Darcy smiled. "CEO, CFO, CTO—you know, your typical Silicon Valley royalty."

"Got it," Jon said after an embarrassed cough.

Darcy thanked him and hung up, then dialed Alton Lane to see what he wanted. It went to voice mail directly. "Mr. Lane, Detective Lynch here just returning your call. The connection hasn't been great, and I couldn't understand the messages you left. Please call me back with anything important."

"The neighbor?" Sorensen asked.

"Yeah. I don't get those messages. Just want to make sure there's nothing weird going on there."

He went back to the placemat and wrote, on the top, in big cap letters, "CANCER."

"All of this is related to cancer. Everything that's happening," he said, thinking out loud.

"Okay..." Sorensen said and waited for him to continue.

"We've got no proof yet, but we're pretty sure that the suicide victims were in some kind of research trial," Darcy said, tapping the circle enclosing the suicide victims and looking at Sorensen for confirmation.

"To do human trials, you need patients," Sorensen said. "What better place to get them than at the office of a doctor who treats those patients you want to target?" He tapped the doctor's circle with his finger.

Darcy drew a line between the two circles and continued: "From the little I remember from college biology, when you do trials you need at least two sets of subjects—a group on the medication, and the control group."

They both felt silent. The waitress refilled their drinks.

"But some of the people Johnson killed didn't have cancer."

359

Sorensen rested his head on his hand, his elbow taking half a table.

"I know," Darcy said, putting the pen down and finishing his last fry. "I don't remember Saffron mentioning being on any medication either," he said after a few seconds. "Let me check."

He pulled his phone and started dialing.

"As good excuse as any, I guess," Sorensen said, winking.

"What?" Darcy asked while he waited for the call to go through. When the voice mail picked up, he said, "Saffron, Detective Lynch here." He felt Sorensen's eyes on him and masked his annoyance by turning his body away from him. "I have a few more questions regarding your visits to Dr. Leavenworth. Please call me back as soon as you can."

The waitress came to offer them the best pie in the county. They each took a piece. Darcy went for the mulberry, and Sorensen chose cherry. They both asked for coffee.

"Johnson got almost $80K to kill a group of people," Darcy refocused the conversation. "All of those people are patients of the doctor." He drew another line between Leavenworth and the murder victim's circle. "The only explanation that makes sense is that Curarent Tech paid Johnson to cover up the human trials."

"But that's crazy. Why not just stop it?" Sorensen asked, his mouth full of cherry pie.

Elena came into the diner and walked toward them. Darcy grabbed the placemat and folded it a few times until it was small enough to fit in his jacket pocket.

"Thank you for meeting us. This is Detective Sorensen," Darcy said, and offered the seat next to him. "Would you like some pie?"

"Very nice meeting you." She hung her purse on the back of the chair. "No, thank you."

Darcy took out the DMV photo he had of Tyler Warren and showed it to her. "Is this the same Tyler that goes to your sessions?"

"Yes."

"And have you seen him talking to Harper Johnson a lot?"

"No. Not much at all, actually." She thanked the waitress for the steaming coffee and continued: "I think the most I've seen them talk was when Tyler brought a puppy to the session looking for somebody to take her. Harper did."

"Tyler gave him the puppy?" Darcy thought about his new dog and how skinny she was and wondered if she'd have been better off with some rich friend of Warren's.

"Yeah. Tyler asked him about her every once in a while."

Back in the car, Darcy pulled the placemat out of his pocket and handed it to Sorensen. He opened it on his lap and held both ends tightly so it wouldn't fly away.

"Does this car have a top, for Chrissakes?"

"Yep. I only use it when it rains." Darcy glanced at the scribbled paper for a second and then said, "Warren knows Harper from the support group. Then they also have contact at the shooting range...It's farfetched, but if I were Warren, I would think Johnson was a pretty safe recruit."

"To kill people?" Sorensen lifted one of his hands in protest and almost lost the place mat. "I guess greed is a powerful motivator," he said, grabbing the paper again.

"You know what's a better motivator?" Darcy asked, glancing at him. When Sorensen looked back, he said, "health."

CHAPTER 83

Saffron had a hard time screaming with her mouth taped shut. So did the other two women, but they were all trying. After a few minutes Saffron managed to stop, her chest heaving every time she breathed. Still hyperventilating, she looked at the blond woman. Her eyes were closed. While she whimpered, she rocked back and forth slightly, as if she were in a trance. Large black mascara tears dripped down her cheeks. The woman with the short hair had also managed to stop screaming. Her eyes were wild with fear. She started moving in her chair, unsuccessfully trying to get loose.

Saffron could not stop playing the images of what Keith had just done to himself in her head. Every time she closed her eyes she saw the large man pulling on his own flesh and slicing it with the knife.

The knife, she thought. *Could I? Oh my God, no way. There's no way I can.*

She stood still, trying hard to not look at Keith bleeding on top of the other man. But she couldn't stop thinking about the knife. She tensed all her muscles and took a tiny jump toward Keith. She kept jumping for what seemed like minutes, only closing the distance a foot or two. Saffron was afraid to look at the other women, knowing that they would be staring at her in horror and frustrated that she couldn't explain to them what she was trying to do.

She maneuvered around Keith's legs and smeared his blood on her trail. She finally reached the other side and looked around for the knife. It was sandwiched between the two bodies. Only the black, rubbery handle was visible. She inched as close as the legs of the chairs would let her and extended her hand as far as she could, but the knife was still a couple feet away.

The smell of blood filled her nostrils, and she thought about the Onion Man at the coffee shop dying on top of her. She shivered and shook her head to push the image away. But when she closed her eyes, she saw Harper pointing the rifle at her and pulling the trigger. The click made her heart stop again, as if it had just happened. Tears filled her eyes, and she would have given anything to have a hand to wipe them away.

She needed to get the knife. She started rocking the chair from side to side and finally got enough momentum to tip her over the two men. She fell awkwardly on top of the older man's shoulder, just far enough for her not to be able to grab the knife. Saffron curled her fingers on the man's vest, but they slipped over the stiff canvas material. She grunted and felt tears reappear again, but this time they were of frustration.

After a few more futile attempts at grabbing the clothing, she pushed her body forward in little spurts, carrying the chair with her. The odor of blood made her mouth taste like copper. She swallowed hard a few times and kept inching away. She finally was close enough to touch the handle of the knife. Her fingers were caressing it, trying to pull it free, but then the man below her grunted. Her heart leapt out of her chest. She remained still for a few seconds, waiting for him to do or say something, but he didn't. *At least he's alive*, she thought and pushed herself to get just a little closer so she could grab the knife.

Saffron finally got enough grip to pull it from underneath Keith. Then the door to the basement opened and she froze, almost losing hold of it. If they found out what she was trying to do, she was sure they would shoot her once and for all. She turned the knife toward her and carefully started sliding it inwards between her wrist and the armrest. She felt it cutting her skin but she went on. By the time Tyler was halfway down the stairs, she'd managed to hide it completely.

"What the hell?" he asked when he saw the chairs where not where he'd left them. He ran down and saw the pile of three bodies and two chairs. "What did you do?" He sprinted toward them. He pulled Saffron off first in one hasty move. She now faced him and had her back to the other women.

Tyler saw the blood on the floor and lifted his foot as if he had stepped on dog poo.

"What did you do?" he repeated, now yelling at Saffron.

Her eyes widened, showing a lot of white. He just stared at her. Then he pulled the tape off as hard as he had done it the first time.

"Tell me." he demanded.

"He...he..." she started, but she didn't have the words to explain what they had just witnessed.

He gave up on her and bent over to Keith. He tried to move him but had much more difficulty than he had with her. Tyler finally rolled him over, and saw the bloody hole in his chest.

"Oh my God." he said. His face turned white with horror. He moved away a few steps and tried looking away but was mesmerized with repulsion.

"What did you do to him?" he asked, but he knew exactly what had happened.

CHAPTER 84

Saffron didn't hear the steps on the stairs and was startled by Julia's voice.

"This is the last one," she said.

The woman walking in front of her stopped in her tracks. Julia almost bumped into her. "Move," she said. But the woman didn't. Julia pushed as she descended behind her. Before reaching the bottom she also stopped.

Saffron had to crane her neck to see them. The woman who had drugged and kidnapped her seemed frozen in place. Even in the dim light of the basement, Saffron could see the blood had drained from her face. Julia took a tentative step forward and then asked, "Is he dead?"

Tyler nodded from the opposite side of the room.

"Is this what happens?"

He didn't answer. He wiped the blood from his hands on his pant legs and then passed both through his hair, leaving a light crimson trail behind. He looked around as if he were thinking about what to do next.

"Tyler, is this what happens with the treatment?" Julia yelled at him, still keeping her distance.

"What treatment?" Saffron heard herself ask.

"Shut up," Julia and Tyler yelled in unison.

Julia stood there with her hands on her hips, waiting for an answer.

"We have to get him out of here," he said to her.

"He's over three hundred pounds. We'll never be able to get him up the stairs," she protested, looking up at the wooden steps.

Tyler rolled Keith on his stomach. Then he grabbed his ankles and tried pulling him, but the body didn't move much. "Help me. I can't look at him anymore." His voice was strained for the first time.

"You, move over there," Julia said to the woman she'd brought downstairs, pointing to the opposite wall. "I need to see you, and if you do anything stupid, I'll shoot you."

The newcomer, a beautiful Indian woman with long black hair, had both hands and feet tied together. She passed the two occupied chairs and didn't stop until she reached the wall. Saffron turned her head toward her. The woman didn't utter a sound, but in the darkness of the room, the yellowish sclera of her eyes dimmed a little.

When Julia was comfortable she could watch her while moving Keith, she walked toward the body and grabbed one ankle. Tyler grabbed the other, and they both pulled. It took them a full minute, but they managed to move him to the east wall, leaving a trail of blood behind.

Out of breath, Tyler said, "You're right. We're never going to be able to get rid of this body. We need to burn the place down."

"Where are you going to take us, then?" Saffron asked.

"Shut up," he said.

"You're going to burn the place down with all of us inside?" she asked, feeling more scared than she thought possible. She heard in her mind the click of Harper's rifle, and for the first time she wished the chamber hadn't been empty. "That's insane. Why?"

"Because you're all already dead anyway, okay?" Tyler said.

366

Saffron couldn't see everybody, but she felt the temperature drop ten degrees as the news settled.

"Just because we've seen you? We don't have to say anything. Just let us go," she pleaded.

"Don't be stupid," he spat her way.

"Tyler, maybe we should just let nature take its course," Julia said, looking at Keith. "It's going to happen anyway. Why do it ourselves?"

He looked at the floor for a few moments. Then he shook his head. "We can't. We don't know how long it's going to take. Besides, what if somebody finds them first?"

"Is this what's going to happen to us?" Saffron said, her voice trembling as she suddenly realized what he was saying. "What did you do to us?" she asked, not able to move her eyes from Keith's body.

"We tried to cure you of cancer," he yelled at her, his voice was strained.

"But I don't have cancer," she said, confused.

"Don't you know anything? Every trial needs two sets of subjects. We tested on both: people with cancer and people without."

"I don't understand. I don't think I'm part of this research. I was never prescribed any medication."

"Nobody did," Julia interjected. "I exchanged some titanium markers for ones that looked identical but instead had the medicine inside. Dr. Leavenworth inserted them when you had the biopsy done."

Saffron wished she had a free hand. She wished she could use it to cup her breast and tell it that everything was going to be okay. But her hands were still tied, and now they trembled. She felt the butt of the knife pressing against her palm and wished she could use it to get free and kill this woman.

"But then it's not too late. Just take it out," Saffron said, as if offering a way out they may have not thought about.

"The device that contains the medicine dissolves once it's inserted in the human body, releasing the medication into the affected area." Julia looked at Tyler, sadness in her eyes. "Once it's dissolved, there's no way to remove it."

"It was supposed to cure people," Tyler said. "We never knew about the adverse reactions until people from the trial started dying...this way," he said, looking down at Keith. After a few moments, he shook his trance off and said, "Come on Julia, I'll tie the new one. You go get the gasoline cans."

"You don't want to do this. You can't possibly burn us alive!" Saffron yelled, pushing her body off the chair, but not really able to go anywhere.

"But tape her mouth before you go, so I don't have to hear her anymore."

Julia remained there, her expression blank, but her lips were trembling. "I don't think I can," she said in a whisper. "I can't burn them alive."

"Julia," he said loud enough to make everybody in the room jump. "We're going to save millions. We are so close. I swear to you, we're close. Qiang just called me and told me she believes she knows what the problem was. She's got a breakthrough. We're going to save the lives of millions of people with breast cancer, I swear to you."

CHAPTER 85

Darcy called Saffron one more time and just asked her to return the call. Then, when the car was roaring on the highway, he decided to call Alton Lane again. The call went directly to voice mail without ringing once.

"That's weird," he said, hanging up.

"What?"

"Lane. I think he has nothing else to do all day but spy on everybody else. I would have expected him to call me right after I left him the other message. Now the call goes straight to voice mail."

"Maybe he's busy. Or he's going after little squirrels and doesn't have coverage."

"Yeah, maybe." The nagging feeling wouldn't go away.

They rode the rest of the way in silence. When they got to the station, Darcy stopped the car by the main entrance. Sorensen turned to him, eyebrows arched.

"I have to check out what's going on with Lane," Darcy said. "Something's not right."

"Suit yourself. I'll work on the warrant for Warren." Sorensen lifted his body out of the low seat and, closing the door, said, "You better be be back when we go arrest him."

"Wouldn't miss it. Quick round trip, I swear."

He turned the radio on and sped away. About forty-five minutes later, he pulled into Alton Lane's private road. Before driving all the way to the house, he left another message, not wanting to get shot for entering his property uninvited.

The sun had started its descent, and now it kissed the top of the trees. It was hot but dry, and the shade felt good as he slowed down in the driveway. He inspected the house over the windshield of his car. He didn't see any curtain move. Lynch got out of the car and rang the bell. Soft chimes reverberated through the empty house. He tried again, but before the noise had died the second time, he had already started walking away.

He patrolled around the perimeter of the house, looking both inside the windows and out into the woods. He listened for noises, but only foliage dancing with the wind and a few squirrels climbing trees disturbed the peace of the woods.

Darcy thought about Lane's calls. Something about cars, something about a gun. The messages seemed strange. He stopped. A gut feeling made him pull his phone out. The screen showed one bar. He went to voice mail and listened to Alton's last message. He cranked the volume as high as it would go.

"Detective…Car again…Checking…hang up… gun…"

"Gun," Darcy repeated. He listened to it again. "*Hang up and gun*" were said by a different voice. He was sure of it.

He dialed Sorensen's number, but the one bar disappeared and the call dropped after the first ring. He tried again while he finished circling the house and headed back to his car. He put the phone back in his pocket and searched for his second clip of ammo in the glove compartment. Darcy checked his gun and put it back in his holster. Then he walked through the woods toward Johnson's house, hoping to find Alton somewhere along the way.

The terrain was uneven and the soil was still a little moist, even though the day was warm. Darcy slipped and managed to hold on to a trunk before falling. The surface was rough and it scratched his palm. He steadied himself and proceeded. Two large scratches turned pink under the dermis but didn't bleed.

Through the trees he saw Johnson's house appear. Lane was right: there was a light blue SUV parked in the driveway. He walked a few more feet but stopped before leaving the tree line. Still no bars on the phone. He opened his stance and watched for a few seconds.

The SUV appeared empty. The doors were closed. The house seemed quiet. There were no lights inside. He walked along the tree perimeter to check the back. He still found nothing. He retraced his steps so he could watch both, the driveway and the house. After a few moments, the front door opened, and a woman walked out. He almost ducked out of reflex but instead hid behind a large tree and watched. She was too far for him to see her well. He strained his eye and wished he had binoculars.

Her stride was resolute. She didn't look around, just walked straight forward, grounding each step and moving her arms as if she were marching. She vanished behind the SUV. Lynch wondered if she was going to get something from the car, but a second later she reappeared and continued walking straight down the driveway toward the main road.

After a few seconds she disappeared from his line of sight. Darcy waited, wondering if she was going to come back. But then he heard a car. A black Tesla appeared on the private road and headed toward the house. The woman was driving it.

She parked behind the blue SUV and before she got out, the trunk popped. She pulled two red gasoline cans out of it and walked back to the house, carrying one in each hand.

As soon as the door from the house closed behind her, Darcy pulled out his gun, left the protection of the trees and ran toward the car, trying to stay low so she wouldn't see him if she looked out the window. He hid behind the car and peeked into the trunk. There was one more can. He then ran behind the SUV and finally made it all the way to the side of the house.

He backed himself against it, and concentrated on slowing his breathing. Then he walked quietly along the wall toward the first window. When he reached it, he moved slowly toward it, increasing his view inside the house. The glass was dirty with dust from the inside and soil from the outside, but he could still see clearly enough. The dining room table was pushed to the side. There were no chairs anywhere he could see. There was a trapdoor in the floor, propped open.

Fuck, I can't believe we missed that, he thought to himself, remembering the thorough search he had done with Sorensen when they first came to Harper's house. *I thought California houses didn't have basements*. He shook his head, trying to not get too worked up for having missed it.

The place was deserted. He couldn't see the woman. He ducked under the windowsill just in case and walked to the next window. He got a better view of the kitchen and the trapdoor, but besides a dark hole and a few steeps, he couldn't see anything else.

Darcy crept around the perimeter. The bathroom window was translucent. The bedroom windows had the curtains drawn, but he could still see a little around the edges. Then the front door opened again, and he froze. He heard footsteps on the porch, down the steps, and then the walking sound died over the soft ground. He walked toward the corner of the house and peeked, trying to see what she was doing.

She reached the car, pulled the remaining can, closed the trunk, and walked toward the house again. He hid behind the wall and waited to hear the front door close behind her.

CHAPTER 86

Tyler grabbed the duct tape from the floor and told the Indian woman to sit in the empty chair. He secured her while she cried silently. When he was done, he walked toward the woman who wouldn't shut up and pulled on the duct tape to cover her mouth. "Shit," he said when the silver tape ended and the brown cardboard base appeared. A couple inches of tape wouldn't do the job. He looked around for more adhesive, but there was none. Everybody was quiet, almost stoic, so he moved on.

"Where do you want these?" Julia said when she came downstairs.

He let go of the empty roll of tape and said, "Just set them by the stairs."

She placed the gasoline cans on the concrete floor and went back upstairs.

He stood in the middle of the room and looked around as if he couldn't remember what he'd been doing before the interruption. He surveyed the basement but specifically avoided looking at the women tied up. His gaze stopped on the older man he'd brought down earlier. He still rested on the floor, facedown. Tyler stared down at him. Then he followed the trace of blood toward Keith. After a few seconds, he closed the distance between them and kneeled down to pat him, soaking his hands in Keith's blood. He searched between the man and the wall and below him, just in case, but didn't find what he was looking for. He gave up and stood, wiping his hands on his pants again, and turned to Saffron.

"Where is it?" he asked.

Saffron didn't answer. Just looked back at him.

"Tell me where the knife is."

She still didn't say anything.

"What were you doing by the body when I came down?" he asked her, his voice rising.

"I wanted to see if he was still alive." She kept her eyes on him. "I wanted to help him."

"You're lying," he yelled and walked to her. Before he realized what he was doing, he felt his hand slap her face with such force that her lip broke and new blood tainted his hand. "Where do you have it? Tell me."

He made a fist with his hand, ready to use it. He stood there, looking down at her, waiting for her response.

"I don't have the knife," she said again, sucking the blood on her cracked lip.

CHAPTER 87

Darcy turned the corner and stopped to listen for noises coming from the house. He heard steps fading. He looked through another window, but it only gave him a view of the second bedroom. He walked by the door and peeked into the living room window again. The house was empty.

He retraced his steps and checked the door. It was unlocked. He turned the knob slowly, trying to anticipate any screeching noises that would give him away. He finally heard the bolt give in, and he pulled the door toward him one inch at a time.

He only opened it wide enough for his body to go through. With his back to the wall, he slid in and heard steps coming from the basement. He looked around quickly, but there wasn't a good place to hide before the woman reappeared. He opened the entry closet and jumped inside. He heard her reach the landing and stop. He wondered if she was staring at the open closet door, if she knew something didn't add up or was different than before. But then he heard steps going toward the kitchen, moving away from him. The faucet turn on, and water started running in the sink.

Hoping that the noise would mask his presence, Darcy stepped out of the closet and walked toward the middle of the room. Both of his hands cupped his Glock, which was pointing at the woman's back. He crept slowly, measuring each step. But then the old wood creaked under his weight, loud enough to prick the woman's ears.

She turned around. Her hands were wet. Darcy kept pointing the gun at her with one hand while he brought his index finger to his lips, indicating for her to be quiet. He walked toward her while she wrung her hands to make them dry. When he reached the entrance for the basement, he looked down, but there was nothing to see except three red cans of gas forming a perfect line by the last step.

"Are you alone?" he whispered.

The woman just stood, not saying a word, not giving up anything with her eyes or facial expression. Darcy asked again. She nodded slightly. He didn't believe her.

He looked down in the basement again, searching for anything that would give him any indication of whether they were alone. From the corner of his eye, he saw her moving her hands. He looked back at her and said, "Hands where I can see them." Out of reflex he spoke louder than he'd wanted to. *No more stealth presence*, he thought.

He moved away from the basement door toward the bedrooms so he could keep both the woman and the basement entrance in his line of sight at the same time. *I wish I had two eyes,* he cursed to himself.

Before he had a chance to get a full view, a man with a gun appeared from the stairs and said, "Drop the gun."

"I'm a deputy sheriff. You need to drop your weapon right now," Lynch said, switching the aim of his gun from the woman to the man. He recognized him, it was the Curarent Tech CEO.

Tyler Warren stopped and took a few steps down slowly, with his gun still pointing at him. When Darcy looked back at the woman he saw she had managed to pull a gun of her own, and now they had the advantage.

"Don't be stupid, both of you. I'm a cop. I can take you both down before you have time to cock the gun. Just put the weapons down," he said, trying to sound a lot more confident than he felt.

"Darcy?" he heard somebody call from downstairs.

"Saffron?" he asked after a second, trying to make sense of the voice.

"Oh my God," she replied.

"Are you okay?" he asked her, still keeping his eye on both barrels.

"Yes. We're okay."

He flinched. "'We?' How many people are down there?"

"Six. There are six of us here."

CHAPTER 88

Right after she denied having the knife, they both heard the wood creak upstairs far away from where Julia was running the faucet water. The man named Tyler looked suspicious and stared up the staircase, probably expecting to see someone other than Julia walk down. But nobody came. Saffron watched him listen and then saw him pull out a gun. She wanted to listen too, but all she could do was focus on the gun she was sure would soon point at her head.

Then a man's voice upstairs said, "Hands where I can see them," and Tyler seemed to forget all about her and the knife she was hiding. He started moving toward the stairs while she listened intently at anything that came from above.

Saffron looked at the other women and saw hope in their faces. She felt the knife press against her palm. She wiggled her hand a little until she was able to grab the butt and started to move the switchblade up and down against her ligatures. Every other move or so, she felt the knife cut against her skin, but she didn't care. It didn't even hurt. When Tyler disappeared up the stairs, her movements accelerated until her hand was freed from the tape.

As soon as she started working on the other hand, she heard the man upstairs say, "I'm a deputy sheriff. You need to drop your weapon right now." The voice sounded familiar. She knew him. She froze. It couldn't be. She listened intently as she cut the tape around the other hand and then her feet.

She stayed seated for a few seconds, trying to listen for Tyler's steps walking back down. But then she heard the voice again say, "Don't be stupid, both of you. I'm a cop. I can take you both down before you have time to cock the gun. Just put the weapons down." And she couldn't help herself but smiled.

"Darcy?" she yelled, mostly to make sure she wasn't dreaming it.

"Saffron?"

"Oh my God," she replied.

She knew everything was going to be okay. He'd come here to rescue them. She didn't care if Tyler came back down. She got up and walked to the woman with the short hair first. Taking the tape off of her mouth Saffron whispered, "Please be quiet. We have to act quickly." The woman nodded, and as soon as she was free, she went to work on releasing the Indian woman.

"Are you okay?" Darcy asked from above.

"Yes. We're okay."

Saffron started freeing the woman with the blond bob. She looked terrified and emitted guttural sounds, as if she were an injured animal.

"'We?' How many people are down there?" Darcy asked her.

"Six. There are six of us here," she responded, not needing to check first.

"Is everybody okay?"

"No. One person is dead and another one may be. I'm not sure."

Then, to the blond woman, she said, "Shush. Everything's going to be okay. The police are here." She kept saying it as she worked on getting her loose. "You have to stay here until it's safe to go upstairs, okay?" Saffron wanted to make sure she understood, so before she cut the last binding, she looked into her eyes and asked her again.

"Yes," the blond woman said, nodding at the same time.

Saffron cut the last binding. The woman jumped out of her chair, pushing Saffron to the floor, and started running toward the stairs, screaming, "Save me, save me."

CHAPTER 89

Darcy was trying to figure out what his next move should be. He had two guns pointing at him. He only had one, and he knew he was not a good shot anymore. There were six people in the basement. One or possibly two were dead.

Loud steps and a desperate voice shouting "Save me, save me" filled the house. A blond woman came running up the stairs so fast that Tyler didn't have enough time to react. She steamrolled him, pushing him down. He fell forward, stopping the fall with his hands. The gun went off. The bullet fired in Darcy's direction but missed him by a couple feet. The blond tripped over her own shoes and fell down a few stairs, grabbing onto Tyler's shirt, making him fall backwards with her.

The woman in the kitchen, still aiming the gun at Darcy, was now focused on what was happening on the stairs. Darcy used the distraction and ran toward her. The front door opened. She looked up. Darcy looked backwards and saw Sorensen's large body fill the door. The woman pointed the gun at the larger target.

"No!" Darcy said, jumping toward her, as she pulled the trigger.

He fell on her, making sure all of his weight landed on her smaller frame. He heard a rib crack, and she screamed in his ear. She still held the gun in her hand. Darcy grabbed her wrist and squeezed until she let go of the weapon. He shoved it to the other side of the room and looked back at Sorensen. "Are you hit?" he asked, looking at his partner sprawled on the floor.

"I'm okay. I don't think I've ever kissed the floor this fast."

He got up and walked toward them.

"Stay away from the basement. Warren's there," Darcy warned Sorensen.

Sorensen stepped a few feet away from its entrance, walked toward them and oversaw Darcy putting handcuffs on the woman.

"I don't know what you're doing here, but if you don't let us leave, I'm burning the place down with everybody in it," Tyler said from downstairs.

Sorensen looked at Darcy, searching for corroboration.

"I saw three cans of gasoline downstairs," he whispered.

Sorensen pulled his phone out. "We're fucked," he mouthed to Darcy, showing him that there wasn't even a bar. Then walked toward the door to see if he could get better reception.

"I have five people here. You come down and let me tie you up so we can get out of here, or I'll start the fire right now."

"We can't come down. You'll shoot us the moment we step on the stairs," Darcy said.

"I won't. I don't want to kill people. All I want is to leave with my sister."

"I tell you what. Let the hostages go first, then we can talk."

"Don't be patronizing. Come down right now."

CHAPTER 90

Saffron cursed herself for trusting the blond woman. She knew she was way too freaked out to be able to do anything but run. She watched Tyler push her away him and get off the floor. He froze in place when he saw they were all free from the bindings.

Saffron wondered if they could take him if they jumped him at the same time. Tyler focused on her first, as if he had just read her mind, then he waved the gun, aiming from one to another at random.

Tyler picked up one of the red cans and lifted it toward them. "You. Come here," he said, talking to the woman with the short hair.

She hesitated for a second, but when he aimed the gun at her, she started walking toward him.

"I want you to empty the can on the floor, starting on that corner." He pointed to where Keith laid facedown.

She grabbed the can but didn't get a grip on the handle, and it fell on the ground. The can flopped and everybody stared, waiting for it to spontaneously combust. When nothing happen, Tyler yelled, "What are you waiting for? Do it now."

The woman walked toward the corner and started pouring gasoline. The stink instantly filled the basement, completely masking the stench of Keith's blood.

Tyler picked up another can and shoved it in Saffron's direction.

"Start on the other corner," he said, pointing to it with the gun.

She took the can and started walking very slowly.

"Wait," Darcy said from upstairs.

Saffron stood still, barely a few steps from Tyler. The other woman stopped pouring gas. Saffron turned to face the stairs.

"I'm going to come down. But my partner is upstairs holding your sister. If you shoot at me, he'll kill you both. Do you understand me?"

Tyler looked back, taking in the basement, smelling the gasoline mixed with the sweat of fear.

"Okay," Tyler said.

"One more thing. I want you to come to the bottom of the stairs so I can see you."

"You think I'm stupid?"

"No, but I'm not either."

Saffron saw Tyler hesitate. He was thinking about his options. After a few seconds, he turned toward the Indian woman, grabbed her arm and twisted it behind her. She screamed in pain.

"If you hurt anybody I'm not coming down," Darcy said.

A second later Tyler walked behind the woman toward the stairs. He was glued behind her, with the muzzle of his gun pressing against her temple.

"If you try anything funny, I'll shoot her."

"I'm coming down," Darcy said and started descending, planting both feet onto each step before continuing to the next one. His gun was drawn but pointed downward.

As he descended, Tyler moved backwards toward the wall behind him and away from the stairs, dragging the woman with him.

Saffron watched as Darcy appeared. He was methodical, careful, and as soon as his head was below the ceiling, she saw him take in the basement, all of it.

"Okay, now I'm here. Why don't you let her go upstairs?"

"I can't do that."

"What, you really think you're going to kill us all and walk away? As we speak, backup is pulling into the driveway." He said this and let it set for a few seconds. "You only have one option. You need to surrender and let everybody go."

"You don't understand. We're so close. We have the cure for cancer. These people are already dead, and you're going to kill many more from the disease if you don't let me go."

"They're not dead. You can choose to let them go."

"We are, actually," Saffron said. "We were this asshole's guinea pigs and he screwed up and now we are all dead, just like him," she said, pointing at the man bleeding on the floor.

Saffron saw Darcy shake a shiver as he started to comprehend the women's fate. He looked where she was pointing and saw two men: The large one was lying in a pool of his own blood, the other one was soaked in it.

"Is that Alton Lane?" Darcy asked, recognizing the vest and pushing away the thought of Saffron's fate.

Nobody responded. Nobody knew.

"Who is he? Is he dead?"

"No. The other one, Keith, is dead."

"Why did you kill him?" he turned to ask Tyler.

"I didn't. He was dead when I got here. He killed himself."

Saffron saw the gears turn in Darcy's head. She saw how he was making the connection from the cancer to the suicides to the people in the basement.

"That's what all of this is about? To get rid of the evidence that you screwed up an unapproved human trial?" Darcy asked Tyler.

Tyler didn't say a word. He looked exhausted, defeated.

"Listen, if these people are already dead, then let them go and spend what little time they have left with their loved ones."

"No." Tyler shook his head. "I can't do that. You'll never let me finish our work."

"Tyler, you have a son." Darcy saw Tyler's surprise fill his eyes. "Wouldn't you want to spend your last days with Lucas?" he pushed.

Saffron saw Tyler flinch. He looked sad, as if he finally realized these were people with lives and families, not lab rats.

"All I wanted was to save people," he said under his breath.

He loosened the grip on the Indian woman but before he released her arm, he shoved her toward Darcy. She tripped and fell forward. Darcy met her halfway and managed to stop the fall. In the meantime Tyler grabbed Saffron and now pointed the gun to her temple.

"That one can go up," he said to Lynch, pointing at the Indian woman.

Saffron understood that Tyler wasn't going to face Darcy man to man and would always use one of them as a human shield.

Darcy steadied the Indian woman and guided her toward the stairs. She started to climb. They all watched. Saffron's heart was beating so hard she was sure Tyler could feel her pulse against his arm. The muzzle of the gun pressed hard against her head. She remembered the knife. It was in her pocket. She wondered if she could kill him just because he had killed her, if that would make her feel any better about being dead. She questioned if she would have enough time to get the knife and stab him before he realized what she was doing. Before he could shoot her.

She shifted as if she was losing her balance. He readjusted his stance after her. Then she dropped the can of gas on the floor and leaned a little, grabbing the knife from her pocket. This time the noise didn't startle anybody. They all looked but then went back to watch the Indian woman leave hell.

Saffron gripped the knife with all her strength with the blade toward her and drove it into Tyler's leg. He screamed and bent over. Saffron tried to get loose, but his grasp was too strong.

"What the fuck?" he yelled.

Both of his hands were occupied, so he couldn't pull the knife out. Saffron fought to get free, but he wouldn't let go. Tyler pulled the trigger. Saffron froze.

The sound of the bullet leaving the barrel and crushing bone filled the air. Saffron's body flew backwards, falling onto Tyler's chest.

Darcy ran toward them. He kicked Tyler's hand as hard as he could, sending the gun flying across the room. It came to a stop on Alton's shoulder. Darcy took Saffron's hand and pulled her off the floor.

"I'm alive?" she asked, wanting to hug him.

"Yep," Darcy replied kneeling down to check Tyler's vitals.

Saffron looked and saw a clean bullet hole on Tyler's forehead and blood spreading underneath his head. She didn't feel pity for the man. She looked back at Keith and wished again that Harper hadn't run out of bullets so soon.

CHAPTER 91

Sunday: Two weeks later

Saffron circled upwards in the parking lot across Best Buy until she found a spot on the fourth floor. That was the easiest place to find parking in Santana Row. As she walked, she could hear the band playing in the courtyard outside of Starbucks. She smiled and for the first time in a week, she realized her muscles weren't clenched anymore. Saffron was the first one to arrive. She went inside in case any of the others were there, but the place was fairly empty. Most people were sitting outside, enjoying the warm sun and the music.

She felt a chill run through her back. She'd noticed that she still felt that certain sense of uneasiness every time she stood in line to order coffee. She looked over her shoulder and then she took half a step to the side so she could see the door and the large windows that were previously behind her. She wondered if she would ever be able to enjoy a cup of java in one of those large dark brown leather chairs without fearing somebody would shatter the glass with massive bullets, trying to get rid of her. *Maybe it's time to quit caffeine*, she thought. But she knew she wouldn't.

As soon as her order was ready, she grabbed it from the counter and walked outside, sitting at a large table with six chairs. She pulled her phone and checked work email. Her inbox had 2,288 unread messages. She selected them all and marked them read. She knew she would never be able to catch up, so why not start from scratch?

A woman's shadow settled on the table, and she looked up.

"Hello Saffron," Roona Moore said.

Her black hair was shorter than Saffron remembered but still cute and stylish. She stood and hugged her. They both sat. Saffron nursed her coffee. Roona sat across from her, staring down at the table.

Finally, she said, "I think I'm going to be okay."

Saffron's eyes lit up. "Yes?"

"Dr. Leavenworth met with all of us." She looked at Saffron for a second, then looked away, resting her eyes on a woman playing with a small child by the band.

Saffron waited, hoping Roona would tell her more without her having to probe.

Finally, Roona locked eyes with Saffron and continued: "She said that the Sheriff's Department let her talk to the researcher who started this whole thing, and they thought that we may be okay if we got mastectomies." She crossed her arms around her chest. "I'm not sure if everybody opted for the option, but I did. It wasn't a very hard decision, considering the alternative." She looked to her right, as if she were back in the basement and she could see Keith bleeding out in the corner.

"I still can't believe they did this to us," Saffron said.

"Me neither."

"Detective Lynch told me that when they arrested Julia and the researcher, they told him everything." Saffron paused to ensure Roona wanted to hear it. When their eyes met again, Roona nodded almost imperceptibly. "They thought they had found the cure for breast cancer but they didn't have enough data to prove it, so the investors started pulling out. The

CEO, Tyler Warren, was convinced that if they could show positive results in humans, they would get the investors to jump back in. So he convinced his sister, Julia, to exchange the regular titanium markers with the ones with their medicine, and the rest is history, as they say."

"Heeeeloooooo." yelled a voice from across the courtyard.

They both looked. It was Tami Lynn, her face fully made up, her blond bob bouncing as she hopped toward them. She had a wide smile splashed on her face, and she was waving both hands as she ran in small little steps, keeping amazing balance on spike heels.

"You look great," Saffron said, appreciating the flagrant contrast to the hysterical woman in the basement. She looked down at her cleavage, a little too pronounced for a woman her age.

"I think we all look better in the light of day, darling. That basement was a horrible, horrible place."

She extended her hands, expecting the other two women to grab them. Once they did, she squeezed them, then smiled again, showing a hint of rosebud lipstick on her front teeth.

"Okay, what can I get you? I need some serious caffeine."

After repeating Roona's order, she walked in to get the drinks.

Saffron and Roona exchanged glances and laughed.

"I like her much better this way," Saffron said.

Roona nodded. "It almost feels like it never happened."

"I feel that way most of the time, except at night. I still have to leave some lights on at home."

"Me too. Weird."

Padmini Kapoor showed up last. She demurely sat down to the right of Saffron after saying good morning.

Tami came out of Starbucks carrying a tray with three cups and a few bags with pastries. "I figured you may want a chai tea, so I got you one, just in case," she said to Padmini.

She took the steaming paper cup, probably too shy to refuse. She placed it in front of her and smelled it deeply. Her shoulders moved back, relaxing for the first time since she'd sat down.

"So, who's taken Dr. Leavenworth's offer?" Tami asked.

They all nodded except Saffron.

"Good. Me too," she said, then, straightening her back, she added, "And then I opted for a bit of enhancement," moving her shoulders as if she were in a salsa club.

"I should have thought about that." Roona said, laughing.

"So what's the story with you?" Tami asked Saffron.

"Well, I learned from Darcy." She stopped and looked around, "Detective Lynch—"

"We know, dear. He saved our lives," Tami said.

Saffron went on: "Apparently there were twelve people in the control group. They killed eight, and they tried to kill me a few times before they realized that the side effect only occurs when the patient actually has cancer."

"How could they not know about this before?" Padmini asked with a strong accent.

They all looked at her.

"I don't know. When they arrested the researcher—Qian Li's her name, I think—she said that they only learned of the side effect when people started killing themselves in that horrible way."

The four women shuddered at the same time.

"Then they just assumed that it was the medicine, so they figured it would happen to everybody in the trial. The researcher kept trying to find out what had gone wrong, but the only thing she was able to find was that the drug only interacted with the cancer cells, creating the side effect. But didn't interact with noncancer cells, so that group was okay. She called Tyler to tell him, but he never picked up."

Silence overtook the table.

"By the way, what happened to that man with the black and red checkered shirt?" Roona asked.

"Alton Lane." Saffron said. "He was the neighbor of the guy who tried to kill me. He's ok. Got a bad concussion, but was released from the hospital after a few days."

"He had the knife Keith used—" Padmini said.

"Enough about this," Tami cut in. "I'm glad we're all okay." Looking at Saffron she asked, "So, what's the story with Detective Lynch?"

Saffron blushed but couldn't hide a smile. "What do you mean?"

"Oh, pleeeaaazzz. Look how coy you are. We all know you two have a thing. And I have the perfect dress to show my new girls for the wedding."

She shook her boobs again and they all laughed, a little embarrassed.

CHAPTER 92

"Three yards," Sergeant Stella yelled. "Three rounds, center mass."

Darcy fired holding the gun with both hands and counted one-one-thousand, two-one-thousand, three-one-thousand. *Okay, three rounds in less than four seconds. I guess I'm still okay*, he thought. He holstered the Glock.

"Repeat with emergency reload and strong hand only," Stella said, his voice steady and loud enough to be heard through the earmuffs.

Darcy dropped the magazine, grabbed a new one from his holster and slammed it in the gun, counting the fourth second as he fired the last round. He repeated both exercises under Stella's directions. Then he was allowed a few seconds to shake up his tense body. Darcy rolled his shoulders, moved his head from side to side and stretched his hands. The shooting range was empty. All the lines were dark except his. The only two people in the entire place were him and Stella, though his large body could have counted for two.

"Seven yards," he announced.

Darcy took a step closer to the shelf and reloaded each clip. The target moved further away.

"Three rounds, center mass, stay aimed in."

Darcy counted the seconds.

"Three rounds, center mass, transfer weapon to support hand and fire three more rounds. Stay aimed in."

Darcy fired, counted, changed hands, fired, counted.

Each time the instructions got longer, more complicated, more detailed. Some of the shots were aimed at the head, some at the chest, all timed. Darcy was wearing plain clothes under the bulletproof vest. He felt the sweat soaking his shirt, sliding down his temples. As soon as he was able to holster his gun, he wiped his face with his sleeve.

Stella didn't provide any feedback. Darcy had no idea how he was doing. All he could do was follow each instruction, aim and count the seconds.

"Fifteen yards."

Darcy saw the target move again. He blinked a few times, hoping his good eye would adjust and focus.

"Draw and fire three rounds, center mass, in six seconds. Scan, and assume a high ready position."

Darcy aimed. *One-one-thousand.* He blinked, but he felt as if he had something in his eye. *Two-one-thousand.* He blinked again. *Three-one-thousand.* He focused and exhaled, then fired as he counted. The last round hit the target as he reached, *Six-one-thousand.*

Stella yelled more instructions. The ear protectors felt heavy on Darcy's head. He was drenched in sweat.

"We're almost done, Lynch."

"Any feedback?"

"You know better than to ask," he said, but his voice was affable.

Darcy wondered if he felt sorry for him because he was doing badly. He shook the thought and forced himself to concentrate.

"Twenty-five yards. This is an untimed exercise," Stella instructed.

Darcy exhaled. This was the last one.

"Aim in prone position, fire six rounds, center mass. Move to kneeling, strong side prone position, and fire three."

Darcy got set and fired. Before he had reached the sixth second, he knelt and with his right side in prone position, fired the last three rounds. He holstered the Glock as he reached the twenty-fifth second. It was nice to know he could do it under thirty, even though the exercise wasn't timed.

He unhooked the bulletproof vest and started unbuttoning his shirt. Stella came behind him.

"I'll send the results to Virago right away," he said, extending his hand.

Darcy took it and returned a strong grip. "Thank you. I know you didn't have to be here today. I appreciate it."

"Buy me a beer sometime."

"You got it," Darcy said, heading toward the bathroom to change his clothes.

When he came out he was surprised to see Virago in the front room, chatting with Stella.

"Good morning, Captain," he said. "I'm not sure if it's good or bad that you're here."

She had the targets rolled in her hand. She placed them on the counter and walked toward him.

"Detective Lynch, I guess your worst nightmare is now official."

Darcy's color drained. He had hoped to pass. Maybe solving the murder cases, maybe working on putting Warren's colleagues behind bars made him realize this was what he really wanted to do, what he was really good at doing. He didn't want a desk job anymore. He sighed and met her eyes. She was a good seven inches shorter than he was.

"I told you," he said.

Before he could continue with some self-deprecating commentary, she interrupted. "You have now passed and will no longer be on desk duty."

She smiled and extended her hand.

Darcy stood there, not comprehending the words he'd just heard. "I passed?"

"Indeed." She still had her hand extended.

"Holy shit!" he said fighting an urge to hug her. He took her hand in both of his and then turned to meet Stella.

"Thank you," he said.

Stella punched him on the shoulder.

"Detective Lynch, I'll see you bright and early tomorrow. I want you there when I give Sorensen the news that he no longer has to look for a partner." Virago said.

"Oh no, are you kidding? Why did you have to ruin this moment so soon?" he asked, smiling.

"Funny, that's exactly how he feels about you."

"Still? Even after I saved his life?" Darcy complained.

"He's like a goldfish. He has a very short memory," she said and walked toward the door with the targets under her arm.

"Captain," he called after her. "What's my score?"

She looked at him over her shoulder and smiled, then walked out without saying a word.

Thank you!

Becky Roth – Thank you for helping me spreading the word about my book in social media. Thank you for reading my book and for being so incredibly positive about it. You always made me feel good about what I wrote.

David Sierra – Thank you for sharing with me so much information about biomedical startups, animal and human trials and the FDA processes.

Deborah Rome – Thank you for reading my manuscript from cover to cover, for all your feedback and for keeping me sane all these years.

Don Lee – Thank you for telling me that my first idea was stupid. It was! Thank you for reading my book, for brainstorming new ideas with me and for keeping me honest about all the medical stuff. Finally, thank you for brainstorming titles with me over margaritas (I still remember that title that made us laugh so hard).

Donald J. Pliner – Andre, thank you so much for hosting my book release party at the beautiful store in Santana Row. I love all my Pliner shoes and can't wait to see what's new next season!

Eric – Thank you for reviewing my book, calling me on some "cliché" stuff and for telling me that you were up until 2am finishing it!

Jasmine, Arturo, Kathrina and Atish – Thank you for brainstorming title ideas with me. It was hard, but we had fun!

Jeremy Franzen – Thank you for all the brainstorming adventures and for the copious information about guns. Thank you for replying to my texts at all hours of day and night as I bugged you for information I knew you had.

Jim Last – Thank you for pointing out a mayor flaw with my evidence and several other things that after changing made my book more realistic.

Joe Torre – Thank you for sharing so much of your firearm knowledge, for the tour of the gun range and for reviewing the hunting scene. It wouldn't have been the same without your help.

John (Jack) Zowin – Thank you for the many hours you've spent with me sharing your vast knowledge and your 30+ years of experience at the Mountain View Police Department. What started as research has turned into a friendship I'm forever grateful for and I will cherish forever. Frances is incredible too and I love the throw she made me!

Jonah Parsons – Thank you for being so positive and awesome! I wouldn't have had the guts to embark in the e-pub and POD worlds if you wouldn't have been there with me through the whole process. I'm forever grateful and I'm looking forward to doing this many more times.

Kevin Metcalf – Thank you for all the connections at the SJPD, for all the info on self-publishing and for keeping my book honest with police procedure and local terminology. I don't know anybody who has less patience for BS than you, and my book is now a much better one because of your feedback.

Marcus Trower – Thank you for fixing my manuscript. Your suggestions were always on point, and oh my God, I can't believe how many POV violations I had! Lastly, even though I almost died when I saw all the red, after I accepted all the changes, my manuscript was much better. You are the best copy editor in the world!

Mark Nelson – Thank you for all the time you spent editing my book and helping me with research. This book would have not been the same without your feedback. Thank you for letting me vent when I thought I would never be done.

Mary Bennion – Thank you for your brainstorming ideas! Darcy would have never become who he is if it wouldn't have been for your backyard, your copious amounts of wine and you being you! You are amazing and I'm forever grateful that we are friends.

Melissa Gena – Thank you for the amazing website, the back panel copy (Oh My God, I'm so thankful you wrote that for me!) and thank you for being so wonderful and easy to work with! I'm also looking forward to doing many more books with you.

Miguel y Soraya – Thank you for having so many great friends who were excited enough about my book to want to help me in different ways. I love you both and I'm so happy you are in my life.

Mischa Lluch and Virginia Sardon – Thank you for the amazing cover. I know it took a lot of work and effort to come up with something that represented my book and also was a powerful way to grab people's attention. All the options were incredible and it was really hard to pick one! But I LOVE our final choice!

Mormor and Sara – Thank you for always being so positive and encouraging in everything I do.

Mos – Than you for being the best mom in the world! Nothing would have ever been written without your daily help! I cannot thank you enough for all the encouragement and for all the support reading my first crappy drafts and still telling me that it was good and I needed to go on. Thank you for brainstorming with me, for walking through different ideas and scenarios and for pushing me to continue every time I was ready to give up. Thank you for introducing me to ThrillerFest, thank you for going with me every year and thank you for inspiring me to write. I can't wait to read your books in English!

Pos – Thank you for being the best dad in the world, for always encouraging me to write, for making me laugh when I wanted to cry in desperation and for sharing your world of writing with me.

Santa Clara Sheriff's office – Thank you for letting me learn about the Sheriff's Office by allowing me to go on a ride along. It was an incredibly useful experience and I learned a lot of valuable information that made my book more real. Thank you, **Deputy J. Piazza** and **C. Markovic** for sharing your shift with me.

Shut up and Write 3pm (San Jose) – Thank you guys for showing up on Saturdays! This book wouldn't be done today if it weren't for this great meetup and all the people who come to it!

Sourabh Mishra – Thank you for reading my book, for providing such valuable feedback and for all your support and encouragement. It meant the world to me.

ThrillerFest – Thank you for the most fun and valuable conference I've ever been to! I would have never embarked in this endeavor if it wouldn't have been for the inspiration of so many incredible authors

Varela – Thank you for taking the time to meet with me and explain so many different aspects of police procedure. This book wouldn't have been the same without your help.